CRAIG MARTIN

Percy Hare and the Girl in the Game

An early legend of the Lafayette town

First edition

This book was professionally typeset on Reedsy.
Find out more at reedsy.com

Acknowledgement

Some of what follows is real, and represents real people who once lived and breathed and walked the streets of Lafayette, Indiana, and real places that still exist today.
Much of the rest is bullshit.

But the bullshit is ever so much more fun.

It must be noted that this all comes to us from the inspirations of local contributors – a reclusive and somewhat ill-tempered artist named Warren Stavros, a community-minded arts supporter named Shelley Lowenberg-DeBoer, and well-loved local pundit and historian of the odd, Harry Brown.

Credit must be given to Sean Lutes and his regular postings at Preserve Historic Lafayette. Many notions in this book sprang from old photos and accounts of the "Old Town" that Sean describes so lovingly.

I

Part One

"The Irishman's Cigarillos"

Chapter 1

Percy felt the gentle reminder of Evaline's presence, as her foot traced its way absent-mindedly down his furry leg. Less sensual than admonitory, he knew the old gal's message. "Watch your eyes, old sir. That *is* my daughter."

Clearly, she was indeed. Nineteen-year-old Esther Wells, playing croquet in the side yard with her young friends, was so much modeled in the image of her adopted mother that she seemed a younger reproduction of her. Save for her flaming red hair, styled in the manner of her mother (with several curls further than respectfully advised by societal norms), Percy could readily see the posture and carriage and laughter he knew so well to be that of his longtime friend Evaline Wells.

His large, soulful eyes perhaps lingered over young Esther for too long. Most eyes did. But it was the pitch of his ears that alerted Evaline to his attentions. The elder madam was a student of body language and physicality, having addressed the physical form in strangers across the country for more years than she cared to acknowledge. It had served her and kept her out of tight scrapes on innumerable occasions. And though Percy's was not the characteristic male form, she had known it intimately enough and for long enough as to divine his thoughts as clearly as any other.

Percy was a rabbit. Or a hare, more accurately. He had appeared one snowy evening in the darkened corner of Tolbert's saloon. As quiet and subdued as the darkened shadow to which he clung, it was only the glow of his thin cigar that illuminated his muzzle and his large eyes. Evaline, a beautiful and seasoned courtesan over forty years old at the time, had sent her girls home for the evening. The saloon stools were empty of anyone but

3

tired old coal haulers who were unlikely to produce the coin necessary for a woman's time.

Curiosity alone informed her that this short creature, standing on his hind legs and leaning with the casual hitch of a seasoned "sport," was worth the approach. Until she drew near enough to address him, she feared he might actually dart back out into the cold. He held fast. His ears picked up from the collar of the small coat which was pulled up close to his chin. Somewhat wide-eyed at her mature beauty, he nonetheless drew casually on his cigar as she approached.

She pulled up a stool and sat beside him. Not opposite him, as he expected, to lean in as if she were addressing a child. No, this one sat beside him and simply said, "With four rabbit's feet, I imagine I'm four times lucky to have you near on this cold and terrible evening."

He replied, "In truth, many rabbit's 'feet' they're selling are actually the rabbit's knob."

With hardly a pause she replied, "FIVE times lucky, then! So what'll I call you? And what will you have to drink, my furry friend?"

Seventeen years of closest friendship and myriad adventures later, Percy sat in the summer room of Evaline's fine home on Prospect Hill. It was the fall of 1883 in the burgeoning Wabash river town of Lafayette, Indiana. An Indian summer day warmed the crisp leaves still clinging to the glowing yellow ash trees in Evaline's yard.

Percy was more than a little intrigued with the blooming flower named Esther, who was guiding her younger friends through the run of a croquet course in the grass. As opposed to their lighter, shorter outfits, young Esther was fully presented in women's long sleeves, grass-sweeping skirt, high collar, and exaggerated shoulders and bustle. But beneath all the fabric and structure, it was clear that her womanly attributes were considerable.

The children were all offspring of Evaline's lady friends. As such, each was illegitimate – all children of passing fancies and failed precautions. But all were subject to the warmest care from their unique band of mothers/courtesans, dressed well, fed to satisfaction, read to, and amply loved.

CHAPTER 1

Esther, at nineteen years, was the oldest. She was also the only child born to a married couple, though it had not served her any better than any of the bastards at play around her. Little Esther had appeared in Tolbert's saloon one day nine years ago in the company of her young, ne'er-do-well parents, who were making their way aimlessly down the Wabash-Erie Canal in search of opportunity. They were immature and short-sighted, quickly becoming inebriated on the local grog and stripped of their savings in a one-sided game of chance.

In a cruel twist of fortune, Esther lost her mother that afternoon after a bizarre accident involving a spittoon, a newly waxed floor, and a collapsed balcony in the saloon. Evaline turned up that night and soon learned of the sad case of little Esther, minus a mother due to the accident and promptly abandoned by her father, who had moved on down the canal to avoid both local authorities and those who had pocketed his debtor's tabs. Evaline, struck by the girl's large, expressive eyes, was moved to take the girl home with her. Eventually she adopted poor little 10-year-old Esther and gave her a home.

Not for one moment had Evaline regretted her choice. Esther fairly blossomed from a frightened, ill-kempt waif to a brilliant, sunny-dispositioned pixie, constantly at play and ever in search of adventure and mischief.

The arrival of her teenage years saw the eyes of more than one of Evaline's male friends wandering too long over young Esther. Percy was not the first, and he was likely the least for which she needed to be concerned.

At that very moment, from the corner of her eye, Evaline caught a well-known figure making his way down the prominent Ninth Street thoroughfare. At present, he had the awkward gait of a man not watching where he was going. Colonel Mel Wigglemann (retired) was a seemingly decent but easily distracted gentleman, who lived further up the hill and thus higher up the financial stratosphere than Evaline. He possessed power from his wealth but fragility of his emotions. And he was clearly fixated upon the vision of young Esther bent over in the yard. He stumbled over a break in the slate walk in front of the house. Though she chuckled, Evaline noted to herself that he bore observation.

But now it was time to send Percy on his errand. Besides, her housekeeper Mrs. Trincotti would complain incessantly about the fur Percy was undoubtedly leaving on the fine horsehair lounge chair. At this time of year, he was generally molting a bit in preparation for his rich winter coat.

Evaline was as anxious and gleeful about the plan they'd formed as one of the children in her yard. She was anxious for Percy to enact it as soon as possible.

Percy was up from the lounge and signaling his departure before it was requested. One of his unique gifts, Evaline would point out repeatedly, was knowing when to be in the right place and when to not be in the wrong place. He always seemed to sense the precise moment in which he would be best served to be elsewhere. Before Evaline could delineate her instructions once again, the hare had already pressed a furry kiss to her blushed cheek and was nearly to the door.

Percy was as trusted a courier as could be, and she knew she could rely on his discretion. And his clever thinking. In a hard scrabble town like Lafayette, Percy had lived a surreptitious life in the shadows and narrow byways. He had encountered all sorts of riff-raff and scoundrel along the Lafayette streets. Hardly had they given him pause. He was shifty and quick-witted and fleet of foot. As a relatively smaller hare in the world of men, that served him well.

His human counterparts, though much larger and customarily aggressive, were generally dim-witted and too fogged of alcohol to take great concern of him. He was, in fact, about to seek out and force an admission of guilt from one of the most dim-witted and fogged characters along the canal – and in so doing he would set in play another of Evaline's twisting, city-wide games of cascading fortune.

Evaline had come by information through one of her cohorts in the house (the girl herself obtaining it from an amorous "appointment"), that would hopefully change the fortune of a local river trader. Today's game might be called, "The Irishman's Cigarillos."

With Evaline's end game foremost in his mind, Percy set out via the pantry door, seeking to evade the young ones. Children in general were his agitants, as they were generally quicker and smaller and more difficult to slip than adults. Too often he found himself being hugged and snuggled by a well-meaning young girl. The young girls were far too likely to want to make him a pet and far less likely to recognize he was a grown and mature hare who had not the time nor the inclination for their adoration. But young Esther caught his escape, knowing the sounds of the house, the pantry door, and the porch. She hissed at him slinking low behind the hedge along the walk and gave him a beguiling smile and a small wave. It was meant to let him know she'd caught him and, though she could, she wasn't going to spill his presence to the children.

"Dammit." he thought to himself. "Girl's too clever by half. And far too attractive to be too clever. Mark it. Sense and caution around her or she'll bring you up short someday."

But Winks Bubher awaited his treatment. And that was the order of the moment. So he treated the girl to only a few fleeting shadows of his passing down the hedge. Percy plucked his stick from the bush in which he'd stashed it. The high end of it bounced momentarily above the hedgerow, then plunged below it, until there was no sign of him at all.

Chapter 2

Percy's stick, a long thin "switch" plucked from a field willow, served numerous purposes and had become a ubiquitous accoutrement. Only reaching a yard in height himself, Percy's four or five foot stick extended his reach considerably. It allowed him to absent-mindedly tap along the paving stones to mount a progressive walking rhythm. And though he often used it to gesture and point and flourish to effect, he could also use it to mount a swift and sharp defense.

The back streets of Lafayette, to which Percy clung in sensible reserve as opposed to walking the larger thoroughfares, were rife with dogs and cats both domesticated and feral. Many of them had felt the sting of Percy's stick across the snout when they approached too closely. Against fearful barking rage or silent stealth, Percy's stick unerringly found its mark and sent stymied "four-leggers" scattering (as he came to refer to them, being a two-legged pedestrian himself). If not completely rebuffing them, these lashes at least bought him precious time to remove himself from attackers, either by distance down the lane or by height to which he could scramble over fences, bushes, trees, or structures.

Percy was well-practiced and well-defensed, so much so that his passage through town was hardly delayed at all by any number of assaults. And he found the stick also gave him purchase in the more challenging affront of larger attackers, such as human men.

Harry "Winks" Bubher, for one, had felt the sting of Percy's stick on more than one occasion. His disdain for the hare was palpable. If inquired of, Winks' reply as to whether he knew the famed Percy the Hare was always and only, "we've met."

Evaline's "game" unfolding this day was to begin with the hapless Winks himself. Winks was employed by the notable Colonel Wigglemann, and as such carried an unnecessary and unearned level of prominence in town. To clarify, Winks' prominence rarely exceeded the back streets, the muddy alleys, or the back rooms of the town's saloons. He performed any number of tasks for the Colonel, who maintained investments in shipping on the Wabash and Erie Canal but who also had a heavy presence in the drinking and gambling establishments along the canal's passage through the district. Winks clung to his status as the Colonel's right hand with pridefulness and anxious defense.

Percy, though a simple and unassuming hare, furred all over, bare-footed as upon his birth while yet cloaked in a man's small jacket, noted both Winks' pride and anxiety. And he dedicated himself to the exploitation of that anxiety with affirmed purpose.

✶✶✶✶✶✶✶✶✶✶✶✶✶✶✶✶✶✶✶✶✶

The alleyways leading downtown from the Prospect Hill area were clear and dry this sunny morning, giving Percy a delighted skip in his step. Far too often he found these same byways heavy with mud and manure in the rainier times of year. So a clear dry day, with wildflowers peeking into the lane at the margins, was welcome and appreciated.

He made his way down the hill into the upper sections of the downtown area. Though there was a trolley line or two, these streets were much less congested than downtown, which fairly bustled with activity. The horses, carriages, trolleys, vendors, scrappers, and odd shinemen were all too much to keep track of. Oh, and the cops. The buttoned and brassed men of civil order seemed especially keen to track ol' Percy's comings and goings. So ol' Percy avoided them like plague.

Near the corner of Ferry and Eighth Streets, a square, muscled dog housed

9

there seemed to anticipate him this day, exploding from behind a wooden fence just as Percy passed. Percy used his stick to balance as he stepped blithely up a stack of discarded boxing along the fence. The dog lunged and crushed his face into the stack. If the beast had pulled back with a mouthful of splinters Percy would not have been surprised. And, clinging to the tip, he just as effortlessly rode the stick on a gentle arc to the ground, where he sprang ahead of the round-faced dog and distanced himself quickly.

As the canine's heated bark faded slowly behind him, Percy saw the gently sloped rear porch of his friend Barkey Smith's house. Barkey lived in a poorer stretch of housing reserved for the city's Black population, along with his wife Kess and their five children. The porch was shielded from the brilliant, dry sun by a purple-leaved plum tree, giving it a somewhat pinkish glow. He made his way through the back gate, leading to a yard where a robust pig quickly ambled over to him. The pig was smart enough to sense good things coming to him when the standing hare appeared. As was his habit, Percy planted his stick to stand in a knothole by the porch pillar and stepped through the open door without formality.

Barkey stood at the sink, washing a number of root plants, while his wife Kess was doing some darning of clothing at the table. Percy headed directly to her while Barkey glimpsed his passing just above the table's edge and was startled.

"Dammit, rabbit!" he cried.

"Hare," said Percy.

"I damn near stuck myself with this knife seeing you, thinking you was a beast from the yard!"

"Percy!" Kess exclaimed. She so loved when the hare came to visit. He was much kinder than any man had ever been to her, possibly even her own husband, and they had enjoyed a mild flirtation for years.

Percy gave her a kiss on the cheek, to which she giggled at the tickling of his fur and whiskers.

"Well, I ain't no beast from the yard – and if I was, how would you allow me to ever get so close as to molest this fine and delicate young woman?" Kess giggled again, knowing that Percy's words would raise Barkey's jealousy.

"Rabbit..." Barkey started.

"Hare, please."

"Rabbit, I have had my fill of you flouncing in here as you please to lay attentions... (seeing Percy nuzzle himself to the back of Kess' shoulder and now raising his voice) upon my wife! Now distance yourself before I use this knife as it is intended."

Acknowledging him only barely, Percy perched up on a chair at the table and addressed Kess.

"How is the air treating you, dear?"

"Oh, it's fine recently – it's fine." A gentle smile emerged and lit her countenance. He could tell she was in genuine good spirits. Too many days he had found her to be troubled and sad at this very table, skin damp and sallow, straining for air from the lung affliction she regularly suffered.

"The dry weather helps her, you know," said Barkey. "Seems to breath so much more easy. Look at her eyes. Ain't they pretty when she ain't struggling?"

Staring directly into her eyes, Percy said, "Yes, they are quite lovely today." Kess felt herself blush, oddly affected again for the unknownth time by the furry little man-creature.

"Hey!" he suddenly started, catching both of his hosts off guard. "Speaking of beasts from the yard..."

"Oh, now whatchoo..." Barkey interrupted, seeing this shift as an all-too recognizable conversation they'd had before.

"I need to borrow the pig."

"No! Now, Percy..."

"It'll be but an hour or so."

"Dammit, Percy – you're gonna get my pig shot one of these days. Now, no."

"And he'll be fed, well fed. You know he will."

"What good is a well-fed fat pig gonna do me, when he's laying shot down the street and I gotta try to fetch him?"

"He won't be shot."

"How you know that? What are you, some fortune teller who can see the future?"

"No, Winks wouldn't have the balls."

A pause. "Winks? Whatchoo gonna take my pig all the way downtown to cause trouble for?" Turning back to the roots, then back again to Percy. "Winks? Really?"

Silence for a bit. Percy sat silent. Kess attended to her darning but, keeping her head down, rolled her eyes up to glance at Percy and smirk.

Barkey's thoughts continued aloud, "Winks, he got himself a big ol' garden there, don't he?"

"Yup," Percy replied. "He's got darn near the whole block. Bastard took over his neighbor's yard to extend it last year. Took down the fence between their properties and set it up again to keep the man's kids out. Cut out half of the children's play space and the man couldn't say anything for fear of what Winks would do."

"Fuck, Winks."

"Barkey!" Kess exclaimed indignantly. "Not in this house. I won't have that talk, now."

"My regrets, my love," Barkey quickly apologized. "I forget myself. But you know that man has tasked me."

"I do," said Kess

"Mm, mm, mmh," Percy muttered, to acknowledge the history between Barkey and Winks. Kess again turned her eyes to Percy, seeing his game.

As a black man, running in much the same tavern business as Winks, Barkey had found himself at disadvantage on occasion. His encounters downtown with Winks and his crew were mismatched, usually by sheer numbers and by Winks' presumed superiority as a white man. In truth, Winks was far inferior to Barkey in standing. Not many would defer to the former over the latter if they had their choice. But choice was not always in the corner of a black man, no matter how wise or fit or even-tempered he may be. However, owing to an altercation years earlier that had not gone so well for him, Winks would never confront Barkey directly, and both knew it, so an uneasy balance had been informally struck years ago.

Barkey didn't like stirring up unnecessary trouble. That, too, didn't usually go in favor of the black man. But he liked stirring Winks' trouble – he liked the idea of it no matter what might fall from it.

"Now, don't let none of this come back on my door…," Barkey began.

But Percy, who always knew when it was time to be going before the time arrived, was already up and planting a fuzzy kiss on Kess' cheek and moving to the door. By the time Kess realized she'd simultaneously felt a soft caress across her vast bosom, and Barkey had the chance to word his caution to the hare, Percy was in the yard steering the pig to the gate.

Chapter 3

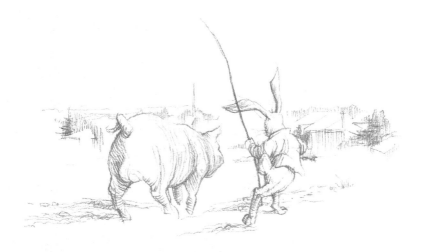

The pig, which in truth had no proper name, had been christened "Charley" by Percy months ago. Barkey never saw the need nor use in naming an animal meant for slaughter. But Percy didn't employ that perspective, preferring to see the pig as a business relation.

The two had been out before, causing ruckuses in various yards about town. Percy had even had Charley down to the Tippecanoe Courthouse once, to enjoy the mayor's green garden, tucked into an alcove on the lawn of the great stone building. Charley had no sense of speech or civilized manner, so he was not a true companion. But Percy enjoyed walking with him and steering him to a targeted destination and seeing the pig assault the particular vegetation there to his heart's content.

A pig is a relentless mover and plods along with seeming purpose, though with no real intent. Percy led him by the stick, the shaft simply laid lightly along his side and the point out before his face. Never was there the need to strike the pig – it perceived the intent from the stick's presence alone and would easily keep moving as indicated.

Together the pair made their way along the back alleys behind the tight log dwellings along the Pearl River, which was less of a river than a fetid trough of waste water. They crossed the river at the viaduct near St. Boniface Church and headed north into the downtown neighborhoods.

Occasionally a child or a loose dog (equal measures of simple-mindedness to Percy's mind) would jerk to a halt at the sight of them and stop to watch them trundle by. At one juncture, a mangy little terrier took more than a passing interest and began to haltingly lunge at Percy, barking loudly. With a quick snap of the willow branch he sent the little scruff scurrying, whimpering over a stinging atop its black nose.

Later, at Ferry Street, an annoying child attempted to alert his distant companions to the sight of the pig and the hare. A similarly quick snap of the willow branch to the child's behind was all it took to allay the soiled urchin's ambitions. He watched them pass, quiet and dejected.

At Cincinnati Street, Percy spied his goal and steered Charley toward a gap in the wooden fence to the side of Winks' yard. The pig looked up at Percy, huffing and snorting from his stroll through the town. The hare tapped at the edge of the gap in the boards with the tip of the willow stick. Charley investigated the gap with his quivering snout, and there discovered the scent of the vegetables lying aground in the yard beyond. He nudged his snout further into the gap and the boards creaked argumentatively.

Percy smiled. The pig pushed once and again into the fence gap, splitting the weathered lumber in short bursts. Now that his reward was at hand, Percy knew damn well that Charley would be undeterred in his pursuit of it. Turning the corner on the yard, Percy proceeded up Fourth Street, meaning to circle to the other side of the garden. Behind him, he heard a great crack as the fence boards gave way. And he could hear shards of wood clattering to the pavement.

He scarcely needed to watch the pig's process through Winks' garden. He could hear it plainly from outside the fence. The voracious sounds of the pig making short work of the neat rows of cabbage and beans were viscerally satisfying. He grinned a broad smile, making his way past Winks' front porch before passing the house next door – there, the neighbor whose yard Winks had rudely accessioned for his garden expansion gazed at Percy with wide wonder.

Clinton Pardoo had often heard rumors of an upright rabbit making his way through the city as one of the populace, but to date he had not laid eyes upon him. He was quick to leave his rocker on the front porch, heading through the front door with morning paper clutched in one hand. "Mabel," he cried, "I swear, this is the damnedest thing!"

The windows on the Pardoo house were all open on this warm autumn morning, so the sounds of the interior made their way easily to the street. The reply to Clinton's exclamation, barely heard from the back of the house over the sound of his children squealing with glee, was "Clinton, as damnedest things go, I may have you beat!"

As Percy rounded the corner on the yard and passed the side of the Pardoo house to the north, he heard a chorus of amplified cries:

"Awww, Momma said a bad word!'"

"Now, that'll be enough..."

"Momma! PIG! PIG! Piggie, look!"

"I see it dear – ain't he something? Look at him go! He's a hungry piggie, isn't he?"

"Mabel, dear, look here. Look, out the window. He's heading to the back yard – look!"

"What is it, dear?"

"Look, there. See? The rabbit – with a jacket on! Walking around the house!"

"What? Well, now, I *will* be damned! Would you look at that. Though I believe that would be a *hare*, dear."

A quiet reply of "Thank you!" came from outside the window.

Percy had circled the two houses and reached the back garden again from the far side. At the fence, a few of the Pardoo's neighbors had begun to gather to appreciate the spectacle.

"Gosh! What's happening here?" Percy made a showy appearance. Hopping to the top of the fence, he took in the scene below and crossed his legs atop a fence post. In the garden, ol' Winks was attempting to wrestle the pig away from his vegetables. He leaned his entire weight against the pig and pushed at it with his foot, all to no avail and to nearly no impact. The pig feasted unabated upon the garden.

"Goodness, Winks," Percy said with false curiosity. "How ever did the beast gain access to your harvest?"

"Rabbit!"

"Hare."

"This is your doin', ain't it? Where'd this pig come from?"

"Well," Percy assured him, "I can't at this time give you any accounting for how he got here, but I do believe I recognize the pig as being the property of Barkey Smith."

There passed a moment of pointed silence. Several in attendance recognized the impact of Barkey's name.

"Barkey?! Well, what's it doing here?"

"I believe what the pig is doing here is... eating."

Winks' neighbors chuckled at this. In truth, some were just as charmed to watch the talking hare as the ravenous pig, and would have laughed at anything to come from his mouth.

"Don't be a smart ass, Percy! Get him out of here! You know the pig – call to him or something!"

Percy was nonplussed, throwing his paws up and saying, "Oh, I don't believe I can alter the pig's trajectory in any way. He and I are not well acquainted, really."

For a moment, the pig paused and looked up at Percy, leaving all who had gathered to think that perhaps the pig had indeed understood Percy's words and perceived them as a slight. In truth, no one was more surprised than Percy himself. But the pig promptly dove back into his earthen meal, ending the suspicion.

Winks was getting pretty worked up by this point. "Well, he and I are gonna know each other pert' well damn soon now. Tanya, fetch my shotgun," he called to his wife.

Tanya Bubher ambled slowly from the house with no shotgun. She strolled forth with her arms crossed and a corncob pipe pinched between her lips.

"You ain't gonna shoot that pig," she reasoned, "'cause you and I both know you ain't gonna provoke Barkey over this."

"Oh, ain't I?"

"No, you ain't. That man is a tree you don't wanna go barkin' up."

Winks acknowledged this slowly but fumed at being publicly rebuked by his wife. Before he had the chance to turn his ire toward her, Percy interjected.

"If I might, I'll confess. I may know more about the dilemma at hand than I at first let on."

"Oh, really? Do tell," Winks replied sarcastically. "And do it fast, dammit!"

Tanya noted flatly, "He's headed for my rutabagas, Winksy. I better not lose them."

"Percy!" Winks pleaded.

Percy explained, "I believe there is a connection here – a 'thread' if you will – that runs from Captain Lark O'Connor to Colonel Wigglemann to you and finally to this here pig."

"What? What's Lark and the Colonel got to do with this?" Winks protested, but his fading rage and tone betrayed the dawning of his understanding.

A week earlier, the Captain had piloted his flatboat back into Lafayette town, following the Wabash and Erie Canal. On board were a variety of ordered goods he'd picked up from as far away as Toledo, Ohio. It wasn't a booming trade for the Captain, but it represented operation and payment. As it entered the downtown district, the flatboat ran aground on a pile of tree stumps that had been discarded by someone clearing a lot to the north.

The canal was in its waning days and the reduced traffic enticed some to take advantage of it as a dumping space.

The flatboat's prow struck the stumps and the hull rode up the obstruction, rising out of the water. The stern pivoted and eventually jammed into the earthen bank of the canal, wedging it firmly in place.

Teams of workers from everywhere along the city docks and the downtown district ran to assist the Captain and his crew. As the canal waters continued to flow and the boat's cargo began to shift across the leaning decks, the fear of many was that the entire boat would flip and be lost.

"Now, I am not well acquainted with your employer, Colonel Wigglemann," Percy continued, "But I *do* know that he is a strong advocate of fair play. Why, I've heard that he threw in the New Year's pot in Cowell's game in St. Louis because at the break he found a card on the floor at his feet. Threw in his entire night's winnings, lest he be accused of holding cards.

"And I know that he is particularly bothered by thievery. So… *if* you in fact have any ill-gotten goods in your possession – say for instance, a certain box of cigarillos obtained from the colorful Irishman's errant flatboat – then it would seem I would be doing you a favor in relieving you of such goods. Would I not?"

"Oh, would you now?" grunted Winks. "Even though all knows that ol' Lark might damn well have just misplaced them cigs and not knows where he lef' 'em."

"True. That may be so. But it may not. There's suspicion about that with your men all about the boat when it was grounded, lending a hand to free it and all, that there may have been, in the confusion, a… *light touch* applied to the cargo. Lark says the manifest was true when it left Logansport and that is such a short scoot down the canal for them to have gone missing. They did, after all, come all the way from Cuba – only to disappear on the Wabash Canal?"

Alarmed at the accusation, Winks spouted "My men ain't done…"

"Now, now, you see my meaning, don't you?" Percy continued. "Wouldn't it be prudent for you to be able to look the Colonel in the eye, regardless of what fate truly befell ol' Lark's cigs, and say in all honesty and with clear

19

conscience, 'No, sir. I do not have the missing cigarillos and know not where they are today.'?

Winks was somewhat distracted to what Percy was illustrating, by being more concerned by far with the greedy progress of Charley the pig through his garden.

"Now, Winksy, if I were to leave here today with said missing cargo, and with this voracious pig, which I suspect I might be able to deter from its destruction of your garden, I feel I would be doing you the distinct favor of, at the very least, clearing your conscience."

Tanya Bubher had perched herself on a stump near the back door of the house and, pausing her relentless drags on her pipe for a moment, she offered, "He ain't wrong. Clearing ya' conscience is good for ya' soul. 'Cause if that pig clears much more of my rutabagas I'm gon' feed *you* to him."

"But T," Winks began.

"Get them cigs, sir. The hare's got ya today."

Winks turned back and forth between them, trying to find his way through the conundrum. All the while, the snorting, snuffling pig's incessant munching drove him to such distraction that Winks looked as though he'd burst. Suddenly he leapt toward the house yelling, "Alright, dammit! Hang on a minute. But firs' stop that damn monster from eating my whole yard!"

Hopping down from the fence and heading toward the pig, Percy said, "Technically, I do believe this would be your neighbor's yard, would it not?"

Winks exhaled heavily through his nostrils and turned hard, stomping into the house. Percy whistled loudly at the pig. It glanced up at him but dipped its head back to the half-finished rutabaga on the ground. Percy reached out with his willow stick and gave it a quick sting between the eyes. The pig scooted backward, having received the message. It huffed heavily once, contented with its engorgement and resting for a moment.

Percy glanced up at Tanya. She turned and dipped her head to him saying only, "Nice play, hare." Percy bowed to her in return. She said, "I'm winking at ya, but it's the wrong eye." And she tapped the stem of her pipe to her eyepatch and cackled loudly.

A broad grin animated his furry face.

Winks stomped back onto the porch with a dark leathery package in hand. He held it out to Percy, then changed his mind.

"No, I ain't a-givin' it to you, rabbit. How do I know you won't make off with it yourself? Then I'll be screwed double."

Percy pondered a moment and came up with a solution.

"Is that wrapped tight so it won't get wet?"

"Sure. Right off the boat and they don't want 'em wet. They're still in oilcloth."

"Then I've got a way to get those cigs right to the captain's door with him being no more the wiser as to who brought them or where they've been hiding. Do you have a man who can follow instructions?"

Winks pointed to a dopey, child-like man seated on a barrel head, who was distracted and squinting at something up in a neighbor's tree. "Pudge'll do it. Yo, Pudge!"

Pudge looked up slightly dazed.

"Go with the rabbit," Winks ordered, handing him the package. "You gotta make a delivery."

"Terrific," said Percy. To Pudge he said, "The pig and I'll meet you on the street."

Pudge hopped down from his perch, looked confused, and asked, "What pig?"

Percy looked out at the large pig seated in the freshly trenched earth, then he looked up at Winks as Tanya cackled ever louder. He asked, "Do you have another one?" He pointed at Pudge, "This one's broken."

Tanya staggered off her log and cackled loudly. A whistle escaped her haggard lungs as she laughed. She reached out to take the oilcloth package from the hapless Pudge.

"I'll take 'em m'self – I need a stretch. 'Sides, this hare makes me laugh. Charmin' bugger," she snickered.

Chapter 4

"Look," Tanya began as they reached the murkier depths of lodgings along the river's edge, "You gotta know that Winks has got it in for ya. I been with the man for long time now – too long prolly. And he pisses me off righteously most days. He ain't a terrible brilliant man, but he's seen me through some of my worsts."

"Understood."

"But the man has a terrible temper and ignores no slight. So what you done to him – times 'afore and now this today..." She snickered again, distracted. "Look at that pig's ass a waddling! He ate himself a good 'un today. Like a field plow, he was. Well, anyways, he ain't gonna forget, ol' Winksy. He'll be on ya sometime."

"I know."

"Keep a wide eye out for him, would ya? Hate to see anything happen to ya."

"I'm obliged of you to say so."

Percy stopped near a stinking juncture of the putrid Pearl River. They nodded to each other and Percy winked at the leather-faced woman. She snickered and repeated her joke.

"I'm winking back at ya, but it's the wrong eye and all." And she tapped the stem of her pipe to her eyepatch.

Percy lay the willow stick along the pig's back and over the ridge of his face. Holding it there sent the message that the pig should stay put, and surprisingly the pig seemed to grasp the intent.

"Right, here's what you do," Percy explained. Pointing to the wrapped package he said, "Take this over the Brown Street bridge to the west side of the river. It's quieter over there – not so many folks around. She's more likely to answer there."

"Answer? Who is this you're talking about?"

"Just listen – you wouldn't believe me anyway. Don't worry, no harm will come to you."

"Harm? Ha! Ain't nobody 'bout to harm me," she replied. To punctuate it, Tanya produced a glistening knife blade from the folds of her clothing, brandishing it and flipping it in her hand with a flourish, and slipping it quickly back out of sight.

Percy made a mental note not to ever challenge Miss Tanya, or to allow her to believe he'd do so. At least not while within her arm's reach. She looked to be alarmingly adept with the blade.

"The piece is clearly your hidden advantage, dear. But you'll likely not need it. This'll be a simple delivery.

Now, once you're on the other side of the river, turn up the river to the north. And you'll only need to make it around the bend a hundred yards or so. You'll see an old twisting willow laying flat out over the river."

Brightening quickly, Tanya offered, "I know that one! I had an old beau that met me there 'a time to time. We used to…"

Holding up his hand to interrupt her, "Details, madam, might best live in your own memory."

"Got it. Yup." She snickered again despite herself.

"Now, back to the tree. On this tree there's a forked branch that should be low to the water. Balance your dark package out there on this fork and step away. Then find yourself a flat rock or piece of bark. I guess you could use your hand. But slap the water, hard. Three times. Pap! Pap! Pap! Got it?"

"Got it. Why?"

"You'll see. Just slap the water three times and step back out of sight. You'll not want to spook her."

"Spook her? Spook who? Who is this timid soul?"

"A friend," Percy replied flatly, already launching the pig trundling on his path. "A special friend who will take the cigarillos back to Captain

O'Connor."

"But how?" She called after him. "What am I to make of this? Are ya jesting me?"

"Not at all. Just do as I say – I'm sure it'll be well."

Staring after him, she was not at all so sure of what was to transpire. Tanya had certainly been presented with some odd assignments in many odd places through the years. But this was new.

She puffed on her pipe steadily as she crossed the covered bridge over the Wabash. The sun shone through the gaps in the structure, and at the open end of the bridge lay a framed canvas of golden trees lit with the sun of Indian summer.

She turned right along a footpath that traced the shore of the river. There the golden yellow leaves scattered in the wind before her and bounced across the surface of the tall grass. Just as Percy described, the tree lay before her, somehow keeping its foothold in the soil while leaning nearly flat out over the river. The forked branch was at the end of a sturdy arm of the tree, requiring her to carefully make her way some ten to twelve feet out over the water. There she balanced the wrapped cigarillo package and made her way back to shore. Low to the ground at the base of the tree, a scooped boulder invited her to sit and await the unknown contact who would take the package.

She puffed peacefully on her pipe a moment before realizing she'd forgotten something. Under some reeds, she saw a flat piece of tree bark. Leaning up off her perch, she grabbed the bark and made her way to the water's edge. Keeping her thin-leathered boots dry, she lay her hand on a rock and leaned as far out as she could, and slapped the bark to the surface of the water three distinct times.

"There," she said quietly, "now let's see…" And the water broke violently under the tree. The piece of bark flew from her hand high into the air and she staggered backward and fell roughly into the soft mud.

A large flat head with an exaggerated beak popped up from under the wrapped package and lifted it free of the branch. The head turned toward the open river, then turned back toward her. Under the shadow cast by the package, she could make out a dark, glassy eye that seemed to examine her and then wink at her. She gasped. An exaggerated splash revealed a fish-like body that extended a full six feet beyond the head. A wide, flat tail slapped the water, and with a series of high pitch squeaks and rapid clicks, the creature pushed away from the shore and rapidly made its way out into the current. The package was perfectly balanced atop the creature's flat head and, though the oilcloth wrapping glided close over the surface, it never came in contact with the water. At least not for as far as Tanya could still make out, as it passed through the shadow the Brown Street bridge cast over the water. The package was headed back into town atop its watery host's noggin.

Tanya sat with her mouth agape for quite some time. She felt the stem of her pipe against the roof of her mouth, levered against her bottom lip. She noticed finally that her fingers had sunken into the mud until they were completely swallowed in it.

She'd heard folks talk and joke of the Wabash River dolphins, and she'd never begrudged anyone their folklore and children's tales. She'd certainly never encountered one, or anything remotely suggestive of the sort. But there it was. Or there it had been, not ten feet from her, in the shallows of the river bank. And there it was now, a ghost under the water, whisking away that little package of cigarillos. The package that seemed to float of its own accord along the sun-drenched surface of the Wabash.

A shocked grin slowly spread across Tanya's face.

(*Author's note: according to local folklorist and historian Harry Brown, the Wabash River Dolphin, long considered a regional myth, was trapped in the upper Wabash River region when the glacial melt and inland waters receded. The dolphins were referred to as the "river buffalo" and their hides provided area Native peoples with waterproof moccasins and raingear.*)

Guiding the pig home toward Barkey's house again, Percy paused on First Street to peer down between several low dwellings toward the river. He scanned up and down stream in the intervals, looking for any sign. The pig snuffled and snorted along at a steady pace, slowly separating himself. Percy worried over allowing too much space to form between them, but kept his eye peeled toward the green water sliding along, glistening under the late morning sun. Then a small dark square floated into view. It might have been any sort of flotsam or river debris. But Percy recognized its squared shape. And that it seemed to float almost independent of the water itself. He grinned and ran to catch the pig before it disrupted a trash can in the alley.

****

Captain Larkin "Lark" O'Connor sat at the dock next to his river boat. A Civil War veteran, steamboat builder and navigator, Lark was one of the last of the river captains, a storied breed of men along the Wabash and Erie canal. He and his brother Jim were well-known in Lafayette, where they'd operated steamers for decades.[1]

Recently, however, his reputation had been bruised by a series of unfortunate events. Two years before the Wabash canal incident, in April 1881, Lark's steamer "The Joe Segner" sank 30 miles south of Terre Haute. The ship had been overloaded in Terre Haute before heading south toward Evansville and at a sharp bend at a river lunge it had simply listed and sunk. Lark hadn't been on hand, entrusting the mission to his brother Jim. In hindsight that had proven to be an errant trust. When several important shippers learned their products had been pitched headlong into the river, the O'Connors' business prospects suffered a serious decline.

Jim O'Connor had been at his brother's side since childhood. Not nearly as charismatic as his elder brother, nor as wise a river steward, nor as clever and entertaining a drinking man (he in fact became dull and very much slowed by drink), Jim had maintained a solid allegiance to his brother, though he had sunken regrettably into his shadow. Lark loved the man and constantly endeavored to support his brother through morbid bouts of melancholy, self-doubt, and drunkenness. But he struggled to maintain faith in his brother's ability to competently serve their interests.

By the 1880's the steamboat industry was beginning to dwindle, as trains were becoming a more preferred method of transportation. But Captain O'Connor persevered, pleading the case for the consistency and reliability of his decades-long service. That was a case becoming more difficult to defend with recent events.

The recent flatboat incident haunted Lark deeply. Realistically, he could never have been expected to know of the submerged tree stumps. He felt the derision and mockery over the incident deep in his heart. The Lafayette community had been more than his home – it had been *his* town to be celebrated in, to be lauded at bars and public events, to be approached at church for handshakes and claps on the back for decades.

Now it felt foreign and coldly distant. On top of the insult and embarrassment of the grounding, there was the issue of missing merchandise. That one particular package, one not of great scale or relevance but more of trust and elite status, had gone unaccounted for. He and Jim had searched personally after the first mate admitted it could not be located. It was with deep regret and collapsed confidence that he was forced to report to his wealthy client that, having made the trip all the way from the island nation of Cuba, it had been lost somewhere in his care.

Sitting each morning at his dock on the river, not far from his house on the corner of Smith and Wabash Streets, he drew momentary relief from the smooth and steady flow of the water. The sound and the feel of it sustained him and led him closer to a sense of his true and well-earned value and his "place" in the world.

It was then he heard in his head, and repeated aloud, the words of his beloved grandmother in times of frustration, "Ohhhh, *cocklebur*, my sweet Larkin!" And then her constant refrain, "My apologies for the indelicate language." The memory of her brought a smile that pointed his cigar toward the brim of his hat.

The sun spotted through the trees on the eastern shore behind him and danced across the water. He drew deeply on the cigar, letting its richness fill his lungs. He followed it with a sip of brandy that warmed his throat and chest. With his eyes closed, he breathed deep and sighed. And something clattered to the wooden boards of the dock at his feet.

It took Lark a moment to register the shape and the wrap of the package. He lunged to his feet, looking for the deliverer of this blessing. Unexpectedly, the water surface exploded beside the dock and the river dolphin raised its head, mouth open as if smiling broadly at him.

"Elsie!" he cried out. The dolphin launched into a loud and rapid series of clicks and squeals, and shook its head rapidly. The two had been acquaintances for years, up and down the river. Lark never knew what it was that allowed him to recognize this particular dolphin, but it may have simply been its familiarity with him. Most folks scoffed at the suggestion of their existence altogether, assigning them to the realm of children's fantasy or to the tall tales of boatmen like Lark. But he knew well of them and indeed felt a close kinship with this particular creature.

"Where did you come from? And how did...?" The thought of where the dolphin obtained the package and its skill in presenting it so pristine and dry boggled his mind.

Quickly, he pulled at the ties and wrappings over the box and examined the cigarillos inside. Perfect. And dry. And waiting to be delivered. Before doing so, he bent to rub Elsie's head. She rose and squeaked and cooed appreciatively. Then she followed him to the shoreline. There his neighbor had a fenced minnow pen. Lark grabbed a scoop hanging on the fence, scooped out a pile of squirming minnows and flung them in the air. Elsie rose and caught most of the flashing silvery fish in the air, then dove to snag those that fell free near her in the water. He waited until her head cleared the water again and tossed another scoop of minnows.

Then Lark grabbed the box of cigarillos and ran off toward their intended owner.

[1]*Information on Captain O'Connor was obtained from "'Lark' O'Connor: The*

Last of the River Boat Captains" at Forgotten Stories of Greater Lafayette –
https://lafayettecitizenjournal.com/2020/04/03/lark-oconnor-the-last-of-the-ri
ver-boat-captains/

Chapter 5

Percy waddled Charley back into Barkey and Kess' yard, the pig having lost some steam over the last several blocks. It had been a long morning for an overfed pig and a long walk from Winks' garden. Charley nosed down into a shaded, muddy corner and flopped to his side. Percy flung the gate closed and dragged his stick along the picketed fence, making a clattering noise to signal the owners of his return. They hollered out and looked for him, but only the waggling tip of the stick above the fence row showed him passing at the end of the block, heading northeast.

****

Hesitation nearly steered him along another path, but soon Percy felt the irrevocable pull of visiting Baby Alice's house at 13th and Elizabeth Streets on his way out of town. He couldn't avoid his conflicted feelings about seeing the place – and her – again.

Baby Alice[2] was the closest thing Percy had ever known to a love of his life, and she was still his greatest regret. Even now, eight years after her death, he felt the tug of both affection and guilt at her passing. He usually felt as though he had come to a reconciliation over it. She had certainly assured him repeatedly that he was not to blame. But each time he saw her he felt the same regret well up in him until he was nearly overcome. He imagined that now, in the full light of day, she'd be less likely to call to him.

As he rounded the corner onto Elizabeth Street, only a house away from the former brothel, Percy could sense the stillness in the air to which he'd become accustomed. It was literally as though the air stopped moving through the trees and the sounds of birds were hushed near the home. He was never surprised by her, because it was as though she was near him even before he approached. He'd heard others express some of the same feeling, though they, as people, were not as well attuned to it as the hare.

As he drew near the house he could hear her tones. Never so mournful as to be considered *haunting* really, they were close to a hum and nearer to singing. And today, like most days, they formed slowly into the soulful whisper, "Percy."

Looking up into the window of what once was the first-floor dining room, under the shadow of a tree and past the glare of sunlight, he could make out the blue light pulsing and growing brighter as he gained a more direct view into the room. The light, which seemed to emanate from chest height, soon illuminated her lovely face. Her delicate, wispy hair moved as though in a gentle breeze. She looked at him and called his name again. Still walking, he smiled at her and she reacted with a pretty smile and a warmth he could feel from the sidewalk.

Her words formed slowly. "Care, Percy." Then, "Be careful, Percy."

He wrinkled his brow, not knowing why she would be concerned for him. It was a beautiful day, wasn't it? He'd just pulled one over on Winks. And fed a pig. And successfully, from what he could see, called upon assistance from Winks' own woman and the river dolphin to return Lark's cigarillos. A fine day. Why should there be "care?"

"Won't you stay with me today, Percy?"

"Not today," he replied. "But soon, my love. Soon."

"Care, Percy!" Alice said with a bit more urgency. What followed was less distinct, but it sounded to him like, "Mind your home."

He marked it, though it made no sense to him at the moment. People were always cautioning Percy to take care. Tanya Bubher herself had done so earlier. It was natural thing, for folks who looked upon him as a small helpless woodland creature in a rough and uncaring town. But this was

Alice. Baby Alice. More than almost any other voice, he took hers to heart.

****

The hare was afforded more breathing space by the greater distancing of homes in the expansive eastern section of Lafayette. His pace slowed, his gait became more loopy and relaxed. He left plotted roadways, and the houses soon disappeared altogether. The ground began to rise and turned to loose, gravelly clusters of native prairie. Percy's eyes followed the land's contours uphill and wandered up into the mountainous white clouds in the azure sky. In his mind, Percy ascended into its hillocks and inclines until climbing out onto the great white expanse of it glowing in the sun. It was so brilliantly illuminated that Percy eventually had to look away.

He was wandering home. Or to what he referred to as "home." Being who he was (or *what* he was?), Percy had never felt the need for much of a permanent residence. Generally he cobbled some things together into a shelter, sometimes of more substantiality than others. At the most, his dwellings were little more than lean-to's which embraced a tree for backing and support. He had been known to relocate a shrub next to his setup and maintain it by watering for a bit more wind break or shade. Of course, by the time the true Indiana winter would set in, he had generally located a much more significant and man-made habitat and would have coerced an agreement for his stay there by agreeing to provide some service or other to the owner. There might have been, on occasional years, some "unsolicited lodging" of which usually none were any the wiser. Those were adventuresome intervals. But today, still basking in October 1883's autumn warm spell, Percy's setup was still his summer arrangement in Barbee's Grove.

White settlers found their way into the Great Lakes region via waterways that criss-crossed the central prairies and forests and flowed eventually to the great Mississippi artery. Through their addition of the Wabash and Erie Canal, which only connected the upper Ohio and Indiana region through a more direct water route, the town of Lafayette had maintained its dependence upon the river and thus clung primarily to its banks.

At the eastern reaches of town, the ground rose up into a series of hills and ravines down which rains had trickled back to feed the Wabash River for a millenia. Those ravines also fed the elusive Pearl River, which squirmed its way southwestward through town, dipping below ground at several points and eventually helping to flush the wastes of the accumulated Lafayette townsfolk into the Wabash.

At the steepest point to the north lay a naturalized wooded area known as Barbee's Grove. The grove had clung to the hilltop for longer than there was memory. It was a fair-sized woods. Percy found it a delightful spot, replete with berry bushes and edible plants. Townsfolk were amazed that there were paths through the forest just "naturally" lined with berries and edible plants, like a Garden of Eden. In truth, spaces like Barbee's Grove had been purposefully maintained and altered by Native peoples for centuries. But sure, it was easier to think of as one of God's miracles. Percy allowed them that. As long as they would just leave it and him alone.

Percy crossed the Toledo, Wabash, & Western Railway line cutting southwest through town and began to climb toward the grove. The trees rustled silently, tossing over fans of their foliage in the sunlight and sprinkling their leaves into the breeze. Still, amidst all the natural beauty, there was something that raised his hackles.

Something didn't feel right, on this gorgeous sun-splashed day, but he couldn't put his finger on it. He kept a wary eye out and scanned deep into the shadows under the trees. He slowed his step and became more purposeful with it. Though not yet alarmed, his ears stood high, trying to register anything that felt out of place.

"Mind your home," Baby Alice had said.

He made his way to the furthest reach of the wood, where it was most dense just before opening over a ridge that allowed a resplendent view of the northern valley of the Tippecanoe region. This was his "place" –

safe, quiet, beautiful, rich with the scent of wild ginger, and more dense with underbrush than folks generally cared to venture through. And yet the closer he came to it, the more the signs of an encroachment became apparent.

Percy stopped and crouched in his path and "disappeared" to take in everything around him. He remained still and avoided any impact on the space around him, not on the dirt or the air, the scent, or the insects. Each of these things were significant indicators to anyone skilled at reading them. And other than the denizens of the woods themselves, he knew he was alone in these skills. He could sit reading the telltale signs for hours if need be. He'd once located a native hunter simply by silently reading the air for twenty minutes. The man turned out to be on the far side of an ancient elm not thirty feet from Percy. He was stealthy to be sure, and certain that he'd heard an approach. But he never saw Percy that day and moved on in time. All the while, and for quite some time after, Percy had sat as still and silent as a rock.

Before him, through the brush and tall, thin trees, was located the spot on which Percy might now be leaning back into the curve of a root at the base of the old hemlock tree, if not for the intruder he had yet to see. His eye scanned each small branch and the status of every rising plant stem. Eventually, he saw it. As it turned out, it was none too hard to spot.

A path through the grasses had been plodded down by a large man. And a berry bush had been pushed aside. He'd used something to do it – a stick or cane would have worked. He'd broken several of the branches and misshapen the bush for the time being. Following the path now with his eyes, and never moving a hair on his head, Percy saw what he'd been searching for. A face in profile hovered behind a cluster of leaves, about fifty feet from where he crouched. A mature man, well-dressed and coiffed. Casual and confident even, or at least putting on that appearance in his high-collared trappings of success.

He appeared as casual and expectant as if in a doctor's waiting room and simply expecting to be met. Percy recognized him from a few times when their paths had crossed and more in truth from reputation and dealings with his subordinates. In fact, Percy had just that morning had a productive dealing with one of the man's subordinates, Mr. Harry "Winks" Bubher. For there, in the further reaches of the Barbee's Grove woods, virtually in Percy Hare's parlor, sat Col. Melvin (Mel) Lafayette Wigglemann. But why?

[2]*According to Jon Anderson at the site, This Is Indiana – http://thisisindiana .angelfire.com/indianahauntings.htm – Baby Alice was a doomed "lady of the night" who died a mysterious death in the days when the brothel she worked for was thriving. "To this day, the story of Baby Alice continues to earn Lafayette the reputation as one of the most haunted places in Indiana.*

Back in 1875, Baby Alice died due to 'congestion of the lungs, produced by debauchery and exposure,' (a direct quote from the newspaper article on her death – Lafayette Journal). The paper then ran a story on sightings of a mysterious, dull blue light appearing late at night in the darkened brothel's windows. Occasionally, the light would escape the brothel to roam free in the surrounding yard.

Speculation grew among the townspeople that the strange light was, indeed, the ghost of Baby Alice. But why would her spirit haunt the brothel? Stories began circulating widely, and soon it was believed that the tragic figure blamed the nature of her work for her death, and the pulsing blue light in her hands was actually her heart and lungs.

Those neighbors in the surrounding houses that weren't excited by the idea of living next to a real live ghost were desperate to get rid of her. They tried everything, from magic potions to actually shooting at the vague figure that floated over the grounds. The other women who worked at the brothel became scared for their lives and eventually fled the scene, vowing never to return. The brothel's owner put the house up for sale and claimed it would never again be used for such sinful purposes."

Chapter 6

Col. Wigglemann[3] was the son of Nevlim Wigglemann and Calpurnia Leggurs. It is interesting to note that Mel was born just one year after the town of Lafayette, Indiana was platted and just one year after Marie-Joseph Paul Yves Roch Gilbert du Motier, the Marquis de Lafayette's triumphant tour of the United States in 1824 and 1825. It is thought that Mel was conceived during one of the many wild and uninhibited celebrations marking the Marquis's visit that occurred in nearly every town and village at the time.

After retiring from service in the Mexican-American War, the Colonel went directly from the U.S. Army to the Gold Rush camps of California in 1848. It was believed that his fortune was made in panning for gold, but he eventually arrived in Lafayette hoping either to run for state office or to invest in canal shipping on the Wabash and Erie Canal.

As well as his canal shipping interests, the Colonel owned a few taverns throughout town. And, it cannot be overlooked, he had dabbled in entrepreneurship with the invention and promotion of what amounted to a "massage chair." Patented under the name "The Wiggler," and advertised widely in publications of the day, the chair unfortunately failed to catch on and the business foundered.

Percy took in the situation with extensive consideration. The Colonel appeared, to Percy's exhaustive observation of the surrounding woods, all without moving, to be alone. No dogs. No men. No protection visible, other than his walking stick, though it wouldn't be surprising to find the

Colonel with a small derringer on his person.

As Percy watched, the Colonel lit up a cigar and puffed a great cloud of rich fragrance up into the tree canopy.

"Well, he's damned casual about his intruding in people's affairs." Percy thought. "But the man has a fine cigar, I'll give him that. Might as well get on with this."

He approached as silently as the gentle breeze, until he was at the edge of the small clearing he himself had formed as his "parlor." He drove the end of his stick into the soft ground and presented himself.

"Hallo." Percy said.

The Colonel started so that he coughed on the draught of his cigar and sputtered.

"My apologies! You startled me! Damned if I didn't hear anything of your approach!" Rising, "Again, my apologies. I owe you an introduction. I am Colonel Mel Wigglemann, retired."

He stood and extended an outsized hand, which Percy considered for a moment before placing his much smaller paw upon it. They shook amicably. The Colonel was a tall man whose bearing was undiminished in the natural setting. Percy felt his own diminutive size very acutely for a moment, looking up at the Colonel until the man took his seat again upon a fallen log.

Percy offered, "I know of you, sir, and it is a pleasure to finally make your acquaintance. I think." The Colonel's eyebrows raised. "Well, you *are* in a place where few have found me or, should I say, where few have been bold enough to venture and make themselves at home."

"Ah! Fair enough. Please forgive my forwardness. I meant no affront at all. It just occurred to me that it might be time for us to meet."

"Oh?"

"Yes. I've heard tell of you about town. Oh, and from a number of different sources. So don't fear that my judgement has been too much colored by my Mr. Winks' accounts."

"Indeed. Good to know."

The Colonel smirked. Then he held out his cigar for consideration and offered one to Percy, who still seemed wary.

"You would be doing me the favor of joining me in smoking off the last of this particular batch. You see, I have just received a new order and I hate to be put off from something new for finishing off the old."

"Do you now?" Percy wondered, almost to himself.

"Yes. The new order is for cigarillos, newly shipped from Cuba. Biting but very agreeable taste. Very invigorating. As I understand, they have recently made their way, rather circuitously, through Lafayette via the canal and a few other, shall we say... colorful passages."

He looked slyly at Percy and implied his knowledge of the day's events.

"Oh. Yes, I imagine so. Well, by all means, I would be happy to join you for a smoke."

"Splendid."

The Colonel lit up Percy's cigar, and the two sat belching out clouds of rich smoke. The colonel was a large figure in black, perched on a fallen log, legs crossed as if seated in a fine conservatory. The hare was a much smaller figure, perhaps half the size of the former, in greys and earthen tones, his ears swept back behind him as if combed gracefully.

A couple of late in season goldfinches peeped and flitted quickly through the smoke in the clearing looking at Percy, as though making sure he was alright.

After several minutes they spoke again. "Ol' Lark O'Connor is a fine man," the Colonel said.

"The finest," said Percy. "I've known him a number of years and have traveled extensively with him throughout the region. Always a gentleman and a fine steward of brandies."

"Really? I did not know that about him." A smoking pause. "Oh, by the way, a very fine effort on your part to retrieve the cigarillos."

Word had traveled quite fast, Percy thought. "Thank you," he said.

"No, thank *you*. I mean, aside from them being *my* damn cigars – stupid Winks – more importantly, Ol' Lark didn't deserve that misfortune. The grounding of the boat was not his fault and I fear he'll pay for it in people's suspicions for some time.

Oh, and the pig," he continued. "Capital work there! However did you manage to steer him to your intent?"

"I assure you, Colonel," Percy said with a near straight face, "I merely encountered the pig in passing as it was laying waste to Winks' garden. I believed I knew its provenance and simply offered to do my part to put things into balance again by returning things to their proper possession."

"Very well said, that," the Colonel replied. His face revealed how charmed he was with this well-spoken creature of the wood. He nearly chuckled just listening to the words coming out of his furry face.

They smoked a while.

"Shame that Ol' Lark has seen the best of his river days," the Colonel remarked.

"Oh?"

"Yes, well, the river and canal are no longer the preferred fares, are they? The trains are where folks want to ride nowadays. I guess it was inevitable. The river brought us here, the canal knifed in on a more efficient path, but the trains are taking us now where the waters don't flow. And there's lots more country inland to be seen and grabbed up.

The canal has gone shamefully bad, don't you think? Why, it's damn near impassable at some spots due to neglect. And the stench of it rivals the Pearl trickle through town at times. Shame."

Percy nodded, "I suppose so."

"Yes, Ol' Lark was the king of a bygone era," the Colonel surmised. "But I suppose to all things come change, eh?"

They smoked a while. A red squirrel barked above them. It seemed offended by all the smoke drifting up through the tree branches.

"How far have you been with him?" the Colonel asked.

"I beg your pardon?"

"Captain Lark – how far have you traveled with him? I remember him telling me he's been to the gulf off of New Orleans and north into the Great Lakes."

"I've not been that far actually." Percy scratched at the ground a bit. "I confess I'm a bit of a homebody. I like to go... but then I like even more to come back. I've seen the Ohio River with Lark, and Toledo on the lake, but that was my limit."

"Your limit, you say?"

"Yessir. You see, I was born, if memory serves, not a half mile from this very spot. Lived in the general vicinity all my days."

"Honestly? Why, you strike me as much more of a cosmopolitan fellow. Shame. There're many fine places to visit for an enterprising gentleman such as yourself. Why I could make introductions for you in such places as, say... St. Louis or Cincinnati, and you'd be..."

"... I'd be as out of place there as if I was standing center stage at the Dryfus Theatre downtown," Percy interjected. "Wouldn't I?"

The Colonel nodded. "Yes, well, possibly. But I could easily see you onstage at the Dryfus as well. You're a fascinating character, Mr. Percy. But in fairness, I acknowledge that may owe to who you are or... *what* you are, eh? A rabbit?"

"A hare."

"My apologies." He wasn't aware of the distinctions between "hare" and "rabbit" but he recognized the value to the hare. "And I assure you it is not my intention to diminish you for being what you are, sir. In fact, the opposite – to praise you for the rather amazing feat of being born a hare and leading the life you have lived. Or at least the life I've heard you've lived."

"Well, sir. I will dwell upon the compliment in that. In truth, I confess I myself don't realize sometimes the full extent of where I've been, as opposed to where I might not have been."

"Hmm. Perhaps a lesson for us all," said the Colonel, chewing over the semantics he imagined were very wise. "I'd toast you on that if I had a drink."

"Another time," said Percy.

They puffed together a while.

"Out of curiosity..." Percy began. "What kind of life *have* you heard I've lived?"

"What? Oh, well, nothing too specific, to be honest. But there is a bit of a 'mythos' surrounding you, Mr. Hare. Mostly escapades in which you've been involved, I guess."

"Do tell."

"Well, for instance, the bits about you and Denleroy Füdd, for one!"

Both gentlemen chuckled at the mention of his name.

For a number of years in the 1860's and 1870's, Percy had been the nemesis of local lawman named Denleroy Füdd, who pursued Percy regularly for bits of petty thievery and assorted back alley transactions. In his younger days, Percy had been more flagrant in his disdain for the law. His craftiness and ability to outsmart his pursuer had led to a storied relationship with Mr. Füdd – a relationship that was even highlighted for local theatre-goers to comical effect, in several vaudevillian plays presented by the Early Apotheosis Theatre.

"Why, there was tell, and I hope you'll dutifully set me right if I cite it incorrectly, of a night in which Mr. Füdd's head ended up in a mule's ass. Am I right to that?"

Laughing heartily, Percy replied, "It was a dark night and little was to be seen in the stalls. But while giving me chase, and upon a series of rapid and unfortunate missteps, Mr. Füdd was kicked by a mule he'd spooked and was indeed thrown headfirst into the hind quarters of a large molly mule across the way." The Colonel roared at the mental image. "If I'm not mistaken, the molly's name was 'Agnes.'"

The Colonel expelled his breath rapidly through his nostrils and fell to his knees laughing. It took him quite a while to recover his composure and his feet, and he did so with his cigar held aloft out of the leaf litter on the ground.

Finally resuming his seat, the Colonel said, "You slay me, sir! That anecdote alone must have solidified your reputation."

"It may have, sir. But I insist that I had no hand to play in it, other than leading old Denleroy on the merry chase that led him to the stable. It was the irritable mule himself who is owed credit for the steerage of the kick."

"Indeed," said the Colonel. "Capital bit of insight there."

PERCY HARE AND THE GIRL IN THE GAME

After a pause, and more puffing on the cigars, Percy asked, "I wonder what ever happened to old Denleroy? It's been some time since I heard tell of him."

"Well, if I'm not mistaken, I believe he headed to Cincinnati. And now he's a security patrolman for their baseball team, the Red Stockings. It's a good bet he's still as hapless as ever."

"But likely not stomping around with that old blunderbuss any longer," Percy added. "God, he was fond of blasting that thing about."

The Colonel asked, "Did he ever catch you?"

"With the blunderbuss?" Percy replied.

"Ah, well, with that too. But was he ever able to detain you? It seemed he made it his life's ambition."

"We all have ambitions, don't we?" said Percy. "And I do regret to say that I stymied old Denleroy's fully. Never caught me. With either shot or handcuff. Poor man."

"Poor man, indeed. A lesson there, I think. 'Know that your goals are obtainable. And just.'" offered the Colonel.

"Well, I would offer that his goals *were* 'just' in the scripture of the law." Percy said. "Perhaps just not obtainable."

They smoked a while longer, as the sun shone almost directly overhead, yet filtered down upon them through a glowing veil of tinted foliage.

"I'm curious – now, forgive my prying and stop me when you wish…" offered the Colonel.

Percy made an open gesture, inviting the Colonel to proceed. He'd shared a bit of comradery by now with the Colonel. And while he remained prepared to bound off in an instant if he felt any connivery from him, Percy was feeling more relaxed around the Colonel as time passed.

"Again, owing to your reputation, I feel my curiosity is piqued and I must ask. You have… well, I'll just say it. You've quite the reputation with the ladies."

Percy looked at him somewhat innocently and produced a sly puff of smoke out the side of his mouth.

"They say you have quite the way with them. Now, I don't mean anything improper, mind you. But they say you are quite charming and at ease with them, and that the women find your company both entertaining and... dare I say it... somewhat salacious."

Percy looked at him without expression, waiting for the Colonel's intentions to be revealed.

"Now again, don't take me wrong. I confess I speak outside of the bounds of propriety sometimes. Or at least out of the bounds of common sense my wife tells me. And I can certainly see the wholly unique charms of a fellow who is furred and pawed and somewhat diminutive of stature who can yet speak as clearly and conduct himself as you do. I can see the appeal, I really do.

"But since it's just us two out here," the Colonel continued, "Honestly, I'd be remiss if I didn't take the opportunity to address some of what I've heard."

Percy offered for a decent pause.

"For instance?" he said, rolling out the carpet.

"Well, I've heard tell that some of your friendships and acquaintances are with those of the courtesan variety of woman. Personal masseuses, ladies of the evening, escorts of certain houses, etc. For instance, from what I hear you've had a few paramours in the houses, is that right?"

"I've had some very close friends among those ladies," Percy allowed. "Challenged as they are to provide for themselves, and sometimes others, within a system designed to make use of them, and then to conveniently overlook them, and which is, at the same time, wholly discouraging to their very presence, and so utterly hypocritical..."

"Sorry, sorry!" the Colonel interrupted. "Again, I have neglected to make my meaning clear and presumed your understanding before one was established. I completely agree with you about much of the system as you describe it. And I am not one to look unfavorably upon such women.

"Nor am I one to look unfavorably upon their services. I will tell you, Mr. Percy – may I have your trust as a gentleman on this?"

Percy nodded affirmatively.

"I have myself enjoyed the solace of time spent with some of the finest and most understanding women of the variety. More than once. They saw me through some difficult times with discretion and caring. I would never fault them."

He seemed to ponder that thread for a moment and whether it made an impression upon the hare.

"Um, and you, sir?" the Colonel breached. "Have you ever…?"

"Absolutely." Percy said flatly.

The Colonel sat on his thoughts again for a moment, though Percy knew the direction they were taking.

"So, how does that work precisely? I mean, with you…"

"No, we shan't be going there, sir," Percy stopped him.

"Good man! Very noble. I forget myself."

"Let us just say that the ladies have found in me a… bit… of a *novelty*. Not a lot more. Suffice to say the physical logistics of intimate relations with a gentleman of my size and species are… challenging."

Quiet puffing on cigars. A small woodpecker seemed to tap out the timing of the pause, and then a silence fell, as if the woods itself awaited Percy's continued remarks.

"That being said…" Percy paused, "I *have* shown a proclivity for certain acts of… intimate friendship and an empathy for… the *pressures* and *anxieties* of the female nature. With this understanding, I have been honored to have been entrusted on occasion with… relieving these pressures in a way that many – well, let's say *some* – women, to preserve modesty, have found to be very… rewarding. When pressed into service."[4]

Leaning forward from his log, the Colonel exclaimed with genuine admiration, "Bra-vo, sir! I commend your discretion. And I am surprised to find that we actually have something in common – something I truly had not anticipated until just this moment."

Percy was undeniably prideful of his reputation for bringing "relief" to his troubled female counterparts. So he was immediately skeptical of the Colonel's assertion of an understanding of the "female nature." The man was a large, blockish lummox and hardly seemed capable of such an understanding.

Indeed, as he explained himself, the Colonel revealed that he had only a tangential awareness. He recounted that a number of years earlier he was interested in something that could only be described as an early version of the massage chair. For women.

Colonel Wigglemann had poured his life savings into The Wiggler. Unfortunately, either the cultural climate or the chair itself had not provided the proper *seating* for successful commercialization. The Wiggler failed to sell as well as had been hoped, with the Colonel taking a sizable financial setback.

"You don't say!" answered Percy. "It may, or may not, surprise you to know that I have heard of The Wiggler."

"No!"

"I'm surprised and not a little disappointed," Percy continued, "that I failed to make the connection in the name – 'Wigglemann' and 'Wiggler.' And… it may bring you some solace to know, I have at least a few female acquaintances (pausing to reflect) – perhaps three or four – who in fact extolled its virtues."

"Ah, I am in your debt, sir." The Colonel seemed genuinely gratified.

"The house on Elizabeth Street had one in residence."

"What? The brothel? Was that Madam Hortense's place?"

"Indeed. Hortie's girls were fond of it."

"But… courtesans? What might they…?"

"Surely, sir, you can appreciate that *sex* is not always synonymous with *satisfaction*."

Yes, the Colonel had had inklings of such an idea, certainly in the confines of his own marital bed. But the vague expression on his face made it clear that it had not occurred to him that women who made their living by offering intimate relations might not *enjoy* said relations.

"Hunh," grunted the Colonel. "Live and learn." But he was reminded of his intention for the questioning. "Along that line, I hear that you have quite the friendship with the widow, and accomplished madam, Mrs. Evaline

Wells."

Halting a moment, sensing they were entering a new field of inquiry, Percy answered, "It would be difficult to deny that is true."

"I've admired her. For quite some time." The Colonel leaned back and seemed to ponder. "She's been a formidable businesswoman, and I must give her credit. She's both wise and bold. Many would see her as 'vulnerable' since she's no man in her life. And some of those I've seen crushed by her upon that misjudgment."

Percy smirked knowingly.

"What do you know of her?" the Colonel asked, followed all too quickly by, "Doesn't she have a daughter?"

A pause. "Esther, is it?" he pressed.

Percy sat stone still, glancing aside at his new acquaintance. He puffed slowly and deliberately on his cigar, knowing now the path the Colonel had rather clumsily chosen to take. His caution rose within him again.

Speaking of Evaline Wells outside of her knowledge was generally an unwise practice. But to speak of her adopted daughter, Esther, was *never* a smart enterprise. At all. Evaline was dangerously defensive of the girl, now a beauty of nineteen years. And as Esther bloomed, Evaline's ire was increasingly easy to provoke.

After no response from the hare, Colonel Wigglemann added, "Lovely girl, isn't she?"

Percy blew a column of smoke into the lower branches of the tree and looked steadily at the Colonel.

"You know she is." His message seemed plainly delivered. But the Colonel either missed his intent or skated around it.

"I've only spoken with her once..." the Colonel began.

To himself, Percy thought, *"I'll bet Evaline is not aware of that. You're a lucky man."*

"... But from what I perceived, she seems a charming young woman."

Aloud this time, Percy said, "That's true enough." But again, in his mind, "I *sincerely* doubt that was your honest reaction. Charming? Maybe. But more like... coquettish, sharp-tongued, provocative, precocious,..."

"Now, lest you get the wrong impression," the Colonel chimed, "Let me remind you that I'm a married man."

"Not a very happily married one, I'd wager..." Percy thought.

"And a *happily* married one, at that," added the Colonel. "My Edwina has been a treasure of my life," he said without too much conviction. "And certainly a stalwart support for all my undertakings. But you can't fault a man for recognizing a lovely and charming young woman. Am I right?"

The hare flinched and shrugged and allowed that to pass without comment. He settled in to a silent posture, determined to allow the Colonel's words to continue to flow past him, but abstaining from stepping into the stream.

"The thing is..." the Colonel began.

"And here's the thing..." Percy thought.

"Over the course of a long marriage, one finds both a comfortable bond with a woman, one's wife, and as well a... certain amount of fatigue. And, dare I say, an *over*-familiarity. While some like the cushion of being able to finish one another's sentences, due to complete and thorough knowledge of all thoughts, others find it an unwelcome... *assault*."

Percy's eyebrows rose.

"Yes, that much," the Colonel continued. "As if that other person is seated within your head and won't leave, offering you no privacy, and seems intent upon only pointing out your inadequacies. Forever.

"And if, God forbid, a man and a woman are unable to produce any offspring to enrich their lives and... buffer the hostilities... and distract from the inevitable changes brought about on both members of the marital contract by cruel time... then they can find themselves looking one to the other disdainfully. And looking out the window... to newer options, passing down the street."

"Ah!" said Percy, half aloud, "And young Miss Esther is the 'newer option,' literally 'passing down the street.'" He remembered that the Colonel lived further up Ninth Street Hill from Evaline Wells. He would likely have seen the girl in passing and throughout the neighborhood for a number of years.

"Yes. Yes, she is. I offer this to you as a friend, and as a gentleman. I hope you know that," the Colonel said.

"Of course," said Percy, with the weight of his friendship with Evaline, years of it, bearing down on the back of his neck.

"And I do not wish any ill of Edwina. She has kept my house, and my finances, dutifully and honorably for all these many years."

A pause. "But... as with the flowing on of the Wabash, and the diminution of travel on the Wabash and Erie Canal, in favor of the heavily-powered efficiency of the Louisville, New Albany and Chicago Railroad, so too are people, even loved ones, regretfully set aside in favor of newer models."

Percy finally felt inclined to speak, "But sir, 'set aside for newer models?'" He leaned forward, his paw with cigar set upon a large root. The cigar began to ignite some of the fallen leaves on the ground.

"Is that not a bit unfeeling? If such an attitude were prevailing, and were we all to reach an age and weariness of seeming unattractiveness to our partners – would that we all had partners – would not every one of us feel vulnerable to being cast aside so? I don't know your wife, sir, and I feel I scarcely know you beyond the gentlemanly bonds of a shared cigar. But would your Edwina not deserve a better fate, for longevity and commitment alone, than to be 'set aside' as you say?"

Taking to his feet now, the Colonel assured him, "Believe me, sir, I have given this tremendous thought." An ash fell from his cigar to the leaf litter and consumed it in a small flame. "And I recognize the position in which I place myself and my wife. But unhappiness, perhaps to a forest creature who knows no bounds or responsibilities beyond his wooded seat, is unknowable. And regret is overpowering. But... it is winnable. It can be conquered with the pursuit of happiness."

Two small, smoking flames now existed in Percy's parlor.

"As a military man, and a businessman, I have rarely hesitated before stating my aims and directing my forces toward accomplishing them. Here, I hesitated, before you, a gentle and considered hare. Here, I ask for your assistance, with making a thing that is wrong somehow work to the right."

"The right?" Percy replied. "Sir, with your wealth and position, I have no doubt you can make a good many things over in the manner you see fit. But would not a divorce carry with it a societal... burden? Would you not be risking your reputation and honor for, if on one hand happiness, then on the other also ostracism and derision?"

"Divorce is only an option, my furry friend. And only one path." The Colonel seemed surprisingly less ruthless than his words suggested. "I would assume a gentleman of your broad understanding would know that and be quick to answer with alternatives. But whether or not you agree to enable me is less important than you not interfering with me.

"For as I have said previously, I hate to be put off from something new for finishing off the old." With that, he turned to leave, looking at the remnant of his cigar. He gestured with it to Percy, saying, "Thank you for sharing, and for conversing. Good day, sir."

The Colonel left, using his cane to push past the grasses and shrubs before finding the path back toward the train lines.

Percy was perplexed that the man made such an exit, without emotion or allowing Percy an answer or even cementing an understanding of what had just been shared between them.

Two small fires burned at Percy's feet. Primarily smoke and blackening of leaves over the dirt, they yet crept toward one another.

Percy knew now that the life of a woman he'd never met was surely in danger. And he knew that his own life was in doubt, as was the security of his home, having been found by an unlikely wandering gentleman with suspect purposes who had just exposed his intentions seemingly without any fear of recriminations. And Percy knew that he could never come to this home he stood in again.

Plucking his stick from the ground, he stepped out of the clearing just as the small fires gathered together.

End of Part One

[3] *Information on Col. Wigglemann is provided by Shelley Lowenberg-deBoer,*

author of the short fiction essays, "A Short Biography of Ginger Wigglemann" and "Before There Was Ginger: A Prequel to A Short Biography of Ginger Wigglemann."

[4]*An essay by Warren Stavros entitled "The Enigmatic Percy Hare: An early legend of the Lafayette town" provides some context for Mr. Hare's claim. In it, Stavros cites the journal of early Lafayette resident Dr. Francis Gullimore, a friend of Percy's. The journal suggests that Hare "performed an admirable and personal service owing of discretion and perseverance' to the wife of then president of Wabash College (Crawfordsville, Indiana), Thaddeus Cornblau, in the spring of 1863. Mrs. Cornblau reportedly suffered from what was identified as 'female hysteria.' The only accepted cure at the time was the massaging of a woman's pelvis (i.e. her genitals), resulting in 'hysterical paroxysm,' or orgasm. The exact nature of Hare's 'admirable and personal service' is left to the imagination of the reader and seems limited by both his and Gullimore's 'discretion and perseverance.'"*

In continuation of the Cornblau tale, the journal states that Percy "was feted at what was either a faculty dinner or women's club luncheon. The precise nature of the event is unclear, but the presence of a large and notably appreciative female audience is highly suggested. Gullimore writes of 'my friend Percy having generated a response of the female contingent, both vocally strenuous and heartfelt. They employed him individually with tasks and lavished upon him their attentions for several days hence.'"

II

Part Two

"East and West"

Chapter 7

The latent summer weather of October in the Wabash River Valley gave way to a sudden snap of cold and wet in early November. In their Prospect Hill home, Esther and Evaline Wells were cleaning in their parlor. The housekeeper, Mrs. Trincotti, would only go so far in her regular dusting, and after some time the residue of what she left had to be gathered up by the mistress of the home. It was easier to spend the occasional evening this way than to confront the rather cantankerous old housekeeper on her work.

Evaline was warming with a bright fire in the fireplace, while an icy rain fell against the windows. But young Esther burned with a fire of restlessness, the agitation of the young missing out on something. She was working in only her undergarments, tired of the bulky trappings of formal dress and excessively warm from the fire. Her mother was seldom concerned with formality, at least not when they were alone together, and indulged her casual dress.

"I wish it wasn't raining so," moaned Esther. "I want to go out."

Evaline sighed and replied, "It's best that it *is* raining – you don't need to be out at night."

"Nothing good happens *until* night time. You know that, mother."

"Nothing good?"

"Well, nothing exciting anyway."

"Tonight, Esther darling, you'll find plenty of excitement with that duster. And with me."

With resignation, Esther returned to her chore. But her inquiries were undeterred.

"Mother, we haven't seen Mr. Hare in weeks, since October! Why hasn't he come around?"

"Never you mind, girl. He has his ways."

Esther had stopped cleaning and draped herself lazily over the horsehair sofa.

"Why must you lounge over the furniture so?" Evaline complained. "In your undergarments you look like a lonely cathouse girl."

"Maybe I *am* a lonely cathouse..."

"What was that?" inquired the older madam, whose hearing was diminished these days..

"Nothing, mother!"

"I'll not have you muttering under your breath at me," admonished Evaline.

"I'm sorry." And quickly moving on, Esther replied, "I didn't get the chance to talk with him last time he was here. Percy. He's always so slippery and ends up leaving before I can say a word."

"He's a private soul, dear."

"He hurts my feelings," Esther pouted. "It seems he doesn't like me."

"He likes you just fine, dear. Not to worry. He'll find the right time to address you, I trust. When it suits him. He knows you well after all these years but he doesn't take to everyone right away."

Pause.

"But we were such fond friends when I was small!" Esther offered. "Why has he grown so reserved around me now?"

"Because you're not small anymore, dear," Evaline answered knowingly.

"What's that supposed to mean? Will he not like me now that I've grown? How silly," Esther protested half-heartedly.

"You know damn well what that means, girl. Percy is a grown man, er, hare, dear. He knows it's a different thing entirely to play with a small girl than to dally with a young woman. He's being more reserved and gentlemanly around you now."

Esther had had something in mind for quite some time, and she suddenly came out with it. "Mother, what was it like when you used to canoodle with Percy?"

"Esther! You mind your tongue! Why, I can't believe you'd…"

"Oh, mother, I am nineteen years old, not some little school girl. You've raised me in a brothel, so I *do* know how things work."

"You'd better not!"

"Mother, please. Don't be overly disagreeable. Now… what about ol' Percy?"

"That is *Mister Hare* to you."

"Oh, piffle. Quit putting me off, mother. Tell me the truth. You have spent some twenty years around that man, er, hare. Have you not?"

"I have."

"And you have shared some adventures, haven't you?"

"Yes."

"Like the time you smoked out the Knickerbocker Saloon by blocking the chimney."

"Yes."

"And when you felled a tree across the Fifth Street train line at the north end to keep the train from meeting another rendezvous somewhere."

"Crawfordsville. No, it was Monon."

"And when you set Judge Willicker home strapped onto his carriage without his pants!"

"Ahhhh! Oh, Esther, you were never to know about that." She cackled.

"Oh, but I do know, mother!" Assuming a pious effect, "And I know that it was not a very Christian thing for you to do."

"Perhaps not." Evaline smiled slyly.

"What would Reverend Tancey say?" Esther asked slyly.

The two exchanged a knowing glance and burst into giggles at the suggestion of religious impropriety and the Good Reverend. Rev. Tancey had more than once made his way up the hill from his downtown parish to spend a mid-week hiatus of several days encamped in Evaline's house. By the end of it, he would enshroud himself in his formal habit once more and give the girls a fond farewell before leaving for the rectory and his preparations for weekend services.

Esther threw herself over the arm of the horsehair couch and plied her mother further.

"So, what of our little furry friend, Mr. Hare? Come, mother. Tell. Have you been intimate with the hare?"

Evaline struggled to put her off. "Oh, now, must you be so coarse?"

"Mother, please! What is it like with him?"

"Stop, now."

"Is he ticklish with all the fur and whiskers? Is he quick, like they say about bunnies?"

"Esther! Stop right now!" Evaline shouted, "I mean it! Now, have you addressed the mantle? You know I can't reach up there any longer."

Esther dutifully began removing bric-a-brac from the mantle and dusting where each piece stood. She was clearly annoyed with her mother and worked in sullen silence, being slightly less careful with her handling of the delicate pieces than she ought to have been.

Recognizing that the young woman would not be put off, Evaline gathered herself. When Esther had finished with the mantel, Evaline patted the seat next to her on the sofa and said simply, "Come to me." Esther flounced down heavily on the sewing stool next to the couch, rather than beside her mother.

Evaline reached over and stroked Esther's flaming red locks and said, "Listen to me now. You must not ever share this with another living soul. I mean it, my love." Receiving an adequate nod of confirmation, she continued. "Yes. Mr. Hare and I have been intimate."

Esther squealed in as high a pitch as air escaping a pinched balloon.

"I knew it! What was it like? Is he just a furry little dear? You must have nearly squashed him!"

"No," Evaline tried to calm her, "it wasn't like that at all. Don't be taken with an image of him as some stuffed bear to be cuddled and propped on one's pillows. He's a living creature – warm, affectionate, even... impassioned..."

Again, a squeal escaped Esther's mouth and she leaned more urgently toward her mother, taking her hands in her own over the arm of the sofa.

"But... but... know that he is, heaven help me... one of god's small creatures of the natural world and as such... not really equipped to fully... *join* with a woman."

"Oh." It fell from Esther's mouth with an audible sense of disappointment.

"Now, that being said, Mr. Hare – my Percy – is still one of the fondest lovers I've ever taken." Esther's attention picked up. "He is attentive to a woman in ways that are almost… fantastical." A breathless pause stretched for several moments. "And there I'll leave it."

"No!" Esther moaned regretfully.

"I must! I must."

Clutching Esther's hands, Evaline marveled at their softness and youthful, unblemished smoothness. When her own hands had been that delicate, she knew she'd been blissfully untroubled by the weight of relationships, or the daily challenges of living. And now her weathered callouses represented the experience of passing decades and innumerable loves and losses.

"My relationship with Percy, with Mr. Hare, has always has been *more* than that… more than the act of intimacy. He has truly been one of my most dear and important friends. To think of Percy as only a former lover truly only cheapens the memory of what he has meant to me. And what he means to me still."

Esther's eyes welled with tears at her mother's words. She'd never spoken of him that way and Esther had not considered the level to which Evaline's friendship with the hare had grown over the years. Charmer and scamp? Yes. Mischievous flirt? Yes. Irresistible to pet? Shamefully so. But to think of him as endeared as a fond human friend? She confessed to herself she had not afforded him that respect.

The two women shared the moment, holding hands over the arm of the couch.

Then Evaline broke, "And you, my dear, will *not* toy with that little friend of mine. Not in that way. I know you're feeling your wild oats these days, but that cannot happen. Is that understood? I forbid it."

Esther nodded affirmatively, assuring her mother of abiding by her wishes… while secretly longing to know firsthand of the 'fantastical ways' of which her mother spoke.

Chapter 8

Percy was huddled at a much smaller fire in the fireplace at the former home of the notorious madam Hortense LaForge, now better known for its ghost in residence, Baby Alice. The house at Thirteenth and Elizabeth Streets was several miles from Evaline Wells' house, down the hill and through the north side of town. Presently, the house was dark, with the exception of the singular burning log in the fireplace. And the dim blue ball of light that hovered a short way off the floor.

Hortie's house had been abandoned for years. No thinking person was willing to set foot in it anymore, except for the occasional authorities, the caretakers checking upon its physical state. And they would only come in the full light of day, for fear of encountering the well-known Baby Alice there in the dark.

Playing checkers with Alice had helped Percy pass many hours in recent weeks. Camping there in the abandoned house helped him forget about his spot in the woods. And about what he'd learned there with Colonel Wigglemann.

He had to concentrate on listening to Alice's vague words, while watching for flickers of her once bright face. In the darkened room, he could see more shades of the blueish light that seemed to emanate at her core. The glow picked up her features hovering above. And he reveled in watching her smile flickering at him through the dim cyan haze.

Her words came slowly and deliberately. They echoed to him, as if from far away, though her light appeared to be within his reach. The sound of her seemed to travel through layers and layers of gauze, so he ardently attended to each word. And he fought to pay attention, because even in death Alice was a notorious cheat.

"No," he chided her, "That's too far – you can't go two spaces and then jump me."

He heard the sound of her faint giggling.

Then he examined the board before taking his turn. The board had been left behind in the old house when Hortie left and her people gutted it. Ol' Hortie had been scared to death by Alice's appearances, chased out of the house and onto the lawn at her final encounter while Alice seemingly pleaded with her, either for help or, as Percy suspected, just for a moment to listen.

He looked up after a moment of stillness to see her smiling warmly at him, with an expectant look on her face.

"What is it?" he inquired.

"Ev-a-line," came Alice's slow response.

"What of her?" he asked. "I think she's well, up there on the hill."

"No," came the most distinct response he'd gotten that evening. Alice struggled to push more words through for him. He made out the name "Esther."

"Esther?" he asked, "The girl? What would…"

"Edwina," said Alice, following quickly upon the previous name, with a slight and sympathetic moan.

"Edwina Wigglemann?" He was completely puzzled now, but waited for her to explain. And after several repetitions, he finally made out, "You should go to them."

"Why is that?" he asked, looking down at the board.

The blue light appeared in the form of her delicate hand beneath his chin, raising it to gain his attention. It startled him enough that he stared at her wide-eyed.

She simply said, "The game. They will need you."

He furrowed his brow, perplexed by what Baby Alice could be asking of him.

"It's cold. And very wet," she added.

He recognized her sensitivity to the conditions. She had left this world due to exposure over a cold and wet night just like this one. She made him think for a moment. But what he heard next was the sound of one of her checkers sliding across the board and her faintly giggling, "King me."

Back up on Prospect Hill, the conversation had moved on to prospects for Esther's attentions. She was all youthful passion, discussing one man of town or another. Evaline chided her daughter for suggesting what she'd like to do with one of the more handsome clients they'd seen in the house recently. And she reminded Esther that she should be focused, to the best of her abilities, upon obtaining the attentions of a marriageable, and *profitable*, man.

Esther replied, "But mother, the marriageable and profitable ones are many times already married. *Or* they harbor within their trousers little more than the timid toys of a boy."

"Oh, you scandalous child."

"Well, that may be true, but not so *you*'d know," Esther slyly teased.

"Oh, no? I wouldn't know about the goings-on under my own roof?"

Esther held her breath, for fear of her mother's meaning.

"Wouldn't I know... for instance..." Evaline turned and speared her daughter on her piercing eyes, "... about your 'peekaboo' show in the bath at the back of the basement?"

"Gasp!"

"Yes, I knew, darling. I knew that that licentious creature Rebecca helped you with your little game. I knew that that little game of yours brought in more receipts than some of the gals were pulling for a full evening. All the while keeping me in the dark as to what was happening. And all with you at the tender age of seventeen – allowing those boys and men to watch you bathe through the hole in the wall. And I know why too. I had to see for myself, didn't I?"

"Mother! You didn't!"

"Yes, I did. Standing in that basin, in nothing but the lamplight, pouring water down your body. Oh! You should be ashamed. It was a blessing you wore that mask to conceal your identity, or I'd have had to cast you out. Shame on you for allowing Rebecca to indulge you so. That girl left 'afore I took her to the countryside myself to leave her with the pygmy bison. Thankfully no one was any the wiser as to who you were, or how young! Why, I couldn't believe my own eyes… Dear lord."

Esther offered, "I'm sorry. mother – I was young and excitable and didn't know the impact I would have."

"No, I don't think you did. Did they tell you of the poor man they found unconscious against the wall?"

"Yes, they did," she said, fighting back an infectious snicker.

"He'd passed out from pent up desire." Evaline herself smirked. "Poor dear."

Esther pushed ahead, "Isn't it time now – nineteen?" she reminded her mother, "for me to have a better understanding of the world? To get out in it and get a little… *dirty*? Why, you have girls here working their trade who are younger than I am!"

"Yes, but they're not you. They're not my daughter."

"Am I so special somehow…?"

"Yes, you are."

"Do you think I've been encased in a glass cabinet here so I wouldn't be stained?"

"Perhaps you should have been." Starting to smile, she offered, "Perhaps in more than glass – maybe an iron cage…"

"Mother!" Esther feigned insult.

"With a chastity harness!"

"*Mother!* You wouldn't!" both laughing now.

"But should I be placed upon a pedestal? Am I to wear blinders as the horses do, so as not to witness any of it and to remain 'chaste?' Is it fair, mother, to ask me to put myself above these women?"

"No. Now, I will not have you placed above them. I will not. These are good girls…"

"I know, mother, I know. They are beautiful, and smart business women, all. And I would never put myself above them. But don't you see that's how they will see me? If I am not privy to their games, to their work, and if I don't know the things they need to know?"

Evaline was softening her resolve.

"If I don't at least *hear* of the goings-on, know the tell of how to spot a grifter and a con and a flake?"

"How do you know those words?"

"How can I protect myself, mother, from marauding, lecherous men who seek to do their worst with me – out in the town or here in this house for that matter – if I can't identify them with the same keen eye as one of your girls? And how can I be expected to pick up the house operation when you are gone?"

Evaline had lost some of her steam. She knew her daughter was probably right.

"I go out to *learn*, mother. Not to be improper, but to learn," Esther clarified.

Evaline knew the world was not as genteel as many of the elite and their debutante daughters would believe. And she would, in fact, have to call upon Esther to carry on her work in this somewhat particular trade. The prevailing view of the time was that prostitutes and madams were not seen as entirely disreputable – a "necessary evil," as it were, that aided in marital fidelity. But Evaline was no longer a young woman, and there was some sign that public opinion could change.

But how? How would she instill the skills now in her daughter that she'd worked to avoid her even being aware of for these nineteen years?

From downstairs, came the joyous call of full-bodied Mona, the hostess, as a favorite gentleman of the girls entered. "Percy!" she cooed loudly. Evaline could fairly see Mona grabbing hold of the poor hare and hugging him to her like a beloved child.

"Oh, you're soaked through, you sweet sir!" Mona cried. "Come with me and let me fluff you by the fire."

A smile spread slowly across Evaline's face. He would be perfect, her old friend. The hare. No one knew his way around, or could charm his way out of a rough spot, like Percy. If anyone could show young Esther things – lead this girl through the world she was desperate to explore – and see to it that she returned home safely – it would be Percy the Hare. That is, if he himself could be trusted to keep his paws off her.

Chapter 9

Half an hour later. Percy was sitting still and staring at her, with a heavy-lidded, exasperated expression. He couldn't believe that this was what he might be needed for. Is this what Baby Alice was urging him to? He could not fathom why his old friend would ask this of him.

"Babysitting?" Percy sneered.

"Chaperoning," Evaline responded encouragingly. "Perhaps *mentoring*."

He stared, expressionless.

"What, in the fiery hell," he began, "do you imagine that I can teach that child?"

"I'm not a damn child…" Esther blurted.

"Esther! Language, please. And will you please close that robe more securely? Mr. Hare did not come here to see your undergarments." Turning back to Percy, "The *world* is what you can teach her," she replied to him, with some aggrandizement.

"Bullshit!" he answered. "Let me out."

Across the room, young Esther Wells flung herself against the door and latched it to keep him in. She had an excited look in her eye, desperate, it seemed, to see this arrangement finalized.

Evaline explained, "Esther is already out and about town, disappearing and adventuring until all hours." She drew close to him to speak quietly, "Percy, I fear for her. You know how headstrong she is. I need someone to regulate her and protect her. I'm too old to go 'round town anymore and see to it that she's safe. Or not making dreadful mistakes. She's been sneaking out to euchre games in unsavory back rooms on the levee. And she's taken to trolling the academics on campus for fine dinners and nights at the opera."

He actually smirked at hearing this, admiring the young woman's resourcefulness. The academic crowd at the young university John Purdue started in 1869 were some of his own fond targets. They were unfathomably fond of their own accomplishments and completely unable to resist the temptations of wagering their perceived status against the odds of the real world. And they almost always came up on the short side of the bet. He glanced at Esther and she gave him a knowing, coquettish look.

"*Lord,*" he thought to himself, "*those bottled up chalkers* (his phrase for lecturers at their chalkboards) *probably don't know what hit them when that girl arrives. I almost feel sorry for them.*"

Evaline continued, "Percy, this young woman has had no benefit of a father."

"You never wanted one in the room!" he stated rightly.

"No, no, I didn't. But I recognize now that the proper... *masculine outlook* on the world might have been a benefit to her full education."

"Oh, tosh! And what has she been lacking in her education? Latin, perhaps?" he asked.

"Ut linguam Latinam didicerunt (*I studied Latin*)," Esther replied under her breath.

"Mathematics?" he continued. "Biologics? What of all those twisted explanations and calculations am I expected to know and share with her?"

Evaline leaned away from her seat to implore him more closely.

"None of that! Percy, don't make an old woman come to you on her aching knees." She took his paws in her wizened hands. "Your knowledge is far keener and more specific than any of those things."

"Ugh!" he chortled. "I'm no nanny, Evaline. I come and I go as I please, and I won't be saddled with a *girl* at my side." He moved toward the parlor door again, but Esther backed herself against it to block his way. He flapped his long flat foot to the floor in measured irritation.

Turning back, he continued, "A girl who just wants to go out and... I don't know... get herself killed for all I can tell." He continued across the room and leapt quickly to the top of the credenza under the window. "Because that's what awaits her! Out there, where she wants to go, she would be nothing but a target. All that red hair, all of that... *girliness!*She wouldn't last an evening. She'd come home to you in pieces."

Gasping at the mental picture that painted, Evaline cried, "Percy! Don't speak to me so!"

He spun on his perch and said, "There is no other way to speak of this, madam!"

The truer picture in his own head was far darker. As a wily hare, he had escaped innumerable close encounters with the loss of just a bit of fur. But a ripe young woman like Esther would be subject to far worse.

He continued, "She must not go to town, not at night – it is madness. Not alone, and certainly not with me! And so," reaching for the window sash and raising it up just enough, "I will bid you goodnight."

And with that, the hare turned himself sideways and fairly rolled out the window and out of sight. The women screamed as he disappeared. But nothing was heard in response but the hissing of the icy rain on the gabled roof.

"Oh. Percy!" cried Evaline. "What does he think he's doing leaping from such a height?"

"Never mind, mother!" Esther answered, somewhat matter-of-factly. "The gable isn't terribly pitched here and leads one directly to the top of the arbor. From there it's two short jumps and you're into the myrtle. Been down it a number of times."

"You have not!" Evaline cried weakly.

"Oh, but I have mother. And I shall again. I'm too old now for your admonishments, so don't bother." And taking her elderly mother's chin in her hand, Esther assured her, I love you, but he's getting away from me. Don't wait up for me! You know I'll be just fine with our gentleman hare."

She climbed onto the window sill, but Evaline admonished her, "Now, Esther, that's a fine silk robe!"

"Fine mother!" she replied. "Then it'll just have to go. Or stay, rather." And she pulled it off and flung the robe to the floor.

Without an evening dress over her corset and bloomers, and without a proper coat, and with no preparation or hesitation, Esther Wells drew high the window sash and flung herself after Percy, out onto the gable roof and into the freezing rain.

Percy could hear Evaline screaming out for Esther to get back inside. And he could hear Esther running after him in the carriageway beside the house, calling his name desperately. He stopped and closed his eyes, wishing he could bound away before she reached him, but knowing she would pursue him nonetheless. He knew her that well. He turned to see his suspicions rewarded. The girl ran to him in her corset and bloomers, in the rain, with no wrap or cloak or hat. She would chase him down the street dressed that way, and she would catch her death of cold. And it would be all his fault.

"Dammit," he muttered.

"Percy, please! Please go out with me."

"Where do you think you're going dressed like that?"

"I don't know," she admitted, realizing her unpreparedness. "Maybe to play euchre?"

"Euchre!?"

"Yes, I want to get into the Marquis' game," she said assuredly. As she said it, she plucked up her gumption and stood tall in the rain, displaying her confidence. She was already soaked and her bare shoulders shone in the moonlight.

"The Marquis' game?" Percy asked. He couldn't contain his dismay at her hubris. "The *Marquis'* game? They would eat you, child."

About four months prior to that evening, a man calling himself the "Marquis de Lafayette" had arrived in Lafayette town, within a fine black enamel and gilded carriage drawn by a jet-black horse. The carriage was emblazoned with a shining gold fleur-de-lis design that certainly spoke of French style, though he was clearly not of French aristocracy. His namesake, Marie-Joseph Paul Yves Roch Gilbert du Motier, or the Marquis de La Fayette, was a French aristocrat and Revolutionary War hero, in whose honor the town of Lafayette itself had been named. He had also been dead since 1834, almost fifty years. The assumption of the Frenchman's moniker must have been an attempt to grasp some of his cachet and impress the populace of the rural town. But the man himself was less genteel than his namesake.

This man's black hair was slicked back flat across his skull, and his moustache was clipped to an abbreviated slash above his rather pouty lips. His heavy-lidded eyes seemed to cast disdain over everyone, his black eyebrows perpetually pressed low as if to squeeze those he saw from his view. Far from an aristocratic tone of voice, when he spoke it was with the pinched, gravelly coarseness of the Great Lakes region. Percy imagined he had spent time in the back alleys of Chicago or Detroit before turning south.

The Marquis quickly assembled a coterie of both sycophantic society fops and deeply unpleasant riff-raff seemingly scraped from the slime-dripping walls of the canal. The former were drawn to him by his pretentious lifestyle, the latter by his cruelty and harsh business dealings.

Rumor had it the Marquis had established a regular, high-stakes euchre game somewhere in town. Euchre had become the card game of choice throughout the Midwestern states, and few played it with as much ruthless diligence, or as much diligent ruthlessness for that matter, as folks of the Hoosier state. The location of the Marquis' game was unknown to any but those who were invited to attend. Rumors had it taking place everywhere from the upper dome of the new and nearly completed Tippecanoe County Courthouse, to a secret culvert of the underground Pearl River in the hills above town, to a riverboat moored on the Wabash. It was also rumored that Sheriff S. O. Taylor and his men were in hot pursuit of the game, as it had become quite the deadly enterprise. A number of men who were known to have ventured to the game had been found "of poor health" the following day, either cold dead or disabled and unwilling to speak of their experiences.

Esther Wells' willingness to even speak of the Marquis' game brought a clutch to Percy's throat. How did Evaline succeed in raising a young woman of such brass? Percy now understood Evaline's interest in having him watch over her. The girl could get herself killed in a single night in Lafayette, should she determine to step into the wrong corner. But he damn sure didn't want to be the one trying to steer the obstinate young woman from trouble.

They stared at one another through the darkness and the sleeting rain. He had to marvel at her commitment.

Responding to his suggestion that the Marquis' crowd would "eat" her, Esther said, "Well, maybe *now* they might. But I want to get established in the game about town first. Start modest, then go large."

"Go large," he repeated, taking in her aspiration.

"Yes. I'm determined," she replied matter-of-factly.

"Why? What is there to..."

"Because I've never *done* anything, Percy! Because mother has kept me sheltered in this house all my life. I never got to do anything because people looked down on mother and wouldn't allow me to see their children or be a part of anything. But I'm good, Percy! And I'm smart. And I can do things. I know I can."

He could see in her large eyes, and in her set stance, there in the cold and wet, that she indeed had the determination. For a moment, he had a vision of the pitiful form of Baby Alice, returned home in the cold rain on the morning of her death. It chilled him to his core. Esther was a bigger and stronger young woman than Alice, for sure. But he swore he could see her full lips turning blue as the rain dripped down her lovely face. He felt himself giving way.

"Be that what it may," he offered, wondering why he was saying it even as the words left his mouth, "let's pick a night that's less... horrible to begin." He was trying to sound stern and hoped it came across.

She gasped, "You'll do it? Oh, Percy!"

Esther knelt in the rough dirt of the carriageway, in her white bloomers, and wrapped her arms around him.

"Alright, alright," Percy squirmed. But she held him tightly. Her hair, he admitted, smelled quite nice. Even in the bare moonlight it shone red like a fire and was coiffed elegantly atop her head.

Esther leapt to her feet again, smiling down on him and breathing excitedly.

69

With the vision she presented of all that red hair and her décolletage glistening wet, he immediately regretted his decision.

"Good lord, child," he stammered, "you'll be eaten alive." The phrasing he'd given her mother, thus repeated, was meant to lighten the aspect while emphasizing his fear. He couldn't very well tell the girl his true suspicion – that she would be raped and murdered in downtown Lafayette just for looking the way she did.

"Another night," he continued, trying to put her off, "When the weather is more agreeable... and you have clothing."

But she was already running back up the drive and yelling, "No, it's tonight! Wait! Wait for me..."

As he watched the young woman run back to the carriage house, a white figure soaking wet with rain, stumbling and quickly getting back up, Percy the hare thought to himself, "*If you had any sense at all – if you were half the gentleman you profess – you would leave her here for her own good. Be gone before she gets back.*"

But Percy stood in the rain.

Chapter 10

Esther fairly clomped down the Ninth Street Hill in the big boots. Completely concealed under the stolen (or "borrowed") rain gear of the house's carriage man, young Esther was unrecognizable. Even her blazing hair was hidden, tucked beneath the broad brim hat. As a figure, she looked essentially floppy and ridiculous. But Percy took comfort in the knowledge that at least she would not be identified and that, perhaps more importantly, she would be dry beneath the heavy sheathing of the oil cloth rain slicker and wader pants.

"God, Percy!" Esther said excitedly, "I feel like Calamity Jane, out on a midnight raid! You ever read of her exploits? Have you? Isn't she just *captivating*? Have you heard of her?"

"A bit," replied Percy.

"Oh, I'd love to lead her life, if I could. I'm sure there's nothing so exciting nor dreadful or dangerous here along the Wabash as what she faces out in the wild West. But I feel like we're adventuring in her boots, don't you?"

Percy thought to himself that he could envision plenty of dangerous and dreadful scenarios right there in north central Indiana. But he kept his eye on the solitary horse carriage coming along 9th Street toward them. "Damned clomping things," he muttered. "The wild West can keep those ugly, tail-flicking monsters. They belong out there anyway." The carriage and its steed rolled past them unheedingly.

"That's all we're missing, Percy!" Esther exclaimed. "Glorious steeds to race downtown upon!"

But he hated horses. All of them. Percy slogged on through the rain, muttering, "We're not missing a damn thing, girl."

They were heading to Barkey Smith's place, or more accurately, the place Barkey oversaw. The Short Buffalo Tavern stood at Sixth and Main Streets, in a block of three-story buildings. The "Short Buff," as it was known, was not far enough downtown to catch the regular river dregs, but too far uptown to benefit from the heavier flow of ill-gotten cash that could be found along the canal and the river. Barkey liked it just fine. He'd fought long and hard, biding his time quietly and, as a black man, taking plenty of shit along the way before he had earned managerial status at the Short Buff. He'd proven himself time and again to both tough customers and well-pressed suits. Now he stood at the door to an establishment to which he was proud to invite folks. A place known to be a little quieter and a little cleaner. He had come around to hosting some games in the back, but this was not the type of place where the deeper pockets preferred to play. His clientele was a lot less flashy and a lot less sharp to the games being played, both on the table and below it.

At the front of the saloon, near the door, there still stood a walled holding pen in which the owner had once kept an actual pygmy bison, the namesake of the Short Buffalo Tavern. It was certainly an attraction in its time, though a short-lived one. The bison, only the size of a large housecat, was of interest to everyone from regular drinkers to children on their way home from school, who had to be shooed out constantly. But the smell of the thing, and its aggressive manner, eventually led to its removal. It would snort and charge at everyone who stopped for a look, leading to its damn near pounding out its own brains on the holding pen walls. The pen now housed a likeness of the bison fashioned by a local taxidermist, with an approximation of the grass prairie it called home and a sign promoting the taxidermist's establishment.

It was rather quiet that November evening, and Barkey had assumed a seat at the end of the bar closest to the Main Street door. He was casually sipping a short draught, watching the customers and getting a feel for their conversations. Nothing happening here.

CHAPTER 10

Then he noticed a brief flicker of the oil lamp in the back hallway, all the way at the furthest reach of the space. Someone had come in through the back door. No one else picked up on it. But Barkey had made it his job to know when any door or window opened, or to know instantly where a drink had been spilled in the crowded bar, and more importantly, why. He considered the back door for a moment, but he didn't remember anyone planning to visit that evening who wasn't already in house. Someone had known how to access the door too, which wasn't obvious to the uninitiated. The outdoor latch was well concealed and only a few knew of it. He rose to check the visitor.

Stepping out into the room, he moved to have a more direct view down the back hallway and found a large figure there. Wide-brimmed hat, coat collar up, all in dark silhouette against the flickering light of the oil lamp. Rain water shone on the figure's shoulders and hat. Then, under that person, or no, in front of them but lower, the muzzle and flat, broad head of an animal. A long grey rabbit ear rose and twisted, shaking off the rain, then another. A small face with large eyes he knew well peeked over the heads of customers seated midway through the bar. A paw raised in a quick wave to Barkey, some sixty feet away through the din and smoke. Then the basement door opened into the hallway, a black bar that swung out and then closed again, showing no one there any longer.

"Percy Hare," Barkey spoke to himself. "Goddammit. What kind of trouble is that boy bringing me now?"

It was an easy entry to the basement. No one watching the door. A friendly game Barkey ran. He wouldn't put up with the mess of a staged game with goons and all. Percy pushed Esther through the door and directed her down the narrow steps. At the foot of the stairs they turned past a thick, rough-hewn beam and into a long narrow basement. About seventy feet long but only about twelve feet wide, wooden storage ran a short length of the brick walls. The rest was open and dark. Three suspended lamps intermittently cut the gloom with glowing domes of light flickering through a smoky haze. Wooden floor boards ran the length of the room, primarily down the center, laid directly onto the dirt which was still exposed at the base of the walls.

Beneath the second lamp, a round table hosted four players at compass points. A few other gentlemen lounged nearby, one standing and two seated atop round barrel kegs. One of the keg sitters snorted loudly, turned his head, and, laying a finger aside his nose, blasted a snot blot onto the dirt floor.

Esther's boots fell heavily on the floor boards, drawing every eye. They watched as the dark-cloaked figure drew nearer, dripping rain water. Percy stepped beside her and into the light.

A fat man at the table bellowed, "Oh my god, it's the hare! I love the hare! How are you, pal?"

Percy replied, "Grand, Horace. How are you? Still doing your part to rid the river of its oysters, I see?" Horace Grinlow let out a guffaw, picked up a plate from the table, lifted an oyster shell, and noisily sucked out its contents to illustrate Percy's point for him.

"Absolutely." Horace laughed heartily, his humor tumbling from him almost unstoppably. Everyone in the room chuckled. Horace's face flushed red with his laughter.

Esther herself giggled quietly beneath her gear without giving away her identity. She was drinking in the atmosphere and the inhabitants of the room, trying to gauge their acceptance of the new visitors. Her companion was noticing everything.

Percy was accomplished at reading a room – getting a sense of everyone in it and their mood and intentions. More importantly, he quickly calculated the physical space, not in footage, but in possibilities. Metal bar leaning against the wall at the base of the stairs. Unmovable heavy soft sacks at the base of the shelving. Medium tin cans, likely lightweight, on the shelves. Evidence of burrowing in two spots along the dirt floor, either by a pet stowed in the basement or a rodent infiltrating the room from without, but likely the former. One spot on the rear wall which used to hold a window but was now boarded shut. It might still be accessible without much effort, but it was high on the wall.

The room was dry and dusty. Beneath their feet, rainwater dripping from their clothing was quickly sucked into the parched wood. No one else in the room showed evidence of dampening the floor. All had been here a good while, but the lower legs of one man's trousers, the man seated opposite Horace, were still damp. He was a later arrival.

As Evaline Wells would point out repeatedly, one of Percy's unique gifts was "knowing when to be in the right place and when to not be in the wrong place." Before the laughter died down, Percy was prepared to be in the right place. And for leaving it in a hurry if it became the wrong one.

"So what's your pleasure, Mr. Hare?" asked Horace. "Are you here for cards?"

Horace McNeely was a local green grocer. He had a modest place up on North 6th street that he kept well-stocked and was well-trafficked by local residents. He was an agreeable man with whom it seemed no one had a quarrel, though he was known to be a bit handsy with lady folk and especially young women. Percy had hoped they'd find Horace there at Barkey's game, knowing he was a regular. And knowing that the ample young Esther would be as tempting to the old grocer as ripe pink fruit, he was anxious to see how the girl would carry herself.

Gesturing to his companion, Percy said simply, "She'd like to play."

"*She*, eh?" Horace answered, now intrigued. "We don't get many members of the gentler sex out to play cards in the evening. Some don't consider it proper, after all." He leaned back and considered the shadowed face under Esther's hat for a moment, thinking over what the hare had brought to the room on this gloomy night. "Tell me, just who is your friend here?"

As agreed upon, Esther kept her raingear on, with her broad-brimmed hat tugged down low, maintaining an air of mystery. This, of course, also maintained a sense of decency, as she had nothing on under the gear but her undergarments.

Percy opened his mouth to reply, when Esther interjected in a voice made somewhat husky from exposure to the night rain, "Just a young woman who's wondering which of you lugs is going to offer a woman a seat at the table."

A broad grin slid across Horace's face and he turned to the man opposite him, clearly a cohort, and nodded for him to get up. The youngish man with dampened trouser legs hesitated a moment, then rose and gallantly offered his chair. He clearly was none too pleased with being nudged from the game, but he deferred to his elder, and to the auspicious arrival of a woman for Barkey's game. Percy imagined the young man had struggled in the rain to get to the game on time, only to be pushed from the table.

Esther seated herself and the men all watched intently, hoping for some glimpse of her face or her build. The large hat and rain slicker offered none of that, but she loved the attention she was drawing.

Chapter 11

"You'll be my partner, darlin'," Horace started. Then, pointing to his left and right respectively, "And this is Oscar Binchen, and here we have Clinton Pardoo." Both men tipped their caps to her. Gathering the cards scattered across the table, "Oscar and I served in the Mexican war together, and now he hauls ice for pretty much all of downtown. Clinton is a clerk at the Timmons law office up on Third Street." He shuffled the abbreviated euchre deck, which only uses twenty-four cards (six from each of the four different suits – Ace, King, Queen, Jack, 10, and 9). Horace added, "And at our game a few weeks ago I believe, Clinton was entertaining us all with the tale of a rabbit, or *hare* (deferring to Percy), and a roaming pig that tore up his neighbor's garden!"

Horace laughed so hard he found himself snorting for breath. The room as a whole chuckled over the memory of the story. A couple of the men seated along the wall planted their cigarettes between their lips to free their hands and began to clap and hoot their appreciation for Percy's fabled deed.

Percy grinned now, though not allowing the cheers to stoke his ego and still watching them all intently. Esther didn't show a response, being the only attendee not aware of the tale or of Percy's involvement.

At that moment, a boot fell heavily on the lowest step of the staircase and its owner plodded into the room.

"And here's the heroic and fabled pig's rightful owner, Mr. Smith!" Another round of cheer went up as Barkey came into the light.

He smirked and looked down at Percy, speaking low, "Alright. And whatchoo bringing me now, rabbit?"

"What do ya say, Barkey?" followed Horace. "Can we give you our orders?"

"Orders?" Barkey frowned. "I'm just bringin' you a set of whiskeys unless I hear otherwise." They all nodded agreeingly.

"There it is then." Barkey turned to leave, but not before giving a long look at the dark cloaked figure and then at Percy. He looked at the hare with a furrowed brow for a moment, then back at Esther, then back at Percy. Percy just grinned and gave Barkey a wink, away from where the others could see. Barkey exhaled sharply and turned back up the staircase.

"Right!" Horace continued. "We play simple here. And fast. It's a quarter a trick and a quarter a bump. A bump when you fail to attain three tricks, or fail to sweep a loner hand, committing table talk, or getting caught reneging. Getting euchred on a loner hand is four bumps. We tally bumps with chits – we'll use these matches – next to the score cards. Bets are settled at the end of each game. You clear?"

Esther nodded.

"Excellent. Let's spank the horse and get her going." A couple of the men chortled at the comment. "Oh. My apologies, miss, for my indelicacy." But Horace had a grin on his face as he commenced to deal. Then he caught himself before the first cards landed.

"Oop! I almost forgot. Gentlemen – and *lady* – let's see your cash. Ten dollars up."

"*Shit, cash?*" Esther thought to herself. She maintained her demeanor but suddenly realized she'd run from the house without any holding money for the game.

"*Shit. Cash.*" Percy thought, having the same realization. How had he not foreseen this, even while distracted by the girl pursuing him down the street in the rain?

The men dug into their vest coats, unfolded their dollars and stacked their coins into neat stacks on the table. Clinton Pardoo stacked an entire coin portfolio, with a few dollar coins, and a variety of quarters, dimes, nickels, three-cents, and pennies. Esther's mind raced to answer how to ante in on the game. She turned to look at Percy. He had nothing for her but a blank, wide-eyed look. He twitched his nose nervously, his whiskers rising and falling from one side to the other. She could tell his mind was similarly calculating but coming short of an answer.

Seeing no movement from the young woman, Horace said, "Come, now, darlin'. It's only a friendly game, but we do expect to see folks' holding cash before cards are dealt."

"It's ten dollars for the whole night, miss," Oscar Binchen offered, trying to be helpful. "No more."

(Author's note - $10 in 1883 would equal approximately $250 at today's value. Not as cheap a game as she'd been playing with the collegiates, but not the priciest in town.)

There was an awkward pause, and then Esther began, with a little hesitation. "Gents, it occurs to me that my companion and I ran out into the rain this evening, and in our haste we have... overlooked this necessity."

Several of the men seated to the side moaned their disappointment, and a bit of annoyance. Percy thought they had ruined her chance with this oversight. Game over. Try again some other time.

"However," Esther spoke up, and the room fell silent. She reached to her overcoat and began to unbutton it. Then, clutching the lapels, she spread it open, revealing her ample bosom and delicately powdered décolletage, saying, "I may have something here to put up for collateral."

The men seated behind her leaned forward rapidly to get a better view, and then the room fell silent. Not a rustle. Then Percy heard his tongue click against his palate as his mouth fell open. Oscar seemed to be choking on his own tongue. And Percy could literally hear the breath escape the lungs of the rest of the attendees, their eyes feasting upon the dramatically lit soft globes hovering above the stiff white corset within Esther's bulky coat.

She reached a delicate hand up and plunged two fingers into her cleavage, then slowly produced a white silk handkerchief. Percy was agog as he watched her now calmly and masterfully manipulate the room. With a graceful tug, the handkerchief was plucked free of her corset and she deftly offered it forward for the men to read. The embroidered initials 'E.W.' were visible in a lovely lilac-colored thread.

"Would one of you gentleman be willing to offer me ten dollars for *this?*" Esther asked slyly.

A flurry of activity ensued as they all, to a man, dug into their pockets for cash. A young scruff originally seated on a barrel behind her thrust forward a handful of bills that nearly touched her shadowed cheek. Percy could make out her sly grin beneath the wide hat brim.

"It's more than ten," said the scruff. "No matter, it's enough. Have it."

She took the money and offered the handkerchief back over her shoulder to him. Her manicured fingers arranged the stack of bills on the table beside her. The young scruff drew back the handkerchief and held it stiff-fingered as though it were a precious religious relic. He grabbed hold of his barrel with the other hand and turned it, to roll it on edge to where he might have a better view of her, at least in profile. Esther would oblige him, and the room as a whole, by leaving her coat open for the rest of the evening.

She glanced over at Percy confidently. He found himself marveling at her moxie and at that moment was won over. Despite himself, and despite his enormous reservations for the trouble she might cause, he somehow knew that life in the proximity of this young woman had only just begun to show its promise.

Horace's face seemed nearly wrenched apart by his wide smile, as he began to deal two cards to Oscar, three to Esther, two to Clinton, then three to himself. Then he cycled around again with three to Oscar, two to Esther, three to Clinton, and two to himself. He flipped over the top card of the remaining four and set this short group aside where all could see it.

"Auspicious!" said Oscar. "Our new girl conjures up the Queen of Hearts on her first hand. Our Queen of Hearts, all dressed in black." He chuckled and looked to her. But Esther gave him no response, so he awkwardly addressed his cards, having the first call. He promptly rapped his knuckles twice on the table to indicate a pass.

No sooner had the second rap landed than Esther said, "Pick it up."

Horace raised his eyebrows at her initiative, calling him up on her first

80

hand in the game. Oscar grunted lightly as though surprised. He was holding the Jack of Hearts, the highest value card in the hand, though the rest of his cards were of black suits. Horace picked up the Queen and discarded another card from his hand, placing that card face down. And off they went.

Oscar led a weak 9 of Spades, seemingly testing the water to draw forth a trump card too early. Esther followed suit with the Queen, Clinton as well with the King. The hand was his, unless Horace had the Ace or, barring no other Spade cards, a trump card. Horace dropped the Ace and swept the hand to the side.

Horace then led with the Jack of Clubs. Oscar followed suit with the ten, Esther similarly followed with the Ace. Clinton, fumbling in his haste to produce it, flicked the Ace of Hearts from his hand. It flew to the side, lodging snugly in Esther's cleavage. He was mortified. Several of the men in the room snickered and shuffled in their seats.

She simply turned and looked at Clinton and asked, "Would you like me to retrieve that for you?"

Clinton's hand was up, shaking nervously over the table. But, after clearing his throat, he replied "Yes, please." She laid it on the pile for him. Having trumped the hand, he politely dragged the cards to his corner of the table.

Oscar spoke up. "Horace... and... E.W. was it?"

Esther thought a second and realized that yes, her initials would be enough to go by. She nodded silently.

Oscar continued, "We're going to bet that we set you on this hand. Two chits." He picked up two matchsticks and dropped them on the center of the table.

"Oh-hoh!" rumbled Horace, in appreciation for the challenge.

Esther realized it was a foolish bet on his part. Even if he had a high trump card (he was in fact holding the Jack of Hearts which was a guaranteed winner) and his team had already taken a trick, she held the rest of the high trump cards. Oscar and Clinton would only need one additional trick to come up with three of the five tricks total and set them. But she wasn't about to see that happen. Still, she allowed her mouth to drop open, just a bit, as if surprised and frightened by Oscar's bet. She fingered her cards a bit, to suggest she was nervously considering the possibilities to come.

Horace considered Esther for a moment, trying to read her reaction. He couldn't tell yet whether she was genuinely concerned over their chances. But he figured it was early in the game and he ought to test the girl's mettle. Horace likely had nothing to help her with left in his hand. But she had come to play, he figured, so let's see how she liked playing.

"We're going to see your bet, sir," Horace said while pulling two match- sticks and setting them next to Oscar's. "And we'll raise you three more." He added the additional three matchsticks.

The non-tabled men around the room shuffled and grunted their appre- ciation. Both Oscar and Clinton darted looks around the table, from each other to Horace to E.W., trying to ascertain her reaction. Was he bluffing? She had called him up and the onus to hold the hand was on her, but was he loaded to help her? E.W. gave them nothing. They could only make out her mouth and chin beneath the shadow of the hat and she was motionless.

Somewhat reluctantly, Oscar picked up three more matchsticks and set them next to the others at the center of the table, calling Horace's raise. Ten chits in the bet, two more for the winners of the hand, and potentially two more for setting the hand from those who called suit. It had become a fourteen-chit hand.

"Alrighty then," said Oscar. "Clinton, your lead."

Clinton clutched his cards tightly, lest he fling another nervously toward E.W. He'd held a mixed hand with no trump that was not of much value. He led with his highest remaining card, the King of Diamonds.

Horace dropped the 10 of Diamonds. Oscar pondered a moment. He had no diamonds in his hand. And he realized his partner had the hand for the moment, but E.W. would likely trump it when her turn came. Should he trump his partner or let it go? He had one sure trick, but they would need another to set their opponents. Clinton wasn't showing signs of being well-suited to assist, so should he hope for the best on this trick and get the next one? But let the King take the hand? Was that even possible?

Before he knew it, several moments had passed and the other players were hanging on Oscar's hesitation.

Horace lay his finger on one matchstick and pushed it to his right toward Clinton, saying, "I'll bet he doesn't play in five seconds. Five – four – three – two…"

Oscar, flushed and irritated at the challenge, dropped his right bower, the Jack of Hearts. Esther dropped the Queen of Diamonds on top of it. She wouldn't have trumped the hand after all. They would have won it with the King of Diamonds. And he had wasted his bower.

Esther laid down the left bower, the Jack of Diamonds, and the Ace of Hearts. They were the two highest value cards remaining, and no one could have defeated them. Horace guffawed as they took the hand. The rest of the room applauded. Horace smiled at her and laughed heartily.

Barkey appeared at the edge of the light with a tray full of shot glasses, each brimming with glowing golden whiskey. Horace plucked one from the tray and raised it to Esther, then he tossed the whiskey down his throat. Barkey looked at Esther, looked away briefly, then shot his eyes back upon recognizing the wealth of cleavage she was now displaying. Clinton picked up a shot and passed it over to Esther. She took it gingerly and tried not to tipple any onto the table. She held her glass out to Clinton, and then raised it to Horace, and then to Oscar, and then she sipped a bit of it.

Percy watched the proceedings a while, then felt the edge of the tray of glasses nudge against his coat. He turned to see Barkey offering it to him, asking, "You takin' one too?" Percy obliged, took a shot from the tray and tossed it back altogether. He set the glass back on the tray, knowing Barkey wasn't done with him yet.

They looked at each other a moment quietly.

"How's my girlfriend, Kess?" inquired Percy.

With emphasis, Barkey replied, "*My wife* is fine and she sure ain't your girlfriend. Now, you mind telling me whatchoo got going on here?" Barkey shifted the tray toward Esther for emphasis. "Who the hell is that?"

Percy looked over at Esther who was looking back at him. He watched her stoically taking in the room around her and admired her restraint. She was maintaining her composure, not celebrating, but rather gathering the cards, flipping them face down, and pushing them toward Oscar for his deal. It was clear Esther enjoyed the anonymity and concealment of her overcoat, despite, that is, her bared chest. The charming, vivacious young girl was hiding somehow beneath the cloak and the assumed identity of the mysterious woman. And she liked it there.

Percy looked up at Barkey again, considering whether he should be informed that the nineteen-year-old daughter of the most influential madam in town was holding court at a euchre game in his tavern. With her breasts out. In a room full of strange men. It might make him nervous.

"To be perfectly honest, my friend, I'm not entirely sure *who* she is. Yet." Then Percy added, "But she could be trouble." He smiled a big cheesy smile up at him.

Barkey held his glare while turning away, saying, "Oh, lord, rabbit, you're gonna be the death of me."

Chapter 12

Through the remainder of the game, Percy watched as "E.W."'s poise and confidence grew at the euchre table. She was good, it quickly became apparent. And not just at the game, but also at reading the men at the table, their inclinations and quirks and tells. She could easily read Oscar and Clinton. It was immediately clear to her when they had nothing in their hands worthwhile, when they'd been dealt a loner hand, and when they had one good card as a "help" to their partner. Horace was a bit harder to read at first, but she made him out too. By the final hand, she knew she would be playing a loner to finish the game by the way he shifted his cigar from one side of his mouth to the other upon seeing the fifth card in his hand. He hadn't signaled her or done anything improper. She'd picked up on it on her own.

She caught the others up on their table talk, taking chits from both Oscar (twice) and Clinton (once) for what they thought were very discrete signals. She'd made them desperate by her skilled play, but that was no excuse for table talk. She'd even caught Horace pulling an extra card on his deal and then discarding two to get back to five cards showing, with a slightly better deal at his disposal. As they were teammates, she'd let it go, but made note that he was not to be trusted.

She sipped her whiskey politely, allowing it to last and refusing when Horace tried to ply her with more. She maintained both the brim of her hat to shadow her face and the draw of her coat lapels to keep her décolletage visible, distracting the other players. Percy observed the other non-players in the room slowly gravitate to Horace's side of the room, allowing them a better view of the mysterious "E.W." and all her charms.

And when the third game ended, though Percy expected her to protest, they settled up when he indicated it was time. He had to point out to them all that it was well past one in the morning and it would be hard as hell for him to chaperone her home at that hour without raising suspicions of her character.

"Not only that," he continued, "but poor Clinton is going to have a hell of a time explaining to his wife how it is that the grocer's funds will be light this week." This drew a general laugh, as the poor man had played abominably and was now bereft of funds.

"Haw! Haw!" bellowed Horace as the chits were settled and they each folded their bills and change into their pockets. He (the green grocer) clapped Clinton on the shoulder with a big paw and said, "Fear not, my good man. Grinlow Grocers will extend you the credit on the groceries this week and she'll be none the wiser!"

For her part, Esther bid them all adieu, drained the remainder of her whiskey, licking the rim of the glass as she did so, and leaning forward upon rising from the table, to the point where Percy wondered how her breasts were prevented from falling out onto the cards. In a graceful denouement, a single curl of her bright red hair then tumbled from within her hat and hug over her lapel. There was a collective intake of breath in the room, they all rose from their seats as gentlemen, and then the coat was drawn closed.

Before anyone could move from their spot, or even inquire as to when she might return, she and Percy had proceeded up the darkened staircase, forty-three dollars richer and one fine handkerchief lighter, and clomped out again in her much-too-large boots into the freezing November rain.

Thus was born the legend of enigmatic "E.W."

About two blocks down the alley behind Main Street, heading west, Esther asked, "Do you think we're far enough away now?"

Percy, maintaining stride, looked back over his shoulder. As they passed a small blockhouse he said, "Yes. I don't think anyone could see us any longer back here...", upon which he was swallowed into a huge wet hug from Esther.

She held him tightly, kneeling in the wet gravel. She kissed him on his snout and hugged him again, saying excitedly in his ear, "Oh, Percy! That was so exciting! I've never enjoyed an evening so much in my life! Oh, thank you, thank you, thank you!" She kissed him several more times until he separated himself a bit.

"Shhh – quiet now, girl," he replied. She wouldn't let him go. Her gratitude and affection were obvious. And before her soft embrace made his own affection too obvious, he pulled away. "We still must be..."

And as if to illustrate his caution, a group of young men stumbled into the alleyway a few buildings down, ambling drunkenly and loudly in their direction. By their jeers back and forth and by their jostling of one other against a wall in contests of spite and grit, a knife flashing briefly against one man's throat, Percy knew their intent on this inhospitable evening would only be treachery.

"This way," he said quietly, pulling her between two buildings so close that she barely fit.

They made their way out onto Columbia Street and headed further west, hoping the young men hadn't made them out in the darkness. This was one of the larger thoroughfares in the downtown, more open than he liked, so they clung to the shadows until he could find a passage into the alley behind the buildings. They continued a bit further before circling home up Prospect Hill.

Chapter 13

Evaline had eventually drifted off to sleep after a fitful night of worrying over her daughter's welfare. She had kept poor Mona the hostess up with her all the night long, prodding the poor woman when she dozed off and entreating her to keep bringing fresh coffee. Eventually the black caffeinated brew could no longer sustain her and the mature matron of the house collapsed onto the horsehair sofa in the early hours of the morning. Mona was beside her in a thick-armed chair, her feet flung out in front and one shoe clinging at an angle from her foot.

Evaline woke in the parlor in the early morning to find what appeared to be Percy the hare curled up beside her. His head was jammed into the back corner of the couch and his furred legs were curled up beside him. His long ears lay back over his shoulders. One ear lifted lazily and twitched momentarily before settling back down against its companion.

Evaline slowly dug herself out of the sofa and raised her weary, aching body to full height. She wanted to address the hare, but she chose to look for her daughter first. She stumbled down the hall to her room.

The floor in the doorway to Esther's room was damp. At the foot of the bed lay a puzzling pile of wet oil cloth in no discernable form. Puddles of rainwater were settled in the folds of the cloth. On the bed itself was young Esther, or at least her backside suspended up in the air in soiled bloomers. Her head was plunged into the depths of her pillows and her luxurious red hair fanned out around her, her arms straight out from her sides like she was flying.

"Fine," she thought. "The girl is fine. Now to the hare."

When she returned to the parlor, Percy was once again clambering over her window sill seeking to escape.

"Halt, you furred miscreant!"

"Oh, you're awake," he replied cheerfully.

Evaline could only glare at him. Her words roiled inside her, unable to find release.

"She did well, you should know." Percy grinned with a sense of false self-assurance.

Evaline drew a deep breath and prepared to speak.

"Really well, in fact. You would have been proud."

"Proud? PROUD, you say? How dare you…"

"Oh, yes," Percy interrupted. "She won, you know. Against some fairly accomplished players."

Evaline could only sputter, unable to find a starting point.

"Yup, she won alright. Did you know that your young Esther is in fact devilishly good at euchre? Astoundingly perceptive and quick…"

"WHAT. Did you do. With my BABY last night?!" Evaline exploded. He could hear other parts of the house stirring from the vociferousness of her tone.

"Your baby? I took her out to a game, as you…"

"How could you take my girl out into the stormy night…" She faltered. "She won? What do you mean, she won?"

"She played well. Better than anyone at the table, certainly," he offered. "She returned home with an expansion on her stake, that's for sure."

"You took her from my home, in the pouring rain, in her UNDERWEAR! Why did you not send her back inside? What did she have on at this game? How was she not recognized? Oh, my LORD! The Sheriff will be here in no time to take her from me, as I'm an unfit mother." A troubled pause. "PERCY!" she screamed.

True to his billing, Percy knew it was time to not be there. He was once again practically over the window sill when she looked back at him. The panes rattled over his head with her rage. He was fully aware that reasoning with his old friend at this moment, indeed making the point that she herself had in fact *begged* him to take the girl out, would be a fool's error and a grave one.

"See here, all came out very nicely – very nicely indeed," he assured her. "You will want to settle in for the rest of the day – it appears it will be incessantly rainy and grey anyway – not a fit day for going out – and I will check back again soon with details of the evening."

"PERCY!"

From out on the roof now, "I might tuck in downstairs a moment to see if the girls have started any coffee that I can travel with, if that's alright…"

"PERCY HARE!"

This time, in the grey light of the early, blustery morning, she watched him leap from the peak of the roofline and drop silently out of sight.

Chapter 14

The following week, Percy sat on a low branch in Evaline's back yard, eating a late-ripening apple from the neighbor's tree and waiting for a sign that the house was once again approachable. Esther came out the porch door and encouraged him inside.

"Mmmm, no. Not just yet," he replied. "Come, I have some folks I want you to meet."

Percy walked her downtown, with dry leaves stirring around them in the breeze, nibbling away at the rest of the apple core.

"Honestly, Percy," Esther said, "Mother seems to be back in better spirits the past day or so. You needn't fear her."

"Fear? I've never feared the old gal," he replied. Esther smiled as the hare jutted his chin forward, attempting to bolster his male pride. "Respect. I'd term it 'respect,' in that I'm firmly conscious of her capabilities. More so, I'd wager, than you yourself..."

"I'm just saying she's not appearing to be so angry as you think..."

"And I'm saying," Percy interjected, "from an experienced viewpoint on the woman, that she has likely fooled you into a false sense of security wherein you *believe* we are safe when in fact... ah, here we are. Barkey's house."

Esther was still puzzling over Percy's suggestion of her mother's nefarious nature when he introduced her to Barkey and Kess Smith and the peculiar creature for which they were caring.

"They don't look *up*, see? It's the way they're constructed by god. It don't allow 'em to raise their head up." Barkey was explaining to Esther why the pygmy bison[5] seemed confused. It couldn't locate them. They stood looking down on it from outside its makeshift pen in Barkey's yard. And while it snorted and turned as they spoke, it couldn't find them. Percy thought the thing pitiful.

Barkey had been asked by the proprietor of the Short Buffalo Tavern to hold his pet, the tavern's mascot, while he attended to business with brewers in St. Louis. "The damned thing will ignore you," he said, "but it can't make it on its own without feed. Gotten used to it now. And if I put in enough for more than a couple days it'll eat itself sick. Probably blow up its guts." So Barkey had been pressed into watching over it, though it tasked him to do so.

The bison was bothered by every noise and sound, unable to identify the potential intruder or threat. So it grew increasingly agitated throughout the day, especially when the Smith children poked at it or dragged the point of a stick through the dirt around it. The thing would charge headlong at the stick, allowing them to goad it into slamming its head into its retaining walls again and again.

Barkey's wife, Kess, was able to quiet the thing a bit by singing to it in the later hours of the day. She'd gotten it to the point where it would accept her hand for a short while.

"Poor thing! It just needs some attention," sighed Esther.

"Yeeeaaah, maybe. But I wouldn't go gettin' too friendly with it, miss," Barkey answered. "It packs a hell of a wallop when it charges. Damned thing is all head, and solid as a rock."

"Barkey, watch your phrasing," Kess admonished him.

"My apologies," he said, bowing his head to the young redhead.

"I thought it would break my leg, the way it ran at me," inserted the Smith's eldest son, Mal. He stepped off the porch to greet the visitors, shyly averting his stare from the beautiful young woman. A good fellow, quiet and serious like his father, but only sixteen or seventeen if Percy remembered correctly. He nodded and waved a bit toward Percy, who liked the young man very much.

Barkey waved Percy to the side for a conversation. The sun was bright this November afternoon, but the air had the distinct chill of winter. They each had coats and collars up, and the men smoked short cigars to keep their lungs warm. Percy hopped atop a stump in the corner of the yard, mostly to avoid being trampled by Barkey's two younger sons who were chasing wildly bouncing rubber balls. Charley the pig ambled over to nuzzle Percy's furry foot and get a pat on the head. Barkey took a seat on a short stool next to the stump, so the two friends were nearly eye to eye.

"Dat the girl you brung to the game last week?" Barkey asked quietly.

Percy looked over at Esther chatting with Kess and replied, "I hope you'll understand that I'm not really at liberty to say…"

"Yeah, I get that," Barkey interrupted. "She's all secret 'n all. But I'm here to tell, you best watch that girl close. She too pretty to get into the messes them euchre games can bring."

"You know her mother, don't you?"

"Yeah, I sure do. That's another reason you best watch her close. Anything happen to that girl and I know ol' Evaline will skin your hide."

"It was Evaline's idea," Percy offered.

"What, now?"

"It was. The girl wants experience – she wants adventure," Percy added. "She fancies herself a Hoosier Calamity Jane. Evaline thought I could show her things and trusts me to keep her safe. Well, at least she said she did. Look! She's having an adventure even as we speak. Not many folks can say they've seen a pygmy bison up close," he smirked.

"No, no they cain't," said Barkey. "Most folks I imagine want their daughters goin' to finishin' school and all – findin' a husband. Not gettin' adventures." After a pause, he continued, "But Percy, I'm telling you to beware. That girl made quite a fuss after last week. Folks are talking 'bout 'E.W. this' 'n 'E.W. that'. Horace won't stop tellin' tales on her. He makin' things up even, sayin' she hypnotized the room with her… her… you know, her… *titties*," he whispered. "That she might have made 'em spin around and *hypnotized* 'em all!"

Percy laughed loud and hard, falling back on the stump.

"Percy!" Barkey whispered sharply.

Percy sat upright again and saw the women and Mal looking at him, smiling quizzically, wondering what was the joke.

"Percy, I ain't foolin' now!" Barkey went on. "That girl best understand the attention she callin' on herself. You best understand it. 'Cause if you're not careful that girl will be found in an alley with nothin' but a rabbit to protect her."

"Hare."

"Hare, whatever. Take care, dammit. This could be a dangerous game you playin'. Don't let it get out 'o hand, now." They watched quietly for a moment as the two ladies giggled over something and looked to see if the gentlemen had overheard them. Mal was sloping back toward the porch, seemingly embarrassed by their discussion. His brothers raced past him chasing the bouncing balls and giggling.

"Another thing –," Barkey continued. "The Colonel heard tell 'o the game and he's comin' himself next time. Horace invited him."

"The Colonel?" Percy asked. "Wigglemann?"

"There another Colonel 'round here?" replied Barkey. "And the owner is tellin' me to allow in some higher fare folk. Colonel's bringin' his men for security and all. Lookin' like it ain't my game at all, no more."

"The Colonel, huh? I had conversation with him a while back. Did I tell you that?"

"You did? With the Colonel? What's a man like that want witchoo?"

"It wasn't entirely clear," Percy said. "But it seemed he has motives and agendas that he might not want to be made public. Part of his intentions, it could be said – now, I rely on your discretion here – involve that young woman over there."

"Esther?" Barkey whispered, wide-eyed.

"Indeed. Again, you must keep this quiet."

"Percy! That girl – that man – that man is married – he may look a fool at times – but you don't mess with a man like that when he wants somethin'! He got bad people with him. That girl in danger, Percy!"

"It might seem. It also seems she's not alone in that regard, either. But it's all the more reason I should keep her by my side, don't you think?"

"Damn – hell, yeah," Barkey muttered.

They watched the ladies laughing a moment and looking in their direction. A loud thump came from the bison's pen and the ladies giggled in surprise as the force of it shook the walls.

"Esther, how tired are you?" Percy asked.

"Oh, not at all! Mother will be livid if we stay out *too* long – but I'm nowhere near ready to go home just yet!" She crossed the yard and took his paw, "And besides, I'm with you and she knows I'm safe!"

Barkey raised an eyebrow and exhaled pointedly.

Ignoring him, Percy said, "Then come with me, I've got something I want to share with you."

[5] *The Wea Plains Pygmy Bison have been long-rumored and forgotten to history, deemed only to folklore. Evidence was eventually unearthed in the early twentieth century, indicating that great herds of the Pygmy Bison, cousins to the larger American Bison but only as large as a house cat, once thundered... well, let's say "trundled"... across the regional landscape. They were concentrated in the area of the Wea Plains, across the Wabash River southwest of Lafayette. Once thought to be lawn sculptures, many of their fossilized remains decayed on front porches throughout the region and are now lost...*

Chapter 15

Percy led Esther further downtown, crossing Fourth Street and into the alley behind the buildings on Columbia. They were now in the block facing the Tippecanoe County Courthouse, the dead center point of the city of Lafayette. Heading into early evening, the whole area was still teeming with carts and horses, streetcars, and vendors. But the rattling and clattering and calls were greatly reduced on the back side of the block. The sun had been obscured by dull grey clouds which now hung over the dome of the courthouse.

In the back alley, the buildings extended to staggered depths. Percy and Esther proceeded through a pass-through arch and he steered her to a rear door toward the end of the block. The door was marked with a small worn sign that read, "G. W. – Art—." The rest of the lettering was illegible.

Percy glanced around quickly and, satisfied with seeing no one around, told Esther to stay at the door and that he'd be there soon to open it. He made a spry jump from the top of a railing to the second-floor above the door. Clinging to the brick ledge, he found a piece of metal bar wedged into the rotted window frame. Inserting it into the jam, he was able to pry up the window, step through, and before ducking inside, reinsert the metal bar in the crevice where he'd found it.

Moments later, the door lock turned from the inside and Percy waved Esther in. From the entry, a closet-sized door led to a tight staircase they took up to the second floor. At the end of a much wider hallway stood a set of double doors. Leaning aside them was a street sign, which had presumably hung on the front of the building at one time. In large lettering it read:

GEO. WINTER

Artist

Portraiture – Landscapes

Esther gasped in recognition. Her mother had often spoken of the artist Mr. Winter. She'd been an acquaintance of his and had been deeply saddened when he died suddenly in 1876.

Percy was able to jar the door open, the lock having become stiff and the door itself loose in its frame. He and Esther entered through dull light from tall windows facing the courthouse.

The space had been abandoned for years. It appeared to be much as Mr. Winter had left it. The ceilings were tall, maybe fifteen feet, Percy guessed. The windows at the front were nearly as tall, though constructed in two tiers, with a semi-circular arch at the top. Its bare hardwood floors seemed dusty and worn and stained in places from countless smudges of paint. The room was almost forty feet square. Frozen faces looked out at them from framed images and drawings tacked to the walls. There was even a canvas left on an easel against the wall.

"My god, it's absolutely *ghostly!*" whispered Esther. "I feel like we're intruding. Are you sure it's alright for us to be here?"

Percy nodded quietly, assuring her he'd been there a number of times. In fact, he'd spent hours there, alone, sitting silently in the one stuffed chair and sifting through the drawings and paintings at his leisure. He knew of no one who still had access or even remembered what was left there for that matter. It was practically his own museum.

Esther sluffed off her overcoat and hat to a swivel chair. She walked across the room slowly, examining stacks of letters and sketches. She flipped through a stack of canvases leaning against a wall, each an expansive romantic landscape featuring small figures in colorful Native American garb.

"That's right," she said. "Mother called him the 'Indian painter.' He spent a lot of time with them, didn't he? Before they were all ushered away to reservations."

Percy paused and made a sucking noise from the side of his mouth. "*Ushered* is an overly polite way of putting it. They were pushed – driven away."

"How long have you been around here, Percy?" Esther inquired. Then excitedly, "Did you ever see them? Before they were pushed away?"

Percy was looking down at a larger sketch featuring three native figures at the edge of a waterway, one on horseback. He replied, "A few times. Once with old George himself. I kept my distance. George wasn't sure how a speaking hare would be received by the old souls. We both suspected they'd skin me on sight."

"Dear god!" Esther replied a bit too loudly.

"Now, now," Percy continued, "It wasn't as if they were *savages* like some think. George always said his parties were very dignified. Very wise and gentle. But they didn't have any more experience with... someone like me... than the folks around here do. And by the time I saw them, they had become extremely distrustful of white men. So a speaking hare walking *with* the white men, even someone they'd become accustomed to like Mr. Winter, would have inspired a great fear. Not to mention a suspicion of an evil spirit walking amongst them."

"Is that what you are, Percy? An evil spirit?" Esther asked coquettishly. "What *are* you, after all, mister?"

Percy remained silent. Even he himself didn't quite know the answer to that one. He'd found his way to the stuffed chair by the windows and sat contemplating something. On a small stand next to the chair, a small scrap of paper leaned against a snuff box. It was angled at just the right angle to catch the daylight. He had left it just there the last time he visited.

On the paper, a simple bucolic scene had been sketched in pencil. A somewhat circular composition illustrated a curved path circling from a shorter cluster of trees, forward toward the viewer, past a larger tree leaning in to the center, and back into space to a small cabin. The path was lined with small fenceposts, indicated with simple dashes with slooping lines between them. And the small figure of a man was walking along the path away from the cabin, with a farm implement or long gun over his shoulder.

Esther noticed Percy's attention and crossed behind him to look over his shoulder. She had to bend close to see the faint drawing. The scrap of paper was only three and a half by four inches in size.

(Author's note - This untitled drawing by George Winter still exists, now in the collection of the Tippecanoe County Historical Association. The author has studied it personally.)

"Look at how... simply, and elegantly, he applied the pencil line. Sometimes it's just scrumbled and makes a grey body of foliage. And other times it elegantly... it almost *dances* like the branches and leaves on the tree. You see? He's not drawing each and every leaf, but you can still see exactly what they are from just the... clumping of marks. It's fascinating!"

"Have you ever drawn before, Per..." Esther started.

"And see how he bends the path – he almost literally walks you right *into* the drawing! It feels like I could walk right in. And – what? Oh, no. I can't draw at all. I can't make the motions with my paw that you can. Nor can I write my name for that matter.

I imagine Mr. Winter might have sat right here, with the light coming from behind him, day or night, to illuminate whatever he was working on. I marvel at the vision of someone who can take what he sees before him and shrink it to this. And to allow it to retain its simplicity and its perfect rendition of that place, at that time. So much so that all these years later I can be transported there just by looking at it. These simple pencil lines. Marvelous."

Esther had studied drawing in several artist clubs as part of her liberal education. Her mother had original artworks by several noted artists in their home, including George Winter himself. It occurred to her just then that Evaline had never said how she'd obtained the painting. But she could easily imagine that some form of "trade" had taken place.

Esther had been trained to see and assess various images from the formal view of perspective, shape, light, form, and color. But she had never before experienced the sheer joy of an artwork through the eyes of Percy Hare. A rabbit. Or hare, actually. An animal, or "woodland creature" as her mother referred to him. For all of his sophistication and fluency of speech, he had no capacity for art-making, for transferring reality into abstract two-dimensional representation. But it clearly thrilled him – *enthralled* him even. And it was this simple drawing, probably the most direct and least labored over type of work Mr. George generated, that Percy was obsessed with.

She marveled at the gentle man-hare seated beneath her, wondering if this was some of the charm old Evaline had seen in him all these years. She reached to run her delicate hand down the mottled fur at the back of his head, when he suddenly spun his head in the direction of the double doors.

He turned back to her and said, "Quick! Someone's coming. Into the corner."

He led her to a spot by the windows, behind a dressing screen. Instructing her to hide low there, he moved a blanket to cover her.

"We'll stay here, still and quiet."

"But Percy…" she whispered, as he tossed the blanket over her and disappeared beneath it with her.

The doors gave way and drew in with them a thick waft of cigar smoke. Two men entered, in formal waistcoats, cravats, and long-tail jackets. Both had thick moustaches. One wore a hard black bowler hat and looked uncomfortable in his own clothes. Likely they weren't his. The other carried a crisp columnar top hat. They stood for a moment just inside the doors, contemplating the darkened room and puffing out clouds of cigar smoke. Finally one spoke.

"Dis shitty place?" said the bowler.

Top hat replied, "Yup. This is what he wants."

Bowler said, "Old place like dis… It's dark in here. Dis guy was a artist, right?"

"Yeah," said top hat.

They began to work their way into the room, nudging aside a chair and the occasional scrap of paper.

"What's da big deal?" said bowler. "Crappy artist dump. Why here?"

"Oh, I can definitely see it. The Marquis, he likes places with sophistication, with some value. He likes *special*things."

"Think this stuff is worth somethin'?" asked bowler.

"Oh, sure. This guy, Winter, he was pretty famous. Not many artists in shithole Indiana. And his stuff has history. He painted the Indians that used to live here."

"Where? Here?"

"Kokomo. Logansport. Further east of here."

"I was gonna say. I ain't never seen no damn Injuns round here."

"They're long gone. Been gone a long time now."

Bowler walked to the far wall and picked up a medium-sized canvas. Holding it up, he sneered and said, "Dis ain't dat good."

Top hat shrugged. "To each his own."

Bowler tossed the canvas across the room into a pile of furniture.

"Hey, now! A little respect."

"Oh! Oh, I'm sorry," bowler said facetiously, picking up another canvas. "More respect? How 'bout dis?" And he plunged his fist through the canvas. He laughed hard and loud and flung the canvas off of his wrist.

"Nice," said top hat. "Let's go, before you tear up too much good stuff."

Bowler made his way back across the room, kicking a small chair nearly to the windows and then stomping on a sketch on the floor and tearing it apart with his other shoe.

Standing by the door considering things, top hat said, "We'll just have to get in here and clear things out a bit first. Make way for the table. And a gallery of chairs. And put those screens in front of the window so nobody can see in."

"Hey!" Bowler had a thought. "What's wit this woman the Marquis was on about?"

"Ah, the mysterious 'E.W.,'" replied top hat.

"Yeah. Who's she? And why's he all 'bout her all 'o sudden?"

"He likes special things, remember? He probably wants her in his own pocket."

The disinterested bowler was already steaming past him into the hallway. "Let's go, I'm hungry. I wonder if ol' Winksy's got some sluff he's still servin'. If not, I gotta go home. And I don't wanna do dat." Top hat closed the doors with bowler muttering something about "screamin' kids n' all."

Percy listened intently and waited until he was sure they'd left the building. Esther jumped out of the blanket and wrapped her arms around him. She clutched him tight.

"Who were they, Percy?"

"The Marquis' men, but…"

"Oh my, I was so terrified!" she said with a sly smile, hands to her cheeks, now approximating the helpless theatrical "damsel." "They did sound pretty rough, though, didn't they?"

"Yes, they did…" he answered, pondering for a moment what he'd gathered from his first encounter with friends of the Marquis de Lafayette. He looked out into the courthouse square and found the two men heading north on Third Street.

"So, the Marquis likes the finer things it seems – refinement, sophistication. 'He likes *special* things,' they said. Thus, he would seek out a *special* forgotten artist's studio for his private game."

"Should we tell anyone about this?" Esther asked.

He looked at her, genuinely perplexed. "*Tell* anyone? Why would we do that?"

"Well," she offered, "they broke in."

He looked at her and tilted his head. He waited a moment for her to get there.

"Oh… so did we."

"Indeed. No, we don't tell anyone about it – yet." He turned her toward the door to leave. "The Sheriff is out for him, the Marquis, but I've got to think there's a way to play this to our favor. If we're smart. I just don't know what that might be yet."

"I just hope they don't damage anything valuable in here…" Esther's voice trailed off as she proceeded down the hallway.

Percy turned to look back at the stuffed chair and the tiny sketch on the stand. He was quickly back at her side.

Chapter 16

The girl and the hare quickly and quietly made their way back down the small staircase at the back of the building. Percy instructed her to watch at the door and listen a moment before exiting, to be sure no one was around. A cart rattled by on the side street but it was otherwise silent.

He took Esther's gloved hand to lead her toward South Street, but she playfully pulled it back and began to skip away. Teasingly, she looked back at him, singing a made-up tune, "You shan't have me – no, no, you shan't!"

Percy pursued her, to her glee. But he was more anxious to quiet her than to play her game. "Esther!" he spoke, attempting to keep his tone to a minimum.

"Percy shan't have me!" she giggled and spun. "Oh, no, no, he shan't!"

"Esther!" he spoke a little louder.

She giggled and broke into a run, lifting her skirts to free her step. As she cleared the corner of a building onto the South Street walkway, she saw the blackened silhouettes of a fine carriage and horses, and the trunks of small trees lining the roadway, but nothing else. At her pace, she never saw the man who was passing behind one of trees until he emerged and she struck him head on.

Esther spun and tumbled to the ground before Percy saw what happened.

"Goddammit!" the man bellowed in a pinched but piercing voice. He looked down at her, splayed over the pavement. He had a bent cigar in his hand. She was obscured by tousled, dark winter fabrics that had been knocked askew, but in the dimmed light he could easily make out her exposed, fair-skinned décolletage.

"You simple little slut! My cigar is ruined!" he yelled.

"Oh, I'm very sorry," she began. "I just wasn't... *slut?!*"

"Yes," he continued, re-establishing his fur-collared coat atop his shoulders. "A simple little trickster like yourself ought to be more *mindful* (he spat the word with venom) as you flounce yourself about." He extended his boot, which had a shining silver toeing, until it slipped under the hem of her skirt and he lifted it. Esther scooted backward and pushed her skirt back down.

"How dare you!" Esther exclaimed.

"But," he continued, while pulling forth a silver-topped cane resting atop his arm, "We'll soon see to your carelessness. You'll *learn* (again spitting the word angrily) to be more mindful of your surroundings."

The man gripped the head of the cane tightly enough that his leather gloves creaked in distress. With very little preparation, he reached back with the cane to unleash a blow upon Esther but didn't progress far. The hare had taken hold of the cane and quickly secured it by sinking his teeth into the lacquered wood staff and twisting his body around it, while flicking the man's hand away from the handle with his feet. Percy landed deftly, holding the cane before him, and then flung it back across the lot they'd crossed. The man watched it clatter across the ground and spun back toward him.

Percy could literally feel the heat of the man's rage and knew he was not to be trifled with. Percy finally got a good look at him. His breath caught for a moment when he realized it was the self-proclaimed "Marquis de Lafayette" staring back.

The man's black hair was slicked back under a crisp bowler hat. His moustache punctuated his angry lips, which were curled into a sneer. Even in the dim light of the evening, his eyes burned at Percy from under his blackened brow. His entire head seemed to have sunk down within the fur collar of his coat, giving the impression of an angered wild animal crouching for the kill. In his coat, he seemed a tall, lean figure with no definition. Almost a pedestal with a head perched atop it.

Esther rose and began to laugh tauntingly in the man's face upon his being disarmed. She moved to strike him, but noticed his carriage man hulking like a shadow and moving closer.

Fearful that she was tempting fate, the hare said, "Miss Wells, I think we'd best be on our way now."

"Miss Wells...?" she looked at him, puzzled at the formality.

"Yes," Percy continued. "I promised your mother I'd see you home..."

"Ah! It's the hare, is it?" the Marquis' voice seemed to squeeze up from out of some ancient crevice before reaching a loud whine. "The fucking *hare*! Percy, am I right?"

Percy nodded, keeping track of both the Marquis and the approaching carriage man.

"*Wonderful* we should finally meet. I've been hearing so much of you. And somehow you've stayed outside my wake."

Percy had kept it that way for damn good reason, and now he cursed himself for finally allowing such a close run-in. The man had "fingers" everywhere and it was wise to avoid his attention, and his concern. Even a stealthy hare couldn't avoid an organized hunt for long – not with the numbers of men at the Marquis' command.

Percy was trying to imagine why the Marquis was even here, when his men had just been in the art studio scouting the location. He wouldn't have imagined it. They should have been more careful. Why, when the Marquis had sent men out for assignment, would he follow so closely? Was he hoping to find them there and join them? Was he checking up on his own men? Was he that untrusting, even of the people he employed?

The carriage man, Percy was surprised and somewhat relieved to find, was angling away from the conversation, seemingly heading in the direction of the lost cane.

"And *you* are?" the Marquis barked at Esther.

"No one for you to be concerned with, sir." Percy interjected, leaving Esther with a mouth full of words and an annoyed look on her face. "She was negligent and being nothing but playful, and she meant you no harm. Or offense."

She began her intended assault with "I..." but Percy shot her a wide-eyed look and she went no further. He took her wrist and she pulled back again, this time in anger but this time also without success. Percy held fast and began to back her away and down the street. She was deeply annoyed with him but, having never known him to act this way toward her, she was chastened by his forcefulness.

"Where are you going?" the Marquis asked somewhat coyly. "We've so much to discuss. And we have so many common concerns."

"We must bid you good evening, sir. Tonight does not hold the most favorable aspect for my young charge here." Percy spoke with theatricality. "She may be possessed already of a chill to the lungs and her mother…"

"There's nothing wrong with those lungs," the Marquis muttered creepily.

Esther's arm tensed and it was all Percy could do to continue to steer her back toward the rising roads that would lead up Ninth Street Hill to her home. He noted the carriage man had retrieved the cane and was approaching the Marquis. Calmly paced, Percy noted. A large man, and one in no hurry.

"Be that as it may," Percy continued to the Marquis, "her health is my utmost concern and we must be away. Another time."

The pair turned and had placed an additional block between themselves and the Marquis. Esther was fairly sputtering with rage. But Percy was discretely watching behind them and listening for the sound of pursuit, or a gun shot. After an anxious, overly-long moment, he heard from a distance, "Yes. There will be another time."

Esther Wells stomped angrily up Seventh Street, refusing to speak. Percy heard Barkey's words, from earlier that very evening, and repeated them to her.

"Cause if you're not careful that girl will be found in an alley with nothin' but a rabbit to protect her," Percy echoed.

"Who said that?" she asked.

"Barkey. Just this evening." She kept walking. "I should have listened to him," Percy went on. "But I laughed him off."

"Oh, piffle!" Esther replied. "You handled him easily. And I would have shown him what for if you hadn't."

"He had a gun in his breast pocket, just beneath his coat."

"What?"

"And had he pulled it, it's quite likely one or both of us might now be dead."

She froze, facing away from him.

"It chills me to the bone to think of it now," he went on. "And not because your mother would be so upset with me. No," he continued, walking ahead of her now, "but because I am so upset with me. Because you've only just become interesting at all. And things were going to become quite fun in this town again."

He stopped, ahead of her on the walk now. He looked up into the darkening sky, now a deep purplish-blue color accented with graceful black silhouettes from the bare tree branches arcing up through it. He held his paw out, gesturing to the scene silently. And then he spoke.

"You see, what would our friend Mr. Winter have done with an image such as this? How can anyone take this and translate it to page or canvas? I know not how, but I'm convinced Mr. Winter could approximate it, and that the interpretation would both stupefy and amaze me."

His paw stayed out until Esther took it in her own hand and began walking again. She pulled him to her side. Then, while he went on about Mr. Winter's interpretation of the night sky, she took him in both her arms and lifted him.

"What is this? No, no, we won't be doing this now. Young lady, put me down..."

She began to sing her own silly song again, with him clutched to her chest, though now it went, "I shall have you – yes, yes, I shall."

"No, no, you shan't! Now put me down immediately. You wicked, awful child."

"I *shall* have you – *I* shall have you..." continued to ring melodiously down the street.

109

Chapter 17

Evaline insisted they take a carriage to the next game. Percy had to confess, in light of their recent experience with the Marquis, that perhaps walking home was impractical and a more rapid form of escape might be helpful.

Percy hated the formality of carriages. They just seemed to drive up the level of irony. A furred hare seated in a horse-drawn transport where everyone else wore gloves and hats seemed ridiculous. But as much as he hated carriage rides, his truly passionate quarrel was with the mechanism of transport itself, the horse.

He'd always hated them, it should be said, because they'd always hated him. Horses are not entirely stupid, regardless of what Percy might say. They tend to understand people as well as they come to understand commands in time. But horses never understood the amalgam of man and animal that was the short, furry, speaking person of Percy the hare.

Percy had been kicked, or kicked *at* by horses (and mules and donkeys it should be said), more times in his storied life than he cared to remember. Little surprise he avoided them and the pathways they usually traveled as much as possible. But there were times when it seemed unavoidable. And Evaline Wells insisting upon carriage transport for her daughter so she wasn't traipsing home again in the cold autumn rain was one of those times.

"I've arranged for you to leave the carriage and Nemo (the horse) at the establishment of a veterinarian friend," issued Evaline. "You remember her, Rosalind Gullimore."

"Gullimore?" Percy responded.

"Yes."

"Rosalind?"

"Yes. She's all grown up and running a veterinary clinic. Did you know that?" she asked, somewhat pointedly.

Percy turned his head to look at her quizzically. "Why?" he asked. It seemed she was finally exacting her revenge upon him.

"Oh, now, I know you had a... falling out with her at some point. But isn't it time to move beyond that?"

Rosalind Gullimore was the daughter of Percy's long-time friend, Dr. Francis Gullimore, a former dentist in town. Dr. Gullimore had been instrumental in Percy's life, taking him in early as the young hare was entering socialized life in the city and becoming a gentleman-hare. Their relationship exceeded mentor and progeny, nearer more to trusted friends and partners. There is a veritable novella to be written of their relationship, perhaps at another time.

More pressing to the moment was the revelation of Rosalind. She was just a young girl when Percy was coming around her father's dental office. They played together as fond friends until one day when Percy realized she was no longer a child, but rather a fetching, dark-haired beauty. At which point, the hot-blooded young hare made an untoward advance and everything came to an end. Rosalind, young, shy, and embarrassed, rebuked her friend. He, young, brash, and ashamed, departed the family's circle. He'd only seen her one other time since. Two years earlier, in 1881, her father the doctor had died. Percy attended the burial but kept a distance. He thought he'd seen Rosalind, now very attractive and more mature, looking around for him as he crouched in the trees, but he couldn't be sure.

Shoving that history aside, Percy asked, "Where do we leave the carriage?"

Esther, showing off her new and more stylish attire for gaming, answered, "I know where it is. You needn't be troubled with it."

As they approached the carriage, Nemo gave a shudder and an anxious step at the sight of the hare. To punctuate his feelings, the horse dropped a hot turd or two. Esther calmed him while Percy got in the carriage. On the way downtown, Esther barely maintained the reins while showing Percy the new "E.W." costume her mother and one of the other ladies in the house

111

had fashioned for her. For all the world it looked much like the old rain gear she'd thrown on for the first night, but it now had some new wrinkles.

They left the carriage at Rosalind Gullimore's clinic, on Fourth Street between South Street and Alabama. From there it would be a short walk to the Short Buffalo Tavern on Sixth and Main. Not immediately handy, but not so distant that they couldn't make it there quickly in a pinch. And, Percy noted to himself, in the opposite direction from where they might be expected to head for safety, Evaline's house, providing an interesting opportunity to lose a pursuer in the diversion.

Chapter 18

Ambling down the alleyways with him, as Percy still preferred to avoid the main avenues, Esther still looked like a man in blocky outerwear. Long, straight cut jacket and pants, large-brimmed hat. At the back door to Barkey's place, she reached inside the jacket and pulled a tab. Suddenly, the coat was cinched in to her waist, accentuating her womanly figure. And the pants were drawn up into pantaloons beneath the hem of the coat. Beneath, she now showed shapely calves in black stockings.

"What do you think?" she asked.

"Very nice," Percy replied. He would confess she cut a gorgeous figure now and would definitely take the room by storm. He grinned as she placed a stylish black mask over her eyes, something left from a masquerade her mother had hosted the previous year. Likely not many would even see her eyes beneath the hat brim, but it would further conceal her identity in the event the hat came off.

Percy planted his stick into the ground just to the side of the door. This time, the same old trick to enter Barkey's back door was not available. Someone had covered the hidden latch in the wall or removed it. But a small panel slid open at eye level – at least normal human eye level – and a voice asked them their business.

"Our business?" Percy asked, annoyed. He couldn't be seen through the small opening well over his head, but he went on, "Euchre is our business, you imbecile."

Esther looked at the partial face through the opening and said, "I'm here to play."

The voice inside asked, "What's your name?"

She replied, "E.W.," and a heavy latch inside the door was thrown.

The door clunked and rattled, as the bolt was thrown from inside. But before it could open Percy grabbed her sleeve and whispered, "Things have changed. Be aware! Look around you – know the room. If anything happens, look for me."

Esther's eyes were wide with apprehension but he watched them narrow and become resolute. She stepped in past the doorkeeper, never looking him in the eye. Her stride became that of someone who owned the place. Not regal and slow, like a duchess, but powerful and steady, more as if she were the woman who had paid the wages of every man on the premises and now demanded to be treated accordingly.

They reached the door to the basement and she turned deftly. A man standing there was checking for arms, insisting on holding any weapons in the tavern until the game was completed. His silhouette was blocking the view of the rest of the saloon. He tipped his hat to Esther, allowing she was unlikely to be carrying a weapon, but she ignored him. When she'd cleared the hallway, Percy could see the man was none other than Winks Bubher.

"Winksy! Good to see ya," Percy offered. He half expected Winks to take him by the throat and slam him against the wall.

Winks just glared at him and said, "Rabbit."

"Hare, actually. Hey, how did the rutabagas finish the season? Good crop?"

The room below was much more populated than at the previous game. As they descended the stairs, Percy's fur began to stand on end. For her part, Esther strode confidently to the open chair at the table, all eyes upon her. Percy used the distraction to assess the entire room. This was a much dicier proposition than before.

This time, the room was full of men, and a few other women. Applause broke out as Esther stepped into the lamplight. Suddenly, she was known. Chairs had been set up all around the room. Where there had been only a handful of viewers at the first game, there were now at least thirty people, other than the four strategic players at compass points around the table.

114

There was a cloud of cigar and cigarette smoke clinging to the ceiling and the entire room was under a haze.

Should it become necessary, escape from this room would be difficult at best. Not impossible, but difficult. Percy's one consolation was that Barkey had positioned himself at the foot of the stairs. He nodded to Percy to set his mind at ease. It helped only a bit.

Esther took the same seat she'd enjoyed at the previous match. This time, the gregarious Horace Grinlow was seated beside her to the right, with Oscar Binchen to her left. They'd clearly decided to take her on together that evening. Seated opposite her, and standing as her partner for the evening, was "top hat," the man who'd broken into George Winter's studio with his rough trade accomplice the same night she and Percy were there. Percy recognized him immediately, though he knew Esther had never seen the man's face. Circling the room with his eyes, Percy quickly found "bowler hat" too, standing not far behind.

Horace again made introductions, with top hat being announced by the name Walter Swettenham. He was charming and seemingly well-educated. Percy tried to do the math that would result in him being in barely civilized north central Indiana, working for a man like the Marquis. But it didn't seem to add up. Of course, the Marquis' presence in town didn't make sense either. Esther was introduced only as "the enigmatic 'E.W.', about whom we know next to nothing… but whose presence I value a great deal more than the entire lot of you farting river toads!" And a general cheer went up.

From behind him, Percy heard a familiar voice. "Harry, offer the hare your seat, won't you? There's a good man."

Turning, he saw a short wooden barrel keg seat open and a well-dressed man seated next to it patting its top and puffing on a cigarillo. "Hello, Mr. Hare," he said. One arm was extended with his gloved hand perched atop his walking stick.

"Colonel Wigglemann." Percy nodded. He thought for a moment, then took the barrel seat.

"Will you share a cigarillo with me?" the Colonel offered. "I feel it is owed. And a kindred gentleman of smoking taste is not to be squandered."

Not feeling fool enough to decline a fine smoke, Percy accepted it and a light from the Colonel. His attentions were conflicted between this man he knew not whether to trust and the table at which his young charge was now confronting (on several levels, it seemed) a very new game.

Horace sought to continue his friendly chatter with Esther from the first game in the hopes, it seemed, of managing more interaction with her.

"It's great pleasure to see you – or *not* see you, as the case may be – again, my dear."

He dipped his head to peer a bit under her broad-brimmed hat and chortled a bit with the others. She nodded politely, not giving him any of the precious conversation he sought.

The stakes were explained again, a quarter a chit, though Swettenham commented that it seemed a low-stakes game for such notable players. Horace chuckled and deferred to playing it conservative, claiming, "The Short Buff's game has always been a friendly one. Besides," he offered, "you can always spice things up a bit with side bets if you've a mind to. But…" he continued, as Swettenham opened his mouth to interject, "any such sides must be agreed upon with a player's partner. Agreed?" And it was by all players.

When cash holdings were called for, Swettenham again commented that it seemed unnecessary in such a "friendly game." But he went along with the others and presented a fold of cash. The rest of the room seemed to hold its collective breath for an outcome that was anticipated since their arrival.

E.W. was the last player to present her holdings. She produced a small set of bills from the pocket of her coat, to the disappointment of the room.

"Oh?" she queried. "I apologize. If that is insufficient, it does seem that it would be helpful for me to possibly have a bit of cushion." It was at that point that she popped the collar on her coat, unbuttoned several buttons, and spread wide its lapels, revealing her bounteous cleavage supported in a black lace bustier. From deep within her cleavage she then slowly drew a gleaming white silk handkerchief, this time embroidered in black thread with the letters "E.W." and a spray of delicate black roses.

"Would one of you gentleman be willing to offer me anything for *this?*"

116

Esther asked slyly.

A clamor arose that almost drowned out her words. More applause, especially from the women, who seemed appreciative of both her flair and her brass. Bills were offered into the air and men began to elbow each other out of the way. But one voice rang out above the rest from the chair next to Percy.

"I'll gladly give you $100 for such a delicate treasure!" The voice was Colonel Wigglemann's and he held the bill at arm's length for all to see.

(Author's note - $100 in 1883 would equal approximately $2500 at today's value – a ridiculous sum for a woman's handkerchief.)

The room fell to a hush, and then an "oooh" of somewhat mocking appreciation of the Colonel's offer. The deal was transacted by a young whore who lifted the bill from the Colonel, carried it to the table, and returned to him the handkerchief.

Turning to Percy, Wigglemann gushed and showed him the handkerchief. "She's spectacular, isn't she? How could I pass this up?"

Percy was perplexed. He tried to read the Colonel for signs. Did he know she was Esther Wells? Was he putting him on, or was he genuinely ignorant of her identity?

It was determined Swettenham would be afforded the first deal by the players cutting the deck in turn. He turned up a King to take the privilege.

As he shuffled the partial deck, Barkey's server from upstairs dutifully set a shot glass of rye before each player. Horace blew a column of smoke upward and leaned in toward E.W. with a greasy grin.

"You know, my dear, there has been a great speculation on the meaning of the initials 'E.W.'" She stoically watched her partner shuffle again and again without responding. "Curiosity consumes us, I'll say. And I confess," Horace continued, "we've come up with some speculative proposals."

Both Esther and Percy hoped he wasn't about to begin citing names from about town, in hopes of stabbing the right one.

"Your girl shows great moxie, you know," the Colonel offered. Percy nodded, ignoring him.

Horace presented, "Of the various options offered, I believe my friend Oscar here has come up with the best solution. Bar none." He chuckled and extended a finger as the entire room listened attentively. "You see, he thinks that, seated where you are, you are offering us compass points – to the 'East' (pointing toward her right breast) and to the 'West' (pointing to her left breast)! Ha! Haw!"

He kicked off a loud squall of laughter throughout the room and commenced to sputtering over his own joke.

"East and West! That's rich, isn't it? Ha! That's what I'll call you now!"

E.W. simply raised her shot glass to him, swung it to the left and to the right, almost as if making the sign of the cross, and consequently recognizing the joke of her own directionality of bosom, and drank a toast to poor Horace, now choking and red with laughter.

Play then ensued, with Swettenham and E.W. off to a quick start, building a lead of 5-0. Then the deal dried up for her, and she was forced to play an assist with only a single off-suit Ace or King in her hand for the next several tricks. Still, she supported her partner admirably, even making Oscar believe she was set for a loner hand when she had nothing of value, and provoking him to call trump of Spades to counter her. He came away with one point on the hand where, had he allowed his partner to call the opposite suit of Clubs as trump, they would have swept the hand for two points.

Swettenham seemed to enjoy her play. He certainly appreciated her skill. And her breasts. His eyes never seemed to leave them, even while dealing the cards.

Chapter 19

The Colonel leaned closely and offered Percy his apologies for their prior meeting.

"I hope you weren't put off by our conversation, sir. Upon reflection I realized that I might have come across as rather harsh in what I confided. Allow me to explain."

Percy acknowledged him but continued to monitor the game.

"I hope you'll remember that I credited you with not only an intimate knowledge of the fairer sex," Colonel Wigglemann began, "but also with a uniquely creative approach to life and living. I dare say you've found a way to skirt past most restrictions that limit most of polite society."

Percy eyed him cautiously.

"And none to the detriment, mind you. For hardly a soul is harmed by the odd voracious pig invading a man's garden. Perhaps more importantly, you've done your business without being seen as anything more than a nuisance or a sly fox. Oh, pardon the reference." Percy looked at him somewhat askance. "Perhaps *fox* was a poor choice... given your..."

E.W. called out Horace on once again dealing himself six cards and discarding two on his turn. She took a chit from him for the transgression. This happened twice in a row, with E.W. catching his discard on the second attempt and holding the cards up for all to see. She threatened to leave the game at that moment with her winnings, earning the respect of the table and the promise of better behavior.

The Colonel continued, "Mr. Hare, I may have left you with the idea that (*whispering now*) I may want to see to my own wife's demise! Far from it! I may have come across as *desperate* for a change in my life, but only within reasonable bounds, I assure you. Please forget I said it.

"Divorce, as I believe I said, is only an *option*. Only one path. And it is not an attractive one at that, I confess. You yourself pointed that out. And I agree."

The first game ended when Swettenham ordered E.W. to pick up a right bower, the Jack of Diamonds, on her deal. She proceeded to play the hand as a loner and obliterated the competition.

"Mr. Hare, Percy, I was only hoping that a *creative* gentleman such as yourself, a man who has brought to our euchre community the wondrous, enigmatic pleasure of this 'E.W.," his eyes lingered on Esther, "would be able to enable me with an alternative... exit to my marital quandary. That you might take it as a challenge, you see."

"I see," Percy finally spoke. "You'd like me to make a game of your exit from your consecrated union. To find you a loophole, perhaps."

"Well, I admit it may sound a bit crass of me, but... *yes!* You must understand that we don't all have the capacity of employing pigs and gardens and river dolphins to our means."

"Honestly, sir!" Percy begged.

"Please! Sir, please keep your voice..."

Percy, suppressing his volume a bit, "I don't know your wife, but I believe she, or any woman for that matter, deserves a better treatment than to be pried from her life commitment by little more than a game."

"Humpf." Colonel Wigglemann thought for a moment. "No, sir. No, you don't know my wife at all."

After settling chits and bets and enjoying a round of bitters, the second game proceeded. The Colonel stayed quiet a while, allowing Percy to concentrate upon his young charge.

Then he turned again to Percy and said, "To be clear, sir, I do not mean that the 'game' need end unfortunately for any of the players." He leaned back into his seat. Then he leaned back again, "Indeed, there need not be a 'loser' in the game that I'm suggesting." Percy found himself admittedly quizzical over the Colonel's meaning.

The game at the table developed relatively without incident. That is, until the last hand. Leading 8 points to 7 and looking to finish out with a dominant hand for two points and the win, Swettenham stealthily reneged on a suit. Instead of playing the suit that was led, he threw a trump card. Having blown up the lead player's hand, he then surreptitiously hid the suited card in the pile of discards.

This, the unpardonable sin of euchre, went unnoticed by all but E.W. He took the trick and the points and the game, while the room celebrated the victory. But E.W. sat unmoving while the others settled chits and shuffled money back and forth across the table.

Percy didn't know the play of the cards. He just knew that her posture and silence did not bode well. Esther turned and looked at him as if for consent. But Percy turned up his open paw, giving her license to make the necessary decision for herself, whatever that might be. He knew to approach her for consultation would weaken her autonomy as a player. But he did leave his perch and take a small step toward the table.

"Gentleman," she said, in a low voice. The room fell silent to hear what she had to say. "I'll leave this for you to settle. But my winnings will remain where they lay, and I'll be taking my leave."

General consternation ensued, with calls pleading for her to stay and to explain herself. Still seated, she said, "My partner reneged on the last hand, trumping your King of Clubs, Horace, when he had the 9 of Clubs to play."

More confusion, as Horace and Oscar recounted the hand and what was played, resurrecting the cards in the gathered tricks in front of her and Swettenham, and coming to the same conclusion she had. Throughout, Swettenham stared at her dispassionately, never looking away and not saying a word. Both Horace and Oscar offered to let her take all her winnings apart from the last hand and she resolutely declined.

"I'll not have them. In truth, I suspect that my partner may also have dealt from the bottom of the deck on more than one occasion, but I don't know that with absolute certainty. However, given his cavalier play in the last hand, I'm inclined to believe my suspicions. I'll leave the game with naught but the Colonel's purchase funds in my pocket, and I'll thank you for a ..."

Swettenham placed a hand on the table and rose slowly. Percy recognized the awkwardness of the gesture. No one would rise from one hand like that without business in the other. In a split second, he knew the man's play and left his feet. Swettenham was even more deft and swift than Percy anticipated. The knife left his open hand from waist height, as though propelled by an unseen mechanism. Percy reached for it, fearing he was already too late.

Horace would later say he would always remember the vision of the knife midway across the table, suspended in mid-air, a blinding flash of quicksilver on its deadly course directly into E.W's face. And the hare's reach into space, coming straight at him.

And then, a moment of blurred confusion later, Percy striking him full in the chest, with cards, cash, and coins crashing after him. From the floor, he and Percy looked upward with the others to where the knife had been diverted and embedded itself in the corner of the ceiling, shaking like a tuning fork.

Percy had barely touched the knife with his paw, but it had been enough to tip it from its path, slipping just past the brim of Esther's hat. The velocity of the throw had caused it to strike the wall with such force that it careened directly upward into the ceiling, where it bit an inch and a half into the aged oak timber.

Percy was quickly up atop Horace and leapt away enraged. Horace would later offer to show his audiences the scars in his thigh where the hare's claws had dug in as he moved on Swettenham. Upon seeing his strike miss the mark, the cad had sought to throw his chair into a group of those nearby and make for the stairs. He didn't get far.

Barkey rounded the corner when Percy took flight across the table. He found Swettenham with his hand still extended and embedded his mallet of a fist into the man's ribcage. Something in there gave way with a pronounced snap.

In quick succession, a black shrouded figure then drove a fist into Swettenham's face and a furred foot drove his head into the brick wall. Barkey hadn't even seen her get up, but E.W.'s fist turned the man's nose at such an angle that it too snapped and blood spattered against the brick wall. And Percy's foot dug three long scratches into his cheek and thrust his head like a melon against the wall. Swettenham emitted a pitiful moan and collapsed to the floor like wet sand.

Percy landed at the lip of the table where Swettenham had sat. He turned to see Esther standing next to him, holding her striking hand in pain. The viewing crowd was crushing upon them, trying to reach the stairs. But Percy could sense, more than actually see, the thick hand of Swettenham's accomplice reaching for him. Twisting in mid-air over the table, Percy landed his feet in the face of bowler hat and shoved him away through the crowd.

"Percy, here now!" Barkey extended his thick arms and swung himself into the room, like a large heavy door blocking their path. He waved Percy and Esther through and they struggled up the stairs.

At the top of the steps, a large heavy arm swung out at them, missing Percy and catching Esther's large hat as she quickly ducked beneath it. She and the hare took each other's arms and ran out into the night. Winks came away with only the hat.

"The carriage!" Esther shouted.

"If we can make it there," Percy answered, quickly plucking his stick from where he'd planted it outside the door. "First, into the dark."

One of Winks' men laid hold of Esther's sleeve, but a snap of Percy's willow stick split open a gash across the man's nose. Percy pulled her across the lot and headlong into a darkened space under the overhang of a shed. As they passed into darkness, a gun shot rang out behind them. Percy could hear Barkey hold up his man, saying, "Not at her! Don't shoot her, you idiot! The boss'll have our asses."

"Are they shooting at *us?*" Esther asked.

"If they are, I don't feel like discussing it with them! Run, girl!"

She was much taller than Percy and had a longer stride, but the hare kept apace of her easily. A cacophony of noises erupted everywhere around them, as game attendees spilled out into the night and Winks' men gave pursuit. Neighborhood dogs began howling, horses bedded behind the homes along South Street bolted and whinnied in annoyance and fear.

Percy led Esther on a circuitous route, around homes and sheds, under dark sheltering trellises of winter-dormant vines, ducking low along fencerows. All the while, they were making their way back to Fourth Street, where they'd left the carriage. A few buildings short, behind Alabama Street, Percy held her up, pressing her against a wall and signaling for silence.

"I'm in such pain, Percy," she whispered. "My hand may be broken."

"Sorry for that, dear girl," he replied quietly. "But that was one hell of a blow you struck, I must say." He smiled at her for possibly the first time she could remember in years. Her heart leapt in her chest and she wanted to enfold him in her arms.

"By the way, why don't you make yourself look like a man again?" he said quickly.

"Heavens, I forgot," she answered. Reaching into her coat, she again pulled a tab and the waist expanded and the legs of trousers descended over her shoes. She appeared for all the world to now be shaped as a man. But without the large hat, her flaming red hair spoiled the full effect. She threw her collar up and hunched low.

Percy looked north and east around the building. He listened carefully to the sounds of extended noises of the street for signs of continued pursuit. Hearing none, he drew Esther out across Fourth Street, restraining her to a leisurely pace.

"Shouldn't we hurry a bit?" Esther asked.

"No, my dear," Percy assured her. "We're just making our way home from the theatre, aren't we? Only someone of suspicion would clatter home in a rush."

They ignored Nemo's agitated prancing when Percy came into view, climbed into the carriage, and headed slowly back to Prospect Hill.

"You're so *creative*, my Mr. Hare."

"Yeah, that's me," he answered, thinking of the Colonel's use of that word. "I'm a veritable artist. And like most artists, I'll likely not be truly recognized until well after my passing. And you, my dear, – my Calamity Jane – you can say you knew me when…"

Seemingly expressing his disdain for the hare's musings, Nemo the horse lifted his tail in front of them and dropped several hot road apples as they rounded the turn onto South Street. Esther giggled and pulled Percy to her side.

He said simply, "Yes, Nemo, I would agree."

End of Part Two

III

Part Three

"New Year's Eve"

Chapter 20

From Elizabeth street, the large bay window reflected the white expanse of new-fallen snow. So new it was untrodden upon at five in the morning, the snow represented a blank slate. In the bottom row of panes, to the right of center, the face of a large hare stared with large, unblinking eyes into the brilliant white. The emptiness allowed him to think through the "game" that had been suggested for him.

The former home of the notorious madam Hortense LaForge was still and quiet and cold. Percy had allowed the small fire he'd built the night before in the dining room fireplace to dwindle. His winter "camp" was working out well, as no one ventured into the known haunt and he could at least enjoy the shelter. In the years since her passing, and the subsequent abandonment of the home, he'd avoided staying there. Baby Alice, the resident spirit and Percy's lost love, preferred he not sleep as much as a hare would have preferred. But it was not as bad as he'd imagined. The entanglement of the resident spirit was usually brief.

"Why would he concern himself with me?" he asked. "A hare. If I *had* told anyone he wanted to kill his wife, which he then dissuaded me of, what consequence would it have posed for him? Why would he bother to explain himself?"

The blue light glowed next to him, in the shadow beyond the window. It pulsed and drifted as he spoke to it aloud. To her. Occasionally Alice would speak back to him. He would gaze into the blue haze and hear words she pushed out to him. "The game," she seemed to be saying. "The game" and then "of women." "Checkers" was the last thing he could make out, before she diminished and faded away.

"Have you tired of me?" Percy asked. "Or is it just too difficult to stay visible? Probably the latter."

He turned again to look into the snow. "Why 'the game of women?' Like 'checkers?' Obviously, one jumps over the other and takes it," he thought. "Is it that simple, though? The Colonel wants to jump over his wife with Esther and just remove her?"

Hearing some light scraping and having grown tired of the impertinent mice that felt at leisure to meander under his feet, Percy turned to the fireplace while shooing them off. But what he'd heard was the checkerboard laid out on the floor. Its pieces were moving, seemingly on their own. He watched and moved closer. The pieces were lined up for the start of a new game. Alice could be incorrigible. She wanted to play almost throughout the day. But this was different, as she didn't wait for him to play.

First a red piece moved, then a black from the other side. One square at a time the same two pieces alternated and progressed across the board toward each other. But then they diverted *around* one other, so one never had to "jump" the other. They kept moving until they each landed again on the opposite side. Unscathed.

"They *replace* each other? They just go somewhere else? No one taken?"

He pondered this a while longer in the bright silence.

✳✳✳✳✳✳✳✳✳✳✳✳✳✳✳✳✳✳✳

Esther, while as precocious and headstrong as ever, at first resisted the notion of venturing out. That is, for perhaps an entire morning after the incident at Barkey's game. By that evening, with her hand wrapped from the damage she'd inflicted upon herself with her one terrific punch (no broken bones, thankfully), she was pestering her mother to help her find Percy the hare. She wanted to show that she would not be cowed. She would not be bullied. She wanted to play. And she wanted to hug him again and again

130

CHAPTER 20

and thank him for saving her life. Where was that hare?

Percy stole the opportunity of the girl's recuperation for some much-needed time with his own thoughts. He'd seen knives brandished before. He'd been in rough scrapes. It was no matter to him. But he was concerned for the girl. For the young woman, that is. He could hardly call her a girl anymore after what he'd seen of her. He was concerned for her and, truth be told, *by* her.

He'd admonished himself for feeling the way he was beginning to feel toward her. She'd hugged him tight all the way home in the carriage that night. And it had felt good. Unexpectedly, she had reined old Nemo the horse to a halt halfway home and fully embraced him, sobbing uncontrollably. He had convinced himself she was still frightened by the events that had transpired. But he suspected she could throw off that fear rather quickly.

He couldn't allow this. He wouldn't allow it. He'd allowed himself the luxury of feeling something toward a young woman once or twice before. A lingering blue ghost stayed with him, in his heart and mind, to that day. A hare with regret – a "creature of the forest" that *should* by all rights be carefree and light-hearted in its innocence – that was a sorry thing, he admonished himself.

When it had happened, he could have ignored Alice's madam, ol' Hortie, and gone after her. She'd told him to "be a man," ironically. That was the life of a whore and Alice was tiny but strong, she'd said. He'd feared the worst from the beginning, when she was offered to a man for an evening out in the undeveloped county. When another local farmer finally returned her the following day, she'd been abused and abandoned in a field, nude and alone in a sleeting rain, for half the day. She was found wandering aimlessly, pale as a ghost... calling the name of her true love. Calling for her Percy. Alice lasted fifteen minutes by the fire in his arms before leaving this earthly realm.

****

Percy stayed away for a week. He stayed away from Esther. He stayed away from Baby Alice. He considered leaving town. Maybe he would jump a train again, like he'd done many times in the years before, just to see where it took him. But he was getting older now. That type of adventuring seemed to be behind him. There was no longer a taste for it. He found a wooded spot north of town and hunched down against a tree and just watched the occasional crane overhead and stared at the cold blue sky for a week.

But just when even his old friend Evaline was beginning to fear for him, and she'd known him to be good for a sulk from time to time, Percy reappeared one day on their screened porch. It had been closed off for the winter, but there he was one morning, drawing on a thin cigar. Evaline wrapped herself in a quilt, pried loose the frozen lock on the porch door, and joined him on a rattan loveseat.

"Oh, Mr. Hare, you're feeling human again, aren't you?"

Without looking at his dear old friend, and with tears welling in his eyes, he said, "Is that it? I wondered what all this bother was."

Chapter 21

It was now the snowy morning of December 18th. In the month since the near-tragic game at Barkey's Short Buffalo Tavern, the elusive 'E.W.' had gone on to play again. Barkey had insisted on having them back, heart-sick over the results of the last game. He'd convinced the owner to allow him to control who came and who played. Now there were Barkey's trusted fellows at the door and Barkey himself positioned as a mainstay in the room. He stood in the center of the gallery, large and solid, never taking a seat. He was so silent and steadfast that Percy joked he could have been mistaken for a pillar supporting the floor above.

Esther had wanted to venture out to other games in town, but Percy and Barkey were adamantly opposed to it. She assured them that they could research who would be in attendance and where those games were being played. If Percy sensed anything at all out of place, he could insist they take their leave. There had been no further incidents. And they'd gotten no word on the whereabouts of Swettenham, or the bowler hat, or of their employer the Marquis de Lafayette for that matter. But it was clear from word on the grapevine that he was looking for them.

This bright, snowy morning, Evaline and Esther, as well as all the ladies of the house, were anticipating the Christmastime holiday. It had them all in a more jovial mood than ever. To Percy, it signaled the need for necessary caution because joviality usually led to someone picking him up and hugging him.

It was almost a contest among the ladies, to determine who hadn't yet held Percy the hare and whose turn it was. Today, it was Marguerite, who went by Margo. She was relatively new to the house and a bit older than some of the other girls when they started. She was tall and pleasant, mostly shy in demeanor.

Against his custom, Percy went to the front door that day. He was met by a group of the ladies who had seen him coming up the walk. They encircled the entry and stood smiling over him. It was always a treat when Percy Hare came to visit. Suddenly, as he was greeting the ladies in turn, Margo scooped him up and hugged him to her tightly.

"Ooooh!" she said. "You're right, his fur is very soft. Oh, I just want to cuddle you all day, Mr. Percy."

"That won't be necessary," he replied good-naturedly.

One of the other girls said, "I just like that tail – look at it, all fluffy…" As Margo held him up, this girl commenced to fluff it with her fingertips.

Heading into the parlor with him in her arms, Margo cooed, "Oh, Percy, I want you to be *my* boy. Won't you? Evaline's had you oh so long now. It's only fair she give someone else a turn," she said, directing this to the madam herself.

Evaline smiled at the spectacle of Percy trying to politely free himself from Margo's embrace while the other girls crushed in on him, claiming it was "my turn" – "no mine!"

"Alright ladies," Evaline finally said. "I think you've harried him to his wits end now, and certainly given him plenty of options to consider. Please put our friend down now, Margo."

Reluctantly she did so. But it could be heard from one of the group as they left that she would love to wear poor Percy snuggled inside her bloomers and walk about town all day. "My, I'm fraught with sensation just thinking of it!" This illicited an explosion of excited laughter.

"Charming," he said.

"Yes, but… truth be told… not a terrible idea in my mind's eye," Evaline teased. "As a matter of fact, I think we almost…"

"Where is Miss Esther this fine bright morning?" he interrupted.

"Oh, you old poo! Well, as a matter of fact, she had a caller this morning. She's out on a sleighride."

"A what? A caller?"

"Yes, and it's someone with whom you are acquainted, I gather. Colonel Wigglemann."

"*What?*" he looked at Evaline nonplussed. "How can the Colonel...? What? How can he be calling? He's a married man, Evaline."

"Yes, he is. And he is filling a role for her, for which she has no earthly father. Much like you, Percy. Filling a role for her."

"What, pray tell, is *his* role?" he asked dubiously.

"Well, he is chaperoning young Esther *in the light*, you see. In the light of day. You are her night consort. He is the day consort. He came to me a week or so ago and inquired about her. I was of course suspicious at first. But then he made the case that Esther is a young woman on the verge of joining society – perhaps even a bit late in doing so.

And in light of her having no father to escort her and introduce her at social engagements, parties, and such, he offered to take on the part."

Percy contemplated this for a moment, staring into a large plant. He had a bit of a sneer on his face and made a sucking sound against his teeth.

"I assure you, Percy, I was none too keen on it at first. He's always seemed a bit of a clod and a somewhat pretentious man. But I admit he *is* a man of means. And he has access in places I myself cannot go."

"So you gave him your daughter," he chided.

"No! Now don't be that way," she urged. She leaned forward on the settee to address her diminutive friend. "I know she means a great deal to you. And I know you're being protective of her. You wouldn't be the man... the hare I know if I thought you weren't going to have this reaction. That's why I didn't say anything to you about it in front of Esther. It would ruin things for her if she thought you didn't approve."

Percy wanted to yell at her – to tell her all the things the Colonel had said to him – to point out that this was a ploy to wedge himself into Esther's life – to eventually use her to *jump the checker*... but he opted against it. This was the part of the world, *society*, in which he was not invited to play. This was where he had to bow away. This was where he had to leave a mother to decide for her own daughter's well-being and the place that young woman might hold in… that word again… society.

Evaline watched her old friend pace the room with these thoughts charging around in his head. She knew he had his reasons for suspicion. He always did. And she trusted him. She also knew that the old hare had a crush on the young woman. And she knew no good would come of that. She knew of experience. A hare can love, but a hare can't stay.

"Well," he finally spoke. "I wish her well. And I hope her ride is enjoyable. I hear the chestnut vendors are out in the town."

"They are," Evaline said. "But now Percy, don't be…"

"If you would, please tell Esther I'll call again later tonight. I understood she wanted to find a different game this evening, aside from Barkey's, and he believes he's found one."

And he left. Through the window, she could see the end of Percy's stick rise as he plucked it from the snow. Then it was flicked back and forth quickly, snipping off a few leaves from the branches of her holly bush as he descended the front walk.

A moment later, several of the ladies entered the parlor. Margo, with hands perched up on her hips, said in a faux pout, "Shame on you, Evaline. Did you upset my rabbit-man?"

****

That evening, Esther said, "You're being more quiet than usual, my friend."

He only patted her arm to indicate all was well, as she held out Nemo's reins.

"I hope you're not jealous of the time I'm spending with Colonel Wiggle-mann."

"The Colonel?" he asked with false disinterest. "I gather he's an interesting fellow. I know little of him."

"You know enough," she replied flatly.

He allowed the comment to drift into the snowy trees as Nemo clomped steadily on.

"Mr. Hare…" she began.

"I believe one is expected to enter this saloon from the Ferry Street side alley," he interrupted, "So we'll have a bit of a longer walk tonight. After we leave the carriage."

"I suppose so."

"The snow is still thick and slushy, so it'll be slower going. We may have to take that into account. Should we need to make a… rushed exit."

"Mr. Hare…" She paused for his interjection but none came. "Percy, you are aware, I hope, of what you mean to me."

He kept his eyes on the horse's flank and swinging tail.

"You are my absolute fondest friend." Esther continued. "I adore you. You have seen me through this gaming adventure with steadfast commitment. You've watched out for me, and steered me, and pulled me back when I got too far ahead. And you saved my life, let's not forget! I still don't know how you managed it – you were sterling!

And all the while, you have allowed me something no one else has – not mother, certainly. Nor the Colonel. You have allowed me… *independence*! You have allowed me to walk, and not be led. You have allowed me to play, and not point out the cards for me. You even allow me to drive the carriage, for heaven's sake."

"Well, in truth, Nemo wouldn't listen to me anyway," he offered.

"Oh hush, before you make me love you more…"

Percy's animal heart leapt in his chest. He swallowed hard. He quieted himself by reasoning that this was just a young woman's manner of expressing devotion and thanks. She didn't really *mean* that. Not in that way.

A quiet pause while they rounded onto Fourth Street and neared Rosalind's clinic.

"Now, let's discuss New Year's Eve," Esther began anew.

****

The New Year's celebration in Lafayette in the 1880's had grown into a two-day social agenda. Throughout the downtown area, residents participated in New Year's Eve celebrations on a wide scale of activities based upon economic status, from the very rich to the deeply poor. Churches greeted the new year at midnight by ringing their steeple bells. And there were a lot of churches scattered throughout the downtown area. New Year's Day itself was the time for gala entertaining and open houses throughout the more prominent homes and neighborhoods.

Evaline and Esther Wells had secured an invitation to a New Year's Eve event thought of as the "Event of the Season," being presented at the Opera House on Fourth and Ferry Streets downtown. In preparation, Evaline's house had been abuzz with activity.

Mona, the full-bodied hostess of the house, was also an expert seamstress and had fashioned gowns for the ladies to wear. She employed a couple of the girls to help pin and stitch as necessary. Other ladies experimented with hairstyles and makeup for both Evaline and Esther, most of the effort being expended happily on young Esther. Evaline professed that she was too mature to be concerned with the effort. "Any color you slather on this old wrinkled potato would just be a waste of fine product," she explained.

Much concern was addressed to the Wells women's intended chaperones for the event. The Colonel admitted that his marital obligation was to his wife Edwina, of course. But the woman was notoriously averse to social engagements and she begged off. She offered her consent however, freeing the Colonel to act as Esther's consort. In order to clarify his commitment, he insisted upon wearing the "consort's button," a boutonniere lapel flower in blue, traditionally meant to represent his "unattainable" or unavailable status. This was only proper.

Evaline one day informed Percy Hare that he would be attending the event as well, as her male escort. He promptly informed her that she could kiss his fuzzy-tailed ass. But she persisted, saying that Mona had been busy at work on a set of proper duds for him. It would hurt her feelings terribly if he refused.

"As well," she said, "you are my oldest surviving friend in this world and

I'm *asking* you, in light of all we've shared, to accompany me. There isn't a decent man in town, at least not one with any sense, who would be seen with me. Tongues would be flapping everywhere over the wag walking with the old whore."

"Stop calling yourself *old*," protested Percy slyly.

Evaline gave one of his long ears a playful tug.

"So you prefer to walk with a short hare?" he asked.

She bent over to him and took his paws in her hands. "Yes. Always," she said sincerely. Looking into his eyes, she said quietly, "I'm getting older, Percy. How many more opportunities might I have to get about town with my favorite boy?"

Percy nodded to her respectfully and consented to attend. Overhearing the exchange, Esther clapped and bounced on her toes, unable to contain her excitement. "But," he insisted, "no damn pants. Or shoes." This triggered another long entreatment from Mona, who was anxious to fit him with his own adorably small and stylish pair of pants. But he held steadfastly to his statement and she was forced to relent.

Chapter 22

On the evening of Monday, December 31, 1883, the rather odd quartet of Colonel Mel Wigglemann, Mr. Percy Hare, Mrs. Evaline Wells, and Miss Esther Wells made their way to the Lafayette Opera House in the Colonel's fine enclosed rig.

The Colonel's stableman and driver, Mr. Poutch, struggled a bit to define the path of the carriage horse, Pinthistle. The mare had taken one look at Mr. Hare approaching the carriage and gave a start. Ten minutes later, she continued to stutter and hop occasionally on the way down Ninth Street. Percy allowed that he would be happy to work it out with the nag, providing they could stop the carriage and allow him to locate a stout stick for the conversation. Evaline assured him that wouldn't be necessary.

The group disembarked at the Opera House to a festive scene. The façade of the building was festooned with decorative garlands swung from the upper balcony and a high central window. Large open torches were mounted from the wall and paired doorways, casting a dramatic flair over the surroundings.

Endless pairs of attendees emerged from their shining black carriages and paraded from the street, up the stairs and through the doors, glimmering in their finest apparel. The men shone in black coats, with starched white shirts and white ties. The women floated in atop wide gowns and bustles, hair gathered high in elaborate, twisting coiffures, and off-the-shoulder gowns displaying elegant, creamy white necks and décolletage.

There was so much bustle and activity, with horses and carriages and pages shouting and clicking of heels on the pavement, that Percy was nearly overwhelmed. He looked about him nervously, feeling very small. This world was hard-shelled and too shiny. Too much artificial light. And he was at the disadvantage of viewing it from waist high.

Just then he saw beyond the torch glow to the opposite side of the street. There the more common folk had gathered to watch the elegant set enter upon their "kingdom." In the shadows, he thought he saw Tanya Bubher and her eye patch. It almost looked like she was trying to signal him, but then she was gone in the darkened crowd.

Evaline urged him to take her hand. She looked more beautiful than Percy remembered. It had been years, perhaps a decade, since he'd seen her "done up" and she didn't disappoint. Gone were almost that decade's worth of aging and worrying. Her eyes were bright again and dramatically lined. The madam's lips were a brilliant crimson and her teeth shone brightly. She was wrapped in a fur stole over which her white gloves shone. He took her hand, but she mostly led him up the steps into the hall.

Esther fairly stormed the proceeding with her appearance. Both Mona and Esther would have preferred to dress her in the newer "Aesthetic" dress style, consisting of a loosely-fit waist, puffed sleeves, and, most importantly, lack of a corset or heavy petticoats and bustles. But Evaline wouldn't hear of it. She thought the style interesting, to be sure, but perhaps ahead of its time here in Lafayette along the Wabash.

Instead, Esther appeared resplendent in a shimmering yellow evening gown, with shoulder straps, a very low neckline, and an abbreviated but sumptuous train. The contrast from her voluminous bust to her narrow waist to the exaggerated swell of the lower skirts – all, mind you, in a stunning if seasonally-inappropriate glowing yellow – made Esther a veritable torch among the fireflies.

Inside the Opera House, the entryway bustled with attendants taking away women's wraps and men's cloaks in a candlelit setting which sparkled of golden accents surrounding the room and door mouldings, as well as numerous sculptural adornments. This gave way through three doorways to the immense inner lobby. The space rose four floors in a vast open atrium, with separate boxed meeting lounges on both sides of the atrium. Each lounge "window" had richly patterned curtains, between which could be seen lighted candelabras and decorative statuary in gold leaf and bronze. From every level of the atrium dripped holiday garland. It criss-crossed most heavily on the second floor over their heads, thinning with successively higher floors. And in the center of the space hung an enormous lighted chandelier suspended with seemingly thousands of crystal droplets. The chandelier itself was nearly two stories in height.

Two lengthy and gracefully curved staircases led to the upper level, meeting there and embracing a ten-foot winged marble angel standing over a large clock with a brilliant gold face. The entire staircase was also festooned on either side with garland.

It was breathtaking. So much so that the management had tuxedoed attendants in place to move among the patrons and politely invite them forward toward the bar and lounge levels, lest folks congregate too long in the entry.

Percy found himself as awed an anyone by the opulence. He could never have dreamed of it all, right here in downtown Lafayette, behind the hopelessly bland façade of an easily overlooked blocky building. The sharp blacks and whites of the men's coats, and the rich and diverse colors of the ladies' gowns set a stark contrast to the daily browns and dull blacks one found on the city's mud-strewn streets.

As might be expected, he was deeply suspicious of it all, to the point of near resentment. His mind began simple speculative calculations on the cost of things around him, from clocks to walnut stair rails to gilded statues to the garland itself. The labor and expense were incalculable and he gave up on it. So great an expenditure on this, when so much of the town *he* lived in was forced to scrounge and steal for what little they had.

It disgusted him. And yet enthralled him. Just when he felt like backing away, he found Esther's delicate gloved hand stretched out to him. He looked up her long arm to her beautiful face smiling at him, her hair glittering with a bejeweled tiara. He took her hand and continued along.

Chapter 23

At the top of the staircase was suspended a backdrop with columns and a painted romantic landscape. It was an idyllic setting of the Wabash Valley, with trees and birds and the river itself gleaming as it snaked into the distance. A river dolphin appeared to be breaching on the water. Guests were lined up to pose in front of the scene for a photographer, whose occasional explosive flash was blinding and further disorienting.

Groups of people were gathering across the mezzanine. A call of "Three cheers for the old year!" went up. "Hip, hip, hoorah!" And a number of party-goers surged forward to join the toasts. Percy was nudged aside and found himself pushed clear of the Wells women.

A large wash of skirts and dress trains flowed past him. When it cleared, Percy suddenly found himself face to face with Lafayette Mayor F. E. D. McGinley and two of his cohorts. The mayor grinned contentedly down at him. Percy looked around for Esther but the landing was too congested.

The mayor's cohorts seemed distracted by the social logistics of keeping their man informed of each passing constituent, and that person's respective job or position. But even they stopped to look down upon the tuxedoed hare before them with bemusement.

F. E. D. McGinley was a lifetime politician. At least he seemed a lifetime mayor. He'd served Lafayette as mayor (and served himself within the position, it could be said) in 1869 and 1870; he'd returned in 1873 and 1874; and then again in 1881, 1882, and 1883, and would continue in the new year of 1884. What no one knew then, or would be little surprised to hear, was that he would be back as mayor from 1889 through 1893.

144

"Mr. Hare!" the mayor announced. "It is a *true* honor." He extended a big, beefy hand to Percy, who shook it obligingly.

Where and when the mayor spoke, it drew attention. Conversations quieted around them as the mayor greeted him. People turned to see. Percy had rarely felt so exposed and scrutinized. He stood his ground and nobly raised his head, while trying to get a glimpse of Esther anywhere nearby.

"Mayor FED," Percy greeted the dignitary. He was the only person who got away with making the mayor's initials into a name – a name that coincidentally indicated the man's devotion to food. "Life is treating you well, I take it?"

"Ha! Yes, I'd have to say that it is."

"At least you're looking well... fed," Percy said, almost under his breath.

The mayor bellowed with laughter. His large, vested belly shook such that the gold watch chain slung across it to his vest pocket bounced and flashed. Everyone around them laughed. When the mayor laughed, others laughed along. They'd begun to draw a crowd, the two of them. The novelty of Lafayette's illustrious and long-time mayor conversing with Lafayette' notorious and little-seen gentleman hare was a great attraction.

Percy continued to glance everywhere, anywhere the crowd gapped, for a sign of Esther.

"Say, when are you going to visit me in the courthouse again? You know, it's damn near finished now, they say. But they've been saying that for nigh on three years!" He belched forth in laughter again, turning only slightly to see if others had joined in.

"Still," McGinley continued, "I've been in the office for months. My rooms are done. So when are you going to join me for another cigar?"

Percy considered the mayor and his broad moustache staring down at him. He leaned in.

"One of two things must happen, sir. As I think of it, possibly both."

"Oh? And what are those?" the mayor looked around, as if to cull others into his interplay with the hare.

"First, the Sheriff must catch me up."

A surge of laughter went up. He interrupted and continued.

"Or…" people quieted. "Or, you must get a better brand of cigars. Preferably both, I say."

He delivered the last part walking through a sea of applause and laughter, giving the mayor a salute as he left the circle. On his way, he caught the eye of the mayor's wife, Delores, who was standing dutifully behind the man. She gave him a sly look and raised a glass of champagne to him. Percy would admit to the vision in his head of a lascivious look she'd once given him in private… in front of the fireplace at their opulent home… on a snowy evening… with the mayor attending a council in Indianapolis…

Percy winked at her, causing a titter of laughter among her lady cohorts. The hare was quickly out of sight, but the blush on her cheeks lasted several moments longer.

Percy couldn't locate Evaline and Esther in the crowd and realized he was at a poor perspective, being so low to the ground. So he leapt atop a balustrade at the corner of the stairway. From there he found his party on the far side of the upper gallery. Evaline was in discussion with some notable gentlemen, with Colonel Wigglemann standing behind her. Percy recognized the gentlemen as belonging to the banking and judicial crowds. The madam was holding court with them, and a couple of the much younger men clearly were enamored of her bearing and confidence.

Esther was nearby, surrounded by a group of young men, over whom she was holding court. By their cut and swagger, they likely held early positions of bearing and influence. The jockeying and gamesmanship on display, even without hearing their conversation, was to Percy's mind rather pitiful. Esther simply glowed between them all, her yellow gown illuminating the space and her flaming red hair acting as a torch for their attentions. Percy could see men of all ages just beyond her circle turning their heads in admiration as they passed.

The Colonel stood looking dour and seemingly unimpressed by the lot. Percy thought it must have been killing the older gentleman to watch the young bucks vying for the attention of the one he himself so desired. But he stood firm to his post. Percy noted that the Colonel was briefly visited by two young men. They were a different breed, serious and dressed inadequately for the occasion.

Esther cursed to herself for having lost Percy in the crowd. It seemed he
was just too short and too easily obscured. She suddenly caught his eye as
he perched above the crowd, clinging to a pillar. She smiled at him, relieved
to know he was within sight again. She signaled him toward the bar by
holding up her glass of champagne and nodding in that direction.

Offering her apologies to the swarm of young suitors, she moved forward,
dodging the attentions of various men. She logged them into two categories
of address: 1. "Service," as in "May I offer you an aperitif or an hors
d'oeuvres, miss?" and, silently, "*Oh, by the way, what a magnificent pair
of breasts you have!*" and 2. "Suitor," as in "Good evening, pleasure to make
your acquaintance" and, somewhat less discretely but still to themselves,
"*Oh, by the way, what a magnificent pair of breasts you have!*"

Esther found herself being edged gradually to the outer walls of the room
in the flow of the crowd. And then a man strode purposefully toward her
and there was a third look. This one, she would call "Menace," and it said,
"You're coming with me."

Without even addressing him, Esther skirted the menace with quick
thinking and a friendly maneuver. As luck would have it, the Good Reverend
Tancey, downtown cleric and regular at Madam Wells' house, was standing
directly in front of her. She threw her arms out in celebration of seeing him
and drew him into a warm hug, while turning him about to stand directly
in the menace's path. She quickly bid him adieu and offered a desire to see
him again soon, leaving the good Reverend (and two of his parish deacons
with whom he was conversing) well befuddled. Quickly, she found a way to
pass on through the crowd.

"Where is that hare?" she asked herself. She leaned into the throng in the
direction of where she'd last seen him.

Almost immediately, two pairs of strong hands took hold of her arms on
either side.

"Oh no, not more of you," she sighed.

"Unfortunately yeah," one of the men replied, "Now let's make this easy, shall we?"

"I agree," she replied. With a well-placed boot heel to the arch of the man's foot, she dispatched with the menace on her left. He collapsed, allowing her a free hand to take the nearest glass of champagne from an unsuspecting matron and dash it into the eyes of the second menace, to her right. She moved quickly away from them, knowing they wouldn't be down for long. And there would certainly be others coming her way.

Where was Percy? There was laughter and frivolity all around. But no direct sign of him.

Percy had lost Esther again in the crowd. He meant to hop down from the balustrade to find her, but came face to face with Rosalind Gullimore, who approached with a male companion. Percy literally gasped at seeing her. She was certainly no longer the awkward young girl with a slight overbite he'd known all those years ago. Before him stood the same soulful eyes, the girl with the same unassuming demeanor, but now in the carriage of a dark-haired beauty. She wore a deep rose red gown with a vivid red nosegay flower.

He nervously looked back and forth from Rosalind to a spot in the crowd where he thought he'd seen Esther's yellow gown.

"Percy! Oh, I'm so glad to see you!" Rosalind looked genuinely flustered. She reached for him and took his paws, caught between the urge for the warm embrace of a childhood friend and the propriety of the situation. It didn't help, Percy thought, that her clearly disapproving companion stood hulking over her shoulder.

"Oh, Percy – where have you *been*? I've agonized over not seeing you." The look in her eyes reflected her words. She stared at him intently and her eyes became glassy with tears. Percy's heart was being tugged between Rosalind's very apparent longing to see him again and his obligation to locate Esther. He looked up across the room and could just see Esther searching the room for him.

Esther found herself again in the company of two more menacing men who

148

took firm hold and began to steer her. In only three steps the way was blocked and she was looking into the glaring eyes of the Marquis.

The benefit of improved lighting made her cringe at his appearance. His eyes hid beneath heavy, low eyebrows. His nose was long and pointed and his mouth clenched in a tight bow, just above which clung two angry, perfectly manicured black slashes of moustache. Scars at the edge of his left cheek and a small puncture wound on the right side of his mouth attested to a violent past.

"Hello, again, Miss E.W." he croaked at a lower volume. His voice was raked and nasal. Before continuing he pressed the head of his walking stick into Esther's bodice, tight to her belly. He leaned in.

"Let's not make this difficult, shall we? I just want to play the game."

Across the room, for the first time in a while, the hare found himself without words, looking into Rosalind's eyes.

"Percy, you don't need to..." she assured him. "I just need you to know that I miss seeing you so..."

"You do?" he asked. "I'm so... I'm very..."

"Don't. The past is the past, dear friend," Rosalind assured him.

The Marquis practically hissed into Esther's face. "If this becomes difficult, the hare will be done away with. Immediately. I'm in no mood." He grinned at her slightly.

Esther felt chilled in his presence, and felt his walking stick pressing into her diaphragm, restricting her breathing. But she surprised herself with uncontrollable laughter in his face.

"Humph. I believe you'll find the hare well able to take care of himself."

"Perhaps," the Marquis answered. In a growl, "But what will become of your mother, dear? Have you considered it?"

Afraid that her reaction could be too readily seen, Esther offered a little more than hopeful assurance, "She is with Colonel Wigglemann at the moment."

"Yes," the Marquis hissed, "He told me he would be so."

"Darling," Rosalind's beau interjected over her shoulder. "Don't make theatre of this. Look around."

Some had begun to take notice of the pair, he perched atop the balustrade and she entreating a hare in a tuxedo and holding his paws. Percy looked again for Esther and thought he saw her red hair heading toward a side door.

"Please, Percy, just come and see me soon, won't you? I'd love to visit with you."

"I will," he assured her. "I apologize, Rosalind, I really do…" Looking across the crowd again, he saw Esther surrounded by a couple of men who looked out of place in the stylish crowd, being led through a side door from the landing. She caught sight of him just as she passed out of sight. Her worried look ignited his urgency.

"I must go!" he said as he leapt in that direction, over the heads of an older couple. They never registered him and continued their discussion with the owner of a local hardware and furnace store whose eyes grew wide following the arc of the airborne hare.

Percy tore across the room cursing at his own lack of progress. To surpass a large group, he hopped around the party-goers and bounded off the wall and down again. Encountering a particularly large hindrance, Percy jumped to the man's shoulders and pushed off from there, over the heads of those with whom he was holding court.

The man, Horace Grinlow, howled, "By god, there he is now! It's the very one I was talking about…" whereupon he began to guffaw and laugh violently. "I wonder where his accomplice is? That mysterious young woman… *E.W.!*"

Another thirty feet to the door and Percy struck it hard enough to be heard. He wrenched the handle and flung himself through the doorway. There he was met with a crushing blow from a wooden chair. The blow threw him against the wall. He looked down the corridor, seeing only a blur of yellow, and lost consciousness.

Chapter 24

Cold air filled his nostrils and slowly revived him. When his wits came back to him, Percy jerked to attention but found himself restrained. He was in a box, or rather a crate. He could see through the sides but his vision was still cloudy. The pressure in his head felt like it was being pinched in a vice.

He began to move. Whatever he was in began to move. He was able to turn and pull himself to a seated position. His front paws were tied together. He peered out through the spaces between the boards but was unable to get a bearing on where he was. Clattering of a horse's hooves. And of wagon wheels on brick pavement.

"Where is Esther?" he wondered. *"Where the hell am I?"* He began to spin in the crate like what he was, a caged animal. He was looking for a weakness in it, somewhere.

The wagon seemed to be emerging from a confined space onto a wider, more open space. Suddenly, he heard a coarse female voice fairly scream, "Percy! Percy! Watch now..."

"Mrs. Bubher?" he wondered aloud, recognizing her voice. *"Mrs. Winks?"* Looking through the crack, he could see her across the street, winding up and hurling something at him.

The knife drove through the board in front of him and wedged there. Three inches of the blade protruded in toward him.

"Ha! Got it! There ya go, rabbit. Told ya – ya need a knife!"

Percy reached out to the blade and dragged his ties over it. They were severed fairly quickly. He unwrapped the bindings and squeezed his hand through the gap between the boards. Grasping the knife by the handle, he was able to maneuver it free and pull it back inside.

Using it, Percy began to chip away at the board the knife had penetrated, eventually weakening it. He immediately set to work at the board beside it. Once adequately carved through, Percy leaned back and kicked through the planks. Moments later, he stood atop the crate, aboard a wagon being drawn down a darkened street. There were other crates on the wagon bed, but they were filled with simple trade goods. No sign of Esther. The driver, having heard the crate being split open, turned around and yelled, and reined in the mule leading the wagon, but Percy was already gone.

Percy looked around him for recognizable aspects. Over the tops of the buildings, he saw the dome of the newly finished courthouse, standing starkly against the night sky. Now he knew the wagon was headed east. It looked like Ferry Street. His suspicion was that he would be needed back in the other direction.

Back down Ferry he ran through the melted snow and general muck in the street, toward the throngs in the downtown square. At the alley behind the Opera House, Tanya called to him from the shadows.

"Ya got out! Good man! I tried to signal ya before. They got 'er, Perce. They got the girl. That who you're lookin' for?"

"Yes, where did they go?"

"They had 'er tied like you. They went that way." She pointed down an alley running behind the buildings facing Fourth Street. They were heading south, in the direction…

"I think I know where they're going," Percy said, distracted. Then, "I beg your pardon, madam! I owe you a great debt. How did you know what was happening? How did you know where I'd be?"

"Ah, ol' Winksy – he spilt his guts tonight, he did. Old fool. Says they was teamin' up on ya tonight, to make you and the girl pay. Said they was settin' up a *special* game for you two tonight."

"A special game, huh? Who's *they*? Winks and the Marquis?" he asked.

"Yeah – how'd ya know? Ooh, them Marquis' bastards – them's who got ya, ya know…" Tanya replied. "Them's the scum of the earth, they are. Winksy's guys ain't so bad, just dumb like he is. Don't usually mean no harm.

Just lookin' to take advantage of folks when they can. But them Marquis' men – they're ugly, Percy. You're lucky you got away."

"Yeah, well I'm going back now," he replied. Tanya looked at him, boggled, from her one good eye. "Look, Mrs. Winks…" he began.

"Don't call me that," she protested.

"Alright, sorry. Mrs. Bubher," he deferred.

"Tanya!"

"Okay then, Tanya. I beg your pardon, ma'am – but I must ask… why are you doing this? Why help me?"

"Ha!" she cackled loudly. "Don't make no sense, does it?"

Percy shook his head.

"Well, like I say, ol' Winksy, he ain't all bad. But he don't think right." She turned and spit, and wiped her chin. After a second she said, "What it is, is, I'm worried with him going in with this Marquis fella. Worried he won't come home. Worried when he does come home he'll be dead to me. You see?"

Percy nodded.

"'Sides," she went on, "you're a clever little fella. A right good time y'are! Ha! What's it gonna hurt, I trip Winksy up a bit?" Tanya cackled hard, forcing her to cough something up on the street.

"Alright then, ma'am," Percy resumed. "I require your assistance. How friendly are you feeling, this New Year's Eve?"

"What? More? I already give ya my knife," she answered saucily.

"I need you to pay a call on a gentleman to join me tonight," he said with urgency. "Could you do that? It's not far."

"You havin' a party?"

"Somethin' like that," he offered. "More of a game. And you're invited."

"Hot damn!" she answered, slapping her skirt and giving a loud cackle.

Inside the grand soiree, Evaline had grown somewhat concerned. She hadn't seen Esther or Percy in a while and could not find them anywhere. The noise of the conversations, the laughter, and calls for toasts was deafening.

"*Where is she, Percy?*" she spoke quietly to herself. "*Have you located some adventure somewhere? Some game or other?"*

The Colonel stood nearby, his hands clasped behind his back. He turned and smiled at her reassuringly, as if recognizing her concern.

"Looking for our companions, ma'am?" the Colonel asked. She tried not to let her concern be too visible. "I haven't seen them in a while myself," he continued, "but I can have someone make some inquiries. I'm sure they're about. The hall has many side rooms, so perhaps they've found some social sport with which to become engaged. Cards, or that 'Forfeits' game of assigned tasks, or the like. You know, I was once assigned to be posed like a statue and had to hold it far too long. What a great laugh we had."

"*Ugh,*" she thought to herself, "*Well, if need be at least I can find my way home safely enough with this fool.*" Then, out to the hare, as if she could message him directly, "*Still, I'd feel better knowing you were both safe. Percy, my good, good, dear friend – Esther's well-being is everything there is. I hope you know that. I hope you're seeing to her.*"

The crowd around her and up the staircase began to swell with the song "My Bonnie Lies over the Ocean" and she and the Colonel joined in with them.

"*Oh, of course you are,*" she thought. "*The girl's just got a wild bur in her corset and probably led you stumbling away after her.*"

Chapter 25

The square around the Courthouse was filling with people now. The hour was nearing midnight, and the dawn of a new year was almost upon them. Percy allowed himself to be swept along with the revelers onto Fourth Street.

A block further north of the Opera House, a crew of men labored behind a street blockade. Theirs would be the very special honor of presenting the River Dolphin Marionette, a traditional experience to downtown Lafayette. The representation of the legendary beast was the highlight of the night, and one that residents of all ages and social classes turned out to witness.

The marionette was more than fifty feet long and suspended upon poles over twenty feet tall. Skinned with colored tissue, and lighted from within with lanterns suspended inside its framework, the dolphin would be paraded through the street around the courthouse to signify the turn of the new year. As the crowd was prompted to count down the seconds, beginning with the strike of the courthouse clock at 11:59 pm, the River Dolphin Marionette would suddenly emerge onto Main Street to circle the courthouse square once completely. Then, depending upon the stamina of its handlers, it could be counted upon to wander the downtown streets for another subsequent hour or more, to the strains of the ringing church bells.

To avoid being slowed by the crowds, and potentially trampled by them, Percy made his way south down the alley behind the Fourth Street buildings. Eventually he turned and crossed Fourth Street, finding his way to the rooftops above the Columbia Street buildings, running westward. To reach them, Percy "fenagled" the back door to the building adjacent to the Lafayette

National Bank, having acquainted himself with one of its tenants years before and knowing his way to its roof access.

Each building along the Columbia Street Courthouse block had a different character and appeal. And a different roofline. Percy looked down upon the throngs celebrating in the Courthouse square and made his way from one building up or down to the next. Eventually he arrived at a building toward the end of the block, with the next highest roof.

Looking down onto the back doorway from the roof, Percy saw two men standing there. He saw one of them point to the sign at the back door and ask the other, "Who's 'G. W. Art'?" The other one shrugged.

Winks' men, Percy thought. He knew then that he was right. That George Winter's abandoned artist studio was the "special" place set aside for tonight's game. And, as they'd cast him off in a crate, for what purpose he couldn't know, Percy knew the Marquis' focus was on young Esther herself. That gave him a chill.

Percy moved to the front of the building's roof and peered down over the façade, upon the crowds gathered in the Tippecanoe County Courthouse square. People flowed through the lamplit streets, over the trolley tracks and through the loose, snowy slush. The tracks were bare and ignored, whereas on a usual day pedestrians would be dodging the clanging trolley cars and cursing the horse turds. He must commend the city this once. They had done a fine job clearing the square for the evening. "Well done, Mayor FED," he thought.

From the far side of the square, Percy heard a trumpet call that echoed through the downtown corridors. The trumpeter made the call sound like a large beast, stuttering and wailing to make its presence known. Suddenly the crowds began to move toward the opposite corner of the square, flowing now up over the courthouse grounds. They didn't want to miss the beast.

The crowds gathered and became very boisterous at the corner of Fourth and Main, the opposite corner of the square from where Percy stood. Torches and lamps met them there, in a glowing hive of activity. The River Dolphin Marionette was about to emerge onto the square to signal the new year. Percy noted the time on the courthouse clock, 11:58, but he kept an eye running through the crowd for the man he hoped was on his way.

Soon, a few figures stood out, moving in the shadows on Columbia Street, in the opposite direction of the celebrants. They pulled a small box cart behind them. A large man, a younger, smaller man, and two women in full skirts. A group was not expected. Percy waited until the recognition was made. This was a group he welcomed. He whistled to them from the rooftop.

Barkey Smith kept walking determinedly and waved up to the hare. Alongside Barkey was a stout young man Percy recognized as Barkey's eldest son, Mal. Percy wouldn't have expected him to be brought into danger. But it showed Barkey's concern for Esther that he brought his young muscle with him. Mal was pulling the cart.

With the men, the two women were a bigger surprise. One was Kess Smith, who, to the best he could make out, was singing something and walking alongside the cart. She looked up at Percy and blew him a flirtatious kiss while singing. The other woman, who was hobbled a bit and puffed steadily on a pipe, was Tanya Bubher herself. She'd been sent as the messenger. Whether she meant to stay and help or just sit back and watch was as yet unclear.

Barkey and team rounded the corner on the building with a head of steam. Percy ran across the roof to the rear of the building again. Winks' men saw Barkey and team and grew nervous. One of them tugged at the exterior door to the studio, which was securely locked. Having this confirmed, Percy began to make a delicate climb down from the roof to the second-floor window above the door. Soundlessly, he lowered himself, window frame by brick gap, until he was clinging to the brick window ledge on the second floor.

"Here now," said one of the door guards, backing away from the imposing Barkey as he approached. "You can't... you can't be here!"

"Now, Billy, you scare too easy," said Barkey. "You and Willy here..."

"It's *William*!" said the other door guard, an indignant young scruff.

"You two," continued Barkey, "need to get on home now. It won't do for

157

your women to hear you out in league with them scumbags what I think are in there."

As he had on the night of his visit with Esther, Percy found the piece of metal bar wedged into the rotted window frame. He pulled it free and inserted it into the window jam, where he began to pry up the window. The heavy old window rose in its frame, over the heads of the men positioned at the door to the old studio. He snuck through.

The debate continued outside the door, with Billy and Willy doing their best to stand fast in the face of Barkey's determined authority and larger form. To his credit, Barkey wasn't trying to intimidate them, though he was clearly intimidating. His intent was to convince Winks' two half-witted henchmen that they would be better served at home for the New Year's Eve.

"Ya oughtta see the beast comin' down the street, is all I'm sayin'," said Barkey. "'N ya oughtta be with you women on New Year's."

"And I'm gonna make sure your girls know where you been, instead o' with them tonight, buying 'em roasted nuts and such," croaked Tanya. As she stepped into view, the two dimwits pointed and acted shocked.

"You! You... you're Winks' woman!" cried Billy. "Hell, we'll tell on *you*! He'll be so *pissed*!" He and Willy seemed pretty content with themselves, until Tanya unleashed a loud cackle.

"Ha! Oh, go right ahead, boys. Ol' Winks'll not halt me up for my doings! Ha! He knows the trouble I'll unleash on him – what I harbor behind this here patch!" She tapped her eye patch with her pipe stem as she spoke, chilling them to the bone as she cackled on.

As their expressions fell, the door latch was thrown from the inside. Percy stood there and held the door open.

Billy and Willy made a move for the door, but Barkey stepped before them. Reaching out, his simply flicked his middle finger under Billy's nose, hard, sending him reeling backward to the ground. Willy helped him up and the two staggered away, realizing that facing Barkey was not worth their trouble.

Percy led the group up the narrow stairs to the second floor. Mal worked with his mother, lifting the small wheeled cart up the steps. There was considerable thumping and bumping, leading Percy and Barkey to urge quiet.

"What's in that?" Percy whispered to Barkey. Then, with alarm, "Did you bring..."

"Brung ya a surprise," assured Barkey quietly. "Keep movin' now."

Looking around the wall, they were surprised to see no one on watch at the studio doors, which stood open. Instead, the guards had moved just inside, out of view of the hallway. Apparently these men were interested in a view of what was transpiring.

Inside, he could see a suspended oil lamp over a table in the center of the room, both new additions since his last visit. Percy watched from between the legs of one of the door attendants. Several men stood around the room, all dressed in black formal wear. They all seemed focused upon something on the floor.

In the pool of light, Percy saw Esther in a heap, swaddled in the fabric of her own yellow dress. She was face down, arms stretched out in front of her.

Esther slowly pushed herself up, her hair tumbling out of its arrangement awkwardly. She crouched there a moment, seemingly regaining her bearings. When she raised her head, Percy could see that she'd been struck. Her eye was somewhat swollen, her cheek was flushed. She tossed her glowing head of hair back from her face and, with amazing resolve, she rose slowly to her feet.

Esther's stance, in bold defiance of the men who surrounded her, awed Percy. But his heart ached as she balanced herself, her hand trembling slightly on the table top. He counted ten men in total. Some of them were Winks' men. He didn't recognize the others and assumed they were with the one man speaking – the man seated at the table, facing the door.

It was the Marquis de Lafayette. He looked up at Esther, sneering as he said, "The dress is ruined now, isn't it? Look, there's a tear in your bustle. Poor dear. Let's see her without it."

"No!" she screamed defiantly, as two men approached her. Esther yanked her arm free of one of them, and shoved the heel of her hand into his eye.

The other man grabbed both of her arms from behind. The first thug had recovered and extended his hand, intending to slap her across the face. But the Marquis interrupted him by simply holding up his hand as he began to speak.

"That'll be enough," the Marquis ordered. He spoke in a pinched, tight-throated voice, Percy thought, as if he'd had a particularly wrenching toilet experience and his voice got stuck that way.

"Sit down," he said to Esther chillingly. She did not move. In a forced voice, that seemed to come through his teeth, he repeated, "I said... sit... down." No movement. The same thug stepped forward with his hand out to strike her again, but the Marquis begged him off.

"No. I said that's enough." He gestured politely to Esther to take the seat intended for her at the table. "Please," he offered. This time she didn't fight him. As she came further into the light, Percy could see her eye taking on a flushed, pale shade of reddish purple and bruises were already forming on her bare arms.

"SO," he pronounced loudly, "I take it I have the privilege of addressing the mysterious 'E.W.', do I?" The Marquis manipulated his moustache and stared at her. Suddenly he bellowed, "DO I?!" at a force of volume that caused Esther to cringe and even made several of the men flinch. Esther sat quietly, looking at the table surface.

"Eh, no matter," the Marquis said casually. "You're not here to talk. You're here to play. You see, you seem to have made quite the show on the town – at least at the euchre tables. So we'll see what you're made of, won't we?"

He began to shuffle the abbreviated deck of euchre cards and continued to address her soberly, making small talk. But his intent was only just submerged by his words.

"Does your mother know you're out at night making a killing at the tables? Your mother's the old whore up on Prospect Hill, no?" A pause to gauge her reaction. "No? Hunh, I thought that would garner a response. Well," he added, beginning to deal the cards to Esther and the other men at the table, "Here's where I'll expect something from you."

He laid her final two cards on the table and released the corners hard, flicking them to the surface.

"You will play a game or two with us, here tonight. There will be no money involved, though my fellows here have, as you can see, laid out their pocket money. You won't need it, fellas, but we'll leave it out there.

But little miss – Miss 'E.W.' – if you win a hand, you can take the money. You can take it. But if *we* win, you'll offer us something else. First, my friend Swettenham here – oh, yes, you've met, haven't you? It seems you broke his nose a while back. As an aside, he didn't take well to that – not from a *girl* – not at all." A snicker went up from the other men, but Swettenham maintained a steady stare.

"But if you lose, when you lose, Swettenham here is going to cut off that pretty dress. The next time you lose, he'll cut off your fancy knickers, and stockings, and so on. And when he's run out of things to cut off, I'm going to send him to cut the clothes off your rabbit friend. And by that, I mean, skin him. Alive. And from him, Swettenham will make me the finest rabbit stew. He knows how. And you and I will eat it, right here, in the morning, watching out the windows as the sun comes up on the courthouse and a brand new year. How does that sound?"

Still no reaction from Esther, though Percy thought he saw her eyes wetting with tears.

"So," the Marquis continued, "you're going to want to win, my dear. You won't. But you're going to want to. Because if you don't… once you and I have enjoyed our New Year's rabbit stew, my fellas are going to pay a call to your mother's house."

"Why?!" Esther finally broke in. "What do you want with me? With her? Why are you so concerned with me?"

"Because," he leaned in and hissed. "You're in my grounds. My field. I control the games here in this piss river town! You have assumed you can have your way, but it's not so. We tried to send you a message and all we got for an answer was a broken nose and a fine blade lost in a ceiling rafter. And you *kept playing*! As if you owed nothing to no one. *You're wrong!*" he bellowed into her face.

Behind him, Percy heard the cart rumbling quickly to the doorway.

"Right!" cried Mal as he entered the room, pushing the cart before him. The young man had heard enough. Barkey saw him through and didn't seek to stop him. All eyes swung to Mal, who threw a forearm into the back of the head of the man nearest him, knocking him to the floor. His partner took a single step toward Mal before Barkey grabbed him by his coat lapels and simply tossed him backward into the room. Young Mal stood more boldly than Percy had ever seen him, and called out, "Got somethin' for ya! Here!" Mal threw open the bolt on the facing panel of the cart, but then stopped.

"Hold there a second, boy," Walter Swettenham spoke loudly from the far side of the room. They looked up to see the dapper fellow, a pair of blackened eyes peering out from his bandaged face. He had pulled Esther out of her chair and his arm was wrapped around her waist. A glittering silver blade point was poised at her throat.

Mal and Barkey froze. Percy caught Esther's plaintive eyes from across the room, clearly frightened but resolute.

"I think you'll want to give this some thought…" Swettenham began.

"Ah, shit!" Tanya screeched, stepping through the doorway. "Too much damned thinkin', I say!"

"Tanya!" Winks bellowed, shocked to see his wife limp into the room. "Whattya think yer doin'?"

"Ah, hush, ya great fool," she answered him. With that, Tanya gave the cart a heavy kick with her boot and its gate panel dropped open.

A heavy snort and a puff echoed from within the cart, and a hell spawn of brown fuzz clattered out across the floor. The pygmy bison stomped and huffed in place, pawing at the wood planks. It was clearly aggravated with being penned in for the shaky journey downtown, but certainly didn't look like the awful threat it imagined itself to be.

"Ha!" Winks laughed. "Whattya think *that's* gonna do?"

Mal reached into his pocket and pulled out his younger brothers' rubber balls. Flinging them out into the room, he said simply, "This."

The small rubber balls bounced in lively arcs in front of the bison. They served as the only visual stimulus it required. And it charged.

162

Chapter 26

In its blind rage, the bison struck out for anything in its view, which was limited to only two feet above the floor. It chased the balls as they bounced into sight, and crashed forward like a living cannon ball. It struck one of the legs of the table, shoving it into the Marquis' chest and snapping off the leg. The table collapsed, sending cards, coins, and chits flying. This in turn gave the bison all the more bouncing irritants to pursue. It trumpeted an angry warning as it began to storm around the room.

Swettenham lost his focus for a second and Esther took advantage of it to free herself. She ducked away and dodged his swing when he attempted to slice at her with his blade. The knife was driven into the wall just over her shoulder. Esther jammed his knife hand to the wall and held it there, while with other hand she pummeled Swettenham's bruised face again and again. His eyes promptly rolled back and he crumpled to the floor in a heap.

The bison turned toward a pair of legs and smashed into one man's shin, splintering his tibia bone. Men shrieked and attempted to either vault over the hooved fury or jump onto chairs. Winks Bubher hurried to get on top of a chair, but in his haste he tipped it over and landed roughly on the floor. He was met with a heavy charge to his ribs. The beast then backed up and drove its rock-like skull into Winks' own, knocking him silly. Tanya released a high, squealing laugh that echoed everywhere.

The room became a flurry of activity, with Barkey, Mal, Tanya, and even Kess stepping into the fray. It became difficult to keep track of the separate bodies, all the while stepping lively over the pygmy bison when possible. Kess had an iron skillet that she used very effectively, bringing it to bear upon more than one combatant. A couple of Winks' men pulled billy clubs and began swinging. One of them clipped Tanya's shoulder and she winced in pain. Realizing what he'd done and who she was – his own boss' wife – he stopped to apologize. Tanya clenched her pipe in her teeth and plunged her hand into the man's mouth. She took firm of his lower jaw and pulled him down to where she could address him. He was clearly in a good deal of pain, as he scabby fingers stuck under his tongue and with her hold she could steer him where she liked.

"Bump," she began. "You ain't smart enough to be here on your own, with your little club. You best take your ass on home now, 'afore I tell your girl what you been doin' and with who! What you think she'll be sayin' if she know you hit a woman with your club, huh? Think she'll look kindly on that? Think you'll be getting a New Year's toss, do you?"

The man called Bump tried to shake his head no and gurgled out an attempted response.

Flinging his head backwards, Tanya screamed, "Then git! Git on home!" And she followed, "But gimme that club there first."

From the card table side of the room, a shot rang out, and then another. One derringer, held by bowler hat, had fired errant. The other, held by the Marquis, had struck a glancing blow to Barkey's chest. It ripped through his coat and took him to his knees. But it hadn't penetrated and he assured Kess he was alright.

The Marquis took aim again, but Esther's stylish, buttercream yellow boot kicked up through his hand and sent the gun high in the air. Bowler Hat seemed to struggle with something between his feet, and with a snorting trumpet sound the bison took out his legs. Bowler Hat fell awkwardly, his chin smashing against the upright edge of the now-collapsed table.

Esther moved for the Marquis, but he was making a fast exit into the shadows. A furry paw grabbed her hand firmly and pulled her aside.

"We have to go, Calamity Jane!" said Percy. "We have to get you out of here!"

"Percy!" Esther exclaimed passionately. She fell to her knees and hugged him tight to her. "My Percy Hare! You came for me!"

"Well, of course I did, you silly girl. Your mother will kill me if anything should happen to you."

"IF anything should happen...?" she replied sarcastically, looking about as a glass jar exploded against the wall behind them and men and women struggled all around the room. "Percy, isn't it exciting!" Esther gasped.

"Yes , well, that's one view. Good for the periodicals. But let's go!" Percy urged her. As if to punctuate this, another gunshot rang out, causing everyone to duck their heads.

Tugging Esther forward, he made an irregular path across the room, dodging fighting pairs and listening for the rumble of an oncoming pygmy bison. As they reached the entrance doorway, Kess rushed them and pushed Esther aside. A silver blade hissed between them and embedded itself in the door frame, just inches from Kess' face. She immediately inhaled in quick surprise, emitting a rattling, rasping gasp.

Percy took both women by the arms and dragged them into the hallway. "You need to come with us, Kess!" he urged. "Your air – you gotta get away from this."

"NO!" Kess spat, with the breath she could muster. She slouched to the floor, gasping heavily for each breath. She signaled back to the room and then pointed to where she lay. Percy understood. Her husband and son were in there and she wouldn't leave them. She tried to assure him with a look that she'd be alright and she waved him on. But her eyes were anxious and wet. Kess began to cough out hard and gasp for air to retrieve afterward.

Percy got close to her and smoothed the sides of her face gently with his paws. He planted a big, soft, hare-muzzle kiss on her cheek and spoke quietly to her while he nuzzled her cheek. She kept coughing, and shook nervously while sucking in any breath that would come. She broke out in a cold sweat that made her chest and arms glisten. But she listened and put her hand on his shoulder.

"Remember – slow, sweetheart... *slow*," Percy said. "One breath at a time – slow – "

Kess struggled, but tried to slow her breathing. She looked deep into her friend's eyes as he coached her through each anxious breath. Tears were running down her face. He wiped them away repeatedly and assured her it would pass. "It's almost over now," he seemed to repeat too many times as she continued to struggle. Sounds of the struggle in the studio continued, and they did their best to ignore it.

Finally, her ragged breaths began to come more slowly. Kess closed her eyes and began to concentrate on each one. She'd gotten through the worst of it. Then she pushed him away, and waved for them to go. Percy leaned in for one last kiss of assurance. Kess pulled him to her and planted her lips fully onto his. Esther was wide-eyed, and she couldn't deny wondering what that felt like, being kissed by the hare.

Chapter 27

Percy and Esther exited the building in the alley behind. It had begun to rain on the New Year's downtown, an icy wet rain that was slickening every surface. They turned and ran to the east. Percy heard something behind them and turned to see the Marquis and Bowler Hat running toward them from a hundred feet away. A shot rang out and careened off the bricks next to them.

"Through there!" Percy said, pushing Esther headlong into a tight alleyway. He helped her as best he could, but her wide skirt was an incredible burden while trying to run.

"We'll have to lose the hoop frame when we can," he said. "But not now… over there."

When they rounded the corner on the block, they found a work wagon with its horse unattended. Percy recognized a broken crate in the back as the one he'd been held in a short time earlier. The driver was nowhere to be found – Percy thought he must have gone to report to the Marquis. Before they'd even reached him, the horse gave a start and a nervous whinny. Esther assuredly commanded his reins and the wagon bolted out onto Fourth Street, headed back into the New Year's revelers, who had not been easily put off from their celebrations by a little rain.

"We'll have to turn away, and go up Columbia Street," Esther said. "There are too many people."

"No!" Percy objected. "Look, there's a path."

"Up the sidewalk?"

"Yes, we can tuck in beside the crowd and lose them."

"Lose who?" asked Esther.

"Them," he replied matter-of-factly, pointing to the Marquis' elegant black carriage coming down Columbia at them from the west. "Ahead!" he cried.

"Oh, Percy – I don't know," Esther worried. She steered the horse over and the wagon climbed up onto the walk along the buildings. Startled revelers, now pushing the River Dolphin Marionette up the street to rescue it from the rain, jumped away from Percy and Esther's clattering wagon. Those supporting the suspended puppet were jostled, causing it to shimmy and twist. The wet tissue was quickly shredded from two segments, namely over the dorsal fin.

Percy and Esther were forced to duck under awnings as they passed. The wagon wheel clipped the edge of the wooden newsstand, shoving it aside. A squeal went up from the anxious crowd and the horse bayed out his displeasure with the plan but Esther pushed him forward.

At the end of the block, the now shocked and angry crowd yelled and hissed at their intrusion in the festivities. As the wagon passed, the celebrants reached out and slapped its sides and shouted obscenities. Esther tugged the reins hard and sent them around the corner and east up Main Street, ostensibly away from the crowds. There were stragglers in the street, but they quickly dodged the vehicle.

They passed through the Fifth Street intersection, glad there were no trolleys running that evening to congest the roadways. Percy looked down the block in the dark, and wasn't sure what he saw.

As they approached the Sixth Street intersection, Esther asked, "Are we clear, Percy? Are we free yet?" Looking down Sixth Street, he saw a shadowy black hearse of a carriage with gold markings on the side slide quickly down Columbia in the same direction they were headed.

"No," Percy replied. "We're not. Faster now!"

The steeple bells of churches throughout the downtown area were still peeling loudly to celebrate the New Year. The bells of the 2nd United Presbyterian Church, at the corner of Sixth and Main, were clanging right over their heads as the wagon clattered past. Esther couldn't hear what Percy said. Percy grabbed the reins in her hands and gave them a quick snap.

The horse bolted ahead at a gallop.

As they passed Ninth Street, Esther was fearful of the wagon's breakneck speed. The horse was in his pride, stretching his taut haunches to their fullest for the first time in quite a while. Esther feared they would never be able to evade any impediments at that speed. Percy feared they would never lose the Marquis and his henchman.

Percy continued to see the fast-moving stylish carriage keeping pace with them a block over on Columbia Street. Thinking ahead, as any self-aware hare would do, he knew that the two roads would begin climbing the hill out of town. Eventually, Main Street would meet the edge of the hills and veer to the right to merge directly onto Columbia. And there the Marquis' carriage would intercept them. But the hare could sense the trees ahead in the darkness, and he forged a quick but desperate plan, leaning on his experience with his time in Barbee's Grove.

Just past the Toledo, Wabash, & Western Railway line, Percy leaned in close to Esther and urged her to reduce speed. She was happy to do so. But suddenly he called for her to pull the wagon to the left, clutching at the reins to assist. Esther panicked, unable to see into the black hillside beyond the house on the left, the last dwelling at the edge of town. She protested, but Percy pulled the reins to straining and the horse headed where he too was uneasy to tread. The wagon was plunged into darkness.

"Percy! I can't see what's before us! What are we running into?"

"Quiet now," he urged into her ear. "I can see a bit better. And I know the residents here, but I don't want to alert them!"

"Oh, good," Esther replied. "Will they shelter us?"

"Well… no," he admitted. "I don't know them as well as that."

The wagon ran along an open yard and then plunged into the woods at a narrow trail entrance of which he was well aware. The way was so compact that as they reared the horse to a sudden halt the wagon became embedded in undergrowth on either side.

"Leave it!" Percy urged. "Quickly now." He took her hand and helped her through the rear of the wagon bed and down.

"Turn about," he urged her. "We need to rid you of this bustle and hoop.

169

You'll never make it through the trees in all of this." He reached up under her waist coat and began tugging at ties and clasps.

"Ooh, Percy," she giggled. Then teasing him, "You've never been so forceful before. I *knew* you've wanted into my skirts, but..."

"Oh, hush, girl!" he said, as her full skirt flopped to the leafy ground.

Esther squealed sharply in mock surprise. And instantly a voice called out from the darkness nearby.

"Halt! Wh - Who goes there? Rabbit? Is that *you*, damn ya? What are ya up to there?"

"Get down – quickly!" Percy exclaimed to Esther, pushing her headlong to the wet ground. "Nanflass, don't fire, you old fool... I've a young wom..." he yelled hastily. But before the words could reach old Nanflass' nearly non-functioning ears, a blast exploded through the brush nearby. Pieces of it ripped at small branches and the few remaining leaves, before dozens of pieces of shot thudded into the sideboard of the wagon. And the hindquarter of one friendly larger-than-normal hare.

"ooooOOOOOOWWW! Goddammit, Nanflass! You shot me in the ass!" Percy screamed. The horse was extremely startled at the blast and rose up, but was too well ensnared in the brush to escape.

"Ha!" Nanflass celebrated. "I told ya, didn't I, rabbit? If ya came through here again, I'd blast ya to kingdom come!" Nanflass made his way through the brush to find Percy. "Ha! Blind shot, no less! Well, done me!"

Percy pulled himself up on the spokes of the wagon wheel, smarting at the buckshot burning in his hide. Esther could barely make him out in the darkness but she sought to assist.

"Nanflass – I have a young woman with me, you old fool! You damn near took her with me to kingdom come."

"What?" Old Nanflass replied.

"Don't shoot again, sir –" cried Esther. "I beg you!"

"What? A woman? Why would ya bring a woman out here? Oh! Is she one of yar tramps? Eh, Mr. Hare?"

"Certainly not," replied Esther. "I am a lady, sir. And as soon as we finish getting this damn bustle off, I will show you so."

"What?" asked Nanflass, unsure of what he'd heard.

"Yes, dear" Percy grunted. "Perhaps not your best turn of phrase."

Esther giggled into her glove at the recognition of what she'd said. But she reached out for Percy in the darkness.

"Oh, my dear – are you hurt?"

"Yes," he grunted. "But no matter, we must keep going. Esther dear, the Marquis could figure things out and be here at any moment. Turn about for me."

She did so. And hooking his claws into the ties of the bustle, he began to rip through them. After three ripping tugs, the bustle and hoop frame fell free of her.

Nanflass caught up to them finally and asked their business.

"Dammit, man, we're being chased by some very unsavory characters..."

"I don't care, ya bloody creature. Ya've done your worst here too many times and I've warned ya, haven't I? I've warned ya! Now get! Get off my land!"

In truth, Percy *had* indeed done some of his worst to old Nanflass, with whom he'd quarreled for years. Percy objected to the old duffer proclaiming this part of the woods to be "his" in such a possessive way. Anyone who spent time in those magical woods would normally understand that their charms belonged to anyone and every*thing*, including every meandering bug and flitting bird.

So Percy had taken to... spoiling some of the Nanflass family's things on occasion. Garden vegetables, rain barrel, etc. In the interest of brevity and grace, it will just be offered for example that Mr. Hare had, at one or more occasions as he passed through, wiped his own soiled arse on bedsheets hung on the line to dry. No matter now, the harm had been done – and now paid for.

Ignoring the still quarreling Nanflass, Percy assisted Esther with stepping out of her dress frames, and the two of them made their way uphill into the woods. Percy thought he heard a carriage's wheels rolling in on the bend of Main Street. He urged Esther quickly through the partially frozen, partially muddy muck of the forest.

Sounds from the roadway behind them echoed up into the trees. A gunshot rang out, and the pair dropped low beside a tree. From the orders being issued, it seemed the Marquis had meant that shot to signal another group of men coming up Main Street. When they found the Marquis, they split into two units and left what sounded like two carriages and their accompanying horses in the street.

Another booming shot rang out. This one sounded like Nanflass' blunderbuss blasting into the tree canopy. He likely was trying to get their attention himself. There was some yelling and it almost sounded like the old fool indicated "Ya'll find them up the hill there, I'd wager!"

The icy rain hissed in the trees and the leaf clutter around them. But they were well on their way up the hill.

Chapter 28

Percy reminded himself, *"You said, 'Sense and caution around her or she'll bring you up short someday.' That's what you said. 'Sense and caution. Bring you up short.' And yet here you are, in the spreading wake of her effect, with an ass full of buckshot. Well done, you damn silly old hare."*

Esther in partial dress and Percy with an ass full of buckshot made their way north through the trees, until the ground began to fall away again at a steep angle. Percy would have preferred to stay within the tree cover and follow it northeast, further into the trees, but the Marquis' men would likely be cutting in from that direction.

Stumbling down the decline, they soon found themselves on open ground, exposed to the moonlight. Percy hopped uncomfortably without relying too much on his left flank, still stinging from the buckshot. Esther supported him while struggling with the wet rocky soil. The rain then began to fall in greater volume, hissing as it swept over them.

Gaining momentum on a steeper bit of slope, Percy clung to Esther's bloomers to signal caution. And he was only able to whisper a weakened "Wait!" before she fell headlong over a short ridge. As he tumbled after her in the darkness, he heard her land heavily, six feet below.

Esther's breath was expelled from her lungs on impact, her face mashed into the now slick, soft earth. She had the presence of mind to avoid crying out, though it took her a moment to gather her senses after the impact. The hare dropped at her side.

As the rain pelted the ground around them, they both raised themselves unsteadily. They listened for the sounds of their pursuers. They heard nothing from the ridge above, but found no comfort in it. Percy did what he could to help Esther to her feet.

Esther eventually rose from the icy muck, stepping into the moonlight. Her skin seemed as pale at the moon itself and her bloomers were practically incandescent white. Percy urged her to head west along the base of the ridge.

He could finally hear the voices of the men across the top of the ridge but was unsure if he or the girl could be seen in the dark.

Slick mud was starting to slide down the escarpment and Esther staggered through it admirably. In the moonlight, she glowed a ghostly white in front of him, while accumulating a smattering of darkened stains. He recognized her brilliance would be a detriment. He would have to hide her somehow. And he knew he couldn't keep going much longer. The buck shot was hobbling him and he was bleeding fairly badly.

They struggled on for a while. Percy kept his ears cocked for sounds of pursuit. Through the hiss of the rain, he heard only the echo of an occasional call, until suddenly a sharp "there!" rang out, followed by a general hubbub of noises.

Without turning to look, he would be unsure whether the pronouncement meant someone was hailing a companion or whether they had seen the girl's white undergarments. He pushed forward with abandon, not caring either way. Haste seemed a momentarily better path than clarity.

His haunches burned with pain but he struggled to catch up with Esther. As the ridgeline curved a bit back to the south, she seemed to be moving out from the slope to less treacherous ground, but Percy feared that would still put her in sight of the Marquis' men. Above and behind them, he feared he could hear a man's path through the underbrush atop the ridge.

With that, he caught sight of a cleft in the muddy wall to their left. Instinct told him there was a chance it was more than it appeared. He grabbed Esther's gloved arm to slow her. When she turned, he silently gestured to the cleft and ran at it. Plunging in, he found his intuition rewarded. A small pocket lay tucked inside the earthen wall.

Percy spun about and found Esther's fearful face peering in.

"No," she stammered, "I couldn't..." The crevice seemed barely wide enough for her face, let alone her whole body. "Into the *ground!?*"

"Come! Come now!" he urged, reaching out for her.

Her delicate hands reached through but she was clearly unsure of it. Percy took her by both hands and tugged, pulling her roughly through the slick gap. She was painted with mud instantly, and her open bodice in fact scooped it up, filling quickly with mud that slid down the inside. Together, they pulled her legs up into the crevice and tucked them in alongside her.

Percy could see out into the moonlit field, and watched for a moment as the eerily lit rain washed heavily to the ground. He dug his hand deep into the earth and covered the girl's white undergarments with darkening mud. He lay back in exhaustion and plunged his face into a delicate white cotton pillow.

Moments later, he knew not how long, Percy awoke, being pressed to the girl's bare neck. She sobbed and clutched him to her desperately, for the first time revealing her fragility. She fairly screamed his name, fearful he was dead, and pleaded for him to wake.

"I'm awake silly girl!"

"Percy! You're alive!"

"Yes, now quit your catterwallin' or we'll be found out!"

"We're trapped here now – how will we get out?"

"Getting out will come in time, have care now. Look about. Can you see anything?"

"I can't see a thing! I can't even turn my head it's so close in here..."

"Then no one will see us either. Doesn't that make sense? We're breathing... and there's at least a bit of room. Hold tight and be still. No one will find us here for a while, and we'll leave before it collapses on us..."

"Collapses?! Oh, Percy, what kind of a..."

"Oh, dammit, hush girl!"

Esther seemed to draw an astonished breath in the darkness. "Why, Percy, there hasn't been anyone who's spoken to me in such a manner..."

"Then it's well overdue," the hare finished. "Now hush."

She clutched him to her warmly. Quieted now, she continued, "Percy, what about Barkey and Kess, and Mal? Do you think they're alright?"

"I don't know. But if I know Barkey, they'll be fine. He has a knack for coming out of rough spots in good shape. And he'd never let anything happen to his family." After several silent moments, he found himself sighing, "Dammit, my ass hurts."

In spite of herself, the girl giggled at this and hugged him sympathetically to her bosom. He squirmed uncomfortably, in the flush proximity of her plump young breasts. This was not the circumstance, he argued with himself, to take an interest in the girl's charms.

"Why, Percy," she cooed, "I now see the fascination the house ladies have shared over your fur! The feel of it is quite... stimulating!"

"Dammit." He muttered into her cleavage.

****

In the dim light of dawn, the muddied creature lurched toward the simple rig, coming to a halt alongside the new road scraped into the base of the hills just west of Barbee's Grove. Though walking erect, the miserable creature was barely recognizable. But this had to be the inimitable Mr. Hare.

"You alright there?" the driver inquired. Both he and his rig were nondescript – brown and worn in appearance. He appeared to be simply hauling mercantile goods on the wagon.

"Well enough. Can we take travel with you? Up the hill on Ninth Street?"

"Us?" asked the driver.

Percy gestured behind him and said, "I've got someone with me. But she's frightened. And chilled."

"Mercy. She'll catch her death out here."

"That's what I fear. I need to get her home right away. Have you got a blanket? Or a cloak? Something large enough to throw over her?"

"Yes, here." The driver produced a thick woolen horse blanket from beneath his seat and handed it down to the hare.

176

"I'll be back soon. Stay here." said Percy. Then, stopping in his tracks, "And can you keep watch for any...? There have been men threatening us all night."

The driver noted his emphasis and the distinct limp as the hare passed back into the mist that hung low that New Year's morning.

A few minutes later, he saw a larger form now at the hare's side. The young woman was covered in the blanket and the two of them made their way gingerly through the muddy field. They paused a moment and the driver scanned the horizon in all directions before waving them forward.

Percy and the driver helped Esther into the carriage. She was muddied from head to toe. She concealed herself in embarrassment and seemed as tired as if she hadn't slept all night.

Seeing the pair secured behind him, the driver steered his rather haggard looking horse out onto the muddy, near frozen road. They progressed in silence until they came to the top of the rise at Burlington Street. To their left lay the wide-open lands to the east of Lafayette. To their right, Burlington changed names to South Street and headed back into town. The driver hesitated there a moment, long enough for another, finer carriage to emerge from the icy fog.

Shifting to look, Percy made out the form of Pinthistle, Colonel Wiggle-mann's grey mare at the head of this carriage. Pinthistle, as was her habit, became instantly perturbed by the sight of the upright hare and jostled about until the driver, the Colonel himself, quieted her.

"Dammit," muttered Percy. "I should have known we'd see him."

Esther gasped and whispered, "Percy! He knew I was being taken last night! I think he's been working with the Marquis."

The Colonel spoke, "Thank you, Orville, I'll take them from here."

The driver tipped his cap to him and replied, "Thanks ya kindly, sir. I best be headed back home 'fore the wife gets distressed."

Wigglemann handed the man some coins and then extended his hand to Esther to help her down from the wagon.

"Shall we return you to your mother, then?"

Esther glared at him, remembering the Marquis' remarks from the night before suggesting he knew what would transpire. She was also appalled to be seen by him in such a state, looking as she did. She clutched Percy's paw tightly.

"Where is my mother?" she spat at the Colonel. "You were supposed to see her home…"

"She *is* home, my dear…" he interrupted.

"Don't call me that."

"… and awaiting your arrival. I assured her you'd just slipped away for some game or other last night – harmless fun. But little did I know the level of… *debauchery* to which you'd be subjected." He looked her up and down, assessing her ragged appearance.

"Debauchery?" she cried. "Assault is more like it. Why, we were lucky to get away with our lives – and you know it full well!"

"I know nothing of the sort, my dear. Why, had I known I would find you in such a state…"

"Oh, bullshit!"

Percy clutched her hand as a caution. Indeed, the Colonel seemed taken aback by her expletive. But he let it pass and extended his hand again to help her down from the wagon.

"Regardless," he acquiesced. "Getting you home would seem to be the order of the moment."

Esther looked to Percy and their stomachs sank, seeing the other in the growing morning light in the pitiful state they were in. They realized they had no other option than to accept his ride. He was not about to sentence the girl to another long struggle through the countryside, and she knew his wounds would limit him. As it were, he might only have a short time to get medical attention before his rabbit's luck ran out.

The Colonel, it was clear, had played a larger part in the evening than anyone had recognized. He had simply waited them out – for what purpose was yet to be revealed. But while he appeared to be offering his assistance, they suspected his actions would ultimately be in service to himself alone.

After they'd gotten underway, Esther spoke, "Colonel, I must apologize.

My dread over the evening's events must have got the better of me. And, I should mention, I fear for you as well, having been out all night in this cold and damp."

Percy smirked at her false concern. God, this girl could wheedle her way out of anything, he thought.

"Me? No. We'll not speak of it," the Colonel assured her. "It is you we must be concerned about dear." Esther stiffened at the man's continued use of the unwanted term of endearment.

Reaching into his jacket the Colonel pulled forth a flask of whiskey and offered it to them both to restore a warmth to their insides. Reluctant at first, they both pulled from it liberally.

Seated in front with the Colonel, Esther reached out to her little friend Percy in the open wagon behind her. He winced at every movement and shake of the carriage.

"Well, my Percy kept me safe. All night. I must say I've never been more terrified in my life – but I never felt safer than huddled with my friend Mr. Hare."

"Mm," the Colonel nearly grunted in ineffectual appreciation. "Commend-able."

They plodded along in silence for a while, while the light slowly grew. Everything was wet and slick. In places there were lingering patches of icy snow. They made their way down South Street to Ninth and turned up the hill at the Fowler estate on the corner.

Percy and Esther were each thinking silently of the moments to come at Evaline Wells' doorstep. They knew there would be questions to be answered, and not just from Evaline Wells, but also from the citizenry that had taken in some of the evening's events.

They began to see folks out walking and greeting each other on a busy New Year's morning. Passersby waved to the carriage and looked to its inhabitants. The day would be filled with visitors and congenial socializing. People would soon be calling throughout the neighborhood unannounced, eating, and drinking liberally.

What news would be shared? What tales of the previous night? What would people make of Esther's wild ride, her making a way through the night in the presence of villainous scum such as the so-called Marquis de Lafayette, and, it would be noted, with the rather infamous Percy the Hare as her companion?

Worse yet, what would any of them think if they saw and recognized Esther in her current state – disheveled, muddied, and half clothed?

"Colonel, could we not take a less traveled route home?" Esther asked. "One with perhaps fewer public eyes?"

The Colonel drove on with no response.

"Sir!" Percy emphasized.

The Colonel finally reigned Pinthistle to a halt, tied off the reins, and reached into his jacket again. He had parked the carriage at the juncture of Ninth Street and State Street, which angled off to the east. Several prominent homes marked the intersection, and a loose crowd of morning pedestrians were nearby.

He turned to Percy, this time a small pistol in hand, and said, "This, Mr. Hare, is where we part company."

"No! What are you doing?" Esther cried. "Percy is my friend. He saved me! He kept me alive and in one piece. Why would you...?"

"He knows there's a price to be paid, my dear," replied the Colonel, keeping his voice low. "Don't you, Mr. Hare? He knows, as do I, that today – right now, this morning – is perhaps a time more fraught with danger for you than all of last evening."

Percy sat unblinking, stoic, and tired. He didn't object. The Colonel continued.

"He knows there will be uncomfortable questions. Questions no young woman should ever have asked of her. There will be suppositions. And rumors. You must be free of them at all cost."

"Are you somehow concerned for my reputation?" she asked. "Because it should be known that I am not!"

He ignored her. "We must have an alibi for the bad behavior of last evening."

"The Marquis!" Esther offered. "Surely he will be seen to be at fault, won't he? Not Percy!"

"Perhaps, my dear," the Colonel assented. "But no one knows of the kidnapping, do they? At present they only know of your scandalous performance in the wagon on the streets of downtown. What questions are asked will be of what led a respectable-looking young woman to crash about the streets in such a way?

"The question of *why* will be present in all respectable minds – and it will not be a great leap to answer the question, '*Who is this E.W. woman after all?*'" He looked at her knowingly. "Not a difficult connection to be made, dear Esther. My dear *E.W.* Galivanting about town until the wee hours, scantily clad, and gaming with rooms full of men!"

Esther was confused. She finally knew what he was saying was true, but held to the notion that another outcome must be possible.

He continued, "So we are left with no other choice." Standing from his seat, the Colonel pointed his pistol directly at Percy and loudly proclaimed, "I heard Percy Hare and his cronies abducted a young woman from the ball, but I wouldn't have believed it of you if I weren't seeing the evidence of it here – with my own eyes!"

Percy held his tongue while passersby gathered, knowing the Colonel to be in command of the situation. He hated him for the suggestion, and for the assumption that he would be the natural sacrifice. And he despised the man for holding a weapon on him, after having taken a shotgun blast to the ass for her – for the sacrifices he'd made for this sweet, incorrigible young woman.

Yes, he now found her sweet. And warm and tender-hearted, and beautiful, even covered in mud as she was, though still headstrong and impudent. She had, indeed, brought him up short after all. And he was wounded and would need to be treated soon. His ass burned and he was light-headed from weariness and blood loss. Time was wasting while daylight was dawning upon them.

He turned to look at Esther.

"Percy, don't go!" she cried. "I need you!"

"See how the trauma inflicted upon her, and the exposure this poor child has endured, have produced in her such a hysteria!" Wigglemann exclaimed.

Tears were streaming down her face. She knew Percy was already gone from her. His thoughts were written upon his oddly expressive face. He had only to follow the Colonel's directive, step down from the carriage, and disappear behind some shrubbery.

Instead, he ignored the gun and moved to her, placing his paws lovingly on either side of her mud-smeared face. And he kissed her full and soft on the lips. Those who had gathered gasped at his assault upon the poor young woman. The Colonel fired his pistol into the air, sending folks scattering.

When Esther opened her eyes again, Percy Hare had already exited the carriage wagon and was disappearing behind the shrubbery.

Chapter 29

The Colonel fired another shot from his pistol up into the trees in the direction of Percy's escape.

"Did you see him?" he called to those nearby. "The degenerate creature has much to atone for, and now I fear he has made a retreat!"

A few men gathered anxiously, seeing an opportunity for athletic response and, perhaps, valor.

"As much as it pains me to do so," the Colonel began. "I must relay to you that events have played out this past evening that might have brought ruin upon the young daughter of one Evaline Wells." He gestured to Esther as he spoke. She attempted to shrink into the blanket wrapped around her. "But those who would bring pain upon the young woman have, I assure you, been thwarted! Follow me as we accompany her home, won't you?"

A rousing cheer and gloved clapping rose up from the crowd gathering on Prospect Hill. They followed the carriage excitedly.

From her tea room, Evaline Wells heard the commotion and looked out upon Colonel Wigglemann rousing the crowd with waves and lifts of his hat while his carriage came to rest at her front gate.

"Oh, what foolishness is this?" Evaline moaned. "That goddamned man."

The crowd cheered when Esther stepped down from the carriage bench and a portion of her mud-smeared leg came into view. Wives averted their husband's eyes from the unfortunate girl's unseemly exposure.

Evaline sighed, "And must that girl always present herself in little more than her undergarments? Sweet Jeezus!" She swept across the room to the front door. "Before God and all his disciples and the whole damned neighborhood!"

Esther was hustled up the front walk of the house and into her mother's arms. Her mother hugged her tightly and whispered, "It's lovely to see you again in one piece, my sweet. But might I ask where it is you've been showing your lovely bottom *this* night?"

"Mother, not now," said Esther.

The Colonel began his oratory, "Mrs. Evaline Wells, an entrepreneur of high acumen throughout the region..."

A few took momentary humor from this assertion of the madam's noble "entrepreneurship" but kept it mostly to themselves. Even Evaline herself suppressed a snicker.

"...was accompanied by me to the fine celebration at the Opera House last evening. And it is from there that a group of ruffians of the card sharp variety laid hold of Mrs. Wells innocent young daughter, Esther, and absconded with her to an as yet unknown location."

Evaline snorted loudly at the word "innocent," and Mona, the house greeter giggled. Esther, still in her mother's embrace, scowled up at her and pinched the back of the madam's arm.

The crowd became disquieted and calls went up for further explanation.

"The details are yet to be ascertained as, I'm sure you can appreciate, the poor child, rather, young woman, has been in quite a state of distress since being discovered this morning."

Much nodding and sympathetic sighing.

"It was I who discovered her, young Esther, alone and in rather poor condition, but, it should be noted, remarkably *intact*, early this morning..."

Both Evaline and Mona, as well as Esther herself, had to suppress snorts of laughter at the word "intact," as that description of her maidenhood, while truthful, could never fully account for the girl's lascivious nature.

"... at the outskirts of town near Barbee's Grove. As her occasional guardian and chaperone, I am honored to be the one to return her home. And for her surviving the chill trip home in my carriage I will be eternally grateful."

Considerable applause erupted, and several calls of "heroic action."

"It must be noted," the Colonel continued, "And I share this not to shock or horrify you good people with the threat it might portend, but of the ill-inclined group that threatened poor Esther is someone with whom many of us are well acquainted. Someone many of us see on a daily basis. Someone we should all be aware has a hidden nature only previously suggested by his frivolous and carefree actions. And for his part in this evening's dangerous developments, for the inconsiderate treatment of a poor, defenseless young woman...,"

"*'Defenseless'*, my dear Aunt Fanny," Mona muttered.

"... We should all be on the lookout for, and protective of the general order for, that unique character of..."

"Oh, he's not going to say..." Evaline muttered to herself.

"Mr. Percy Hare!" The Colonel emphasized his point by firing two gunshots into the air. General consternation went up amongst those gathered there – the ladies covering their disappointment and memory of their own personal flirtations with Percy with mock horror, the gentlemen acting as if they knew this to have been his nature all along.

"Oh, close the door, Mona. I've heard enough!"

Hugging her mother tight, with true affection and in celebration of finally finding some warmth in the entry and in her embrace, Esther sighed lightly and closed her eyes for a moment. Hearing the door shut behind her, she reminded herself of the continuing concern.

Esther stood tall and let the horse blanket fall from her shoulders. She handed it to Mona, who seemed less than charmed with the dirty offering. Evaline gasped at her daughter's appearance, her flesh and undergarments caked and smeared with brown mud from hairline to ankle. Some of the ladies of the house, who had gathered with the commotion and were peering down from the stairway balcony above, began to snicker at the sight of the bold young woman who now brushed dried mud from her arms while she spoke with her mother.

"CHILD!" Evaline cried. "Where in the hell... and how did you... oh, sweet Jeez... it's getting all over the floor... Wait! Where was Percy in all this?"

"I'm trying to tell you, mother, he's in worse shape than I – and he's out there alone! I've got to help him!"

Outside, Percy had been spotted. "There he is!" cried the Colonel, pointing to Percy peering over a fence. "The bold, inconsiderate beast that he is, gloating over his part to play in the attempted ruination…"

The rest could not be made out over the noise of the gathered throng, which seemed to swell as one in Percy's direction.

"Take him!" one woman cried.

"Careful, he looks wounded and could be dangerous!" warned a man nearby.

Esther had found a reserve of energy now, and was taking the steps up from the main entryway two at a time. Evaline called after her desperately, climbing the stairs with all the speed her gown and her age would allow her.

"Child!"

"I'm not a child, mother!"

"Esther! Young woman, where do you think you're going now?"

Esther had found her 'E.W.' outfit, the fitted raingear they'd created for her gaming persona, and was pulling it on when her mother caught up to her.

"Mother, that bastard – that dumb Colonel – he'll have them all out hunting poor Percy! He's been shot, mother! Percy's shot!"

Evaline gasped at this. Her old friend was agile and tough, but he could still be hurt.

"I've got to find him before anyone else does. Oh! Oh, mother, I'd almost forgotten." She drew Evaline close and, with a girlish, whimsical smile, whispered in her mother's ear, "Percy kissed me! The Colonel was separating us and making a sacrifice of Percy – and he was the most gallant, the most romantic little man…"

Tears began to trickle down her muddy face. Seeing the mix of emotions on her daughter's face, Evaline reciprocated with her own tears. They giggled a bit to each other. Then Esther sniffed and wiped her eyes and said simply, "He's out there. I must go find him."

"You'd better," replied Evaline.

"So! How do I look? Can you tell it's me?"

The clenched waist of the coat offered a pronouncement of her exaggerated female form, which might be a giveaway. Evaline encouraged her to relax the belt and look more like a man.

"Good idea."

"And leave the mud on your face. You looked bearded."

"What else?" asked Esther. Just then, a waifish brunette from down the hall appeared in the doorway and presented her with two pistols.

"Constance!" exclaimed Evaline.

"What?" asked Constance with false innocence. "Calamity Jane needs her irons, don't she?" Constance was Esther's fellow reader of Calamity Jane serials. The two had swapped book installments with each other for years.

Esther's face grew into a wide grin. She grabbed the pistols and brandished them up into the air like a brash gunman.

"Esther!" cried Evaline.

"Oh, mother, not to worry," assured Esther. "I know my way around a firearm. From 'Uncle' Delbert. You know, the man you told me was your cousin or something..."

"I recall, girl," snapped Evaline. "How did..."

"He was a bit of a shootist. Did you know that? I was just a girl, but he used to take me out to the Wea Plains to plunk bottles from tree branches."

"What? And when did this...?"

"Mother! It's not of importance right now, is it? I need to find that poor hare."

Then she shoved the pistols into her pockets and ran down the hall to the upstairs parlor, to the corner of the room, and threw up the window sash.

Turning to her mother and a host of young women who were gathering to watch this swashbuckling performance, Esther said simply, "Don't worry, mother. I'll bring him home to us."

With that she clambered through the window and out onto the gable, which led directly to the top of the arbor. From there it was only two short jumps and she was into the myrtle and gone. They could hear her whoops and calls and a pistol shot echoing through the neighborhood.

The crowd was no match for Percy's agility and speed, even hobbled and in great pain. He quickly distanced himself into a neighbor's yard, past their barking canine, across the street, and up the drive of another home. But before he got far, he glimpsed the anxious but sympathetic face of someone he recognized. Rosalind Gullimore, the young love of his younger self, urged him, "Percy! Go to father's old clinic, Percy! You'll be safe there!"

He had to give this consideration. Though still unsure of what his reception might be in the Gullimore family, the old dentist's clinic was attached to his old friend's home. It had been shuttered for years now since his passing. No one would expect him there. And, it was becoming increasingly clear to Percy, he would indeed need someone's help. Whether he could put his faith in a former love interest became a secondary concern to whether or not he could even make it there safely.

Percy made a bit of a show of his escape, actually circling back on his pursuers, a couple of young men eager to be seen in a heroic light, before hopping blithely away. After making a few popup appearances along the block, he made his departure through the trees behind an outhouse and proceeded down the hill toward the downtown neighborhoods.

There he changed his purpose, now being careful to *not* be seen. Percy dodged any passersby at considerable distance and avoided pets that could be alarmed to his presence. His buckshot-laden hindquarter was stiffening and he was feeling feverish and weak. He arrived at New York Street and the unremarkable home and clinic of his former friend, Dr. Francis Gullimore.

Knowing it to always be unlatched, Percy pushed open the basement access window at ground level and slid through. He allowed himself to tumble down a pile of unused furnace coal in the basement and lay there exhausted. As he looked up through the open window, into the first blank grey sky of 1884, a single snowflake wafted through the window and fell towards him. Bloodied, still covered in mud, and now blackened with coal dust, the fugitive hare watched the snowflake tumble through the chill air. He was unconscious before it touched his face.

CHAPTER 29

End of Part Three

IV

Part Four

"3 E.W.'s"

Chapter 30

Esther did her best to track Percy through the woods above town. She took clues at first from the reactions of the locals who were pursuing the hare through the neighborhood. Several calls of "He's here!" pulled folks in one direction and then back in the opposite direction, past the large homes and woods. But Esther recognized these as false flags, signs that the hare was leading them on a pointless chase.

His general path seemed to be back down the hill toward downtown, so she continued that way looking for sign. She kept the large floppy hat pulled down low to hide her face. At one point a couple of young toughs clambered over the edge of a ravine, eager to follow a hunch that Percy might be just where she believed he was.

Esther pulled her pistols and fired off through the trees, back in the direction of the homes on Ninth Street. She made sure she fired high into the canopy.

"Wahoo! That was him!" she grunted in as manly a tone as she could muster.

Waving the toughs over, she ran in the direction she'd just fired, adding a couple more shots to punctuate it. They excitedly skirted her path from higher in the ravine, thinking they were gaining the advantage over her and that they would ensnare the hare themselves. She allowed them to pass back up into the wooded yards. When they had fully taken the unseen bait and chased it out of sight, she turned back down the slope.

She suddenly remembered a Calamity Jane episode she'd read in which the heroine had assisted a posse in pursuing a bandit through woods in winter. Calamity had paused to carefully assess the woods and eventually her patience paid off with a sighting of footprints the men had missed. Esther noted there were still pockets of snow that had survived the rain in the denser wooded areas. Here she eventually found his unique footprints and even, worryingly, some drops of blood.

Patiently she followed along, and when the snow cleared she could still identify his track in the wet soil. She eventually reached New York Street and followed muddy paw prints to a building alongside a modest home. No sooner had she approached the home than she heard a door slam shut to the rear of the building and a woman came into view, heading through the rear yard into town with a bundle in her arms.

Instinctively, Esther approached and pulled her guns. She had no real proof that this woman had Percy, but that didn't stop Esther from charging into the yard. She ordered the woman to halt and when she turned, it was clear she held a bundle that was very Percy-sized.

"Hold it right there," Esther said. "What have you got?"

"It's just a sick animal – I'm a veterinarian." The woman was hooded but clearly seemed frightened to see Esther's pistols aimed at her.

"Veterinarian?" Esther replied. "Wait – are you Rosalind? Miss Gullimore?"

"Well, *Doctor* Gullimore, actually…" tossing her hood back from her face. "But yes! And who, may I ask…"

"Miss Wells! Esther…" she said, tipping back her large floppy hat to show her face. But she still had a mask on as well. "You know my mother."

"I certainly do. I've treated your horse – Nemo, is it? – more than once."

"Yes!"

"And to answer your next question," she moved closer and whispered urgently, emphasizing her bundle, "Yes, this is your friend Percy – our friend Percy – and I'm desperate to get him to my clinic so I can care for him. Can you assist me?"

"Of course!"

"But we must go quickly! I think I saw some of that mob circling up the hill there behind you a moment ago. And I'm so afraid for him! Some rube was firing pistols!"

****

He was bathed in heat. There was a warm woolen blanket under his head that smelled sweet. Percy's eyes lolled open slightly. Things were blurred, but there was a momentary blue glow. Then three shadowy silhouettes could be made out. The closest one bent to him. A gentle hand smoothed back the fur on his face. He couldn't remember any single touch feeling so comforting.

"Alright, lazy bunny," said a warm, resonate voice. "You've been sleeping long enough."

Another voice addressed him, "You've been sleeping for three days now, haven't you?"

"Three days," Percy muttered, his dry tongue sticking inside his mouth. He tried to come to grips with the length of that absence of his wits. He slowly raised his eyelids and attempted to rouse himself. The loss of time worried him. What had he missed? What had gone by in his absence?

The same hand passed over his furred face again, this time gently wiping away his drowsiness. But it stayed above his eye on the side of his face, reassuring him to stay down and calm.

"Percy. Percy, my old friend. It's Rosalind."

"Rosalind," he croaked.

"Stay still now. I've been very concerned about you, old hare. Scared to death. But you're tougher than your size, I guess."

His head was swimming. But he could remember being shot and running wounded through the snow. That was memorable.

"Where?" Percy muttered. "Where are we?"

A second voice spoke, "We're in mother's house, back up on the hill." He recognized Esther, who seemed anxious for him and couldn't hide it well enough.

"I had to find someone to care for you, Percy," Rosalind answered. "I've got too many furry friends in the clinic at present. And... I didn't think John would be understanding of you staying with me."

"John?" he asked.

"My betrothed," she offered. "You met him briefly on New Year's Eve."

"Ah." A pause. "Asshole," he muttered.

Esther and Evaline snickered and fought to suppress a laugh.

"Well, I'm sorry you see him that way," Rosalind smirked. "But I just didn't want to venture the conversation with him. Esther here, and her mother..."

"Who else is hurt?" Percy interrupted.

"What? Do you mean Esther?" Rosalind asked. "She's right here, and she's fine, as far as I know. Right?" Esther nodded.

"And Evaline...?" he asked.

"She's fine too, Percy. She's right here."

"And Barkey? And Kess! And Mal?" he sputtered. "And, um, Tanya? Mrs. Winks?"

"They're fine, dear." Rosalind assured him. "Now don't get all worked up. Everyone made it through alright. We went to check on them just the other day, Esther and me."

Rosalind settled him with a hand laid over his furry face. She smoothed back his fur and ran it the length of his floppy ears. This seemed to immediately quiet him, his breathing and his heartbeat. He lay still and sedate, like a puppy next to its mother.

"Dear Percy, I need to be going. I only stopped to check in on you," Rosalind began. "But I'm so very glad you're a bit better. You need to eat something. You're wasting away laying here. I'll be back tomorrow to see you, so eat up. And if you need anything, or start feeling worse, I'm relying on you to let the ladies know. Won't you? Will you promise me you won't just try to be a strong man and suffer silently?"

She stroked his face again. He consented to her urging, unable to muster the energy to object... He was having trouble keeping his eyes open.

"What ladies?" he asked, seemingly forgetting anyone else was in the room.

"Esther, dear. And Evaline. Or... Mona, or any of the others. The house is full of ladies, and they're all eager to look after you."

He closed his eyes again, for what he thought would be just a moment.

With a gesture, Evaline assured Rosalind there was no need for further explanation. He wouldn't remember it anyway. She could go.

Rosalind gave Percy a light kiss on the nose before turning to leave.

"Rosalind, Dr. Gullimore, are you very anxious to be on your way?" asked Esther. "I wondered if you might like some tea. Or some sherry. And conversation."

Evaline sighed at what she thought was her daughter's all-too-transparent intent, as she gathered damp rags and left her to it.

Chapter 31

Esther showed Rosalind into the music room, where a small piano sat, as well as an intimate two-sided couch and small chairs. As the two sought to become acquainted, a couple of the house girls strode past the doorway, laughing loudly, in only their corsets, stockings, and garters. Rosalind averted her eyes and seemed embarrassed.

"My apologies, Doctor," Esther said nervously, rising to close the door. "I forget that the nature of this house is not one everyone is accustomed to."

"No problem – no problem at all," Rosalind assured her. "You're right that I'm not accustomed to it, but I would hate to think of myself as prudish." She chuckled. "You know, maybe I am a bit of a prude after all! I don't think I ever saw my own mother or sister in their corsets more than once or twice, and only when they were sick and I needed to assist them."

The two laughed a moment and Esther offered Rosalind a glass of sherry.

"As I think about it," Esther said. "Those two young women who just passed – I don't believe I've ever seen either of them fully *dressed*! How odd!"

They laughed again, and Rosalind proposed a toast.

"To women who can be comfortable just as they are!"

"Cheers to that!" replied young Esther, who seemed nervous nonetheless. After a moment, she continued, "I'm eager to talk with you, you must know, because you've known our Mr. Hare for much longer than I have."

"Well I suppose I have, but we haven't communicated for quite some time," Rosalind replied. She sensed a bit of jealousy on the younger woman's part and wanted to dispel it. "Unfortunately, we have been a bit estranged for a number of years. But we were very close for a long while in my youth."

"What was that like? That was when your father was alive, I take it. I hear they were close friends."

"Goodness, yes," Rosalind gushed. "He was practically a member of our family. Most days I awoke to find Percy at our breakfast table – and many times he was in front of our hearth having a smoke with father when I was sent to bed."

"That sounds somewhat familiar," Esther smiled. "That scene has played out here in this house any number of times. But how was your mother with that relationship?"

"Oh, she was not overly keen on it, if truth be told. It did seem to her, she would tell me later, that she was not her husband's best friend. That there was another with whom his time was split. So that she hardly felt that she held that special place in his heart."

"Mmmm, that must have been difficult."

"I'm sure it was. But I must say that Percy was aware of it and he was very sensitive to my mother's feelings. At times when she felt alienated from my father, she would suddenly notice that Percy would go missing for several days. He would make himself scarce. And it was always timed to her feeling lonely for my father's attention."

Esther smiled her appreciation of the gentleman-hare. Rosalind seemed to share it. They raised their glasses together and clinked them in a silent toast.

"May I be so bold as to ask..." Esther began.

"What happened?" answered Rosalind.

"Yes. Between the two of you. If that's not too forward of me."

"Oh, certainly not." Rosalind gathered herself and took another drink of sherry. It warmed her enough that she felt her reluctance immediately fade. She held the younger woman's hand, knowing how fully Esther was smitten with Percy. How fully the adoration of that wily gentleman-hare could swell a girl's heart to bursting.

"Percy and I were practically raised together, it seemed. He was older as a creature, but young of spirit. He was at turns our playmate and then my father's companion and cigar and pint mate. That was the unique kind of creature a gentleman-hare can be. But eventually, as was to be expected, I grew out of childhood and began to mature.

"Percy was on a ride somewhere. I don't know if you've heard of it, but he used to ride the trains for weeks and months at a time. Just hop aboard and see where it took him. I can't recall where he'd been that particular time, but he'd been gone for an extended period. In the interim, as young women are wont to do, I came into 'flower,' as my mother called it. Percy returned to find me no longer a girl but a woman in his friend's home. For the first time, I had shifted to bridging the divide between his playful, young side and his mature, rakish side.

"And I knew it, of course. Of course. I had a woman's... *form* suddenly, and I was curious about its effects. I'm ashamed to admit that I likely made a show of it to poor Percy. And he did not weather it as well as he might have.

"He made an advance that was somewhat... *untoward*. It was just clumsy, really. Not harmful. I was shocked that my friend, my playmate, had taken such liberty. But as I say, I had teased him into it with no care for his feelings. No thought to where it might lead. And I reacted badly when it led to its inevitable result.

"He was appalled. He couldn't bear to think of what he nearly did to me – what he nearly did to my innocence, to my trust in him. So he ended things with us, with the whole family, ashamed for his behavior."

"Because he loved you," Esther sighed. "His little furry heart loved you. And he still does, I'd wager."

"Love?" Rosalind considered this a moment. "No. I think not."

"No?"

"Not that way. I don't believe so. Not with me. We were very good friends. *Very* good friends. But we'd never achieved any level of intimacy at all."

Rosalind considered Esther's hopeful face and smiled. She decided to give the girl the present she'd clearly been hoping for. It was deserved.

"No, he never looked at me the way I've seen him look at you." Esther seemed to stop breathing before her. "And I'm not sure the hare I knew – who, understandably, was a younger version – would have gone to the lengths and dangers on my behalf to which he's gone for you."

Esther felt her heart swell until she was nearly swallowing it.

"Oh, piffle!" came a soft retort from the doorway.

"Mother!" Esther cried.

Evaline continued. "Doctor, I came to say the weather would seem to be turning wet and icy again, and your mare out front seems nervous.

"And I apologize for eavesdropping. But you must know, the both of you, that that hare will be a hard one to nail to the floor, no matter how infatuated you become with him. I've told you before – 'a hare can love...'"

"... but a hare cannot stay!" Esther and Rosalind finished.

Chapter 32

On her next visit, two days later, Percy asked Rosalind, "So, what's my prognosis, doc?"

"Better," she replied. "You were in sorry shape when I found you. But after I removed the buckshot pellets and dressed your wounds, you made your way back fairly quickly. Quickly enough, I guess, to go crawling about the house at night, I hear…"

"Oh. Yeah, well, I went to Evaline's room, to sit by her fire."

"And drink port."

"Yes. She offered and I thought it would be rude to decline. And indeed, it's medicinal, isn't it?" She shook her head no. "But this morning it feels pretty awful. My leg, that is. Have I done something to it?"

"Probably just aggravated it," Rosalind replied. "Maybe re-infected it. I'll put something on it."

"Ooh, that sounds… painful," he said as she peeled back his bandages.

"Possibly."

While she worked on him, he looked into the fireplace. He watched the flames for a distraction.

"What are we to do with you, Mr. Hare?" Rosalind asked. "People are all about looking for you, do you know that?"

"Me? Is that so?" he asked facetiously.

"It is. Sheriff Taylor himself is said to be out for you."

"The Sheriff? Well, that is noteworthy. I've not received his attention in some odd years. But a girl gets run out of town and now he wants my head, eh?"

"Apparently," replied Rosalind. "Now, personally, I can't imagine the Sheriff would think you're responsible."

"You can't, can't you?"

"No. It doesn't make sense."

"Well, what does he know?" Percy inquired. "Does he know about the Marquis and the kidnapping?"

"Probably."

"And how we got away, into Barbee's Grove?"

"Probably not all of the particulars, but enough," said Rosalind. "The Sheriff has met with Colonel Wigglemann."

"The Colonel! Ah, shit!"

"Percy! Please!"

"So he doesn't *really* understand what played out. Not *really*. Not if he got it from that man. And yet," Percy offered, "it is clear enough to him and to folks in town that *someone* has to be to blamed for it, eh? So... the hare will do. The hare will have to do. Because, as the Colonel suggested, if there's going to be a 'good' girl, then there has to be a 'bad' hare."

"Now, Percy," she chided him, smiling. "That's enough."

He quieted himself, but seemed to turn sullen.

"I mean," she continued. "Since when have you concerned yourself with what the populace in this town have to say?"

"Ooooh, good point made there," chuckled Evaline, who had just entered.

"I apologize, Miss Gullimore," he said.

"Doctor. *Doctor* Gullimore," inserted Evaline.

"Ah, yes. I apologize. Perhaps I find myself more anxious than I imagined. Lying here while the good *Doctor* rubs this burning goddamn ointment on my ass – what *is* that, by the way? It burns like hell! Maybe I'm missing my good manners in light of it all."

"Oh, settle yourself, Mr. Hare." Evaline produced a blueware plate of food. "I brought you some things to eat. Help yourself. It seems you've gotten your appetite back."

"I am quite hungry, in fact," he replied. Percy raised himself up on one elbow to consider what she'd brought.

"I confess to there being some general 'rabbit-like' things, like carrots and lettuce."

"No offense – you can't go wrong there," he offered.

"But," she continued, you being a more sophisticated creature, there are other things here that may be to your liking as well. Bread, cheese, pâté, even crisps."

"Marvelous. All very agreeable," said the hare.

Rosalind offered, "I seem to remember you being partial to peach cobbler at one time."

"Mmm, that is a fond memory which seems like forever ago. Do you make them like your mother did?"

"No. No, I don't. Now eat. And rest. And be a polite guest."

Rosalind began bundling up her medicinal supplies for departure. Then she stopped and turned and slid into a reclining pose on the settee, her hands still full of bandages. She appeared lost in thought. She turned her head to look at him, with a wry smile on her face.

"However... do you know who makes a terrific peach cobbler?" She paused provocatively.

"No," Percy said, growing suspicious of her intentional pause. "Will you please tell us?"

"I have a friend," Rosalind began. "An unusual friend, to be sure. And I think...," with a more provocative pause, "Yes, I'm sure of it. You would like her."

Rosalind studied him and grinned at a scenario seemingly playing out in her head – one of mismatched chemicals being brought together in a bottle for dramatic yet undetermined effect.

Chapter 33

"Wigglemann?!" Percy asked. "Mrs. *Colonel* Wigglemann?"

"Her name is Edwina. And believe me, Percy," Rosalind assured him. "She presents no threat to you. She is almost wholly separate from her husband. They sit together at dinner functions for appearances sake. But she's the most independent woman I've ever known. I'd like to fashion myself more like her."

Percy looked at Rosalind as if she were mad. He could barely grasp her suggestion that he meet with the Colonel's wife, but he was actually intrigued with her suggestion that he flit so close to the flame of the imminent threat the Colonel posed. What could she be thinking?

"Fine," Percy said. "Independent women have always held my favor over any other type. But why in the world would I want to appoint myself of this particular one?"

"Proximity," she replied. "And insight."

"A view behind enemy lines?"

"Precisely. And maybe establishing an agent on that side. Like Lincoln did in the war between the states." Percy's face told her he still had reservations.

"Give her some time, Percy. She's a fair woman, though you may find her… bitter in her circumstances. She's been frustrated. Her ambition has exceeded her lot in life. Or more to the point, it's exceeded the horizons presented to her gender. She's very smart. Far smarter than her husband. But times being what they are, she's limited in what she can accomplish. I feel for her, as I myself am in a comparable situation, as a woman veterinarian. Patronage from men who own stock and service animals is difficult to arrange."

Percy considered this a moment. He was sympathetic to the predicament in which Edwina and Rosalind found themselves. Seeing things as he did, from a shorter angle, and from the perspective of a "stranger" to the world of men, he could see the limitations of those who were kept from accomplishing what men could. How easy it was for men to declare themselves a success in this time, with so little justification. How easy it was for them to hold women just outside the door to the same success.

Beyond that, he began to wonder what Edwina might know of the Colonel's intentions. Things they had discussed at Barbee's Grove would be appropriate to share, if difficult for her to hear. Surely, she couldn't know of the man's suggestion to do away with her. How could she know how close she might be to being disposed of? Perhaps that knowledge could cement a bridge of sharing.

Rosalind's wisdom seemed to come into focus. Indeed, he thought, this could be an engagement well worth having.

****

"I don't mind saying, sir, that you fascinate me," Edwina began.

"Indeed?" said Percy, grinning appreciatively.

Her friend Rosalind's note had intrigued Edwina, to be sure, for its brevity and its allure. "A very special visitor will find you later this day." It read. "Please prepare nothing in anticipation of his visit – with the exception of your fine peach cobbler. I ask simply that you enjoy his company with all discretion. Best, Ros." And yet, little did she imagine the small and magical presence with which she would be treated. He stood before her a bit sheepish and uncertain of how to take her.

"Indeed so! You fascinate me, sir, on a multitude of levels and topics... I don't honestly know where to begin. But before I forget myself, here, I must be sure you eat. I've heard you were injured recently."

To himself he thought, *"Why do women fear that I'll forget to eat?"* Aloud he heard himself say, "Ooh, peach cobbler!," finding a slice dished up atop a bale of straw. "I had not anticipated any such treat. Thank you."

Percy had made his way up the Ninth Street Hill neighborhood in the waning light of the early evening. The women of Evaline's house were none too keen on him venturing out on his own, but he insisted on it. He was only just mobile from healing his gunshot wounds, and the weather was inhospitable. There were those still banging around in the woods in search of the ne'er-do-well hare who had so "endangered" young Esther's life only a week prior.

Upon a large sheet, tacked to an elm prominently positioned along Ninth Street, he read, "Watch for Percy the Hare – threat to young girls and children. Caution! He is wont to charm his way into their trust and abuse them egregiously. Find him and still his beastly heart!" He was appalled.

He took his time, and stepped carefully, stopping occasionally under cover to assess any passersby. At the Wigglemann estate, he clung to the edge of the woods observing. He observed long enough to locate the Colonel, situated in the dining room with a newspaper, and a woman who made her way to the barn behind the house. No others about – no staff, no other residents. He made his way to a side entrance to the barn, out of view of the house. Inside, he found Edwina Wigglemann, seated on a bale of straw and leaning forward smoking a cigar like a man. She seemed to have anticipated him, but was nonetheless taken aback when he appeared.

"I imagine, Mr. Hare," she addressed him, "that you have some questions."

He squinted at her, evaluating, and said quietly, "Sure as shit I do." The wise hare positioned himself in such a way that his path to the door was unobstructed. Habit. He still knew not what her reception might be, and it was always best to be safe rather than sorry.

"No, he doesn't know you're here," Edwina assured him, before he could even ask.

"He won't know? That I'm in his barn?"

"Mr. Hare, for the past two weeks, my husband has had a single thick, black hair growing directly out from the point of his nose," Edwina replied.

"He can't see it in his mirror. He is no more aware of it than he will be of you.

"And, to be honest it's more *my* barn than his. I can't remember him ever being in it. As colonels go, Colonel Wigglemann is a fairly *clean-clothed* colonel. Rarely ever gets his hands dirty."

"Still..." Percy continued. "Wouldn't he be concerned?"

"Oh, yes, he'd be concerned... don't doubt that. He's had little to say of you that was complimentary."

Percy chewed on that a moment and considered her. Edwina Wigglemann was an interesting study in and of herself. She wore a man's trousers and had her sleeves rolled up. Her hair was pulled back simply, though it was of a length that he imagined could still be styled upward on her head as was the current fashion. Her shoulders were broader than one might expect, and her jaw was set more strongly than most middle-aged women. She had dark, intelligent eyes and her mouth was bent in a slight sneer. At least while looking at him. She seemed fairly amused by Percy and puffed away at her cigar, taking equal measure of him.

She finally spoke. "Your eyes are different. Unexpected. They are really quite sharp. And intriguing. And hearing a voice come from you..."

"You're wearing trousers," he replied.

"I am."

"They look... good on a woman."

"Thank you. Oh, and do you drink... whiskey and such?" Edwina inquired.

"Very much, and such."

Edwina snickered unexpectedly and began to pour them each a short glass.

"It's only fair, Mr. Hare, as you may have suspicions of me, that you understand the circumstances of my relationship with the Colonel." Edwina sat astride a bale of straw and leaned toward him. "At this point, it is a cursory one at best. We have long since tired of one another. And where he goes, and with whom, is of only passing interest to me. I'm speaking, of course, of the Wells girl, as well as any of his... 'business' associates."

Their eyes met, with no relevant communication being shared.

"We have... an... understanding," Edwina continued. "In truth, I don't believe it is all that different from many other marital situations I know of. People don't always marry for love. And love is not always the bond for husbands and wives. It was never our bond, the Colonel and me. And over the years, especially in the absence of children to fortify our commitment, our 'bond' as it were has become... strained. We are a union in formality alone. There are times we do not encounter each other within that house for days on end. And we have become somewhat... *comfortable* is not the word, perhaps *resigned* would be better, to knowing that there remains not much between us but for the appearance of propriety.

"We go our separate ways, mostly. And we respect each other's unique interests. But it can be difficult, I will acknowledge, when he appears time and again about town with the young Wells girl on his arm. There are uncomfortable questions asked. And this is new for him. He has never taken interest, that I am aware of, in other women – only in other pursuits, like Cuban cigarillos, and gambling, at which he is awful..."

"And the Wiggler chair?" Percy offered.

"Oh, yes that. You know about that? Well, to be honest – since we seem to be sharing in all honesty – the Wiggler chair was in fact my project."

"Yours?" Percy expressed with surprise.

"Yes. But perhaps we'll discuss that another time," Edwina replied.

"If you are concerned," Percy interjected, "In the interest of sharing information, Esther, the 'Wells girl,' is not interested at all in your husband. If that makes any difference..."

"It does not," she stopped him. "The appearance is what matters. And in that, he has made his intentions clear. He intends to be associated with younger *talent*, as it were."

"Well...," Percy began, thinking he might have the opportunity to share the Colonel's inferences with her, but she proceeded in another direction.

"Right!" she began. "So, out of curiosity, what exactly is there between you and the good doctor, Rosalind? Clearly there's something. I gather you two knew each other a while ago, when you were younger."

"Yes, we did."

"And what happened?" Edwina settled in the chair, sipped on her whiskey with some crisps and seemed ready to relish some good scuttlebutt.

"Well, we almost grew up together. I was a friend of her father."

"The dentist," Edwina interjected.

"Yes. Fine man. Did you ever meet him?"

"No. Unfortunately never had the pleasure."

"Wonderful gentleman. We were friends for years. The whole family, really – Francis, his wife, Rosalind, her sister Emily. But… as things go… children grow up, and things… change."

"So, you made a play at young Rosalind, I take it," Edwina jumped ahead.

"Wha… why, whatever would make you…?"

"Oh, come now, Mr. Hare. I do know enough about you and your reputation – and I know enough about the way she speaks of you to know there was something that… came undone between you."

"Really!" he said, with admonishment. Then, "Really?" with surprise that she could read into the situation as she had.

"Yes. And judging by your reaction, and by hers as well to you, there's a fair bit of guilt attached to it. And regret. You feel guilty. She feels regretful."

Percy attended to his hunk of bread and whiskey, and considered her, from the side of his eye.

"*Rosalind* told you?" he asked, circling back.

"Well, she's told me *of* your relations, not all about them. She would never discuss such a thing openly, you know that. For all her beauty, and she is ravenously beautiful, is she not, she is a very chaste and proper young woman. I think she keeps herself a bit too bottled up. But I'll bet there's a boudoir beast within her petticoats!"

Percy was wide-eyed and tongue-tied. He had no idea how to respond. Whether to be upset and offended, or to laugh out loud at her audacity. He found himself, perhaps despite himself, with a wry smile.

"You think I'm right, don't you?" Edwina asked.

"I won't do you the honor of a reply. That's certainly not anything I would…"

"Fine, fine," she ended it. "I understand completely. I mean her no disrespect, sir. Surely you know that. She and I have been friends for years now, and I am wholly dedicated to supporting her practice. The old codgers around here won't think of taking their animals to her unless circumstances force them to. They think the whole idea of a woman dealing with animals is unseemly. Can you imagine? I've heard them discuss it here at my own dinner table."

"Ridiculous," he answered. "Or perhaps not so. I've seen how some of those men, the ones I imagine have sat at your dinner table, have attended to their animals. They throw food at them when they appear hungry and throw buckshot at them when they prove incalcitrant."

"Just so," Edwina agreed. Then, grinning, "Is that what happened to you, sir? Had you become incalcitrant?" She laughed heartily, pointing to his bandaged behind under his coat.

"This was old man Nanflass' doing," he said, delicately patting the bandage.

"Nanflass? Why, that old blind fart. I'll have to make a trip his way to impart my displeasure. Sometime when the weather turns more agreeable."

"I would be much obliged."

They supped and sipped in friendly silence. Percy obliged to take on the pie, as expected. Keeping an eye about him, he listened for another's footstep and watched for a suspicious movement from her. Reading nothing untoward, he wondered what else might be on her mind. He knew what was on his. But how does one approach the topic of a husband looking to shift off his wife for another woman? He noticed something stowed above in the loft.

"As this is 'your' barn, can I be so bold as to guess that *you* might be the rower?" Percy asked, going in another direction. He gestured toward a skiff that was suspended in the loft area of the barn. It was a long, single rower with a beautifully deep, caramel-toned wood hull. "Is that possible?"

"I am. I am indeed." Edwina looked back over her shoulder and pridefully grinned. "I row most nights, in the better weather. Up and down the Wabash."

"Nights?" he inquired. "Is it safe in the dark?"

"Oh, yes. I've never had any troubles. But you see, the reason I go at night

211

is that the river men *definitely* don't think a woman should ever be blading on the river. Not alone. Or really at all, for that matter. They have a deep distrust with women on boats. And a woman alone on a skiff is, to their mind, little more than a whore out peddling herself for all to see."

"I can imagine… that they would think that, I mean."

"And I certainly don't go rowing wearing skirts and petticoats now, do I? It's damned impractical. So at night, in the dark, no one need be any the wiser. I dress like a man. I row. I sing like a man to keep apace. My father taught me, years ago. We used to row all about, my father and me, when I was a girl. But when I grew up… things changed."

"As they do," Percy offered. "Cheers, to women in pants." They raised their glasses and toasted.

After a large gulp of whiskey, Edwina asked, "Have you ever been on a skiff, Mr. Hare?"

"No. Hares do not do water willfully, madam. But cheers to women on the water."

They toasted again.

After a few moments of additional snacking, Percy reopened discussion.

"I don't wish to consume your entire evening, but it's been a distinct pleasure to get to know you a bit." He paused to consider his approach.

"You needn't hurry on, you know," Edwina answered. "It has indeed been a pleasure to make your acquaintance."

"Forgive me. But I feel I have unnecessarily delayed what I needed to know – and make known – knowledge I needed to share with you. And I'm being dishonest not addressing these things."

"Do tell. Oh, and have another piece of pie, won't you?"

He considered himself, and whether he would be hampered in his trek home with a fuller belly. The risk seemed manageable and he accepted a second piece of pie.

"Would you mind sharing with me," he began, "what might be known of Percy the Hare to the authorities? Like the Sheriff?"

Edwina considered him and understood his concern. "Ah, what might a Colonel have said, eh? You know they've met, then?"

Percy nodded.

"Well, as I say, he's had little to say of you that's complimentary, at least in my presence. But in all honesty, I cannot say that he has fed a very hot flame for your arrest. Negligence, disregard for your young paramour's safety – these things he has preached, yes. But I would say the Sheriff himself expended far more energy in the conversation on the Marquis than on yourself."

"Oh. Yes?"

"Absolutely. In fact, at one point I believe the Sheriff chuckled over the River Dolphin street parade and how you sent things flying. Seems you really woke things up."

"Ha! Yes, well…"

"Brought the New Year in with a bang! Bells ringing, hooves clattering, horse manure flung in all directions… I dare say there are those who will be unforgiving about the condition of their River Dolphin puppet. It took quite a thrashing!"

They chuckled together a moment.

"Mind you," she continued, "there is an element of the populace out for you, even as we speak. It seems, Mr. Hare, that you have elicited some distrust over the years that has perhaps come to a head now. Perhaps your actions in the presence of a young girl has finally pushed beyond some imaginary line and taken possession of the more puritanical folk in the old town."

He considered this and remembered the paper bill attached to the tree he'd found earlier.

"But a spry and mischievous gentleman such as you has surely heard such talk before, eh? Yes, I'm convinced you have."

He smirked a bit, and noticed that Mrs. Wigglemann was not exactly sharing in his mirth.

"But those days are behind me now, mostly. And I fear not for myself. Not among these folk. The Prospect Hill residents are for the most part too genteel and too well accommodated to be much of a threat to me. Now, this Marquis fellow…"

Tellingly, Edwina winced at the mention of him.

"He concerns me. And I would ask, from what you've overheard, what sort of threat I should gauge him to be."

"A grave one," she said. "And not one to be taken lightly. I confess to knowing little of his whereabouts – and the Colonel's conversation with the Sheriff would suggest that others don't either. The Marquis seems as great an enigma as you yourself. The Sheriff mentioned reports of his presence, and of his men, variously around town. Oh, and there was concern for, oddly enough, a Black family. I know nothing of them and can't recall the name. Seems it was a common one. I don't know if that has significance to you."

"Smith – the Smiths. And it does. Very much."

"Well, it didn't seem of interest to my husband, so I doubt he has a connection with them. But the Sheriff was interested in locating them. He seemed concerned for their welfare."

This news sunk into Percy's heart. With the Marquis still roaming undeterred, Barkey and Kess and their family would be vulnerable targets. They had fought admirably against the Marquis and his men, on Percy's behalf, and had certainly made an impact. The Marquis would be interested in them. And, he knew, the law of the land being almost exclusively a "white" law, the Smith family would likely be a low priority for protection. It was encouraging, though, that the Sheriff had even inquired of them.

"And that, unfortunately, is the extent of what I am able to share with you, Mr. Hare. Now, I believe you inferred something of interest to me…"

Yes, there was that. He almost wished he could avoid it. But Edwina had shared honestly with him and was owed.

Percy felt relatively unconcerned for his own safety there in Prospect Hill. But there was one particular Prospect Hill resident of which he was cautious. And he was seated not far across the yard in the main house.

"I fear… ironically…," he began. "Well, I am *concerned* for you, Mrs. Wigglemann… Edwina. And I don't know how to reconcile myself to it."

"You fear for *me*?" Edwina asked.

"Sit down," Percy urged her. "I need to share. A bit more whiskey might be helpful."

They sat and they drank, the small gentleman-hare and the lonely independent woman. He told her of his conversations with the Colonel in his wooded home and in Barkey's tavern. It seemed ages ago now. But Percy shared what he knew and why he'd been concerned for her since.

She acknowledged it to be true. And she shared that it only confirmed what she had suspected herself, what she felt powerless to do anything about. She knew a woman of her position would never be afforded the luxury of freeing herself to a new life, at least not through the conventional means of divorce. And she wished to avoid the means of separation her husband might have at his disposal.

Percy reached out his paw to address her, or to comfort her in some way, he knew not how. Before he could, Edwina separated herself from him. They sat quietly a moment, apart.

"He's a bumbling old man, Percy. He's an old fool who's willing to throw away his life for some young debutante, a girl who is entirely uninterested in him. A man who's willing to gamble on losing *both* his wife and the young girl, in order to see himself – for others to see him – as anything but old and inadequate. And as I've said, he's a terrible gambler."

Percy remained respectfully quiet. He offered only his apologies for being the bearer of the news.

"The rowing will take this out of me," she finally spoke. "It's easier to address my thoughts on the river." She rose and hefted her scull out of the barn to the carriage house. From there, she would drive it down to the river access below town.

"Ride with me, won't you?"

Chapter 34

From the shoreline, wrapped in a woolen blanket, Percy watch her out there on the water, in the dark. Rowing. Slicing atop the still, swelling waters. Singing aloud like a man. He smiled at the image of the opposite dark shores and the lights of the Lafayette downtown reflected over the black water like trailing stars. He imagined what folks on the other shore must think of the singing rower in the night, her voice echoing across the water, unseen…

Edwina rowed rhythmically down the river, slicing through the gap in the ice sheets that crept out from both shores. She gained steam and momentum as she powered along, her spirits and more rising. Her energy rose into impassioned tones with her effort. She began to hum in rhythm, building louder, until someone from the shore called to her.

"Rower! Sing us a shanty, rower!"

And she did. She sang louder and more heartily as her scull zipped down the river. She sang for the few people applauding from the darkened shore. Unseen over on the shore…

When Edwina later returned to the wagon, bearing the scull over her shoulder and looking energized and wide-eyed, Percy turned to her and said, "I have an idea. I have more than an idea. I have a plan."

Edwina smiled and said, "So do I. But you intrigue me – now I want to hear *your* plan." They waited until they had slipped back into the barn unnoticed.

Anticipating an interesting discussion, Edwina retrieved the cheese and whiskey from what she'd brought out earlier. And the pair settled in next to the fire stove to share their thoughts. Percy gallantly allowed her to proceed ahead of him. Then he shared what he'd been considering while she was away. Their thoughts were similar, but Edwina was much happier with Percy's idea than her own. It was as if he had heard her own thoughts from afar and simply taken them farther. Much farther.

She was ecstatic. But nervous. She paced the barn interior, asking again and again, "Could it work?" "Is that possible?"

He assured her it could. And it was. He explained in detail. They laughed and drank more whiskey.

At one point, Percy said, "Tomorrow I will need your help with some correspondence, as I am unable to pen things myself."

Edwina grinned. "Of course."

"I have some favors to ask in town. And more visits to make."

Chapter 35

The night ended soon after, as Edwina realized she had better make an appearance in the home. The Colonel was usually not inquisitive of her barn work, but better to maintain regular appearances.

Percy returned to the madam's house and was welcomed by a council of women, all anxious to see him safe and to hear how his visit had transpired. Evaline shared news that in his absence a small band of ruffians had been trodding up and down the street with torches. Apparently they saw themselves as a posse of sorts, looking to protect their loved ones from the "damned rabbit and child molester." The women thought it odd that the posse was committed to being mindful and regulatory exclusively during the evening hours when it was convenient. And they did so with more than one pocket flask of spirits.

Percy treated the women to tales of Edwina's pants (which set them all atwitter), and of her rowing on the darkened Wabash River at night. Then he pulled Esther and Evaline aside to share the seeds of plans he'd come up with. Later, he drifted off to sleep pondering how in the world to bring these plans to fruition and comforted that his old friend Evaline was the craftiest mind and most astute planner he knew of. He felt assured things would be worked out very soon.

Rosalind woke him sweetly early the next morning. The whiskey from the previous evening had allowed him a delightfully restful sleep.

Her first words to him were, "I think today would be a grand day for another visit."

"I do as well." Percy rose and stretched carefully, his wounds having grown stiff during the night. But he was mission-oriented this day.

"He's a busy man and I think we should get an early start to catch him at home," explained Rosalind.

"Agreed." Percy looked out the window, finding it to be still quite early and quite dark.

"Agreed?" she asked. "Do you even know to whom I'm referring?" She paused, and they looked at each other. She pondered him quizzically. Together they said, at once…

"Sheriff Taylor."

Chapter 36

The pair made their way down Eighteenth Street in Rosalind's carriage in the dim morning light. Esther had been wholly beside herself over not being invited to go, but she had a separate societal engagement that day, one she was not pleased to have to attend. And Rosalind was a regular visitor to the Taylor estate, having tended to their pets and livestock for a few years, so her presence would raise no notice from neighbors. Percy was tucked into a large carpet bag at Rosalind's feet, safely out of sight. Her nag never flinched at Percy's presence, apparently having seen all manner of animal and being not at all bothered by a large hare.

On their way, they passed Barbee's Grove. Percy pointed out the vicinity of the mud hole in which he and Esther had spent New Year's Eve. Rosalind was aghast at the crudity and scolded him for placing the girl in such a deplorable condition. He was in fact regretful of the events and the state in which it had placed poor Esther.

Near the corner of Indiana Avenue, not far from Barbee's Grove, they came to the fine home of Tippecanoe County Sheriff S. O. (Stephen) Taylor and his wife Laura.

"Damned if he couldn't have heard the fuss coming from the grove that night, right here from his own back porch," Percy marveled. "It's a wonder he didn't come out looking to see what was the matter. Perhaps throw a few shots into the trees to see if he could hit someone."

Hardly had she knocked at the rear door than Laura pulled it open with a jerk.

"Door still sticks and S.O. hasn't seen fit to work on it – Hullo, Dr.

Gullimore, isn't it odd early to be seeing you here!" she spurted in a stream of words. "Dear God!" And then, more whispered, "Hare, you frightened the life of me – why would you hide yourself behind her skirt to take an unsuspecting woman of fright at this hour of the morning? Come in, you two."

Rosalind and Percy entered and endeavored to clear their feet of any dampness and muck of the yard. Laura eyed him suspiciously, having never hosted such a creature in her home, but having seen him out and about at times and hearing much of him. She fought the door to close snugly again.

"I'm making batches of breakfast already and you're welcome to it…" Laura began.

"AAAHHHhhh! Percy Hare!" A piercing shriek startled him, and a young woman swung around the banister at the end of the hall, running at him with petticoats rustling. The Taylor's eldest daughter, Irene, dropped to her knees and clutched him tight to her. The seventeen-year-old's hair was exquisitely coifed and she smelled delightfully, of lilacs, Percy thought.

"Oh, my Percy! I've heard such things of you! You naughty rabbit," scolded Irene.

"Ouch. Hare. Careful, my sweet." He was still a bit tender on his backside.

She resumed her hug and clutched him tight. Rosalind and Laura exchanged a knowing glance before Laura returned to the kitchen to attend to breakfast.

Irene was rumored to be the most beautiful girl in town, somehow eclipsing Esther herself. And Rosalind took note in her maturation since the last time she'd attended to some kittens at the home. It was not difficult to see why people spoke of her so. She was breathtaking. No wonder Irene was acquainted with Percy – he attracted pretty girls like flies. She gave him a look that said, "Behave yourself" and he shrugged as if helpless in her grasp. Irene stood and took Percy by the hand, following Laura into the kitchen.

As he passed, Rosalind said quietly, "This is how you always find yourself in trouble."

"I know," he replied, grinning only slightly.

"Damned incorrigible," she whispered.

Irene pulled Percy through the kitchen and through a doorway into the dining room.

"You'll sit here next to me, sir. Thomas, move along," she said to her younger brother, already in place at the table and playing with a lead figurine of a Union soldier.

"Hey!" he objected, before catching sight of the standing hare coming around the table. Wide-eyed, he left his seat and backed away. He was half a head taller than Percy but was stunned by him.

"The hare will join me in the parlor!" a declarative voice said. Standing in silhouette in the morning light coming through the tall windows, was none other than Sheriff Taylor.

"Oh, papa, no!" whined Irene.

The Sheriff eyed Percy closely as the furry gentleman deftly kissed the girl's hand, at which she cooed, and then turned toward the parlor.

"Jeezus, you've got brass. Right here in my home, you little...?" the Sheriff muttered quietly. Then, aloud, "Good morning, Percy – long time, no see. I've been looking forward to this."

Rosalind caught Percy's eye and looked worried. Percy said "shit" under his breath. To himself, he thought, "So much for 'knowing when to not be in the wrong place.'"

Sheriff S. O. Taylor was a well-respected and stalwart figure in the Lafayette area, being of an upstanding pioneer family.[6] And in his job he was unparalleled, affecting swift and sure justice while showing ample generosity and kindness to those humble and poor who found themselves in uncomfortable positions that occasionally forced their hands.

S.O. was a casually graceful man who carried himself well. He pulled the parlor door closed and took a seat on a high-backed stuffed chair, crossing his legs neatly, somehow looking very gentlemanly for his vocation. His brow sat low and straight over his eyes. And a large handlebar moustache skirted his lip. One would be wise to perceive him at first glance as an "all-business" sort, but Percy knew him to be a very personable character.

"Good morning, SOT," said Percy, continuing his awkward habit of taunting authority figures, particularly those who carried multiple initials, with a condensed acronym of their own names.

Percy seated himself on a low ottoman and grinned resignedly. He recognized no benefit in feigning innocence around the man. He had been sought after by the Sheriff and he was there to oblige. It did feel a bit like walking into the man's breakfast room was like calling the man's bluff, but that was beside the point.

"SOT! Ha! I'd forgotten your charm, old hare," said the Sheriff. "It's been a while, hasn't it? Maybe since that business with the Pearl River mermaids? But that's been a number of years, no?"

"Gosh, the *mermaids*," answered Percy. "I'd nearly forgotten them myself. Are they still causing concern, the pernicious little bastards?"

"Apparently not. I think once we chased them back up the water source they saw fit to stay there. Haven't heard anything of them in quite a while."

"Anyway, Percy," resumed the Sheriff, "there are a few things I'd like to discuss."

"I imagine so – I as well," replied Percy.

"Here, would you like any bacon, or scones, Percy? Help yourself." He gestured for Percy to help himself to what was on a plate nearby.

Sheriff Taylor continued, "I've a softness for good bread. And, between us, my beloved wife has only recently mastered the particulars of fine yeast. Bless her. But now she's got it!

"But anyway... as one Percy the Hare had been sighted in Prospect Hill on New Year's morning, in the company of a young woman in a rather sorry state, and, additionally, as said young woman and said hare were reported to have played some part in the destruction of the New Year's River Dolphin exhibit near the courthouse, I have been called upon to determine the extent of your role in the proceedings. And in some other proceedings as well."

The Sheriff sat back, grinningly self-satisfied with his wordy pronouncement and chewing heartily on one of Mrs. Taylor's scones.

"Other proceedings?" Percy asked.

"Something happened in George Winter's old studio that night, didn't it?

To be clear, that is what I'm most interested in. Did you know it was still there, after all these years, vacant? And everything still in place? I hadn't the notion. But you and the girl were there, I take it?"

"Well, aren't you a clever fellow," said Percy.

"That's been said," the Sheriff offered. "But I find it difficult to brag on the success of one's common sense. Now… as to why I've been seeking you out…"

Percy stirred a bit, figuring this was when the good Sheriff would be handcuffing him and escorting him down to the courthouse to answer for his misdeeds of, presumably, kidnapping, public mischief, destruction of property, etc. But the Sheriff held out his hand and urged Percy to stay settled.

"No, no, Percy. That's not why I'm about. What am I to do? Throw a wounded hare into shackles and parade him through the town on the back of my horse? No, I think not. Now, while there may be some who would enjoy that sight – and there are some who might say it's well overdue – I say nay. Percy, you're clearly not at fault for what transpired on New Year's."

"I'm not?" replied the hare.

"Certainly not. Unless you'd like to be."

No, Percy shook his head, he would not.

The Sheriff continued, "Now, there might have been some shenanigans that were… inconvenient and caused a bit of turmoil downtown. But clearly, as they say, there are bigger fish to fry. Yes?"

"Absolutely," said Percy. "So why don't you clear me? Make it known that I'm not to blame?"

"Well, I *could* do that, but it may serve us to delay. If you're in possession of the patience. I'll confess I have allowed the appearance of a manhunt – a 'harehunt' if you will – because it serves our purposes as a distraction. While the public clamors for the rabbit's head on a platter, and I appear to be seeking it, the presumed 'Marquis de Lafayette' believes himself to be above reproach."

"Could make him careless."

"Precisely. Now…" the Sheriff began, "what do you know of this Marquis

224

character and his lot? Where are they? He made quite a splash when he arrived in town, in that black and gold carriage, but he has now made himself damn near invisible. You know, we've even located that carriage, in a warehouse down on Second Street, where it hits the canal. But it appears to be abandoned. We watched the property for several days but no one ever appeared for it. Where has he gone?"

"Unfortunately, I know little of him," Percy admitted. "Were I able to be up and about, and not hunted myself, I would gather some news about town for you. He sounds to me, in his voice, as though he is from the lake region up north, but I can't know where. In the waning months of the year, no one seemed to see where he came from or where he escaped to. But he and those men are a rougher squad than we've seen here.

All I *can* tell you is that he has a particular axe to grind with the young woman I've accompanied."

"This E.W. person."

"Yes."

"And who is she?" the Sheriff asked. A pause ensued with Percy unresponsive. "Come now, Percy, I've laid all my cards on the table. Time for you to do the same. Let me assure you, she's in no legal jeopardy from my perspective either. It's the Wells girl, no? Madam Wells' daughter. Correct?"

Percy nodded.

"Once you two were seen together about town that ruse dissolved. But it was fun for a while I wager. And how is it that she has raised the Marquis' ire so?"

"Circumstances, really. And resentment. At first I believe he wanted her to join in and operate under his influence. Probably sought to garner her winnings for himself as part of his team. But that didn't materialize. She pointed out his player as a cheat. He – the Swettenham fiend – didn't take kindly to the accusation and nearly knifed her."

"I've heard tell of this from old Horace," inserted the Sheriff. "And Barkey reiterated it."

"Yes, well, for her part, the girl cracked the nose on Swettenham's face, which no doubt set him against her. But the Marquis himself had a minimal personal dusting with the girl. He only wanted to 'possess' her, if you will. And his rage seems to stem from her keeping him at odds. He seems a possessive and prideful man. And very violent."

"So it's still the girl he wants," posed the Sheriff.

"Undoubtedly," said Percy. "Maybe now more than before. In fact, he was shipping me off to be stewed that night, so he has no use for me."

The Sheriff said, "Well, you have made his life, especially his pursuit of the girl, a good deal more difficult, so his feelings may have changed."

For the next half hour or more, Sheriff Taylor and Percy the Hare enjoyed a conversation on a number of topics. As it happened, Percy had almost as many questions for the Sheriff as he for Percy.

Percy asked how much he knew about the events of the night, and of its participants. The Sheriff confessed he knew only a handful of the players involved. But he was aware of the Smiths' participation and assured Percy that Barkey and Kess had both received medical care, Barkey for a glancing gunshot wound that appeared to have bounced off the man's rib but which had left a fair wound, and Kess for a debilitating shortness of breath. He described her as being labeled "asthmatic." Their son Mal escaped with only some bumps and bruises. And some of those, the young man offered, may have been obtained in trying to re-crate the pygmy bison in its makeshift traveling cart.

The family was being housed in a safe location now, Taylor shared. They were none too pleased about it, as they far preferred their own home and furnishings. But an attack on them had been only narrowly averted a few nights past New Year's. Young Mal had noticed some men gathered near their home and recognized them as the Marquis' henchmen. The family escaped to a neighbor's home, from which they watched the men enter their own home and ransack their possessions. Their pig was shot in its flank but had survived.

"Damn!" exclaimed Percy. "Poor Charley."

"Let me tell you, that's one big, tough pig," laughed the Sheriff.

"Where are they now, the Smiths?" Percy asked. "Are you at liberty to say?"

The Sheriff only reluctantly assured him, "Let's just say they've gone boating."

He added that Tanya Bubher had emerged completely unscathed. She had dragged her husband Winks home by the ear, refusing to let him be seen by a physician, though the man was bleeding from several wounds and though he had been rendered somewhat "simple" by a significant blow to the head. The Sheriff assumed Winks had shaken it off eventually, as he hadn't heard anything to the contrary.

"Here's a full accounting of our situation," Sheriff Taylor said, "I will agree to these things: 1. To ignore your breaking and entering into the abandoned art studio of George Winter on Columbia Street, as it seems you were not the only ones having done so and you were not to blame for any damage done there; 2. the life-threatening carriage ride through the downtown, as again the damage was minimal and no one was hurt – this in contradiction to the wishes of the Downtown Lafayette New Year's Celebratory Committee, which was quite enflamed over the damage to their River Dolphin Marionette; and 3. the complaints of disorderly conduct and trespassing asserted by one Percival Nanflass of Main Street."

"His name is 'Percival'?" Percy asked, surprised by the ironic commonality between them. "Hunh. I never knew."

"Yeah. Imagine that," said the Sheriff. "Regardless, I put him off his declarations. And I damn near wanted to wipe my *own* ass on his sheets before I was finished with him, he's such an ornery cuss. That was you who did that, wasn't it? I assume he was correct – you wiped your ass on his laundry?"

"Yes, but that was ages ago. A couple of summers back," Percy assured him. "And he shot me in the ass by the way."

"Yes, there's that. You could press a charge for *that*, if you saw fit. But, all things considered, I find that to be a moot point at present."

"Agreed."

"Oh!" the Sheriff halted. "And I don't know if you've seen the newspaper this morning…"

"No, I didn't take the time for it."

227

"Well, you may have seen opinion articles calling for your arrest, or heard tell of them. But this morning the ante was raised a bit."

Taylor presented Percy with a folded section of that morning's paper, with an advertisement in larger typeface displayed. The major lines read, "REWARD $50. Delivery of scoundrel Percy Hare. Should be captured alive and prisonered to constabulary." The advertisement was credited to a "Mr. Felix," whom neither Percy nor the Sheriff could identify.

"Hmm, 50 dollars, eh?" said Percy, nonplussed. "I'm not sure, but I believe this is my first reward notice."

The Sheriff seemed surprised. "Are you certain? I would have thought that Denleroy Füdd would have had you on a notice years ago."

"Now that you mention it, that is a distinct possibility. But I can't recall. The good doctor would likely have concealed such a thing from me."

"Dr. Gullimore? Your friend having breakfast out there?"

"Actually, her father, who was also Dr. Gullimore. The dentist."

"Oh, yes, I remember him. But see here – this notice may make your life more challenging, Mr. Hare. Be aware."

"Of course."

"You know what this means, don't you? Who this 'Mr. Felix' is probably connected to?"

"I suppose I could guess…," he met the Sheriff's concerned eyes. "There could actually be a number of…"

"The Marquis."

"Ah. AH! Yes, that would make the most sense, wouldn't it?"

"There'll be yahoos everywhere, all over town looking for you. For that reward."

"Beating the bushes."

"Driving you out into view," Taylor surmised. "Doing his work for him. It's a smart play actually. Nefarious. So please be cautious. And you shouldn't return here again, lest anyone see you and the Marquis turn that to his advantage."

"Well, it *would* seem that you are aiding and abetting a known criminal." Percy grinned mischievously and filed two pieces of bacon into his mouth.

"Oh, you're no damned criminal," the Sheriff replied. "Perhaps just a sizeable pain in the ass." They both chuckled. "Now – as for what I will ask of you in return, my furry friend…" the Sheriff continued. "I should very much like your assistance with a unique… game, of sorts, that I have in mind for our friend the Marquis. We'd best locate him before he has a chance to locate you first, eh?"

Percy nodded in agreement with a mouthful of bacon.

"Come. There are more conversations to be ventured this day, particularly with your friend Evaline. And her daughter. But first, let's enjoy proper breakfast with the ladies here, shall we? It's rather rude of us to have ignored them for this long."

Sheriff Taylor began to rise, brushing bread crumbs from his lap.

"Oh, and do you know this was my last year as Sheriff? I'm just tying up some loose ends. Time for other things. Laura says with the news of the horse thieves we broke up a year ago – quite a well-traveled story, that one[7] – she believes I can harness that for perhaps a better position. Maybe a judicial or political post. You'd vote for me, wouldn't you, hare?"

"Certainly. Several times over," Percy consented.

They both had a chuckle. Voting "irregularities" at the time were rampant. Some folks had a decent living of voting for hire.

"Thomas!" Sheriff Taylor called as he opened the parlor door into the dining room. Young Thomas looked up with his mouth full of sausages, and the women halted their conversation.

"Tell Mr. Hare about that game you were playing with your school mates the other day – 'Where's the Hare?' – was that what they called it?"

[6] *Information on Sheriff S. O. Taylor was obtained from "About Stephen Taylor, a newspaper account:"https://lafayettecitizenjournal.wordpress.com/2020/03/31 /tippecanoe-county-sheriff-breaks-up-multi-county-horse-thief-ring-marshal-a rrested-after-attempted-escape/*

[7] *"Desperate Horse Thieves" story, which appeared in the Muncie Evening Press December 4, 1882 – https://lafayettecitizenjournal.wordpress.com/2020/03/31/t*

*ippecanoe-county-sheriff-breaks-up-multi-county-horse-thief-ring-marshal-arr
ested-after-attempted-escape/*

Chapter 37

Esther Wells stood impatiently near the door of her mother's home, awaiting a carriage visit from Colonel Wigglemann. He was to escort her into downtown Lafayette for a luncheon, and she was livid over being forced to attend. With him. Her Percy had gone to speak with the Sheriff, of all things. And she was worried he might not be allowed to return.

"Your Mr. Hare," assured Mona, the hostess, who joined her in peering out the window. "He'll be on his way soon, dear."

"But by then I'll be gone with the Colonel for this ridiculous luncheon. And I'll miss him!" Esther returned to sulking in silence.

"You can be sure that he is alright, my dear, that he's healthy and sound. I know how much he means to you…"

"I don't think you *can* know," Esther replied tartly. "Percy gave me trust, Mona, something no one else has. He allowed me to step forward on my own. He showed me that I *could* do so."

"I credit him for it," said the matron. "I genuinely do. You are a notable and strong young woman. And lord knows you've a strong sense of adventure. While some may question the wisdom of a woman exhibiting those traits, I wholly celebrate them.

"And while I give the majority of the credit to your mother, I cannot ignore the role Mr. Hare has played in encouraging your innate qualities. His sacrifice is noted, at least by me, and will not be forgotten. And while I'm aware you have found the recent affair unpleasant and unfair…"

Esther grunted in response.

"… It was, however, necessary," Mona went on to say. "Mr. Hare's assumption of blame cleared your name, and served you well. Indeed, he cleared your name before it was ever even besmirched." Pressing the point, she added, "Do you think you would have been invited to this Women's League luncheon today if the cloud of suspicion over you hadn't been removed? In fact, it may have been this whole drama which brought you to their attention and got you the invite."

"Oh, who gives a hang about these luncheons?" Esther moaned.

"*You* should, my dear. I know your mother does."

"I think she fears them," Esther replied. "I think she knows the power they wield in 'polite' society."

"And that they might," Mona added, matter-of-factly. "'Bawdy houses' like ours are only tolerated as a preference over individual streetwalkers and she fears they'll be coming to close the brothels next. It's not beyond their inclinations. So doesn't it make sense for an enterprising young woman such as yourself to join in and change the course of the conversation, if ever, *when*ever, it goes in that direction? Your presence there could be the determining factor in saving your mother's enterprise someday."

Esther genuinely hadn't considered that before and pondered it a moment. Mona, the hostess and keeper of the house and all of its inhabitants, a woman nearly as present throughout her life as her adopted mother, had come through with shining wisdom. Just when Esther had begun to overlook her importance in her life, here she was, naming Esther as the captain of her own destiny, and indeed of her mother's.

"I'm sure you are proud of your mother, and rightly so. But I tell you now, young lady," Mona wrapped her arm around the girl's waist and smoothed her dress over the whale bone corset beneath, "that you will be the sharp and beautiful mind that continues her work and her business through the years to come. And you will be ready for it."

Mona paused a moment before glancing again out the window. She pushed a stray hair back behind Esther's ear and said, "You know, my dear, I'm aware you don't care for Colonel Wigglemann, and I certainly can't say that I blame you. The bastard. And what he did, making a scene of our dear Percy!"

"But...," Esther said, studying her for her intent.

"But, your mother believes the man can still be of service to ferry you in and about through society." In a much lower tone now, she continued, "I wonder though, is that a bit conservative? I wonder, if there might be a way in which he can serve you through other... arrangements. Don't you think?"

Esther considered her curiously.

"For instance, maybe... an enterprising young woman, such as yourself, can use the time you're with him to learn something about doing business. The Colonel's business and assets. How does he do business? What precisely *is* his business, and what are his holdings? From what anyone has seen, a good extent of his commerce takes place beyond what is legal, or what is sanctioned. Oddly enough, this house also operates somewhat beyond the level of what is legal or sanctioned. Maybe... there's... something to be learned... Eh?"

With that, Mona, being a bit shorter than the young woman she had helped raised from the day she was brought through the very door at which they stood, rose up on her tiptoes and kissed the softly powdered cheek of young Esther Wells.

Chapter 38

The river. To go "boating." The challenge, Percy knew, was making it down to the Wabash river without being seen. Sheriff Taylor had suggested it, probably carelessly. If he were seen by any of those who would be bounty hunting him now, he felt he could fairly easily escape on his own. But being seen would endanger those he intended to meet, those who were, for the moment, safe from unsuspecting enemies who meant them harm.

How could a clever hare make it to the river, he thought, if the hare did not wish to be recognized? As a hare? A three-foot-tall, long-eared hare?

He contemplated hitching a ride with Charley the pig, but he'd heard the pig was injured. Or on a horse, upon which he might conceal himself better. But anyone who saw one of these animals, seemingly unattended, might try to keep them. He'd made it to Sheriff Taylor's home and back by essentially acting as Rosalind's carpet bag. But he didn't want to involve anyone else to take him to the river. They'd all done enough, and to anyone looking for him, seeing the hare's friends would be as good an indicator as seeing the hare himself.

Percy sat grumbling over this challenge for the rest of the day, after returning from Sheriff Taylor's. It was a challenge he would meet, he was confident. There were several questions outstanding. But his mood grew darker as the day carried on with no solution. Daytime, nighttime, rain gear, barrels, carriages – nothing was satisfactory. He wanted to just crash down from Ninth Street Hill with no one paying attention, or with everyone otherwise occupied. He needed them to be distracted.

He needed fire.

Not a huge fire. Fire could be dangerous and could spread quickly. He didn't want to bring the whole of downtown into a conflagration. He just wanted a nice, small-but-not-too-small, self-contained blaze. Something that could be sacrificed. Something that deserved to be destroyed. Something that people might even, dare he think it, *enjoy* seeing destroyed.

What had the Sheriff said? That they'd located that gaudy black and gold carriage of the Marquis, "in a warehouse down on Second Street, where it hits the canal." Perfect.

Oh, it burned so nicely, he thought. After poking about a bit in the dark, he'd found the carriage, entered the darkened warehouse and opened the doors. The carriage was a lightweight design, a landau, which had two folding hoods, one at each end, that met at the top to form a private box. In a true performance of ingenuity and physics, Percy had steered the carriage out into the street, clear of structures on either side, and set it afire. The folding hoods, both dense canvas, came to light surprisingly quickly and appeared they would burn for quite some time. He felt he was doing the Marquis a favor. The thing was a firetrap and could have had disastrous consequences for the man, as well as for whatever hapless victim he sought to spirit away in it. Percy would have to declare his service when next he saw the man.

Once the carriage was alight, Percy became more cautious of being seen as he journeyed onward. He made his way deftly and quietly behind the industrial structures on Second Street, keeping to the shadows on the river side of the buildings and trying not to tax his wounded backside. From the bridge at Brown Street, he could see that his plan was working. Throngs of people were heading in the direction of the blaze, running right by him with no awareness of his presence.

As he approached the southern end of town along the river, he hung longer in the shadows, behind sheds, and under overarching trees. He waited and watched for any sign of passersby, or bounty hunters, or indeed Sheriff's deputies before slipping along to the next point of concealment.

Eventually, he arrived at Captain "Lark" O'Connor's residence, on the corner of Smith and Wabash Streets, a short distance from the river. Finding no lights there, he slipped down the road to where Lark docked his riverboat. There he found some evidence of the presence he was seeking, though the windows seemed blocked with blinds, concealing anyone inside.

"Dammit, rabbit!" Barkey growled. He was surprised to turn and see the hare nuzzling the neck of his beloved Kess. In fact the entire cabin was startled at Percy's sudden appearance on the boat, with the possible exception of Kess herself, who never seemed startled by the smooth fur and moist muzzle running along her neck. She reached up and cupped Percy's face with her hand, while he sheepishly looked up at Barkey.

"Ah, Mr. Hare!" called Sheriff S.O. Taylor. "I should have expected you, you crafty bastard."

"Percy!" cried Dr. Rosalind Gullimore, Evaline Wells, and Esther Wells at once. Esther stood and planted her hands on her hips, looking as though she was going to scold him.

Captain Lark simply grinned and chuckled and crossed his legs in the other direction, puffing on his pipe.

"Oh, dammit, Percy!" said Evaline. "I should have known. You are supposed to be at home with the girls, being distracted, so we could be here. And so you wouldn't cause yourself harm. They were all so looking forward to it..."

Esther was silent, seemingly overcome with emotion seeing her courageous paramour slipping from the shadows like a thief. But Percy could see her eyes ignite with jealousy as he planted a tender kiss on Kess' bare shoulder.

"How did you get here, Percy?" asked Rosalind. "If you were seen, we all could be in danger, particularly Barkey and Kess..."

"No one saw me! I assure you. There's a fire up on Second Street and everyone is making haste to see it. Quite a spectacular fire too! But don't worry, Sheriff – it's none too threatening so you needn't run off. Seems someone found that horrible black and gold chariot the Marquis has been parading about in – and they set it on fire in the street! Can you imagine?"

A number of Lark's guests snickered at his clearly being the culprit, and at the brass he'd shown in such an act. Barkey acted as though he were anxious to go see it for himself.

"Well, shit, Mr. Hare," said the Sheriff in mock anger. "I told you that in confidence. And I guess I intimated too much about the Smiths going 'boating,' elsewise you would not have found them, and us. Tsk! It really is time for me to retire. I've become too sloppy in my counsel with suspects." He grinned and re-lit a cigar from his vest pocket.

Percy at once inquired of Barkey's and Kess' health and their children's safety. They were alive and healthy, they assured him, though not happy with the arrangements made for them to live on the boat out of sight. But their children and pets had been safely seen to the home of Kess' aunt over the river outside of Chauncey.

Percy could see in Esther's face that she desperately wanted to grab him up and clutch him to her. He gave her a look of protest which she returned with faux petulance. She mouthed to Kess, "He's MY hare!" Kess smiled and replied, "Oh, you can have his troublesome ass!"

The others had resumed their discussion, with Sheriff Taylor recounting his son's game of "Where's the Hare?" with his neighborhood friends. In it, a group of three participants would stand closely together, side by side, facing "the cop," the active player in turn. Another player, referred to as "the hare," would slip behind the group of three, or "the blind," and conceal himself. Then the "cop" would turn his back and count to five. During this count, another separate "blind" would form. The "cop" would take another look at each group, then turn his back and count to five again, at which point another final "blind" of three would form.

At each interval, it was encouraged that the hare would shift to a position behind a different blind, and the cop would be forced to guess where the hare had gone. The game could apparently become quite raucous and silly, with the players all laughing at the hare shrinking to hide behind his friends and at missed guesses. In Taylor's son's game, even the blinds began to turn themselves about in place with each shift, before popping stiff again and further confusing the cop.

"It's the shell game!" said Evaline.

"We called it 'thimblerig,'" said Lark.

"Same thing, right?" answered the Sheriff. "And these children have made variations of it, depending on the numbers of players available. Sometimes they just stand next to trees or gravestones in the cemetery to act as blinds and hide the hare."

The others sat politely, waiting for more explanation. His intent had not become clear.

"Soooo," he continued, "I'm suggesting a game of "Where's the Hare and E.W.?"

"Gotcha!" said Percy. "When are we doing this?"

The others looked at him quizzically, wondering how he'd so quickly assembled the plan from the Sheriff's brief introduction. They wanted to be caught up.

"Well, there are a lot of details to inquire about, Percy," said the Sheriff. "A lot of permissions and consents. Now sit back and allow me to explain... it could be a... serious endeavor." Clearly, he was suggesting an element of danger, and he was reluctant to be too flippant about it.

Esther took this opportunity to slip across and sit next to Percy, wrapping him up in her arms and cupping her hand over his mouth. She hugged him close and cooed and kissed him, while he put up a perfunctory fuss.

They stayed until all the possibilities had been played out and everyone agreed to their part. This would be quite the operation. The Sheriff earned his reputation that night, corralling all the players into a shared understanding. And it would take place in one week, on Tuesday, the 22nd of January.

There were items to be made, stories to be told, routes to be planned. The women made to depart and planned to take Percy with them. But he deferred, opting to stay and speak with the Captain on his riverboat. Ol' Lark was pleased at this, as he hadn't had the opportunity to have a good jawing with his old traveling companion in quite a while. As it was getting late, he offered to put Percy up for the night and see that he was trundled out under cover in the morning light.

Chapter 39

On the evening of Monday, January 21st, Edwina Wigglemann and Dr. Rosalind Gullimore met for dinner in downtown Lafayette. The doctor shared news of an improvement to her spirits. This was attributed to the resumption of friendly relations with her childhood companion, Mr. Percy Hare. Edwina could appreciate her feelings, having spent time recently with the hare herself and thoroughly enjoying the conversation. The two friends spent three hours together with fine food and drink and laughter. After a point, they began to fear for the gossipers about town who would chat up the lengthy and boisterous meal between two otherwise unaccompanied women. At the end of the evening, Rosalind offered Edwina a ride home in her carriage.

Upon returning home, Mrs. Wigglemann discovered that her house had been burgled. Her husband had himself been out, escorting Miss Wells to a polite social function at the Ball mansion. In the Wigglemanns absence, a good number of family heirlooms had been taken, including a horsehair settee, an antique dining cabinet replete with a set of fine china and silver, and Edwina's entire collection of jewelry, most of which had been obtained from her mother or as a gift from her husband, the Colonel. In addition, the thieves had made off with many items of her clothing, oddly leaving her husband's wardrobe seemingly untouched.

Edwina was sick over the removal of her possessions. She and Rosalind sat in the mostly emptied house and awaited the arrival of representatives of the Sheriff's department. The constabulary were surprised when Edwina presented them with an already-drawn list of all of the lost items. But they shared Sheriff S.O. Taylor's personal condolences for the loss and his assurances that they would exhaust every resource in relocating the lost goods.

****

The following day, Tuesday, January 22nd, was a busy one at the wharfs south of the city.

Captain Larkin "Lark" O'Connor and his brother Jim, along with a small crew, prepared for a voyage of commerce down the Wabash River to Terre Haute and points beyond. First, they had to make room and were obliged to help Barkey and Kess Smith return their effects and family to their home, it having finally been deemed safe for them to do so.

With this run, Captain Lark was hopeful for brighter days in this new year, as he'd had a run of a few years of bad luck. Since the sinking of Lark's overloaded steamer in 1881, the O'Connors' business had suffered a serious decline, further complicated by the near loss of their canal boat just outside of downtown Lafayette the previous fall. Vendors had since shown a lack of confidence in the O'Connor team.

Jim O'Connor, at the helm for both incidents, and prone to morbid bouts of melancholy, self-doubt, and drunkenness, was hoping to restore his brother's faith in him. He couldn't help but feel that Lark was keeping a keener eye on him for this trip. Jim was tempted to address his brother's overbearing aspect, but thought better of it. He opted instead to pay greater attention to his duties and prove himself by maintaining a solidly dependable performance for the trip.

The O'Connors loaded their steamboat throughout the day, in anticipation of a launch that evening.

Chapter 40

In the early evening, a nondescript black carriage made its way through downtown, to the river district. It made a stop on the corner of Smith and Wabash Streets to pick up a rider. Then it proceeded to New York Avenue to take on another. Finally, it mounted the hill at Ninth Street to board additional riders before heading back downtown again.

Inside the carriage, a fair bit of merriment was being had. Three women were clad in black rain gear, each possessing a large floppy hat and wearing black masks over their eyes. These three were, in circuit, Mrs. Kess Smith, Dr. Rosalind Gullimore, and Miss Esther Wells. Miss Wells' mother, Evaline Wells, was seated next to her. Opposite them and between Mrs. Smith and Dr. Gullimore, was one Mr. Percy Hare.

All in attendance were sipping alcohol in some form, ranging from a flask of whiskey to flutes of champagne. They seemed nervous, but giddily excited.

The carriage rolled down Ninth Street into the downtown, and turned left onto North Street. At the corner of Seventh Street the carriage turned right and parked in front of the First Baptist Church. Into a loose crowd of dark figures milling on the walk, a woman in black rain gear exited the carriage, alongside a short figure with tall rabbit ears. "Great cheese!" someone said aloud, "It's E.W. and the hare!"

A buzz rose from those gathered there, as the anticipation for this illicit euchre game and the arrival of the notorious pair had been growing for days. They followed the woman and the hare through the courtyard beside

242

the church, and then into a haberdasher's shop behind a small house, all keeping a wary eye out for the constabulary.

Inside the haberdasher's, the pair passed between two rows of onlookers. Sewing mannequins stood stoically on either side, dressed in coats, high-neck shirts, and cravats. The woman kept her head down, shielding her face from view under the broad brim of her hat. They came to a round table with a single light centered overhead, and one chair unclaimed. The woman, "E.W.," took the seat, and the hare passed into the crowd.

He was a quick and astute study. No one noticed, but the hare took in clues from each and every one of them, even patting into their clothing unnoticed. He registered nearly everything, from pocketed pipes, cigarette cases, combs, and, inevitably, concealed weapons. He looked up at the owner of the pocketed pistol. The man looked down at him and turned out the lapel of his coat, revealing a shining silver badge pinned to his vest. The man whispered, "They're not here – go – quickly!" And he pointed to a swinging panel door leading to the store room.

Percy was shuttled through the store room, essentially a narrow closet, and out a door into the cold again. He passed down a thin brick passage, through an iron gate and out to an alleyway. Making a right turn, he climbed the back steps of a townhouse and found a man holding the porch door open for him. Percy ran through the first-floor level. A family was gathered there on the sofa in front of the fireplace. A small girl in her mother's arms waved very excitedly at him as he hopped through.

"Ugh," he shrugged at the girl's cuteness. But he waved politely in return before leaping out the front door and down the steps to North Street. The fading sound of the little girl's squeal of delight knifed right through him. Or perhaps that was his sore backside being exercised again.

His original nondescript black carriage was coming back down North Street toward him. After letting him and Kess out in front of First Baptist, the carriage had simply circled the long block. The horses drawing the carriage, both seasoned with the constabulary for a number of years and veterans of desperate situations and exchanges of gunfire, both bucked and shied at the presence of the walking hare.

He muttered, "Oh, for crying out loud," to the women inside the carriage as he leapt back inside. And they giggled and handed him a flask of rye whiskey. Esther's eyes were wide with excitement as he clambered back in from his adventure. She couldn't resist the urge to clutch him tight as he took a draught from the flask.

The carriage continued west down North Street to Fourth Street and there passed by the Opera House, the scene of the New Year's Ball and kidnapping. It appeared to be quiet that evening, with the windows and doors darkened and no torches lit on the exterior. At Ferry Street, the carriage turned left and east again. It followed along the exterior until the building converted into the attached Post Office. At the end of the building, a large alleyway opened and the carriage followed this in and came to a halt. The other side of the courtyard was enclosed by the rear of the Fifth Street Methodist Church.

Into a loose crowd of dark figures milling through the open courtyard behind the buildings, a woman in black rain gear, this time Rosalind, exited the carriage alongside a short figure with tall rabbit ears. Percy could make out someone saying, "It's E.W. and the hare! They came!" A buzz rose from those decidedly non-church-going folk gathered there, as anticipation of their arrival at this euchre game had emerged over the weekend. They followed the woman and the hare through the courtyard to the back door of the post office.

Inside the post office processing room, men were shuffling trays of mail to surfaces on the outer portions of the room. A round table with a single light centered overhead had been cleared, and chairs were claimed in succession by men who stepped from the surrounding group. One chair remained unclaimed and the eyes in the room all turned to the woman in black gear and large hat which kept her face shaded, "E.W.," who confidently took the seat. The hare helped her into the chair and then slowly circled the table behind the players, seemingly assessing them. He then passed into the crowd.

Again, he made a quick study of the audience. No one noticed, but the hare took in clues from each and every one of them, including what was in their clothing. This time, he recognized at least one man's face from the attack in the George Winter studio on New Year's. He was one of the Marquis' men. The man avoided making eye contact with him, and another man slid into the shadows before Percy could make him out. Yet another man subtly sought Percy's attention and signaled him from across the table. While the room was occupied gazing at the form suggested under E.W.'s outfit, he turned out the lapel of his coat toward Percy, flashing the shining silver badge pinned to his vest. With short hand signals, he let Percy know there were two "subjects" in the room, three officers, and no Marquis or his lieutenants. He indicated things were in hand and Percy should go. Percy found a darkened passage under the tall work tables. These led him to a standing panel screen, behind which stood another officer. He put his hands together down low and gave the hare a boost up to an open window. Percy was up and out the window, landing on the exterior of the building behind a firewood bin.

Percy found the carriage parked on the north side of a home facing Fifth Street. It was next to the stone façade of the Fifth Street Methodist Church. From the shadows, he examined every detail in the vicinity before approaching, to be sure no one was waiting or watching. The damned horses both shied again at his approach and one nervously dropped several hot turds. He climbed aboard in disgust and the carriage launched out onto Fifth Street heading south. The driver deftly avoided the train tracks lining Fifth. Percy was wrapped up in Esther's embrace as the carriage bounced and lurched. Evaline looked on the pair with a tired eye. They were the last three in the compartment. In a short while the carriage turned left and headed back east on Main Street.

Soon they arrived at the third and final venue for gaming, Barkey's Short Buffalo Saloon. It stood at the corner of Sixth and Main Streets, across the street from the 2nd United Presbyterian Church.

Word of the "secret" venues had been spread by way of subtle mentions among Madam Wells' clientele. The girls spoke of hearing that the elusive

"E.W." would finally be at play again – some men were told the game would be at the haberdasher, some heard the post office, and others said the Short Buff Saloon.

Arrangements had been made for separate "E.W.'s" to appear at each venue, with Percy the Hare at their sides. There had been discussion of the possibility of also presenting separate "Percy's," but finding anyone short enough to approximate the hare seemed unlikely. Barkey offered one of his young sons, but the thought of endangering a child was unpalatable to everyone. And a game would be staged at each venue, with undercover Sheriff's deputies on hand to await the presence of the Marquis de Lafayette and take him into custody.

Esther Wells, the original "E.W." herself, and her companion Percy the Hare entered the Short Buff in their usual way, through the back entrance. Presuming the Marquis had received word of all three "E.W." games that night, and presuming he had chosen to infiltrate each one, it seemed unlikely to Percy that the Marquis would choose to return to Barkey's establishment. His men had been bested there once already, and Barkey had shown himself to be a considerable impediment to the Marquis' plans.

Still, Percy made a lengthy study of the room and its inhabitants while Esther made her way to the table. In spite of himself, Percy found her entrance as enchanting as did every other attendee. He marveled at her brass, her elegance, and the solicitous way she made her way through the crowd, hat brim low, one hip at a time. She turned her head slightly towards him and he caught sight of one exotic eye from behind her mask and in the shadow beneath the hat brim. She blew him a luscious kiss that he was sure others would see, the minx, and he swallowed hard. He turned his attention back to the room.

There were faces he recognized – like Horace Grinlow, and Clinton Pardoo, and the young scruff who had purchased E.W.'s handkerchief in her first outing, and Colonel Wigglemann himself. And there were others Percy did not recognize. The Colonel looked suspiciously detached, choosing not to acknowledge Percy as though he imagined he might go unrecognized if he didn't make eye contact. But what troubled Percy was what he did *not* see.

There was no one in attendance he could connect to the Marquis, but there was also no one he could connect to the Sheriff. There was supposed to be a contingent of Taylor's men at each site and they were to make themselves known to Percy, when an opportune moment presented itself. No one did. Barkey! Where was Barkey? This was his own establishment – had he chosen to be with his wife that night at the haberdasher? He wouldn't blame the man. Percy wracked his memory but couldn't recall. He'd believed Barkey would be here.

At the risk of showing his concern, Percy opted to make a physical cycle of the room, watching faces, listening to conversations, checking beneath people's cloaks without their knowing. As he neared the end of the cycle, his anxiousness growing, he heard something he hadn't noticed to that point. A church bell was ringing.

Chapter 41

The plan centered on the church bells. Each game site had been chosen specifically for its proximity to a church with a bell. The churches formed a triangle in the downtown – the First Baptist Church, at the corner of Seventh and North Streets, near the haberdasher; the Fifth Street Methodist Church, at Fifth and Ferry, near the Opera House and Post Office; and the Second United Presbyterian Church, at Sixth and Main, across from the Short Buffalo Saloon. They were meant to provide alarm bells. Sheriff S.O. Taylor was to establish himself at the center point of the triangle, the Episcopal Church at Sixth and Ferry Streets. In the event the Marquis and his crew made themselves known at any of the locations, a silent signal would go out to commence the nearest church to ring its bell. This would call the Sheriff and all his officers to come to that location.

But something had gone wrong. Percy knew it in his heart. His fur stood on end. No one was here at the Short Buff – no one from the side of the righteous and not even anyone from the aspect of the wicked. No one he could see. The church bell was not the one across the street. It rang and rang and he was the only one who seemed to notice it. Others saw the concern in his eyes but no one reacted. There was no one left to find the source of the signal, to do their duty.

Suddenly Percy felt more than saw someone's eyes upon him. He looked up and found them. A pair of dark-rimmed eyes stared out at him from under the brim of E.W.'s large hat. They hovered next to her own, as if unnoticed. But she was well aware. Esther stared at Percy with alarm, alarm she hadn't been able to express with a gleaming silver blade in her face.

"Hello, hare," growled the Marquis from behind Esther Wells' ear. He rose slowly, tilting Esther's hat up until it tumbled onto the table. The light over the table illuminated her brilliant red hair, gathered atop her head. And it revealed the Marquis' skull, with his jet-black hair drawn taut over the top and slicked down in place. The lower part of his face was obscured by an uncharacteristically scruffy beard. It was a fake, tethered behind his ears. Also emerging into the light was his gloved hand at Esther's throat. The crowd pulled back away from the pair. But there was no panic – there seemed to be a sense that that could put the girl in unintended danger. The room grew quiet. The church bell peeled on in the distance.

The Marquis shook Esther by the neck, seeking to elicit something from her – a cry of fear or something. She didn't oblige him. Percy felt completely exposed. Esther was bravely, confidently, defiantly staring out at him. She projected nothing but certainty that all would be fine. But Percy was more afraid than he'd ever been in his life. It was a foreign sensation, fear. He no longer feared what men might do to him. He'd seen too much and avoided too much grievous harm to fear for himself at this point. But seeing the eyes of this girl, this beautiful young woman, filled with apprehension and defiance, now *that* sent a chill through him. That and the sharpened silver flash that reappeared across her eyeline. He feared for her. And he knew the Marquis was aware of it.

The Marquis' voice creaked out of him like it was being forced through a broken pipe. "No? Nothing? You've nothing to say, whore?" he jerked her neck again. "Fine, I'll content myself with the hare." He paused to shift himself, and spun the blade in his hand in front of Esther's face.

"MISTER HARE! How you vex me, you vile rodent! The people here allow you to scurry across their tables, leaving droppings and footprints, and they laugh it off as if you were a clever, silly, stuffed toy. They ignore the fact that you drink their spirits, before playing with their children, that you climb up the skirts of their women and sleep with their daughters, as if you were a harmless scamp. But you're not, are you? *Are you?*"

"No," Percy replied.

"NO! No, you're not. All it was... The only... Our only intent was to have this girl, this filthy little slut…" he jerked Esther neck cruelly, "To have her work for me. To play cards and flash her tits for me. And to bring the cash *to me!* But no, you had to convince her she was bigger than that…"

"She was. She is," Percy answered.

"No! She's just a girl, hare. She's nothing."

"She's not nothing."

"She's nothing! And she will always be nothing." He rose, with his knife at Esther's face, urging her up from her seat. "And we will be nothing but a memory to this town, shortly. And she, this bitch, will be left over in some ditch outside of town – dead by the time you find her…"

Percy pulled himself atop the table in a deft hop.

"… Or, she'll be dead here, if you prefer." The Marquis stuck the blade into Esther's chest, meaning only to prick her, in the threat of worse. But the blade found no purchase there, skidding over a hardened surface beneath her coat. The Marquis tapped the blade against the surface, then stabbed with purpose, time and again, and only striking the metal plated corset all the "E.W.'s" had been fitted with for their protection.

"Clever," he said. Then Esther drove her heel into the top of his boot, cracking a bone in his foot, then spun back with her elbow, driving it deep into his ribcage. His lungs were emptied at once, but he clung to her throat. He'd now gotten hold of the neck gaiter protecting her, and he brandished the silver blade alongside her face. It drew a thin line of blood.

Esther spun away from the blade but the Marquis held fast to the gaiter. The other players pushed back from the table; the onlookers dove to the far corners of the room. Percy saw his opening and took it, throwing his elongated foot into the Marquis head and sending it hard against the brick wall behind him. Still the man held the gaiter and the blade, slashing wildly while Esther twisted in vain. Percy caught his hand in mid-air, clung to his sleeve, and pulled it away from the girl. Percy went to the wall clinging to the Marquis' fist and felt the blade slip into his side, the knife sliding across his ribs.

Percy froze as he felt the blade removed from his side. He dropped to the floor and landed hard. The pain seared through him. Looking up, he watched the Marquis and Esther struggle as the crowd disappeared into the background. Esther threw her fists at him repeatedly, while he lunged at her, the blade clanging off her metal bodice. One brave soul stepped forward and grabbed the Marquis' sleeve. He slashed at them wildly, missing but forcing the onlookers back. Then he turned and threw Esther back against the wall, almost knocking her unconscious.

The Marquis backed up the steps with his hand at Esther's throat, his knife extended as a threat to any who would follow them. Dazed, she nonetheless kicked and pulled as he dragged her backwards. At the top of the steps, the Marquis thought he heard something and spun to his right. There he faced Sheriff S.O. Taylor and two of his men, all bearing pistols. Esther pulled loose the clasp that held her gaiter closed around her neck, and she fell free at his feet. Spinning back around, holding nothing but the empty gaiter, the Marquis found only a darkly cloaked figure which reached out and slapped him viciously, spinning his head atop his neck and rending him unconscious. The Marquis fell over Esther and down the steps, tumbling awkwardly and heavily. He ended in a twisted heap at the bottom, with his knife blade embedded in his own eye socket, his hand still clutching it.

Seemingly only moments earlier, sitting in the haberdasher's playing a solid game of euchre and having just "set" the other players, Kess Smith heard the church bell begin to ring in the church next door. *Their* bell – the church bell for their game. Looking around, there was no sign that anything was happening, there in the game room or even outside the building. The deputies looked at her and at each other and shrugged. As the bell chimed on, Kess was the one to put together that something was wrong. And her first thought, regardless of whether anything at all was happening there, was for her husband's well-being over at the Short Buff.

She ran out of the room and made the short jaunt to the saloon in no time, with others following in her wake. They found the front door locked. With her breath failing her, both from running and from fear, Kess made her way to the rear entrance. She knew the secret mechanism to the door, and she was through it in no time. There was a considerable hubbub coming from the basement, and the noise seemed to be climbing the stairs.

Just then, the front door crashed in and in ran the Sheriff, S.O. Taylor himself, and two of his deputies, who had also figured out that something was amiss. But the sight of three white men with pistols in hand, coming towards her, sent a shiver down her spine, making her relive a night in Georgia from her childhood which she had barely survived and which her own parents had not.

But then the basement door crashed open between her and the Sheriff's men. The door was flung all the way back to the wall, giving that man, the "Marquis," a clear view of the lawmen – and giving Kess a clear view of the pretty Miss Esther, with that man's hand and a glistening white blade at her throat. When the girl fell from his grasp, that man spun at Kess like a wild animal. And she did the only thing she could – she reached out and slapped the holy hell out of him, and sent him back down the stairs from which he came.

Then she fell to her knees beside Miss Esther, pleading to the Sheriff that he recognize her. *"It's me, Kess Smith! Barkey's wife!"* she'd tried to say, but her air had escaped her. She'd gasped in terror while she and the white girl held each other and the Sheriff's men ran into the basement. Esther told her to hold her head back and open her windpipe and try to breathe slowly, slowly, slowly.

Once the church bell had begun ringing, Sheriff Taylor's deputies made quick work of the Marquis' men at the other staged game locations. They eventually made their way to the Short Buffalo Saloon, after being assured the haberdasher's was a false alarm. Along with them came Dr. Rosalind Gullimore, seeking to attend to anyone needing medical attention as best she could.

The scene was madness, with deputies running about, and game attendees fleeing. Rosalind found Esther and Kess struggling to regain her breathing in the back corridor. They set about relieving Kess of her stiff protective corset to free her lungs. Esther inquired of her if anyone had seen to her mother. She feared she would be alone in the carriage.

Rosalind smiled and said, "Yes, I have," reassuringly. She then recounted a scene she said would live in her memory for the rest of her days. As she neared the corner of Sixth Street from Ferry, on her way from the post office, Rosalind had come upon Evaline Wells alone under a wash of streetlamp light, holding two men at bay with a horsewhip. From Rosalind's description, Esther knew they were Walter Swettenham and William Harlan (who was known to Percy and Esther only as Bowler Hat), two of the Marquis de Lafayette's most senior lieutenants. Apparently, the two men had sought to commandeer the carriage for their escape. After the driver struggled with the pair and was overcome, Evaline had grabbed the driver's whip and subdued them single-handedly until deputies came and took them into custody. When the deputies arrived, the two fiends were on their knees begging for help. The whip had to be gently pried from the madam's hand after badges were presented to assure Evaline of who they were.

Once freed from her metal bodice, Kess was able to join Esther and Rosalind in the silliest laughter they'd had in weeks. Though they begged her to spare her breath, Kess kept crying out, "I'd pay to see! I'd pay to see!"

"Girl, whatchoo do?" asked Barkey. His beloved Kess stood before him, as the stronghold door to the saloon's cooler was opened. Her hair had come slightly undone and the women hadn't completely reclosed her blouse at the neck. "What happened? You lose your air?" She threw her arms around him, unseemly in the presence of others, he thought. But he allowed it. She was still short of breath.

Barkey and the deputy assigned to the Short Buff had gotten locked into the cooler, they believed by accident, as they inspected the property before everything began. But it turned out they were locked in by the other deputy assigned there, who had secretly been in league with the Marquis.

That deputy was found later behind the First Baptist Church with a knife wound to his belly. He had gone to tell the man assigned to the church bell to commence ringing. This had falsely drawn the Sheriff and other deputies in that direction, away from the Short Buffalo Saloon. The man was then knifed for his trouble by one of the Marquis' men. The Marquis no doubt preferred to eliminate his entanglements. As it happened, the Marquis' entanglements had all come to an end now, having killed himself in his fall down the steps with his own knife passing through his eye into his brain. As brutal a death as surely befitted him.

Kess described for Barkey what had taken place there in his absence. Hearing of the trouble inflicted upon Esther and Percy, and the rest of his paying customers, Barkey wanted to fly off in a rage, locate every one of the Marquis' men, and make them pay dearly. She held him back, only by breathlessly describing how she, herself, had saved the day. For, she whispered in fear to her husband, she had slapped her a white man, and she had slapped him *hard!*

Chapter 42

January 22nd had also been a busy and stressful day for Mrs. Edwina Wigglemann. After speaking with a reporter from the Lafayette Courier about the burglary over afternoon tea, she returned home to meet with her husband about the event. Neither blamed the other for the loss, as both had been out of the home for common activities, but in hindsight they wished they had arranged for a housekeeper or the carriage man, Mr. Poutch, to keep an eye on the house while they were away.

The Colonel seemed distracted and unsure of what to say.

Edwina seemingly became distraught once more, becoming impatient with the man's indecision and thinking about the items that had been lost. Eventually she decided to go rowing upon the river that evening to alleviate her anxieties. The Colonel assured her that she would feel much better for doing so. He mentioned having some business downtown that evening and wished her well. He was taken aback when, for the first time in quite a while, she gave him her best and patted his shoulder before leaving.

****

"Percy, this is ridiculous!" Esther chided him. "I don't care what time it is. You've been hurt. We should take you home."

"Just answer me, my dear girl. What time is it?"

Esther located the clock over Barkey's desk and reported, "Nearly half past eight."

"Good lord, we must be going!"

"Percy," said Rosalind firmly, trying to tamp down his energy. "You need to be careful…"

"Ros, dearest, you said I was fine. Just a poke. Correct?"

"Yes, well, a bit more than that, but you've only just stopped bleeding. You need to take it easy," she urged.

"I will, I assure you. WE will! You're coming with us, so I'll be under good care…"

"Me? Why…?"

"And I promise not to exert myself. I promise." He flashed a charming grin. "But we have to get a move on."

"Oh, damn you, you silly hare," Rosalind relented. "But I'm going to watch you carefully." Then to Esther, who looked unconvinced, "I will. I'll keep my eye on him."

"Oh, she's coming too," Percy said. Esther brightened. "We're all going. Come on, we need to get to the chariot."

"Chariot?" questioned Esther.

"Carriage thing. Please hurry."

Having arrived on the scene somewhat late, Evaline watched the trio go, smirking at the capriciousness of youthful women. But she herself knew the appeal of pressing that charming hare to one's side, and she wouldn't begrudge anyone the wonder of his company.

She made her way down the stairs to the gaming room of the Short Buff and found the gaming clientele, or at least the braver few of them, still on hand. Barkey's game regular and local green grocer Horace Grinlow was on hand and holding court. He was recounting the goings on to a deputy, who had heard his story once already, and to others who had themselves been in the room when it happened.

Colonel Wigglemann himself was there, sitting to the side, though in a position of prominence in the room. He listened to Horace with mild interest and a lit cigarillo glowing. But his very nonchalance itself seemed suspect, given the agitation everyone else in the room exhibited at having witnessed a knife fight and an attempted abduction.

Evaline met the Colonel's gaze and acknowledged him out of formality. "See the whole thing, did you?" she asked.

He nodded. "I did."

"Ever leave your seat to help the girl?"

He looked away, seemingly distracted by the burning cigarillo or some invisible person speaking to him out of view.

Evaline grinned and turned to the deputy, "Sir, if you're through here, you've no worries with us. Tell the Sheriff we're all friends here and we're going to keep playing for a quarter a chit." Then she instructed Grinlow, "Shuffle and deal, Horace. We'll have ourselves a friendly game. And who knows, if you behave yourself maybe you'll get a handie out of it for your trouble!"

Horace had himself a hearty laugh over that one, sputtering and turning red in the face as he split the deck to shuffle. Only this one was all too hearty and all too fitful, and, on top of the excitement of the evening's operation, it made for poor Horace's departure from this earth.

Later, Evaline was heard to have said, "Horace Grinlow died laughing, my friend, with the unfulfilled promise of a handjob, as he was likely always destined to have done."

End of Part Four

V

Part Five

"Elsewhere"

Chapter 43

"So, allow me to tell you a tale of the river dolphin," began Percy the Hare.

"Ha! *Another* story of the river dolphin, Percy?" laughed Rosalind Gullimore. "You've been fashioning those legends since I was a girl."

She and Esther were huddled together in the enclosed carriage, with Percy between them, as it rolled west through downtown, toward the river.

Rosalind had heard so many tales from her friend the hare in times past that she felt herself becoming giddy with anticipation. When he'd told them there was another adventure that evening, she knew not what to expect. Now the warm, loving days of her childhood with her friend the hare had been reawakened.

Those days lived on in her memory like instances of magic. And the magic was tangible to both women. Percy sharing tales of the frontier and historic figures, tales of mythic creatures and strange enchanted spots all over the town and especially along the river. These tales always clung to the dubious suggestions of things that couldn't possibly be, they thought. But as always, whenever they developed those suspicions, they would see words being formed from the mouth of a large, charismatic hare who was himself very, very real.

"Surely you don't doubt the presence of the river dolphin," Percy addressed Rosalind. "You being a doctor of animal medicine and all."

"Precisely. The day I see one with my own eyes and can study it to my satisfaction is the day this medical professional will believe in one. But please, Percy, I don't wish to cast shadow over your pending story – I want to believe and be swept away in it."

Rosalind clutched his paw tighter into her gloved hand as they made their way onto the covered wooden bridgeway at Brown Street. They were crossing the Wabash River to the western shore, which was as yet relatively open land, with the exception of the town of Chauncey, which lay further west across the levee, with the new college John Purdue had founded.

The women were now bundled up heavily against the cold on that January night, in their "E.W." raingear with collars turned up under broad hats. As enshrouded as she was, Percy was stunned by Esther's beautiful face, her striking features smiling down on him. Her long legs were crossed and dangled below. She ran her foot along his furred leg and he stammered slightly but finally began his story in earnest.

"The Wabash river dolphin, as I've heard tell from the early frontiersmen, is a clever creature. Long living an idyllic lifestyle along the clear 'water over white stones' – for that is what the word 'Wabash' translates into. The dolphin were forced to learn to survive over time as men poured into the Wabash river valley. Long hunted but revered by the native peoples, it was only when the white French trappers arrived that the river dolphin were truly threatened.

The French were anxious to capture and skin anything they could and send the hides back across the ocean to Europe. You've probably heard that before. The haberdashers on the far continent were clamoring for what they saw as 'exotic goods' from the new world, and they would pay a handsome price for them. Primarily the trappers were concentrated on beaver and mink and muskrats, but they couldn't help but be enamored of the dolphin pelt coats fashioned by the native peoples they met."

"Oh, now Percy," Rosalind interrupted. "You can't mean the Indians…"

"But I do, madam! The natives were seen on many occasions wearing very effective raingear made from the skins of the river dolphin, which they actually referred to as the 'river buffalo' as they were once that numerous."

Esther laughed. "Where are you taking us, might we ask?"

"We're almost there. Now allow me to continue… Unlike their more genteel native counterparts, the French trappers were known to conduct coordinated hunts for the river dolphin. They would line up several boats full of men who would pound the waters with cannon shot or explosives and drive the dolphin upstream to a point of congestion where the dolphin might become ensnared and easier to gaff and pull onto their boats."

"How horrible," Rosalind reacted.

"Indeed. They were savage in their approach. So much so, in fact, that the native peoples – who with great irony white men consistently label as 'savage' – insisted upon not participating in these hunts. They had long felt the river dolphin were elegant, noble creatures and could not abide by such treatment.

Soooo… what would transpire was that the white trappers would thunder along the river heading upstream, while the native peoples would paddle through them, quietly heading about their business downstream. The whites would allow the natives to pass peacefully, as they wanted no quarrel. At least not at that time. Later on, things devolved into a much more contentious state, of course.

But what the trappers were unaware of was that the dolphin that were being driven systematically upstream were then plunging out of sight, turning about under the water, and emerging directly under the canoes of the natives. Hugging to their thin hulls, out of sight of the trappers, the dolphin would then pass peacefully through the melee and emerge downstream unscathed.

Esther laughed gleefully and clapped her gloved hands. "Oh, that's so wonderful!" she said. "Was it really so?"

"Of course," Percy replied, acting somewhat hurt at the suggestion of doubt. "In fact, the tribes' disruption of the hunt and rescues of the dolphin was discovered only many years later. It was one of the points of argument when the whites attempted to drive them off to faraway reservations on land they knew nothing of. Tragic tale."

The carriage stopped at the end of the bridge and they helped each other down. Esther hugged him to her protectively and refused to put him down.

"You're my hurt hare," she cooed. "I need to keep you safe."

He sighed and said, "Alright, dammit. Go that way," pointing down a bramble path running along the river. Rosalind and Esther exchanged a glance, marveling at his consent to being held and carried.

He began again, "I wanted to bring you out tonight for a view along the river. It'll be lovely to see in the January moonlight and, I dare say, it will provide a marvelous panorama for things to play out on the water. As long as the wind is right and the stink from the canal is blown in the proper direction, it can be delightful. And see, the canal runs along the far bank and we are to the western side, so it should be advantageous for us."

The group arrived at a promontory that rose above the river and afforded a clear view both north and south along the curve of the Wabash. At the top, the trunk of an ancient hickory tree had long ago been bent at a right angle so that its body ran parallel to the ground for ten feet before it resumed its natural inclination and rose into a full canopy of branches rising up into the night sky. The trunk afforded a perfect bench for the friends to perch upon and consider the river.

"My Mr. Hare, I must say I'm happy to have you close to me again," said Rosalind.

Percy smiled.

"For years I would hear people speak of you and I would wish, so fervently, that I could just see you again. And when finally we met at the New Year's gala and I was able to look into your eyes again... oh, Percy, I truly thought I would faint away."

"Dear god," said Percy, wrinkling his nose in distaste. "You could author those dreadful penny romance novels, with talk like that."

"Ooh, I love those!" cried Esther.

"Me too!" laughed Rosalind.

The two women pressed in upon him from either side.

Percy reveled in the nearness of them, he had to confess. The smell of their still beautifully coiffed hair. The moonlit glow on their faces. He abruptly ended his own musing and pointed down the river to the south, "Here comes the steamboat of Captain Lark O'Connor and his brother Jim. Isn't it majestic?"

"Why, yes, it is," offered Rosalind. "But do they always travel at night?"

"Unique circumstances," he answered. "Lark told me they had a unique fare which required an evening castoff."

"And do they always travel at that... angle?" asked Esther. "Doesn't it seem a bit... misaligned on the water?"

"Yes, it does, I agree," he said. "I would venture to guess that's because old Jim is at the helm. Have you ever met them – the O'Connors?"

"No, I'm sorry to say I haven't," said Esther. "Not really. I mean, I met him that evening last week – ol' Lark, that is – but not his brother."

"Nor I," said Rosalind.

"Well, they're quite the pair. Steadfast brothers and companions they are. But Captain Lark is the more serious and reliable gentleman. Jim is a bit... *less* reliable it could be said." In his head, he could hear Evaline chuckling knowingly, having made arrangements more than once for ol' Lark to come retrieve his unconscious and buck-ass naked brother from one of her rooms after an extended bender.

Percy related to them the story of the loss of Lark's steamer "The Joe Segner," which sank 30 miles south of Terre Haute, while under Jim's command. And the ensnarement and near capsizing of their flatboat the previous fall on the canal – also on Jim's watch, but not completely to his fault.

"Poor man," Rosalind offered. "I hope he can right his fortunes. It must shake a man's confidence to find himself in such situations time and again."

"It does," Percy assured her. "Which is why it is understandable that ol' Lark generally keeps a watchful eye on his brother and entrusts him with the simpler passages of their journeys. Such as disembarking from Lafayette for Terre Haute. I happen to know of Lark's plans and that is what we see playing out before us now."

"Hunh," Rosalind uttered. "Um, Percy... am I mistaken, or should the ship be going in the opposite direction? If they are, in fact, destined for Terre Haute, which is to the south, why would they be heading upstream, to the north?"

"I thought you would pick up on that," Percy answered. They watched quietly as the ship paddled past them, picking up steam and heading north. "Call me a foolish optimist," he added, "but I'm going to venture that ol' Jim is going to catch his mistake soon. Or Lark himself will."

And soon thereafter, the engines were reduced and the paddles noticeably slowed. Bells sounded aboard the ship signaling, as Percy explained, the intent of a change of direction. The O'Connors were not off to a great start, but it was nighttime and very few folks ashore, if any, would be aware of it. Things would be righted soon enough. It would take some time for the boat to slow enough to come about and make a complete turn but they watched intently.

"Ah, look, Rosalind!" said Percy. "Here comes our friend, Eddie, on her nightly row."

"Eddie? Edwina?" Rosalind reacted immediately, sitting up and straining to look back down the river where Lark's boat had originated. "Where?"

"If you look closely," Percy pointed, "You can just make her out. See? She leaves a thin line of wake on the water."

"I see her!" Rosalind exclaimed. "I always wondered what it was like for her rowing out here at night. Would she hear us, if we called to her?"

"Possibly, but I'm not sure. I think she'll be attentive to her paddles in the water. And she might be making her own sounds... yes, I think I can hear her. Do you hear her singing?"

Rosalind paused with her mouth open, listening intently. They could just hear the sound of a sea shanty chiming over the water as Edwina muscled along.

"She really does have a nice resonant voice, doesn't she?" Rosalind chimed. "And she really does sound like a man, no?"

"Indeed," said Esther. "And look at her go."

They watched her a moment, as she approached their point on the river course. The scull was little more than a thin line as it skated across the surface in a steady course.

"Percy," Rosalind began, "might she not catch up with the steamer soon? She's headed right for it."

"Yes, she will." He seemed unconcerned.

"Well, shouldn't we warn her?"

"I don't believe she would hear us now, with the noise from the paddles.

Besides, I'm sure she knows what to do in the presence of another vessel. It probably happens frequently."

"Percy! I'm concerned – she could run right into them!"

Percy turned to her at that moment and spoke plainly and reassuringly.

"Dear Rosalind – I brought you both here tonight to watch events play out. Didn't I say that?"

She nodded, still concerned. Esther pointed out over the water in agreement with the sense of danger, but remained quiet.

"Consider this our *theatre*. We have seats – you two and I on this tree – to a marvelous new melodrama that is presented here on the Wabash River stage. I don't want to ruin the experience for you, but rest assured that the show is well in hand, and the players, are well acquainted with their roles."

"But Percy, she could be killed!" Rosalind exclaimed.

"Ah," Percy assured her, "but that is not in the script! Watch with me."

"Percy!" Esther cried.

But he pointed out onto the river and said, "Watch."

Edwina's scull had drawn near the steamboat and was now being tossed a bit in its convulsive wake. The steamboat was cavitating as it attempted to complete the turn and head back from whence it came. Edwina could be heard calling out to the small shanties on the shore. Voices there responded to her, though it was difficult to make out what was being said.

Rosalind was beside herself with fear. She clutched at Percy and rose from her seat.

But he simply said, "Watch."

Edwina began to flail about on the scull in an exaggerated fashion. Even Rosalind could tell she was not in serious distress. Then Edwina slapped an oar to the surface of the water – not once, but three times in a row – loud, flat smacks that pierced the darkness.

"Look," Percy pointed. "Another player takes to the stage!"

Across the surface of the water, a fast-moving streak appeared. An occasional ripple and a splash appeared behind it. It was headed straight for Edwina Wigglemann's scull.

Rosalind asked, "Oh, Percy, are you sure she's alright?"

Just then, Edwina exclaimed very loudly, loudly enough to be heard from across the water in all directions, "OH, NO! THE DOLPHIN! IT HAS ME!" And a loud splash was heard as Edwina fell into the water.

Both women gasped, "A *dolphin?*," and covered their mouths with their hands.

"Rosalind, look now," Percy said. "Look now to the side of Lark's steamer!"

By this point, the paddleboat had nearly completed its turn and was pointed directly toward Percy and Rosalind. As it pulled further around, the starboard side of the boat came more and more into view. Percy pointed to the rail on the side of the ship.

In the darkness, on the rail facing west and away from the city, several men could be seen leaning out. One of them slapped a board to the surface of the water, again, three times in a row. A moment later the men reached out and began pulling something from the water. It was a person. That person was quickly wrapped in a blanket and could be seen being ushered down into the hold. The steamboat seemed to resume its rightful course southward to Terre Haute. The engines roared to life again, the paddles assumed a more rapid thumping through the water, and the boat progressed noisily into the night.

"Percy!" Rosalind exclaimed. "Was that Edwina?"

"Yes."

"Is she safe?"

"Yes."

"Did the *dolphin... rescue* her?" asked Esther.

"It did indeed," he said, "It pulled her out of sight, on what I wager was a quick and cold plunge. And I believe its name is Elsie." In the moonlight, he could make out Esther, wide-eyed and grinning at him.

In the boat's wake, the tiny scull could be seen floating errantly in the moonlight. Voices cried out from the shore. It was clear the constabulary was being alerted and a rescue would be attempted. But all the local constabulary were either downtown mopping up after the Marquis' mess or having a celebratory ale at the Knickerbocker Saloon. And the occupants of a small rowboat that ventured out hastily toward the scull but would only find it empty.

Percy explained that little did anyone on the eastern shore realize it, but the hapless rower, Mrs. Edwina Wigglemann, was safe now and huddled below deck aboard the steamboat, warming herself at its furnace. She was surrounded by her recently stolen earthly possessions, on her way south to a new life.

On the western shore of the Wabash, Rosalind asked Percy, "What about her husband?"

"He will be informed sometime soon, I imagine. When they can find him. With the Marquis gone he'll have to reposition himself in... *things* in town."

"Will he suspect anything... about her?"

"No. I don't believe so. From his perspective, his life just got easier."

"Percy!"

"From *his* perspective, I say."

"Where is she going? Edwina. Where is she headed?"

He replied with the only information he had.

"Elsewhere."

After a few quiet moments watching the steamboat push its way along the river, escaping the light from the city and slipping into the wooded midwestern darkness, Percy turned to his lovely companions.

He asked, "Have either of you ever developed a taste for a fine smoke? A friend recently shared with me two very tasteful cigarillos she pinched from her husband." And he produced them.

Neither woman was interested, but both encouraged him to partake on his own. He deferred to another time and pocketed them again. They sat quietly for a moment.

"It was selfish of me. I apologize," he offered. Esther looked at him, unsure of what he meant. But Rosalind understood.

He added, "The wild hare overtook the gentleman it would seem."

"You were young then. A natural inclination, I imagine." Rosalind said.

"Perhaps. Perhaps the original offense – that may have been an instinct. But not the distancing. That's what I really regret, staying away from you for so long."

Rosalind looked at Percy, her eyes full of compassion and yet showing her profound heartache. "I still miss you, my old friend. And not as the girl I once was. But now as the woman I've become, the woman who could use your companionship. Your advice. And your wit."

Esther feared she was a third wheel in the conversation. But Rosalind reached across Percy and took her gloved hand and held it. She meant for her to be part of it too. She meant for Percy to be conscious of Esther.

"You want my advice?" Percy asked.

"Yes. Very much so."

"Well. Lose that hulking lout who speaks at you like you're 'his girl'. You don't need him."

"I suppose you're right. But my mother argues he's a security. That I need a man to smooth my path through this town." Rosalind hugged her arms around both of them. But she was speaking to Esther.

"Smooth your own path," came the voice from between them. "You can, you know."

"Do you believe that?"

"Of course. I wouldn't say it otherwise," he answered. "Do you not remember? You were always the smartest child on the block. The wisest girl in the town. You were an audacious child – it was beautiful to see you speak and think as you learned. This one is the same," he added, nodding his head to Esther.

"Really?" Esther asked.

"Oh, I can see that," said Rosalind. "But this one has bigger dreams than I had."

Percy interjected, "The problem is, somewhere along the way you forgot how brave you are. You overlooked your own strength."

"I lost my Percy," she replied.

"Bullshit. I didn't make you strong. But," he acquiesced, "I should have been there to remind you how strong you are."

Esther burst into tears almost before Rosalind herself.

"I won't make that mistake again," they heard him say, now having almost magically removed himself from the branch and landed several feet away, along the path. "I don't want you to end up as old as our boat-rower there before you decide what you want from your life. Sorry, your *lives*."

The women looked at each other. Both felt like he had blown cool, fresh January air right into their lungs.

"Let's make our leave. I'm becoming frosted," said the hare. As the trio proceeded back down the path to their carriage, they became foggy silhouettes. He could be heard complaining that they were crushing him, he *had* just been stabbed after all, and no, he didn't really like being picked up, thank you very much. Dammit.

Chapter 44

Mrs. Edwina Wigglemann was declared dead and lost to the river on February 5, 1884. Her body was never recovered. The role the mythic "river dolphin" played, or whatever it might have been that led Mrs. Wigglemann to claim that one was upon her, was never determined. It was classified as an unfortunate accident.

A memorial service was held at the river bank the following week. The weather had turned colder again at the end of January, and the river had become partially frozen, preventing the passage of any large vessels. A black wreath was hung from the prow of Edwina's scull, which was floated out onto the center of the Wabash River where it was unfrozen and free-flowing.

****

In the abandoned house on Elizabeth Street, the former home of the notorious madam Hortense LaForge, the dining room was still and quiet and cold, except for a small form on the floor in the dark, sitting under a full coat. No fire had been lit. No resident had been addressed to visit. And still one came.

Before Percy, low to the floor, a dull blue light appeared. It swirled and grew, becoming more brilliant and extending itself toward him. What felt like a delicate hand was laid upon the side of his face and smoothed back his fur. His heartbeat seemed to resonate through that touch, with that of the ghost, Baby Alice. It seemed she absorbed his warmth and wrapped herself around him.

He could hear a delicate "shhhh" sound. Without opening his eyes, he could feel Alice's face very near his. More clearly than ever before, he could hear her voice now.

She pushed her words out to him, as though through an echoing tunnel. "Oh, my Percy," she said. "My handsome, brave boy. You've done so well. The game... turned out. Now... make him 'king' her now..." Her voice diminished, and then "the women. *Of course* they love you."

Percy's heart ached with apprehension, but she soothed him.

"Especially the big one."

"The *big* one?" he asked.

Ghostly hands seemed to cup two large globes.

"Oh." To Baby Alice, constantly petite and frail through her lifetime, Esther probably seemed a very large girl.

"She warms you... good... that you let her. We *all* love you. We always do. Our hare loves us too... but..." She began to fade. "... has never stayed..." was the last thing he could make out, before he couldn't see her or feel her anymore.

"... make him 'king' her now..." echoed in his head.

"Yes, I believe that's in the offing," he said with a grin.

Chapter 45

Esther descended the staircase dressed in almost regal splendor. Percy had had occasion to marvel at her often, but never had she appeared so... mature. Resolute was also a good word. Mona the house matron and Evaline followed her, their eyes never leaving her and smiling pridefully. Esther froze in mid-step, angled classically on the stairs, with her gloved hand gently resting on the bannister, and she addressed him.

"Why, Mr. Hare, what a distinct pleasure it is to see you. You're looking very well." She spoke it with all of the reserve and throated nobility of the very highest society matrons and looked down upon him with their heavy-eyed disdain.

"Ugh," he said. "That's too believable by far."

"Ha!" she exploded in laughter, "I know! Isn't it abhorrent?" She continued down the steps in her normal flouncy manner, bustles rustling and a smile seemingly larger than accountable. She reached for him anxiously.

"I so want to embrace you, my wonderful, gentle hare. But I do not think I could bend to you in this getup."

"You needn't," he assured her. "You have a task before you. Maintain your demeanor."

She looked at him wistfully and clung to his paw.

"I wish you..." she began.

"But I cannot," he finished. "This is your day. Your pronouncement. Your transaction. And I will be right there. In the wings, as it were."

"We'd best be on our way, dear, me and Percy," Evaline interrupted. We'll meet you there after the recital."

Mona approached Esther with her hat. To call it a hat was perhaps an inadequate misnomer, as the thing was bedecked with lace and ribbon and birds' wings as was the style. Mona carried it as though a coronation crown. It was clear it meant a great deal to them both.

"With this, my dear child, you become the master of your fate. You take on the role of your own administrator, your own woman. We've talked this through and you know what it means, what you're doing today."

"Are you sure, my dear?" Evaline asked.

"Mother!"

"My last inquiry on the matter, I'm sorry," Evaline assured her. "I don't know or understand all of the particulars. I likely never will. I just want to be sure that you are ready – that this is the life you want – for you, and me. And for him." She gestured down to Percy beside her.

"It absolutely is," Esther said. "It is, mother. My dearest, dearest Evaline."

The elder madam put her hand to her mouth in a rare show of emotion.

"Good," said Evaline. "Then I'll shut the fuck up. Percy, let's get a move on."

Esther and Percy exchanged a look. Then she whispered to him, "King me," and he smiled an uncharacteristically large smile.

****

"You like to watch, don't you, Colonel Wigglemann?" asked young Esther Wells.

"I beg your pardon?" the Colonel replied. He held the door and gestured for her to pass, as they entered his sizable home. They passed through the entryway, and she led him into the empty parlor, now cavernous and echoing with the recent removal/"theft" of his wife's possessions.

He must have thought it odd when Esther directed him to a chair in the center of the empty parlor in his own home. She seated herself in a similar chair opposite him at a small parlor desk, in front of a yawning, ornate fireplace. Esther's adopted mother, the madam Evaline Wells, appeared, having set a cordial fire in the fireplace. She helped Esther situate the ornate bustle and train of her dress upon the chair. Clearly, this meeting had been arranged.

"Ah, Madam Wells – how good to see you again!" the Colonel said.

"Yes," she said simply, being attentive to Esther's positioning.

"Now, Madam Wells, I've been meaning to ask what has ever become of that scurrilous character, Percy Hare?" he asked with a disingenuous smile. "Has he ever shown himself again? I understand he has been a friend of yours for some time, but I for one would be sorry to hear that he had."

Unbeknownst to the Colonel, in addition to Madam Wells, one Percy Hare was watching the performance from the music room alcove adjacent to the parlor. He was there for backup only, should the Colonel become belligerent in any way. Esther had strictly forbidden him from interfering, so he settled in to watch in silence. He pulled one of the Colonel's cigarillos from his pocket to suck upon for the flavor alone. The warmest sunlight seen in the region in weeks angled through the windows behind Percy and drove through the house into the parlor. Percy kept back against the wall to avoid casting a telltale shadow.

"Do you mean, has Percy Hare shown himself since playing a part in bringing down your ill-advised cohort, the Marquis de Lafayette, not a month ago?" asked Evaline.

"My cohort...?" the Colonel asked, seemingly dismayed at her inference.

"Yes, yes – no time now to clutch your pearls..."

"Now, mother, the Colonel is our guest this afternoon," Esther inserted. "Shall we allow him the benefit of the doubt?" The Colonel wrinkled his brow at being referred to as a guest in his home, but remained silent.

Evaline waved off her daughter's concerns and said simply, "Pay attention, Colonel."

Esther continued, "As I was saying, I've made the observation that you like to watch things happening... but from a distance. You like to set scenarios, and then sit back and watch things play out. It's amusing, isn't it?"

"Why, yes, sometimes I guess I do," he said, unsure of the purpose of her query.

"Would you like a glass of wine, sir? This is a really lovely one from down in Bloomington." Esther began to pour two glasses. Percy marveled at how the warm glow of the sunlight reflecting from the floor lit her skin with a golden glow. The cut glass carafe holding the wine glistened in her hand.

"Though only the time for afternoon tea, I would not be averse to a glass, thank you very much. What's the occasion, might I ask?"

"Oh, I believe I have a proposition in which I might interest you," she replied. Holding up her glass for a toast, she offered, "To… 'beginnings,' let's say." The gentleman and young lady tapped glasses and drank.

He offered, "Sounds auspicious."

She replied simply, "You might think so." Then she continued, "Many times, sir, I've noticed that you don't ever get involved in the scenarios you put in play. Sometimes you don't even seem to have anything to gain. You just… instigate, and then watch. You're practically a producer of your own theatre, aren't you? The 'Wigglemann Playhouse,' one might call it," she laughed and took another drink.

Her directness and specificity in scenario provoked caution in him.

"You see, I've looked into you," she smiled. "And your history. I thought, if I had as much to gain from being chaperoned by you as everyone says I should, then I ought to really get to know whereof you speak – and how you became as successful a man as you are, or as you are suggested to be."

"You looked into *me*? Esther, I'm not sure I understand the meaning of this… approach of yours. I mean, you looking into me? That really suggests some cheek on your part, young…"

"No doubt. No doubt it does, sir. But cheek I have aplenty," casting a provocative look over her shoulder, "It's been said, anyway. Have some more wine, sir." And, reflexively, he did.

Evaline then helped with the removal of her daughter's jacket. She folded it neatly over her arm and stood back. Esther's dress reflected more of an evening look than a more traditional tea gown, forsaking the high fitted collar of women's daywear for a much lower neckline and exposed shoulders.

The Colonel, for his part, assumed a staunch posture with his cane planted before him and one hand atop it. He had not sought as yet to make himself comfortable, nor had he been invited to do so. His gloves and hat remained in place.

"Now." Esther resumed. "As I say, your history is marked by a degree of… shall we say, 'aloofness.' In your estimable service to the country," Evaline provided her daughter with a sheet of paper from a folio, "The record shows it was said of you that you employed a 'Go and Do It' philosophy towards your men. In that, you would develop or accept a plan of attack submitted to you, then direct your men to carry it out, without yourself being engaged or endangered."

"A common practice of leadership," the Colonel interjected.

"Common enough, perhaps, though not very inspirational, hmm? Especially when one then blames ensuing losses upon subordinates who are said to have either provided faulty reports of troop numbers or are said to have given their men the wrong orders. Though their orders were in fact written down and still existed in the pockets of the unfortunate dead."

"Do you mean to denigrate my service? Is that why I've been welcomed into my own home this afternoon?" he asked.

"Oh, Colonel, I mean nothing at all as yet. I'm only recounting what information I've gleaned from service records and all. I mean, you have all those medals of service you've shown me, no? And I am certainly no military strategist. Have a drink."

He did, and she did as well.

"Regardless," Esther continued, "it begins a pattern." She handed the sheet back to her mother. "Here in Lafayette, you seem to have distinguished yourself with the habit of developing stockpiles of goods that have been completely unavailable to other merchants, and being totally 'unaware' of said stockpiles until one of your underlings brings it to your attention. And then, with your most humble of apologies, you generously turn out your pockets, as it were, and make the stockpiled items available for all in the community! And remark for journalists that your generosity is all in the spirit of 'fair play.' How magnanimous of you!"

278

The Colonel tipped his head cautiously.

"Well, it *would* be magnanimous of you, wouldn't it, were it not for the fact that you then publicly rebuke your underling and place responsibility for both the egregious stockpiling and the secret supply knowledge solely upon their shoulders, while claiming no awareness on your own part. And that you then provide those stockpiled goods at exorbitant resale prices, claiming a wide profit from your so-called 'generosity.'"

Esther reached up and removed the pin from the decorative hat atop her head. Her shimmering, vivid red hair tumbled down over her white shoulders. She handed the winged hat to her mother.

Percy loved when that girl's hair fell. It was a silky burning red flow that in itself could overwhelm a man. The raking sunlight from the far side of the house torched it to a fiery heat. He noted that "magnanimous" was the actual word Tanya Bubher herself had used, in full sarcastic cackle, when she described the Colonel's practices and how ol' Winks had been blamed for things several times over. Neither he nor Esther could get over hearing the word come from the crusty woman, who spat it out while chewing on her corncob pipe. So it had stuck in his memory.

Before she continued, Esther turned her head slightly, allowing a few long curls of her hair to slide further along her bare shoulder, and glanced knowingly toward Percy, secreted in the next room. She grinned the most delicate smile. It made him catch his breath. He winked back at her, holding up the cigarillo he intended to light when this was concluded.

"Ah, yes," Esther continued. "The cigarillos. That was an interesting chapter too, wasn't it? Poor ol' Captain Lark. What did he ever do to you? To treat him so?"

"Why? Whatever do you..." the Colonel blustered.

"And you always trumpeting about 'fair play!' Was it fair play to have your man Winks Bubher direct the roadsmen to dump their tree stumps into the canal at that juncture? Knowing the Captain's boat wouldn't be able to pass? Was it fair play to have Winks and his men show up just in the nick of time to rescue the Captain's cargo, and then pocket some of it for themselves? Rather, for you?"

"I'm sure I don't know what you're referring to," protested Wigglemann.

"Well, I'm sure Winks Bubher might be able to illuminate things for us!"

"Winks? Why, the man is a stumbling idiot now, ever since that New Year's fiasco! He can scarcely form words!"

"Ah, yes, the 'New Year's fiasco.' Let's return to that in a moment, shall we?" Esther stood and pulled her hair over her shoulder, making room for Evaline to undo the ties at the back of her bodice. She sipped the remainder of her wine and refilled her glass, encouraging the Colonel to follow along. He did so presently, rising enough to offer his glass for her pour.

"First," Esther continued, "Mr. Bubher, while presently unable to orally communicate, is actually quite adept at expressing himself, by directing his wife to papers, and storehouses, and garages, and all manner of visual clues that can tell the story of the work he's done for one Colonel Melvin Wigglemann."

Evaline removed Esther's bodice, revealing her corset beneath, and began to work on the considerable bustle on the rear of her dress.

"Now that is a scurrilous charge, young lady! And might I ask what you think you're doing? This is highly inappropriate behavior… Madam Wells!"

"Oh, pipe down, you old pervert," said Evaline. "It's not like you haven't watched this before."

"Madam, I have no idea what you mean!"

"Yes, you do. Barely two years ago you paid good money to watch this young girl, who has at least since then achieved the age of consent, undress and bathe herself…"

"Why, I never!" Wigglemann blustered.

"Oh, yes, you did," Evaline continued. "In the basement of my own house. Because my matron, Mona, she's got a prodigious memory on her. And she remembers exactly who paid for a peepshow on the side of my normal operations. An unauthorized peepshow with a seventeen-year-old girl at the time. She could likely tell us the date of it, were we to ask. So spare me the consternation, Melvin."

Esther gently placed her hand atop her mother's arm, indicating the need for a cease-fire in her assault. Evaline helped Esther step free of the voluminous dress and bustle, then said quietly, "Sorry. I'll take my leave now," and delicately kissed her daughter's cheek before disappearing with the dress through the empty dining room.

Esther rolled her eyes toward the Colonel and chuckled, saying, "My mother has a tendency to be a bit cantankerous. I hope you'll forgive her."

The Colonel rose, saying, "Oh, I've noticed, I assure you. And I believe I'll be taking my leave now as well. This spiteful game..." he said while gesturing loosely in the vicinity of her undergarments, at which he tried not to gaze directly, "... has gone on long enough." He headed for the archway into the entry.

"No, you won't, sir. I don't believe you will be going," said Esther. Evaline reappeared. "Not unless, on top of all the rest I've mentioned, you also want to be exposed for your part in your wife's disappearance."

He stopped and spun back, looking quizzical.

"By the way, this is your home. Why would you be leaving?" she added.

"Why... that's... and, yes, why would I? It's ridiculous. I had nothing to do with my wife's..."

"My, but doesn't every indication suggest you had though...?" Esther interjected.

"What do you mean?" he stammered.

"Sit down again."

"What do you mean?"

She waited. When he had finally consented and touched down upon the chair once more, Esther continued.

"I only mean that it would seem odd, I feel, Colonel, to many people, that the furniture and possessions that were 'stolen' from this home on the evening of January 21st just past were in fact, more accurately, 'removed' from your home by movers, not thieves. And that these items have been claimed as stolen property with the Aetna Insurance Company[8]of Indianapolis, with the intention of course that you be reimbursed for the value of their loss. You see," picking up the folio of papers again, "here is a bill to you, 'Colonel M. Wigglemann,' from local furniture movers Ainty Grand & Co., with a list of items to be received. And here is the letter to

Aetna Insurance requesting reimbursement for the loss… of these same items. How odd. Don't you think?"

The Colonel seemed genuinely perplexed by the revelation of the movers.

"But, I never… I wouldn't have…" he mumbled.

"No?" Esther replied. "Well, it certainly would appear you did, according to this."

"But why… the day before she…"

"The day before your wife disappeared? Yes! That perplexed me too. I thought, 'What would be the point of having one's possessions 'stolen' the day before one's wife is lost in a tragic accident? The day before? It doesn't make sense, does it?"

He shook his head no. She held up her glass to indicate he should have another drink. He did so and she joined him.

"Unless…" she continued, "Could the disappearance have been just an oddly timed coincidence? A happenstance that could never have been foreseen? Or… perhaps… the wife found out about the plan to make a false claim on stolen property… and objected… and then was dealt with, in order to assure her silence."

"No!" the Colonel replied, rising again.

"No! Surely not," she answered herself. "Well, perhaps not. But your wife, Edwina, she was known to be an independent woman, wasn't she? And everything we can see would lead one to that supposition." She paused, allowing his temperature to cool. "But please take your seat again, sir." And he did.

Esther also sat, and then leaned down to unlace her tapered boots. This, to Percy, seemed almost cruel on her part, as in this position her voluminous bosom was pushed upward from her corset. If not already stupefied from the revelation of the movers bill, and the rapidly re-emerging question of what had happened to his wife, then the addition of this vision might surely kill the man. Esther turned her head, and she and her mother exchanging a knowing glance. Then Evaline left the room.

Esther turned to him and said, "Now that we're alone…," which was a lie, because Percy sat mouthing on one of the man's own cigarillos in the next room and Evaline herself was just around the corner in the dining room. But nonetheless, "… the 'New Year's fiasco.' The Marquis de Lafayette. We got in a bit over our head there, didn't we?"

The Colonel had wisely, it seemed, chosen to become more buttoned up, ironically as Esther became more unbuttoned. He simply nodded.

"You threw in with the wrong sort and underestimated him, didn't you? Didn't think he would try to murder anyone, did you?"

He shook his head no.

"No, of course not. But you did, after all, see to distracting mother that evening…" Looking up, he was shocked to find Evaline having almost magically reappeared next to her daughter, with a withering look. "… Allowing for the girl to be separated from her and abducted. And then, later, while you may not have been fully aware of what had transpired with the Marquis, you did *watch* and allow us to be pursued and nearly killed on the outskirts of town. And *then* you saw fit to show up when we were at our lowest point, like a righteous angel of mercy, and 'escort' us back home again. But… *but*… you took the opportunity to make a show of us, didn't you? You could have taken us down back alleys and less-traveled pathways where no one would have been the wiser of our passing, but you chose to parade us about as the noble hero, rescuing the 'damaged' maiden – and the immoral hare. And then you watched as you set them against him, that 'cur of a rabbit,' and as the city tore itself apart looking for him."

With a gentle flicking sound, Evaline untied Esther's corset and then pulled it free. Esther sat back in the chair casually in a loose cotton camisole with attached knee-length drawers. The sunlight now caught the side of her face, casting oddly angled shadows over its contours. She looked at the Colonel as if he were a tired old pitiable man. He could scarcely recognize her piercing eyes. The look on his face was one of shock and resignation.

"Well, that's all behind us now, eh?" Esther began again. She became very relaxed and more predatory without the corset. Her new posture appeared to signal a change in tempo. "Let's say it's behind us. Even if the public distrust lingers. Even after the Sheriff has cleared Mr. Hare of all charges. Let's say it's behind us now. Have another drink, Colonel." And he did.

She continued, "Wouldn't it be nice to put all of that behind us? I know I'd like that, wouldn't you?" She leaned over the small desk, which caused her camisole to gap open at the chest. "Start fresh and make something good of all of this?" She nodded exaggeratedly, he followed suit.

"Well, I have an offer for you. An... *arrangement* I'd like to enter into. With you. Here it is." She leaned towards him with her elbows on the desktop, her hands clasped in front of her. "I say we forget all of that... and get married. You and me."

Percy could practically hear the metaphorical skillet panging against the Colonel's head.

"Wh – what?" he stammered. It was precisely what he had wanted, secretly, all along, without ever being able to voice it or imagine it could come to be. How might this young woman, this gorgeous young woman, be leading him along a canal path like an ox – a path not of his choosing at all – and how could that path be leading him directly to his heart's own most secretive desire?

"Now, now, take a moment and let's consider what I'm offering," Esther interrupted, stepping into his thoughts. "Mind you, we will have to wait for a respectable amount of time to have passed, in deference to your wife's departed soul. And this would not be a marriage in the traditional sense. At all. No, this would be a marriage of 'opportunity' – a marriage of 'convenience' as they say. In exchange for keeping mum about all the nasty little things you've done over the years... all the people you've disenfranchised and cheated and deceived... I would become Mrs. Esther Wells Wigglemann – my, saying that out loud, that has some clout behind it, eh, mother? Some *oomf*."

"Indeed it does, my dear," came Evaline's voice from the next room.

"And, with said name," Esther went on, "I would gain access to... societal considerations and levels of acceptance that I would otherwise not. No longer the whore's child..." A quiet cough came from the dining room. "... My apologies, mother... but from that point on, a member of society with some bearing and acumen."

The Colonel's expression had not changed. She was not sure he was still breathing.

"Now, I assure you," she went on, "that I have NO interest in the normal trappings of marriage on any level, in any form. Do not allow your mind to wander, or for your imagination to 'play house' with me here in your large and... (regarding all the emptiness of the furniture-less rooms around them) barren... home. That won't be happening. Besides, I already have a lover with whom I am exquisitely happy." A quiet cough came from the other direction. Had he had his wits about him, the Colonel might have noticed another presence. But he didn't. And he didn't.

"And," she continued, "You seem to have been very comfortable here on your own, keeping to yourself, reading your morning newspaper, meeting with esteemed colleagues. Apparently, you have been independently contented for years, even with your previous wife in attendance, so there should be no noticeable change.

For my part, I will provide for you the picture of a much younger and wildly attractive wife, lending you the appearance of either the luckiest man alive or an astute and accomplished cocksman." His tongue caught in his throat, making an odd sound. She simply extended a finger toward him and said "No." Continuing on, she added, "And, it should be said, I will bring to your dealings a better sense of order and... purpose. No more spiteful self-dealing. More generosity will be in play." With now a friendly, warm smile, "Won't it be nice to know that your finances are grounded in healthy, progressive practices that encourage the community forward, rather than deceive it and cheat it? Won't it be gratifying to be seen walking the streets of the old town, with me on your arm, and folks' hale and hearty welcomes attending us wherever we go? To host your business dinners here again with myself as your hostess, appearing for all the world to be your dutiful and attentive spouse?"

He nodded with an insipid grin.

"However, I will in fact be living in my mother's house for the foreseeable future, and I will, I'd very much like to point out, be enjoying a deeply passionate and all-consuming relationship with another fine little man." Another quiet cough came from outside the room. "But I assure you that will remain a secret, so as not to ruin our marital charade.

"And all of this comes in exchange for your not being exposed as a disreputable cad or for having arranged for your wife's death and/or disappearance, for that will surely cause you utter financial ruin, won't it?"

"But I had nothing to do..." he tried to interject.

"Tut, tut, tut, now – no sense quibbling over these things, is there? It will look like what it looks like, won't it?" He nodded again resignedly. She continued, "There are probably numerous details to be worked out in time. But Colonel, are you agreed to what I've laid out for you today, sir? Do I have your word, as a gentleman?"

He seemed... undone. Unsure of what had just happened – indeed what was still happening – but generally understanding of her meaning and the cost she could extract upon him, even if he couldn't really give it a rational examination at the moment.

The skies to the rear of the house darkened as a heavy, blue-violet cloud had descended. Simultaneously, the creamy orange sunlight from the opposite side of the house intensified, forging a theatrical contrast of light and dark in the room, with Esther at its juncture.

"*OH!* I nearly forgot!" she rose to her feet again, "In addition, once each month, you will be invited to dinner with us all – my mother, and the ladies at the house – after which you and I will retire to the basement for a private... *show* of sorts. Reminiscent of the peep show when I was younger. How does that sound?"

And with that, she loosened the tie at the top of her camisole and, with a gentle shimmy, let it fall to the floor. There was a deafening silence as she stood before him utterly and unabashedly nude. Her hip gently nudged the desktop, adjusting the wine carafe slightly in the angle of the sun and casting shards of reflected light from its cut glass features across her nude form. As he looked on, Percy could only hear the crunch of the cigarillo being bent in his own mouth. Was the magic of this light display only serendipitous, he wondered, or could she have purposely brought it about?

After a long moment, Esther turned her head and said, "Mother, I believe the Colonel is in agreement."

[8] https://www.in.gov/idoi/files/IDOI-Indiana-HistoryofInsurance-2016.
pdf

Chapter 46

Spring 1884. Percy was enjoying a very pleasant, if somewhat bothersome existence. Esther Wells was every charm and grace that had ever been suggested to him by the magic of femininity. They practically swam across her bed chamber together each night, in a wash of supple flesh and ruffled fur and flowing bedsheets. She excitedly clutched him to her every morning, as if rediscovering the world's greatest treasure.

He had hoped the other ladies of the house would become accustomed to his presence in time, and that that would lessen their fawning over him. Unfortunately, the sight of the small gentleman hare seated in the breakfast alcove off the kitchen, reading the newspaper every morning, generated fascination and cooing beyond his reckoning. His passage through the house was unceasingly impeded by cuddles from half-dressed women.

He was desired – he was loved – he was well fed, with food and affection and cordial friendships throughout Evaline's household.

And he needed to get out.

Dammit.

His heart ached from it.

There he was, sitting on a high vista north of Lafayette, overlooking the Wabash. It was a warm spring day, and the breeze blowing through a thatch of his beloved ginger was comforting him. His willow stick, planted into the moist ground, wagged gently back and forth in the wind. The shade cooled him and showed him colors in the early tree canopy of which the paintings of George Winter had always hinted. And yet, all he could wonder was how long would be too long to be away from her. Would she understand?

It had taken him the better part of the day to get there as it was. He was still not a particularly welcome sight about town, regardless of the Sheriff's clearing him of any responsibility for the New Year's Eve fracas. Making his way unaccosted through town required a bit more effort and time. Now that he'd arrived at this glorious view, it would seem a waste to turn about and head home again. But if he did, he would still be arriving quite late in the evening and would have a lot for which to answer.

It had been quite the day though. Earlier, he'd tossed rocks up into the hillside opening of the Pearl River, in hopes that he might agitate the mermaids sequestered there enough to show themselves again. But it was to no avail. Then he'd dislodged a streetcar from its tracks on the upper end of Main Street with a strategically placed piece of scrap iron in the rut. The driver of that particular car had been especially caustic toward him in the past, so it seemed deserved. He laughed, knowing it would take his team of horses and a fair amount of men to realign the car on the track once more. If he could have produced a handful of turds on demand, like the horses themselves seemed well equipped to do, he'd have flung those at the man as well. He'd enjoyed a bottled beer from the Thieme brewery tossed to him from a passing delivery wagon. He couldn't recall the driver's name, but he always had a large toothy smile and always seemed happy to see the hare. And he'd stopped at Barkey and Kess' place and given his regards to Charley the pig from the garden gate. Charley was excited to see him, anticipating a rousing lunch escapade, but he made do with the loose scraps of vegetables and acorns Percy had gathered for him along the way. Percy patted the grateful pig atop his head and soon left, choosing not to disturb his friends or to get caught up in conversation on this day. After waving off his friend Mr. Biggs at the B.F. Biggs Lafayette Pump Works and circling past Baby Alice's presence at the LaForge house (though he could feel her pull and her calling out to him), he headed north through the industrial section along the canal and a sweet-smelling apple orchard just coming into bloom. Eventually he'd arrived at his present locale, and it had seemingly welcomed him as a long-lost friend. He'd planted his stick, settled into the ginger, and listened as late-arriving sandhill cranes warbled high above on their way northward.

It was a full sensory day for the hare. He filled his nose with the scents of the ginger and the grass and the budding trees, and even the river wash, displacing momentarily the aromas of ladies perfume and fine linens and wood fires and rugs. Not that he minded the smell of those things at all; he just needed to smell something else. At times he almost felt "brainwashed" from the overwhelming presence of indoor living.

As the sun sank behind a purple-hued sky, Percy felt the air turn colder. He tucked his long ears down under his jacket, pulled it up higher on his neck, and settled in under a thatch of brambles at the base of a young hickory tree. When he closed his eyes, he imagined Esther's eyes peering at him lovingly from beneath a tumble of her flaming red hair. He blew her a kiss and breathed deep, finding her scent still on his sleeve. He slept like a baby.

****

The next morning, an unusually cold one for the springtime, Evaline was watching Esther and some of the other children of the house ladies playing in her yard. A low spot in the garden had filled with water and frozen overnight, forming a small ice pond. Esther and the younger children were stepping across the ice. There was a lot of slipping and staggering and giggles.

When their little lips began to turn blue, Esther insisted the children go back indoors. Evaline held the porch door for them. Then she closed it behind them to investigate a quiet moment in the still winter air. She could hear something in the air. The reaction of the small birds flitting in the trees perhaps. Something. The old gal had developed some of the hare's senses herself, it seemed. And she knew that he was there. He was watching them.

"Oh, Mr. Hare," she spoke aloud, just enough beyond a whisper that her voice could reach the undergrowth. "I love you so. And Esther loves you too. She's desperate to see you. As am I."

A chill breeze wafted through and rustled the branches. It pushed a couple of errant dead leaves across the surface of the snow. Percy stepped out from the bushes.

He stopped and looked at his old friend from across the yard. "Is she upset with me?"

"No."

"Are you certain?"

"Yes. Come here and sit with me," she said. "You're too far away. I have trouble seeing that far anymore."

They sat on the outdoor furniture on the enclosed porch. He was leery of getting too close to her, fearing her anger on her daughter's behalf, but the older madam simply clutched him to her lovingly and held him tight.

"It was a long night, I'll grant you that," she finally said.

"Oh?"

"Yes, she was up and down the hall several times, and I could hear some crying. But this morning she was up with the children just as she used to be before you came to live with us, giggling and playing and seeing to it they were bundled up right before coming out." It was quiet for a moment. "All is well, Mr. Hare. Have no fear."

"What I fear is that this will signal she is done with me," he said.

Sitting back, she cried, "Done with you?! Hardly."

"Madam, you and I know well the feminine temperament. All may seem well, as you say, and the next moment a lash of retribution could be on the way."

"Yes, well, that is true," she acknowledged. "And I confess as the girl's mother – girl – I can hardly call her that anymore, can I? As that young woman's mother, I did expect something rather more... *dramatic* from her this morning. But she simply looked me in the eye and said, 'He'll be along soon.' As simple as that. And then out the door with the children. And then there you were – 'along soon.'"

"Mmm, I'm still not convinced I won't pay for this," he said.

"Oh, perhaps. I won't go so far as to say there won't be any price," Evaline offered. "She's bigger than you are, and she's strong."

They exchanged a look and laughed.

"But, what I want to impress upon you, my furry friend, is that this is different. This young woman is different now. I believe she is in love with you."

"Love?"

"Yes."

"Truly? How dreadful." A pause. "Love?"

"Yes."

"What could have possessed her?"

"Well, you are rather charming. I suppose."

They laughed and watched a fat robin sift through the detritus under the trees.

"We used to think those robins went south for the winter too," she said.

"No, they never go anywhere. They just stay protected whenever possible."

"You know," she resumed, "It should be pointed out that you are here now. You came back again. You don't fear Esther enough to do without her, do you? Not this time?"

"Not *this* time?" he repeated.

"Oh, Mr. Hare," she said, wrapping him up even more tightly. "I've known you for years and years, haven't I?" He nodded. "And I have fallen in love with you myself a few times along the way..."

"You? Certainly not," he replied playfully.

"... and I've seen you leave more than one young woman behind. Time and again. You doubted them, or you thought they doubted you. It didn't matter which – because you were out the door and down the path. The hare couldn't stay. But this time... maybe the hare got his tail caught in the door, eh?"

He thought long and hard. Then, as if just realizing it himself, he said, "Maybe this time he's just been left without any doubts."

****

His "punishment" as it were was reasonably light. Owing to an earlier suggestion from one of the ladies in the house, Esther was taken with the notion of wearing Percy in her undergarments for the day. That way, she noted playfully, she could keep track of him. She kept him suspended under her petticoats and full skirt, between her soft thighs, for the entire day. The rule was that no one could know he was under all that material, and it seemed all the ladies of the house inquired after his whereabouts. In truth, the "entire day" only lasted through supper, at which point she could bear the soft provocation of his fur against her thighs no longer.

Upon making her apologies and leaving the table, Esther seeming to struggle up the staircase but refused assistance when it was offered. Soon after, she was heard making some sharp exclamations from her room.

"Ah! There's Percy, then!" one of the ladies remarked, to much laughter at the dining table.

In truth, there he'd been all along.

Deep in the night, once they'd exhausted themselves, Percy explained himself to Esther. He whispered into her hair as they held each other tight. She assured him time and again that she understood. That he was welcome to come and go. That it was his *return* that meant anything to her at all, for it in fact meant *everything*. The hare came back. The hare stayed.

****

In contrast, Percy received a note the next morning from Rosalind Gullimore detailing her departure. The note, in fact, came for Esther and she had been asked to pass the message along to "our compatriot." Apparently Rosalind had received word from "a friend whom we watched depart on the river that one enchanted evening." The friend detailed how she had begun a new life far away to the south in a utopian community that knew no restrictions on lifestyle or career choice or even "intimate partnership." It was a dangerous notion – so much so that the friend had declined to share her exact whereabouts in written correspondence. But, having arrived there and become accustomed to things, the friend had had the revelation that her life, her true inner life, had always been meant for something... *different* than she'd ever known. Hence her struggling with a life that never seemed to suit her.

The faraway friend had then invited Rosalind to come and join her. Apparently, it was only through the distance between them and the time apart that her fondness for Rosalind could be revealed and she could even make such a bold offer. She wasn't sure she could say what she desired face to face.

As it happened, Rosalind had had a similar revelation. In her letter, she described for them how her fear, rising from watching the friend depart on the river that night, had awakened in her an understanding of her sense of loss and of her own true desires. It had made her reconsider conversations and confidences shared over the course of years of time. Kicking herself now at the loss of opportunity, she hoped that Esther (and their "compatriot") would understand that her departure would be necessarily abrupt. She knew not where she was going, but transport had been arranged for her, leaving that very evening. She hoped however that the transport would be much less dramatic than the scene they'd witnessed together on the river.

Percy confessed to not having seen this development coming. Esther laughed and said of course he hadn't. She pointed out that, like most men of the age, he hadn't been looking for it or even allowed for the possibility.

****

Over the coming months, the Greater Lafayette community looked on as Colonel Wigglemann was comforted by young Esther Wells, who visited him regularly, with her mother in tow as proper chaperone, at first. Miss Wells soon began to limit his visitors and oversee his affairs, in order to ease his stress and anxiety over his immense loss. When the investigation into the burglary of the Wigglemann home proved inconclusive, Esther assisted him with selecting and purchasing new furniture and settings to replace what had been lost.

The Colonel, it was said, quickly came to appreciate Esther's nimble mind and sharp business sensibilities, so much so that these considerations nearly obscured his appreciation for her beauty. But not completely of course. In no time at all they had developed a very close relationship. By late spring, somewhat surprising news came that the two were engaged. They were to be married in July of 1884, some six months after his wife's untimely demise.

When questions of the propriety of the relationship arose, due to the rather rushed nature of their courtship, many on Prospect Hill answered only, "Well, look at her. Would *you* wait?" Little could they know that the Colonel's wait was only just beginning, and it would be lifelong.

Chapter 47

Ginger Percinia Wigglemann was born April 1 of the following year, 1885, ostensibly to Esther Wells Wigglemann and Colonel Mel Wigglemann (ret). The child's notable middle name was always credited to a distant cousin of whom Mrs. Wigglemann was exceedingly fond.

In truth, Ginger was born to a lady of the household named Gladys whose precautions against pregnancy had unfortunately failed her, as happened occasionally. Having carried with her the memory of a child she'd aborted years earlier, the loss of whom did not ensure the father's commitment to remain with her, young Gladys struggled with the notion of forfeiting this baby. However, she also struggled with the notion of motherhood, having not had a warm example of such in her life until joining the house of Madam Wells. She awaited any signs of maternal inclinations, through the extent of her pregnancy, but none were to come.

Being unable to entertain the male clients in her latter-term condition, Gladys would inevitably be invited to chat in the parlor with Esther and Evaline and play games in the evening. She felt herself unworthy of such leisure but could generally be convinced to enjoy the comfort of the horsehair sofa for the evening. With some pillows and experimentation, they could find a position in which her enlarged belly was comforted and supported, and if only for this reason alone she was glad of the invitation. The women would inevitably note that Gladys' hair was perhaps one or two shades a darker red than Esther's own. Esther would brush it for her at length while they talked.

On such occasions as Percy the hare might join them, for he was generally uncomfortable in the presence of women in the family way, Gladys found him utterly charming. He could provoke her to uncontrollable laughter from the smallest comment, until she indeed suffered fits and tears would run down her face. At this point he would make his apologies and exit, fearful of damaging the already overburdened young woman. When once they tried to convince him otherwise, Percy said, "Look at her! She could rupture at any moment!" This only sent the woman into another uncontrollable bout of laughter, making Esther think he could in fact be right.

One night in March, as she sat uncomfortably in the parlor sofa, she admitted to Esther that she was reluctant to bring this child into the world. She felt no budding urges of motherhood and feared that, even among the affiliated brood of the household's children, loved and cared for by all of its residents, she would be unable to provide the child with the parentage it deserved. That evening, a pregnant seed was planted in Esther's mind.

Upon the child's birth, on an evening charged by a spring storm, Esther took hold of the infant and, holding her snug between Gladys and herself, whispered that the little girl would never be without the love and care of a mother. She herself would fill that role, as the role had been filled by Evaline for her. She informed the Colonel the next morning that they'd had a beautiful baby girl. He was greatly surprised to be sure, but oddly welcoming of the news.

Percy Hare was glad for Esther's adoption of little Ginger as well, and for the relief it seemed to offer poor Gladys to know that she was well cared for. In truth, he himself was relieved, since the child gave Esther the distraction to ease the expectation of Percy's presence. He'd known all along that he was a lover or partner at best and a "spouse" not at all. Though he loved Esther with all his heart, or at least all the heart with which a hare could love, he would not be living the life of waking beside her every morning. Now she had a real devotion in the chubby cheeks and wide eyes of baby Ginger. And on occasions when they lay abed with the girl sleeping next to her, Esther would turn to him and quietly remind him that, no matter what else occurred, and no matter where he ever found himself, he would always be the love of her life.

With young Ginger Wigglemann would rise another era of adventure and ignominious behavior in the Tippecanoe region.

But that is, as they say, a whole other can of worms…

End of Part Five

Epilogue

Many years later, when her mother had become infirmed and her father had long since passed, Ginger Wigglemann ordered a large old lilac bush removed from outside her mother's home. Concealed behind it, the gardeners discovered a small, well-crafted door cut into the stone basement wall. The arched doorway had a sturdy wooden door with a latch but no lock. The door sprang open when the latch was turned, leading into a tunnel to the basement that was far too small for anyone to have passed but a small child. It was unclear if the door had ever been used, or for what purpose it had been installed. The crew cemented over it.

As for our friend Percy Hare, his fate is sadly unknown. For as notable a character as he was, it seemed that one day no one knew where to find him. And the week after that, he was simply forgotten, at least to all but a few. He had made such a practice of staying just outside the notice of most folks that when he disappeared he was scarcely missed. The madam Esther Wells reminded folks that he was a long-lived hare by any standard and he likely, as most creatures of the wood are wont to do, found a quiet place to expire peacefully.

One cold February morning, Evaline Wells was found sitting on the outdoor furniture, gazing out into the vacant yard. The old gal was chilled through and her daughter urged her back into the house. Evaline seemed weakened and unsteady on her feet. Esther had never seen her mother's eyes so reddened and anguished, or so soaked with tears. Little Ginger stumbled in, asking, "What's wong, Gamma?" Esther then noticed a small scrap of paper, only three and a half by four inches in size, on a vacant plant stand next to Evaline's chair. She said she'd found it there just that morning. On the paper was sketched a simple bucolic scene, with a curved path circling from a shorter cluster of trees, a larger tree leaning in to the center. The path was lined with small fenceposts, and the small figure of a man was walking along the path away from the cabin, with a farm implement or long gun over his shoulder. Esther recognized it as having come from George Winter's studio.

Percy Hare left no home or effects, and no photographs of him exist. A few theories emerged – one had him joining a vaudevillian show that passed through the area, stopping in the nearby city of Delphi, Indiana to play the ornate Opera House there – another suggested he had joined the staff at Wabash College in Crawfordsville, though in what capacity was unclear, and there is no record at the college to support this.

And still another account was the telling of "a Negro family, Barkey and Kessandra Smith who, having traveled many miles from Indiana by wagon with their five children, a pig, and a large rabbit, arrived this week in Albuquerque. Having come for the amenable air, Mrs. Smith being among the asthmatic afflicted, they report the area to be much to their liking. Mr. Smith seeks to establish a quality saloon in the area, offering high spirits and a favorite card game of the middle western states, known as Uechre [sic]." (*Albuquerque Sage Times, New Mexico, November 17, 1889.*)

The Very End

Made in the USA
Monee, IL
30 October 2022

16834496R00167